# Good God in Govan

*A memoir*

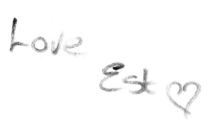

Love
Est ♡

Presented as a non-fiction personal
testimony with historical content.

The right of Esther Baxter Scott as the author of this book
and its contents has been asserted by her in accordance with
the Copyright, Designs and Patents Act, 1988.

First published in Great Britain in 2020

With gratitude and thanks to Bell & Bain,
Margaret Tomlinson
Palimpsest

Typeset in Bembo MT Pro by
Palimpsest Book Production Ltd, Falkirk, Stirlingshire

# Contents

Introduction                                             v

**Chapter 1:** In Heaven                                 1

**Chapter 2:** On Earth                                 20

**Chapter 3:** Three Stairs Up                          62

**Chapter 4:** The Liar, the Witch and the Wardrobe    128

**Chapter 5:** In Love with Life                       164

**Chapter 6:** The Burning Bush                        215

**Chapter 7:** Long Dark Bloody Nights                 232

**Chapter 8:** All Work and No Play                    248

**Chapter 9:** God Meets Me in the Town                257

**Chapter 10:** The Baptism                            282

**Chapter 11:** Life is a Peach                        314

**Chapter 12:** The Backslider                         332

**Chapter 13:** Agape Love                             344

**Chapter 14:** All Work and All Play                  374

**Chapter 15:** The World is a Stage                   413

**Chapter 16:** Half-Hour Call                         445

Glossary                                               465

School Playground Songs                                468

# Introduction

A bizarre and honest account of my life growing up with Jesus, The Heavenly Father, and the earthly father, whom I refer to as The Daddy. Some events will shock and others may hurt, for that I sincerely apologise, especially as some family members have a very different memory of The Daddy.

As a new Christian, when I first questioned the differences between the four Gospel accounts of Matthew, Mark, Luke and John, I was told to imagine four people placed at the four corners of any football match. If the four witnesses were each asked to give a written account of the football game as they perceived it, they would all come back with their own versions of the same game they had just witnessed. In each account there would be discrepancies regarding penalties, fouls and offsides. Players' names and actions would be jumbled, the referee would be judged unfairly, possibly even hated according to the result, and the supporter numbers would be hugely over or under-estimated in size. The four witnesses would not be lying, they would be telling the truth as they saw it from their own corner of the pitch.

This is my version of events from my corner of the family into which I was born. There are siblings, aunts, uncles, cousins, nieces, nephews, friends and acquaintances who knew The Daddy. Many younger than me were not yet born in my time. For any family members who thought The Daddy was the bee's knees, I quote my mother: 'You did not live with him.' Did I live with him or did I just exist? Yes, to both. There were times that were very difficult and I didn't want to be on earth and, when recalling a story or fact, I have been met with the statements 'That's right, I remember that'.

I have been God-conscious from my earliest memory and have never known life without Him. At the same time, I have also always known there is a Devil and evil surrounds us.

Although God was in my life and protecting me, it hadn't occurred to me as a child that He wouldn't save me, as children are saved already. Someone asked me this question once though, which unsettled me: 'If you died tonight, would you be absolutely certain you would go to Heaven?' Although I had known God and Jesus came to take me out to play, I was not one hundred percent certain I would automatically be allowed to enter into Heaven's rest and beauty. We are saved by grace through faith. I am completely Heaven-bound, because of His Word.

God has shown me His salvation plan and the need to fulfil my talents, one of them being the production of this book, a book that explains to you that not only is God alive, He is real and does indeed walk, talk, interact and commune with us.

Many of the testimonies I have to share with you may come across as unrealistic, but I am the one testifying about the goodness and Glory of God, I am involved in the testimony as it's mine and He is involved because it's all about Him. In meeting other Christians, I have heard overwhelming testimonies regarding the goodness and faithfulness of God and heard bizarre stories where I've commented, 'No way!' Yes way, God will do whatever He desires, when He desires because He is the great 'I AM'.

When I was a child, Jesus played at chases with me and ran through the park and up the closes of Drive Road in Linthouse, near Govan. God has allowed me to see dreams and visions and has taken me away many times while I slept. I watched my three angels twice, heard God's voice often and was allowed to be at my own life review at The Great White Throne. Nothing, however, compares to the out-of-body experience I had when I was fifteen years old, while walking from Lochgilphead High School. There have been so many events which have occurred in my life that I've had to write them down and give God the glory where glory is due. I also had to get on with using the talents God gave me, so here you are.

'GRACE' . . . getting what we don't deserve.

**This book is dedicated to**
**Christopher and Sarah**
(The fruit of my womb)
and Alan, my husband

Special honour is awarded to My Mum, Emily, and The
Daddy, Addie. To say I miss them is a huge understatement.
Without them and life's trials there would be
no testimony and no book.

**Also**
The highest praise goes to Jesus for taking me out to play,
looking after me and sending me Angels, for comforting me
and laying down His life for my salvation. No person can
show love greater than Him, thank you Jesus.

To God The Father for becoming flesh and dwelling among
us (as Jesus and The Word). Thank you for hearing my
prayers and looking out for me. Thank you for being our
Creator and for being who you are, The great . . .
I AM.

To The Holy Spirit for being with us every second of every
day as The Comforter, Helper and best friend. You hear us,
guide us, speak to us, warn us of danger, direct our paths,
assist in our talents and take part in our activities and lives.
Thank you, Holy Spirit.

**THE WORLD IS OUR STAGE**
GOD IS OUR PRODUCER
JESUS, THE DIRECTOR
THE HOLY SPIRIT IS THE PROMPT
. . . And the Bible (The Word), Our Script.

## ACT NOW

**God** is our producer
Jesus our director
Holy Spirit is our prompt
The world is our stage
Act now! Act now! Act now!

**There**'s no dress rehearsal
The script is The Word
The costume is the robe
The props The cross and blood
Act now! Act now! Act now!

**Actors** take your place
Extras we must bring
Cast ensemble for the rapture
He's coming in the wings
Act now! Act now! Act now!

**Curtain** going up (speak) 'Curtain up'
Smoke machine, lights and strobes
High expectations
Everyone disappears
Act now! Act now! Act now!

**There** are no tickets required
It's all free
Hands, feet, side pierced for thee
No audition necessary . . .
ACT NOW! ACT NOW! ACT NOW!

## Chapter One

# IN HEAVEN

I only knew Heaven, I lived there with everyone I loved in perfect peace. Peace was peace, love was love and joy was joy. Perfection was beautiful and everything beautiful was perfect.

I ran towards the semicircle of sparkling-eyed beings seated at the kidney-shaped table waiting to greet me. Each glorious spirit had a burning desire to welcome me tenderly into the fold to commune with them for fellowship and instruction. There was no sense of judgement, at the 'appraisal' I'll call it, nor was there anything negative whatsoever as I eagerly approached them, knowing they were every bit as happy to see me as I was to see them. They were all closer to me than brothers, each one totally and completely loving me with a glowing heart.

Even the kidney-shaped table loved me. The curved edges of the table wrapped around me when I entered the hollow to be surrounded by my superiors, who have all wisdom, knowledge and understanding. They look after me as office bearers and have my wellbeing and welfare right at the very top of their unseen written agenda.

As I sit down I am aware there is no chair beneath; I simply sit into nothing but trust. I'm slightly tilted back in comfort as the kidney-shaped table morphs around me as though making a warm and loving reclining lounger.

Everyone and everything loves us deeply and passionately in Heaven. The grass, flowers and trees love and serve us. In turn, we naturally love Heaven and the thought of leaving for an exercise or duty seems rather far-fetched, if not too amusing, at first. Trying to imagine what Earth was like was bizarre because of rules, regulations, sickness, disease, right, wrong and ever-present evil.

My Heavenly mentors are well known to me and I knew them completely and individually by their pure love, characters and natures. I'm aware I won't miss them as Love will follow me in all of my Earthly adventures. Among other things, I am told I will never be alone, 'His' light will shine in the darkness and His Majesty will speak to me in His 'Still small voice', I am advised and assured.

The Lord Jesus is around, somewhere, and I can easily find Him. Living in Heaven is so natural that The Love of God infuses and permeates the whole area. He is always near. Sometimes I would wave and call out His name when He was far off and, no matter the distance, Jesus always heard me. He is totally amazing and always takes the time to respond to my hand wave of worship. When He was out of sight, He was never ever out of mind.

When I saw the King of Kings, Jesus, on a mission and walking on by, I would occasionally run to Him and walk with Him part of the way, chatting to Him or telling Him something, just as I did the last time I met Him when taken from my sleep, to find I was sitting on a wall talking to a friend. She saw Him behind me and smiled the broadest smile ever.

'Jesus,' I called after Him, running, 'Listen to this, I can sing, I can really sing.' I then opened my mouth and let Him hear the most amazing musical tones, tunes, vibrations and melodies, everything I had wished to perfect on Earth, and I sang to Him with all the joy, praise and confidence I could. Jesus stopped, turned around and gave me His full attention. He listened intently as we had our meeting, even though He was busy on a mission.

The supernatural loving and laughing Lord delighted in my voice. He thoroughly enjoyed the praise and waited until I had sung to Him every note in the form of what I describe as opera.

He swung back round quickly in order to continue His journey and laughed, 'I know, you always could!' When He said, 'You always could' in Heaven, then 'You always could' on Earth because your talents, dreams, gifts and creative notions come from, and are confirmed in Heaven with and by The Word of God, in the name of Jesus. You can do it on Earth because The Heavenly Father says, 'My will be done on Earth as it is in Heaven.'

I was ecstatically happy. Jesus threw His head back in laughter, giving the odd side to side shake as if to say, 'Finally, the penny has dropped, she's got it!', and laughed as He continued on His journey down towards The City of Lights below. The little dazzling and sparkling bright lights that shone in the city were people, brighter flying lights would zoom all over Heaven and fly off quicker than lightning, they were Angels, always working, answering prayer and never tiring.

There is no need for lighting in Heaven as it's as clear and bright as you could ever imagine, yet still, there were greater and smaller brighter lights that sparkled and shone as they moved around. Lights followed Jesus and moved out of the way, disappearing, at the same time. There is life in the light and light in the lives of everyone there.

My eyes followed Jesus as He walked down the dusty road around the bottom of the mountain, and a good walk to The City. He is so beautiful you can't take your eyes off Him and the desire to commune with Him and praise Him bursts from your abdomen without pre-empting. 'I know, you always could . . .' It's difficult to ask or tell Jesus something with a straight and sincere face because the answer is revealed before the statement is completed.

His answer is always the same, 'I know,' He laughs. He walked away laughing and said I could always sing. So why didn't I just do it?

I had zero confidence. As you read on, you will see and understand why. It took me a very long time to believe in who

I was. I was nothing, a nobody and I felt the song, 'Nobody's Child' was truly mine. Many years passed before I imagined I could do anything positive or even worthwhile for that matter. My confidence came as it built up slowly with the help of The Saviour, but I sing now without fear of being ridiculed because I do it for God and by the nurturing of The Holy Spirit, thank you Jesus.

When we go to God in prayer and tell Him our problems, He already knows. Having told Him something, or asked Him for something once, there is no need to bleat on about the same thing, the same question, statement or the same complaint. God is not deaf. He already knows what we are in need of. The Word of God states, 'Before you call I will answer.' I might add I am speaking to myself here because I have done that all too often. Not only does God hear us the first time, He already knows what we need and He is waiting for us to come and ask what we will. We just need to thank Him and believe, because we are reminded that the answer is on its way.

Relaxed at the kidney-shaped table, I was being prepared for my journey to the planet named Earth, an amazing physical journey that could stop at pre-birth, our spirit departing from the physical womb child before being delivered, or birth, being delivered to stay on Earth. We could have a disability resulting from medical complications and be on Earth simply to aid other people in their journey for teaching purposes, in humanity, humility, strength, love or whatever that mission is, as decided and agreed beforehand.

Although disability (definitely) is not of God's intention and doing, nature gets to take its full right and course and we learn through the trials and tribulations of it.

Our spirit is on a specific Heavenly intelligence mission and has orders, called or chosen. We each have ministries, talents and supernatural guidance from Heaven.

Exiting the Earth is part and parcel of that pre-ordained mission. It could be near death, leaving Earth but being sent back as it's 'not time', giving us a sneak preview of God's glory. Death, leaving our bodies, or being taken away (from the area). This is being taken back to Heaven without dying, as some people have. I was shown there was no actual final death, we were held in a body for the sole purpose of staying on Earth, that's all. Most people assume we are born to die, full stop, but I was shown a little deeper. I was shown, 'knew', we were sent to Earth as flesh and blood humans who were very small and vulnerable and grown and developed from the seed of man, as planned and planted, to be physically nourished within the womb of the woman. Filled with the breath of the Living God, behold, 'The baby', the gift from and of God. A tiny vulnerable little scrap of humanity, totally dependent on his or her mother for love and nourishment.

A celebration of life mightily explodes and erupts as Angels watch in awe of God's handiwork. In total agreement and arrangement, we chose, with God, our mission to planet Earth and clearly decided whether we would come to Earth for a few seconds, minutes, hours, days, weeks, months, years, or not even come through at all. We choose where to settle and what to learn. It's as simple, natural and as beautiful as that. We would develop our gifts and talents to work with and expand and to praise God because we wanted to. We would enjoy the experience with Our Precious Daddy in the Heavens-God, Abba-Father, Our Creator-The Lover of our souls, Our Healer and Deliverer . . . Our Daddy . . . My Daddy.

My Heavenly mentors were briefing me as I relaxed in the authority of the comforter. They supplied me with instructions and knowledge as they were detailing my entry onto the amazing planet Earth. My parents, family, circumstances, education, illnesses, troubles, dismays and disappointments were clarified and they answered every question in a pure and simple way. I didn't have to go, of course, but I wanted to experience all of God's goodness. I had never known any sadness in Heaven, it is awesomely beautiful there and negativity doesn't exist. I could sense their concerns, though, that I wasn't fully taking in the seriousness of the mission.

'It will be difficult,' they told me but I made it clear I wanted to go. I was extremely excited about the journey, but not quite prepared or sure about the 'Timing' information. Time? How do I master something I don't have control over? I was more amused than confused, that's the way it is in Heaven: fearless, faithful and fantastically funny. Of all the briefing statements and questions, the most important discussion to strike me as odd was the one regarding the 'Silence'. It is easy in Heaven to live with silence and peace, but on Earth silence would have to be practised, I was told. Not that Heaven is silent, silence is not a part of Heaven's make-up by any means. Our special time and place area where God would be found, then, was in the silence on the Earth, to learn the art of listening to God's still small voice . . . Shh.

'Concentration, meditation and participation in The Word is imperative,' I was told, their eyes widening as they leaned forward in unity as they repeated 'The Silence'. I was to find and guard this silence, along with time, above all that I was to achieve on Earth for my own good. If I could master the art of silence I would get along much more easily and quickly. Missions to greet, silence to complete and perfect timing, I whispered over and over.

I would know the perfect timing as I embraced the silence. Within the silence I will hear God, I will learn to listen and He will still be there to hear, see and watch over me, always.

Some of the information seemed easy to understand and the parts I couldn't fathom would come to me as I waited on God, as far as I was concerned there would be no problem, or would there? I would have no real idea until I was actually on my mission, as there was no trial period. There was no dipping of the proverbial toe into planet Earth's sea to test the waters. I couldn't go to Earth twice, one host body only, no dress rehearsal, take it or leave it, and I couldn't just throw my arms in the air and demand to be brought home. I must wait and develop patience regarding the time and God's perfect timing because there is perfection in Heaven and perfection in the order of the harmony of life. There are no accidents or disorder in God's beautiful Heavenly creation, until we step foot on the swirling planet Earth.

Silence, Timing, Patience, I thought over and over again. I had many other orders to collect on Earth by way of God's handbook, which (was Him and) contained His instructions for living and I was to obey the handbook as a guide throughout life and meditate on it at all times, every day without fail. How could a book of instructions be God?

I did eventually receive one of the handbooks on my eighteenth birthday, a pure white little bible that I neither read nor understood, unwilling to peer inside in case it became damaged. I was also given a Gideon's bible in primary school. That one was the old faithful, though I was still unlearned in how to use it and I still didn't get it. To me it was just a book, but God (The Holy Spirit) also met me in the town and gave me His handbook personally, more on that later.

Once I had chosen my wonderful planet Earth parents I knew where I was going. Through briefings I saw in a frame of cloud surrounding them but they could not see me. I was wholly confident in Heaven with my lot but as I began to see my Earthly life unfold before me I started to have doubts and reservations about whether I would succeed or not. My concerns warned me I would have to keep alert and focused because the billions of distractions on Earth were not only real, but very attractive and completely free. The competition on the paths of life of good and evil were fierce, many temporary or everlasting prizes for the gullible, proud and greedy. The takings, spoils and dangling carrots of success or greed would snare and trap us. There was a hissing invitation for all and the path for choosing was left to our own means. I would be helped as much as I so desired, as much as I called out, according to my inner faith, and my mentors went to great lengths to make me understand it would not be easy, I would have to get into silence.

Although it looked incredibly easy from where we were sitting in the peace of The Lord, this Earthly adventure was a whole new ball game, especially when I realised my advisors knew some of the tasks were difficult too. They were well versed and experienced in the school of mortal life and there was nothing hidden from me that would not be revealed, sometimes in an instant, sometimes later on. I was shown silence does not live everywhere on Earth. Silence can only cleave to us if we allow it to do so because there is too much distraction in noise from all of the activities, airwaves, actions and adversities.

I was listening with great sincerity but it's not until you're there and doing the job that the experience comes. I can't not go, I thought, but my mind was read as soon as the thought was hatched. The look of love and concern for me was so overwhelming that I swiftly sat up before bending forward and bowed my head, face down, hidden by my long flowing hair.

I had to ponder and take my time before concluding I could endure this journey. The kidney-shaped table moved away from me as my comforter elevated me gently to an upright position.

As I was playfully swishing my feet to and fro, I saw them differently. They were very much alive, willing and dancing about in a way I had never seen them do before. They looked strong and well capable of carrying me to the hills and mountains of life on Earth. The understanding here was that my feet would carry me all the way, I had dancing, lively feet that were looking forward to getting there. Dancing feet? How come? I would walk in faith, step by step, and was allowed to follow my heart. My whole body would complement each of its own parts and I was to look after them and use them wisely as the body was a precious and delicate gift, I was told. I was to use the gift of the physical body to help and assist others who were not so able-bodied. Although my body was entirely mine, it was also entirely God's and He was not willing to share my body, which is His temple, with others without His permission. Everything I needed on Earth, whether it be physical, emotional or spiritual, would be at my command because He said so. All I had to do was ask in the name of Jesus but I was again warned I would either forget or not remember many of the instructions given. How could I forget? I wondered, as though the statement was untrue. I would not remember, I was enlightened. Weren't forgetting and not remembering the same? I was puzzled.

It was explained that one part of the memory was related to the past and the present and the other to the present and the future. The brain and mindset with past memories was able to store, memorise and recall every minute detail of our lives regarding colour, recognition and understanding. We would be able to recall our past but have difficulty as we aged.

Prompting in recall would work as the information was previously stored. In the present and future part of our memories, our brain naturally stored every piece of information as fact and was able to forward think so as to work out equations. The future part of the beautiful brain and mind could become too tired and slowly fade and phase out, like a light bulb which was on at full glow until someone fitted a dimmer switch to turn the power of the light down. The information was still in there but unless I practised and used it, it could slip away and hide in the closets and secret places. Our body's ability to renew forever would become exhausted as we aged. As we learned formulas we could make, build, enhance and re-create to a point. There is nothing new under the sun that was not already tested or tried, as every idea first starts in The Spirit, in Heaven. Understanding would become too tired and fuzzy.

Some of us would be hugely creative and continue to play with our talents as we freed our minds and emotions and allowed our ideas to fly. As for creation, that is who we are. That new colour of flower or designer dog was already created but it could be duplicated, twisted or tampered with. Messing with design for recognition was dreadfully dangerous and brought chaos, upsetting the harmony of life and living on planet Earth.

I accepted the memory information with a nod of the head as though throwing the memory aside. I had no desire to break or damage any of God's creative intuition or work. The greatest majority of my Heavenly life would become hidden on a deeper realm, deliberately, so as not to influence my earthly journey. All information was stored and recorded in Heaven and would not be deleted. The Holy One would go with me to the entry point, He would be with me inside the womb and He would be with me on my arrival, He would never leave nor forsake me. Jesus would be with me and waiting for me on my return journey.

He would be waiting on me and with me at the same time! How amazing, I totally knew it before it was explained. God would also always cover and forgive my mistakes, be them accidental or deliberate ones.

The Angels in Heaven were hardly seen in their magnificent glory when they were working, only as bright lights with life and strength in them but, man alive, they couldn't half move fast. There seemed to be an infinite number of them and every single Angel is always on a mission at great speed because God will answer before we call. The angels arrive with the request before we have finished asking. Easy for God because He is everywhere and before our time. I thought being a human looked difficult, but the Angels have a terrific ministry of their own. The mission for them was completely and significantly different from ours and nothing stopped them. I was positive I wanted to depart from Heaven to planet Earth and trusted in the full authority of the Heavenly realm. What's more, I had that authority and I was allowed to use it when I had matured and understood the terms and conditions of the laws on earth, laws I had to adhere to on earth as they were put in place by the very nature of God Himself, who appointed judges and rulers over us. When the laws were twisted, misused and abused due to misadventure, mischievous people and sin, then they did not line up with The Word of God. The law to obey solely then was The Word, The Bible. I would become like my guardians and family in Heaven once my mission on planet Earth was complete. I had to dutifully practise this silence with all of my heart, soul and mind, wait in, and joyfully trust in the perfect timing.

My companions sensed some of my concerns and confusion with the silence and time concept and advised me I would manage through prayer.

Assisting others was very high on the agenda with Love right at the very top, and putting myself last was also repeated. I was 'Not' to want anything as I would have all I needed and be given what my heart desired. Heaven is made up of Love, deeply concentrated and so thick that the density is a force which is God and mankind cannot contain it.

My Heavenly mentors turned inward with one another and had their own silent discussion. They were communing with each other but I couldn't understand what they were saying as they were communicating by 'thinking'. To do this they had to look away so I couldn't see into their eyes. They were far superior to me and I understood this to be perfectly natural. I kept thinking of how much I loved each of them but I knew they knew my thoughts and I knew they loved me deeply too. I was part of them. Every so often they would look at me with the usual tender love and they would all smile. I knew not one of them had a negative thought regarding me when I was being discussed, every good thought was for my welfare, growth and help. I was extremely highly regarded and deeply cherished.

Periodically one of the startling bright beaming lights would whoosh, zoom over, take off and totally disappear faster than the blink of an eye. Three did this as I tried to watch them arriving but they were too quick. I concentrated carefully, amusing myself, but I couldn't see or hear them, let alone touch them, they were just gone, zooming away with instructions.

The depth of my brothers' eyes had infinite colours in them, pearls of blues, purples, pinks, greens, even black, and millions of diverse colours which have not yet been named and seen with the naked eye, and millions of shades from that one colour. Colours which were still being revealed and each had a name in its own right which glorified God. Shades of metals, gold and silver, ice and fire, smoke, stones, crystals of every pastel and shape imaginable.

Diamond cut with so much precision that I would see myself multiply in their eyes over and over again and kaleidoscopes of movements which were so mesmerising, yet had life.

Waterfalls, rainbows, snowflakes, bubbles, circles, glass and what seemed like sparklers on the inside, which multiplied from a single spark, quickly became infinite in number and design and continued to explode and kept going on and on just the way I'm remembering.

The multiplication and harmony never ends . . . mesmerised, I would often look into their eyes and just stare at the dancing auras. There seemed to be another world going on in their eyes, another life, another story, another planet, another everything. In their eyes were deep waters of coloured bottomless pools. Dancing jewels, gems and every precious stone imaginable mirrored and reflected beauty which was never repeated, completely different every time. I threw my head back with laughter when I caught myself creeping forward so I could look deeper into their eyes because I felt I wanted to join in, something in their eyes wanted me to join in, it was almost a personal invitation. Then I would catch sight of the face with a raised eyebrow which seemed to say, 'Come any closer and you'll fall in!' They made me laugh so much, it was such a great joy to be called before them, particularly because they were authoritative figures. They had great power from The All Powerful One who refers to Himself as The Great 'I AM', I AM that I AM. I AM all you need. I AM Everything. Everywhere. I AM your Good Shepherd, your Salvation and your Living Inheritance.

It was finally agreed that one of my brothers would go before me to lead the way and help open my earth mother's womb. I was to wait until he returned so I could know, share in, and be part of his experience. He chose the pre-birth experience as it was my destination to be the first-born child, to become the first daughter of my earth family.

Off he went without any recollection or remembrance of his Heavenly duties. We watched on and followed his journey inside the womb as he swam with all his might, beating millions into the womb and burst through the jelly of the egg which was designed by The Creator and given the life and love spark. I marvelled at the miracle of his little beady eyes protruding as they developed and saw what looked like sparks and flashes of coloured lights coming from his growing brain to and from his eyes. His amazing brain was a phenomenal art, a labyrinth of perfection, a secret path, a wonderland place, a mystery yet a world of adventure, a computer file, everything. He seemed to grow immediately to full form and I laughed when I saw him coping with hiccups in the watery fluid-filled sac, even smiling as it amused him and sticking his fingers in his mouth, mouthing often as though talking and communicating. As a tiny little baby protected in his cocoon of the mother, he smiled constantly as he wasn't alone. He had a relationship in the womb which only he and His creator knew of, a one-to-one private and personal divine experience no one else could share, connected to love.

My authoritative figure came back before the delivery, as was his requirement, the miracle of the beginning of life was completely natural yet utterly awesome. There was more to this growing structure than could ever be imagined, constant energy developing from between the brain, eyes and spinal cord, which danced and celebrated in the creation of the forthcoming birth. Electrical currents and water splashed, clashed and exploded as they bounced, yet complemented each other in the dance of this physical creative development. Again I was totally mesmerised at the miracle meeting place of a newborn child from the dark and watery, yet calm and warm living area of the womb I got to see into. A womb the size of a room, the meeting place where The Holy Spirit Himself inhabits on a one-to-one engagement.

I then watched, with deep compassion, as the tiny white coffin which was vice-gripped tightly by the heartbroken man became soaked in tears. He was shaking and crying sore, a dreadful time of bereavement. The Daddy could hardly let it go down onto the back seat. His sister (Mary) took over and cradled the light wooden box in her arms, adding more tears to the top of the lid. He then drove his car to the graveyard. Mother was also heartbroken, forever, on Earth. I was so emotionally engrossed by the Love that I hadn't noticed my advisor, Adam, as he was called on earth, distracting me from the scene I was sucked into.

'There you are,' he said, 'How easy was that? Your turn.' I stared deeply at his radiance. He was so incredibly and stunningly beautiful, I stood amazed. There were no words for his splendour and he wasn't even God. Like a veil, though, my Heavenly heart was tearing in two.

'I'm not going,' I sighed, searching for an excuse to stay. He laughed wholeheartedly at my flippant comment, which echoed, merging with the swishing flowing rivers surrounding us. I had to say it again, 'I'm not going!' He continued to roar and the others joined in, making a laughing orchestra. It was too infectious and ripples were stirring inside of me. I quickly shook my head and walked away because he wasn't taking me seriously. I wasn't leaving this beautiful dwelling place, maybe another time but not right now. I desperately wanted to go for God, but I wanted to stay more, what would I do?

The kidney-shaped table, now suspended in the air, had a rainbow of colour above it. Would I manage? What if I failed? There were no failures in Heaven. How could I come back to Heaven a failure when I knew Heaven was beautiful and perfect?

'Would you like to travel with me?' His voice whispered in my ear.

I turned around quickly as I recognised His Voice but He was too quick and was still behind me. I quickly turned the other way but again I wasn't smart or fast enough. He made me laugh because He was playing with me, toying with me, which brought me into instant harmony with His Spirit.

'Hold my hand,' He said as He pulled me round to face Him and I did. He looked into my eyes as we walked and He laughed as He pulled me into a run which made me laugh too. He was pulling me off my feet, literally, and when I missed my step He held my hand tight and pulled me up and away from the ground.

'Keep your eyes on me,' He said as we were flying through the cosmos without wings. We whizzed and ducked through the deepest valleys and over the highest mountain tops, in through light and out of darkness where we could still see, and circled planets for fun, rocks and rings, trillions of billions multiplied by the infinite. A never-ending universe that delighted to show-case its beauty and splendour. As the thrilling experience slowed, He squeezed my hand twice, which was the signal I could now look away from His face. Words are not always used, there is instead 'The Knowing'. He whisked me through universal space where 'It is what it is' because 'I AM' said so.

As He let go of my hand I stayed where I was, suspended, and we danced in sequence to the music of the Universe as though in the most magnificent ballroom, the cosmos pulsing and flashing to record the scene forever. The applause of the Universe was rapturous and I was chosen to share in this remarkable event by His personal invitation. Our dance was a pivotal private and deep personal experience, where time stood still as we became part of The Creator's wishes, part of His glorious creation and in total fulfilment in the firmament. Dreams and desires were ordered and completed there. The Creator had prepared my destiny in His plan and allowed me my forever inheritance any time I desired.

'Will you leave me?' He asked. I couldn't see His eyes, I lifted His head and saw tears silently streaming down his face and I began to wince in pain as we held onto each other. Love shot through me like a spear and I realised the pain was the tremendous love I was feeling. The love was heavy and unbearable, crushing me. This was the first time I experienced a love so deep it hurt. It was too heavy, a force of super nature which morphed intelligence and separation was agony, as though the tearing of the heart could be felt.

'I'm not leaving you, I'll never leave you, I'm not going,' I assured Him, determined to never let Him go from my presence or lose the experience. 'Never, ever.'

'You are going,' He said. 'You are going and you know you are going, I ask you again, will you leave me?'

'Never, never, ever,' I cried with Him as I held Him tight and laid my head on His chest. 'Never, Lord, but will you come with me? I won't go if you don't come with me.'

'I will,' He told me. He then took my face in His hands as we locked eyes and continued to slow-dance within the Universe. His Love was an overwhelming force above which there is no greater, no other to describe, because there is no other force above Love concentrate.

He lifted me higher with His hands and kissed my forehead, and just at that, a bolt from His being pierced my spiritual abdomen area like a 'punch' of lightning.

'Are you ready?' He asked.

'Yes Lord, I'm always ready when you're with me, you make me say yes, I can't help but say yes, I can't help but love you, I belong to you and you are mine, you are Love.'

'Are you sure?' His question was unfounded, He already knew my heart. Why was He asking me if I was sure?

'Yes, I'm sure, I'm ready to go,' I said, with the assurance He was going with me.

'Come then,' He said, and He flew off without me, leaving me suspended alone in the middle of somewhere.

'Jesus, wait for me,' I laughed. In the twinkling of an eye I hit the ground running.

With His assurance I couldn't wait any longer to get to The Earth and help to heal the heartache of the young married couple who had stolen away and got married on the mother's sixteenth birthday, much to the disgust of her parents, who became my granny and grandad.

My heavenly brother recalled everything about his earthly mission and the time spent in the mother's womb but the experience which blew him away most of all was The love the Earth mother had for him. She loved him unconditionally, embraced her belly and wrapped her arms around him. She cuddled him and sang softly in her joy and excitement at expecting him, longing for the day she would kiss and cuddle him. Preparing for his entry by providing everything he would need to be comfortable on Earth, choosing his soft garments of lemon and knitting his tiny hats and little matinee jackets with ornate baby buttons. She thought of him day and night, desperate to meet and hold his little face without even knowing whether 'He' was male or female. Her baby was loved and nothing else mattered.

She was my earth mother, incredibly beautiful, and I wanted to go to her immediately. My Earth mother was very tender, emotionally fragile, and required much love and tender care herself as she was struggling with her mission. It was clearly pointed out to me that my earth mother would be 'coming back' to Heaven very soon and I totally agreed, without hesitation.

I see the Planet Earth, the oceans of blue and white covered in brilliant white clouds in areas over the separated lands. I see life forms in the waters of the most minute creatures, magnified to perfection. Each and every creature belonging to another in harmony and having their very own song and call of nature. The colours in the deep not too far away from the colours in Heaven, yet undeveloped in their true potential. Millions of primitive life forms, which still have just that, life. Deep-sea life which look like flowers, I notice, when I see the flowers, and the flowers which look like birds' heads, all remarkably similar yet completely and profoundly different. Tiny organisms unknown to mankind, which are a secret and want to keep it that way as they hide in the bottomless crevices. Giants in the ocean which are hundreds of years old swim and splash to wave their presence in honour of The Creator.

Trees clap their hands in praise as they blow from side to side and the flowers bow their heads in humility. The grass stands erect to call His name and geysers blow steam as a 'Hail, Hail' to His Majesty. Fireworks spew from the mountains in celebration of His glory and electrical currents splash across the sky in terrific thunderstorms to 'clap' admiration.

From the ground, shooting stars, comets and asteroids blaze through the dark sky which even make us smile, a reminder to keep looking up, a reminder of how our Heavenly Father loves us and is watching, waiting and listening to us at all times. He reminds me with a punch in the abdomen that 'He is' and also lives inside of me, with the words, 'The kingdom of God is within you.'

I look around and thank God I have no breath yet because it would surely be taken away as I survey His footstool. My earth mother was Mrs Emily Beatrice McGregor Baxter and I loved her before I met her. Memory wiped, I left Heaven to become birthed onto the planet Earth.

SH AL VAH The poetic voice whispers over and over, SHH. My tiny hands and arms are stretched out before me, swimming in the vast ocean of water and air, my brain and thoughts connected to The Spirit holding my hands, SH AL VAH. I am suspended in the purest, deepest, widest, concentrated LOVE. I am pulled very softly closer by the magnetism of LOVE and into the midst of The Spirit again, then let go, completely, but I cannot leave as I drift away because of LOVE.

My Living Loving Holy Spirit shows me He is setting me free. He embraces me and softly blows on me, the wind of His

Spirit pulling and pushing me between the Universe and the natural womb, SH AL VAH. He gently plays with me, swirling me upside down, slowly, very slowly, over and over, I am washed and embraced with LOVE, SHH.

My intelligence is in Him, with me and in me. He lets me go, I'm smiling, I lift my hands to Him on my own as He releases me. I eagerly want Him. He is mine, my forever Daddy. I stretch out my whole body – it's time. He cups and prepares my body and tucks me up, sets me before the entrance of my destination, has one hand on my head on the inside of the mother's womb and the other, like a wing of feathers, on the outside of the womb, watching for me to be delivered, SH . . . AL . . . VAH. I need to stretch myself out, I have been cocooned for too long and my instinct to stretch out is over-whelming, I struggle, I become distressed for a moment, POP. I need air and there is none. I fight for the right to live on Earth.

Finally, the first breath is blown into my tiny body by The Holy Spirit on The Earth and I scream in vibrations. I can't see Him for the bright dazzling lights which abuse my eyes. I scream and scream. I know nothing. I remember nothing. I am nothing on my own. I have just been created in a new dimension, I am a creation of 'I AM'. I scream . . .

## Chapter Two

# ON EARTH

Screaming like a banshee, I was introduced safe and well, I was informed many years later by my beautiful earth mother, Emily. I don't recall my own being 'Born' event that wonderful day I entered onto the big blue marble planet known as Earth. I can only imagine it was a traumatic experience for myself and my mother, coming from a warm snug watery womb into a blast of colder air, after having endured the pain of being squashed through the taut birth canal only to be welcomed by strangers' hands pulling at my head and stretching me silly, out into brilliant bright artificial lighting, adults shouting above and beyond the pitch of my untrained ear, before being rubbed vigorously with a rough towel. Had a sharp instrument poked up both nostrils to drain mucus, held upside down by the ankles and slapped hard on my back until I cried. Bumped down onto wobbly weighing scales after announcing to Emily, 'You have a girl,' before being wrapped into the tourniquet and popped on top of one's mother, who's been in labour for a whole day or longer and was in so much pain that she imagined death coming before a new life.

Phew, that was a labour of love just going through it. Yes, I most definitely preferred the near-death experience and I'm sure I will agree wholeheartedly when I experience my 'Birth' day as I entered this earth, at my life review. The life review I have already seen while standing with the huge crowd. God took me from my bed and placed me in the crowd. It was there I watched my Earth years go by. Over to my right, in the distance, was

The Great White Throne and He who sat on it, The Father God. I was lifted up from the crowd when it was my turn though I didn't get to see who was up before me or who else I knew. I had a quick enough look behind me to see no end to the sea of people also watching the life reviews.

I was lifted above the crowd as though I had floated and everyone could see me and the screen. I don't know what else to call this screen but I was watching my life from birth until the day I left the Earth. I took part in my own judgement and accepted there was no escape. I was watching myself, I knew my thoughts and feelings, my rights and wrongs. I understood the consequences of bad behaviour and the ripple effect of misadventure as I impacted sin towards others I loved and even those I didn't know. A word spoken in anger, lies and blasphemy made its way to people who loved me. What's worse, I could feel the hurt I had caused others as well as seeing their tears in the secret place, which then became my tears. Everything I had desperately despaired of and despised, I had done to someone else. Just as easily as I was lifted up, I was placed down into the slot of the great multitude, fully aware my loving Heavenly Father was looking on from His Throne.

Long before my mother passed away, she told me of her traumatic giving birth events, seven of us babies were born and stayed on Earth and seven went back home to Heaven, including the first-born, Adam. Some left before the scheduled birth due date or stayed for a few hours or days, allowing them to be registered as a citizen in The 'Dear Green Place', [Whose motto is: LET GLASGOW FLOURISH BY THE PREACHING OF HIS WORD AND THE PRAISING OF HIS NAME].

The whole new healthy being gripped her mother's finger tightly in the delivery suite, that was me. I was born in Rottenrow Hospital and taken to my first home soon after, a very dilapidated tenement building in the Gorbals area of Glasgow, which has long since been pulled down. I remember nothing of it and was told very little of the area by my mother, therefore it doesn't hold anything in the way of memories or sentiment for me in my heart.

I did visit Adelphi Street once, only to see what it looked like. There are no houses there, only factories. The street has changed and the area looks nothing like the way it would have done in the smoggy foggy nineteen sixties.

The first house I do remember living in had very high dusty stairs, peeling paint and no wallpaper on the landing walls in the hall. There was a family living in the house underneath us so this has stayed in my memory as being a four-in-a-block with the top house occupied by my parents, myself and my younger sister. This area was Carnwadric, on the south side of Glasgow, and the street, Dryad Street. The solid wooden stairs were so big that I had to hold onto the banister rail tightly with my left hand as I negotiated down them quite eagerly but slowly and in a one foot at a time drill. My little legs found each stair a milestone but the steps outside at the front door were even higher and made of stone. Those steps were scaled in horizontal fashion and cushioned by my backside as I had no handrail to assist me.

The front door was wide open, allowing the chatter, happy squeals and sunshine to breeze in as I was heading down and out to play, after having eaten my own dinner and wearing my younger sister's food as she threw it about me, laughing all the more because I was mad at her. Everyone and everything is so huge when you're a child. I must have been between two and three years old. I had been unsuccessfully trying to feed my younger sister with her dinner and was struggling with the intake of her peas, the last of the little green rollers on her plate which I found difficult to manoeuvre from the spoon to her mouth. Throwing her head back in laughter, she kept slapping them from the spoon and I had to continually pick them up as they scattered in different directions along the floor. The Daddy appeared from the kitchen to investigate the hilarity and planted a kiss on top of her messy-haired little head.

He was smitten by my little sister and laughed at her antics, calling her 'Pan Wan' due to the fact it rhymed with her name. She was in her high feeding chair and laughing every time I carefully and meticulously balanced the tiny amount of peas from her plate onto the spoon. The little patience I had was wearing thin. I complained to my mother about her because I was fed up chasing the rolling green peas along the floor, having Pan Wan in hysterics every time I had to bend down and get them up.

The Daddy was in the kitchen with our mother, and I eagerly wanted to escape to the outside world again to play, and stopped the assisted feeding, taking the dirty peas to the window to feed the little birds instead, and to get rid of them. I loathed peas so I could understand why my baby sister wouldn't eat them either. My hand fitted through the sash window gap perfectly where I let the peas go so I could get out. The quicker the peas were gone, the sooner I was on my way and out to play. I think I 'pead' on the lady downstairs who was sitting in her deckchair, because I heard her yell as they landed, softly and quietly in her big yellow Beehive hairdo. I had no idea why she would complain about that, I thought, as I bumped my way down the last of the stairs and ran off without a care in the world. I didn't turn around to face our neighbour on the way out for obvious reasons, she had been minding her own business [something The Daddy always repeated, 'Mind your own business']. If the neighbour was offended I didn't get to hear about but I didn't do it again, lesson learned.

There weren't many toys, as I recall, but I didn't miss or desire any. Friendships were all that mattered as we played our own games. Using our imagination, we would be who we wanted to be and our friends would wholeheartedly agree and readily joined in with games of Cowboys and Indians, Doctors and Nurses, Mammies and Daddies, or being a big fierce Polis. Before heading out, my mother warned me the doctor was coming and I was to 'Keep my eyes peeled for him.' I was told to behave or the doctor would take me away, especially as I had managed to open a wee bottle of deep violet liquid out of curiosity and spill the entire contents all over my dress, hands and face. I convinced myself that if I just smiled, the doctor wouldn't notice so that's what I did. I hid my stained inky hands behind my back and swayed with a big smile as the doctor came in through the gate and up the path. I looked up at him to see if he was angry but when he smiled back I knew I was fine, not in any trouble and going nowhere. Big fibbers big people are, I thought. Threats are terribly alarming when you are young because you believe everything adults say as you are naive and unwise, just a small child.

My mother's hair got parted with my tiny fingers many a time because she told me she had eyes at the back of her head and knew what we were up to. There was little me parting her long, thick, black hair looking for them. I never did find them but I would keep looking anyway, saying, 'Let me see your other eyes.' I was totally convinced she could see me at all times. When she took her glasses off to clean them one day, I immediately took them from her and shoved them back on her face and told her I didn't like it when she took them off. I had never seen her with the glasses off and she didn't look the same, she didn't look like my mummy. Whenever she cleaned them from then on, she wouldn't do it in front of me because I didn't like it and I only wanted my real mummy, even if she did have other eyes at the back of her head.

As well as the doctor, we saw the Green Lady most days and she'd get a warm welcome with shouts and bawls of 'Here comes the Green Lady' as she went about her business. Marching in her own army with her bag of supplies, she came to attend to the newborn babies. Our Green Lady was stout and severe with a big bun in her hair at all times and not a single solitary hair out of place because it was stiff with hair lacquer, as it was known as then. She had wide slitty eyes because her hair was pulled back so tight that it stretched her face lengthways. She spoke with authority and did not smile, ever. She wasn't our best friend in the world but nevertheless, we respected her, especially when we claimed to know the newborn baby well. We all ran ahead of her, calling out to let the families know she was on her way as she marched with purpose and speed to the house of the newborn child.

Everybody's business was our business and everyone knew and helped each other out then, except for The Daddy, he was a private man. A lot of men were like that, their family life was hidden but children and wives talked to each other for support and shared the gossip. We always knew which neighbours we could rely on for borrowing food like sugar, milk or bread. We also had a good neighbour who would bring us ice-cream and yoghurts on return from his job at the farmer's where he worked. Another neighbour sewed us a cheap new dress for a small price, one per year, usually for the first Sunday of May.

I remember being at the local primary school in Carnwadric a bit later on and queuing up for an injection with the big girls, who had their sleeves rolled up. There were huts in the school playground and I followed the big girls along into the queue, expecting to receive the same medical treatment as they were getting. With my left sleeve yanked up as far as I could get it and great excitement, I was waiting my turn. I could hardly see in front of me because I was tiny but I did notice some of the big girls at the front of the queue were crying. The game was 'a bogey' though, because I was too nosy in trying to see what was going on. I was spotted long before it became my turn and was escorted from the premises by a bewildered adult, back to the play area where I belonged. The primary sevens were receiving an injection which had alarmed some of the big girls so much that they cried, yet I stood there wanting a shot, even if it was sore. It was a freebie and freebies weren't to be sniffed at.

The teacher I had at primary one of Carnwadric Primary School seemed to be wrapped up in worries of her own this day as she sat on a small chair built for children with her chin cupped in her hands. She was in a foul mood and her eyes followed me around the room like a crow, her face dark. We were told to go and choose a box to play with. In the boxes there were large-pieced wooden Jigsaws, Fuzzy Felts, Snakes and Ladders, Meccano, Lego and all sorts of other playbox activities. As we scurried to the wall units to get the boxes out the teacher growled 'Not you' into my face as I crossed in front of her. I was shocked, so shocked that I have remembered her face and statement with clarity to this very day, often wondering what was wrong with her. Bewildered, I racked my tiny brain trying to think about what I had done to make her angry. What was wrong? I wondered, puzzled. I was four and a half years old. Conscious of her peering stares, I leaned on the desk and chatted with my classroom friends, but her eyes followed my every move, listening to my every word. Every now and again I looked at her to find her still staring in disgust. Although I wasn't frightened or intimidated by her, I was aware of being watched and I wondered what she was thinking about as I kneeled on my wee wooden chair. I remember being friendly with everyone in my class and when it came to swapping the boxes with one of my classroom friends, I tried to do it too. 'If you give me that one, then you can have his and he can have hers and . . .' 'Then I won't have one,' a little hurt voice protested as I listened to the wee girl close to me.

I tried to work it out so we could all have a box and be happy but I just couldn't fathom out how to do it. That was the first sign maths was not going to be my strong point. I was fully aware the teacher observed me trying to join in but she just kept the staring up. She deliberately and wilfully tried to leave me out of social inclusion with my classroom friends and I was deeply disappointed in her and decided she was another 'not nice' person, just like The Daddy. She didn't realise I had over four years' experience ahead of her of 'not nice' persons and she certainly wasn't at the top of the list. This one was easy to deal with given that The Daddy was a meanie. Still, I was sad because she didn't like me and I didn't know why.

Not long after the play activity time had got under way the school bell rang and I got out first as I had nothing to clear away, so she unwittingly did me a favour. I loved school as far as I remember, as it was great to play with friends, but I had as much time for the teacher as she had for me, ignoring her so she wouldn't shout at me again. It also meant there was no two-way communication as she was now unapproachable. A chance of a friendship severed at the very beginning because of her horrible attitude to a four-year-old child.

Close by me was a wee boy in the class. Like me, he was picked on and shouted at, not by our classroom friends though, they were just wee bits of weans. He wasn't allowed to leave his chair and often got bawled at for just breathing, so it seemed. I remember feeling sorry for him as he would jump every time the teacher shouted. I would hold my breath as though to make the silence and peace come. He never spoke, he would just get up and wander from his chair and slowly walk away from his desk, a lovely little boy. I sensed he was special and not very well and I remember that day in primary one after he had been off school for a while.

We were told he was not coming back to school again as he had gone to Heaven. I felt really sad but my thoughts were towards the teacher. I was watching her face, her reactions, and thought, 'You are so cruel.' No judgement, just honesty. I thought she was a bad person and I took as little to do with her as possible. Even at that young age I had discernment and could read her like a book. I wondered if someone was hitting her and that was why she was sad because she certainly wasn't happy. It's reasonable to remember alarming, traumatic or exciting events as they stand out well in the memory. My memories are slotted in wherever and whenever I can recall them. I must have only been at this primary school for a few weeks, as I remember starting my other primary school in primary one as well and was there until my primary days were through, until the age of eleven.

When we moved to number fourteen Drive Road in Linthouse, near Govan, the next primary school I attended and was to stay at until leaving from primary seven, was Elderpark Primary School. I had a strict and stern teacher by the name of Miss Gray in this primary one but she was very good, a staunch no-nonsense madam. She spoke 'properly' and walked very tall with an air of grace and authority. I felt safe and secure as I remember walking behind her one day and acting like her as though I was as proud as punch to have her as my teacher. No one messed with this older lady and, despite the fact she hardly ever smiled either, she was strong and fair. Her encouragement was medicine for the soul and I saw her as my protector.

I remember this day being in the boys' playground as Miss Gray's window looked down to the side of the boys' entrance and stairway. The boys and girls were separated by high wooden slats and a gate which was permanently locked by the Janitor. We were not allowed to be in each other's playgrounds and we had no desire to, as girls played with girls.

In the boys' playground I was in the thick of washing the dolls' clothes in a huge square basin on steel legs when Miss Gray appeared at the top of the steps and called me in. I became upset because I hadn't finished the task of wringing the clothes out to hang up and thought I would be in trouble for not doing so. Miss Gray insisted I leave them, telling me someone else would bring them. I remember thinking she was kind to do this as she didn't pressure me to hurry up. I believed in her and trusted her to do what she said. She took on the responsibility of looking after me. Unlike the other primary one teacher, she was interesting when teaching and I very much enjoyed the reading books, *Janet and John* and *The Cat Sat on the Mat*. My first proper reading book was, *What Katy Did*, which I got from the library at the other end of Elder Park, in Govan.

As a family we got weekly comics such as *The Dandy*, *Beano*,

*Topper, Beezer, Mandy, Bunty* and *Judy*. The *Oor Wullie* and *The Broons* comics came from *The Sunday Post* and each Christmas we would get whichever annual was due. I would often stay quiet, reading from an early age. We knew exactly what days each comic came out and we always reminded our mum to make sure she remembered to get it, having to take it in turn in receiving the gift which was stuck to the front page. One week's notice was given regarding that gift from the previous comic and we looked forward to it with great anticipation. When we didn't get the comic our mum would say there was none left by the time she got to the shops. I believe, and understand now, that she didn't always have the money to buy it.

I laugh with friends as we get together and share our childhood memories. I asked them recently if they remembered the school sticks we learned to count on and they all said, 'No, I was dreaming.' I wasn't dreaming, I remember the little sticks well, even from primary one.

Many of my Glasgow friends had a very different school life/ education to me and some started smoking at nine years old, they have informed me. Every day is a school day right enough, no wonder they were forgetful. In those days children were allowed to buy a single cigarette.

Our little coloured sticks were called 'Rods' and I remember the first one was a little white cube, which was the starting square number one. The second was red, double the length of square one, so, number two. I have tried to remember very carefully in order to get this right, the rest are as follows, I think (and may stand corrected): three was yellow, four was pink, five was a sort of dirty yellow like English mustard, six was dark blue, seven was black, eight was orange, nine was a lovely deep blue, my favourite colour then, and number ten was the biggest stick in cream. I used to imagine they were stairs and would let my fingers walk up them as well as build little flat houses. They came in handy for building when I collected a little more than I should have. They were for my homework, stealing indeed!

We children always got a lovely tin at Christmas with toffees or some other kind of sweets and that tin was always kept as a keepsake for our worldly goods. In mine were my rods and 'Chinese ropes' for playing elastics, basically just rubber bands which went in the hair too, pulling strands out at night time as they got tangled up in my hair.

Night time was very cosy as we piled into the bed recess after our supper of tea and toast which was made with the help of the three-pointed fire fork. The fork was as black as the coal itself at the tips, but it assisted in the making of the best toast in the world, especially when we were hungry. A lot of the cooking was done on the fire from heating the whistling kettle to making soup or just boiling water and I don't remember us having any kind of big cooker.

The one clear memory that has stayed with me about being young is the cold. It was absolutely dismal and bitter. With no proper warm clothing, a decent coat, hat, scarf or gloves to keep us warm, our fingers and toes would forever nip and hurt and that was because of the temperature on the inside of the tenement, hence the reason there were coats on the bed. There were no carpets (for us) either for when our feet eventually left the comfort and warmth of the bed, only freezing cold linoleum, known then to us as waxcloth flooring. I would have remembered if we had fancy slippers to quickly get our feet into, nor did any of us have a dressing gown or a bath robe. My younger self would ask, 'A bath robe, what's a bath robe?' Answer: 'It's a towelling garment in the shape of a dressing gown you wear after coming out of the bath so you can get dried quickly.' 'What's a bath?' I have the wonderful gift from God for making myself laugh. My mother used to comment, 'Aye, you think you're funny' in an abrupt tone, but I do laugh a lot now. I think my funny was sarcasm back then.

It was straight out of bed with a quick morning-glory dance to get warm. A bit like when you go on your first holiday abroad and stand on the roasting hot sand with your bare feet.

It's agony because you didn't realise it was so hot and you do a frantic dance trying to get straight back into your sandals. It was very much like that except the waxcloth was freezing cold and we acted in the very same way, getting very quickly washed and dressed before hypothermia set in. 'It's like Siberia in here,' my mum always said. Not too much of the jesting, though, because unfortunately hypothermia did set in, along with tuberculosis before I got through primary seven. Jack Frost, The Tooth Fairy and The Sand Man even did a bunk from our abode because it was too cold for them. Frozen fingers, toes and a runny nose was the norm in our house. It was no wonder we didn't want to get up for school in the winter.

I recall the day our newborn sister number three was brought home and laid in a drawer with soft sheets. The drawer was taken from the chest of drawers from the only bedroom and placed carefully on top of the double pull-down bed settee in the kitchen. We gathered around the bed settee to look at her tiny angelic face. I thought she was a really pretty baby, as babies go, her tiny little pink face with no dry skin or wrinkles. I remember she was a lot smaller than my big doll, Heather. Our new baby was so small I stared in amazement and wonder. Our little sister was named Kathleen by my parents, Kat by myself and 'It' by Pannie who poked 'It' in the cheek with her finger and ordered our mother to 'Take it back'.

Another time when 'It' was screaming, I was told to give her a sterilised dummy from the steamer but Pannie beat me to it and screwed that dummy into her face like a pneumatic drill. My parents saw that Pannie was a wee bit jealous of the new addition and had to be carefully watched. There would be the odd wee nip to startle the bonnie new baby but nothing more serious. Pannie became clingy on The Daddy as our mum cradled and fed our new addition. The 'It'/Kat baby and Pannie soon became good friends as they grew up together. In fact, they became as thick as thieves and would often clype on me for drinking the milk, which was accounted for by hungry mouths.

Given that we had no fridge or freezer (for us) in those days, food was always bought on a daily basis with a little left over for the morning breakfast. We got free milk at school every day, sometimes not so fresh, or filled to the brim with midges in it. We only discovered the tiny drowned flyers when one of our classmates poured her milk down the sink because she didn't like milk. The warm milk was in a triangular carton with a small plastic straw. This only happened in the summer time though, before the school closed for the holidays. The milk was thick with thousands of tiny dark midges and when we all poured our milk down the sink to see if we had midges in our own milk we started a riot, not only in our classroom though. The whole school joined in as everyone was shown the flies, led of course by the theatrical one. Who, me? Answer this question first, one lump or two? Yuck. How long had we been drinking the milk before it was discovered it was full of midge protein and not just calcium. I remember the days when we thought it was cute to find the little birds had poked through the silver top of the milk bottle to get at the cream. Aw, so lovely and cheeky. Not so. The dirty little cream-thieving bandits had been eating earthworms, mealworms, caterpillars, beetle larvae and other food sources before descending on the silver top for dessert, leaving their juicy germs behind in the milk. Second yuck.

As Kat grew up, she was feisty and not afraid of The Daddy, having him wrapped around her little finger. While we were all relaxing on a tartan rug one scorching day in Elder Park, I jumped up and fled in horror as she walloped The Daddy across the shin with a glass bottle of Irn-Bru. She had demanded he open it to give her a drink but he didn't move quickly enough for her liking, so she moved him along. She brought that thick glass bottle down on his shin in temper for not doing what she had asked. I was terrified. She walloped him and stood laughing her head off as The Daddy hopped on one leg, roaming in circles, clinging to the other. The pain wasn't funny but I suppose his actions were. I was too scared to even imagine laughing though, as I stood back in shock and disbelief, waiting for the ripples of the assault incident to reach me. If that had been me who belted him I wouldn't have been here today to relate the story, I always thought. She was always mischievous and loved pushing his buttons for a reaction, which astounded me no end. How on earth could she get away with it?

Everything that happened in the family was my fault, I was told it often enough to believe it. Like the day Pannie was being rather silly and fancied a chase, I guess. She stuck her tongue out and waved her hands above her head at me, turning quickly without a care in the world, she smashed her face into a concrete lamp post. It was a sore one. She screamed all the way home with her forehead bulging and me running after her. It was just one of those moments in time when you knew something awful was going to happen but there was not a thing you could do about it but stand and watch in horror. It was my fault, bellowed The Daddy, for 'Not' watching her. I did watch her. I watched her smash her own face into a lamp post that didn't belong to me, nor did I put it in her way so she could hurt herself, face facts I thought, not lamp posts. When Kat got hurt it didn't matter because she was the kind of child who would get up, dust herself off and laugh. Pannie on the other hand was much more fragile.

Kat had The Daddy at her beck and call day and night and he actually loved that, he laughed at her fiery spirit. No matter what she did to him he always said to my mother, 'See that Emily, she's a wee bissom.' I've often heard that the first-born gets away with nothing and it's easier for the siblings who are born later, I believe that to be true in our family. Not only did I not get away with any nonsense, I would get the blame for everyone else's misadventures, even his own. I didn't want the relationship Kat had with The Daddy, because I didn't like him. I loved him but I certainly didn't like him for battering my mother daily. I've heard many a preacher proclaim, 'It's ridiculous to state you love someone but you don't like them.' I say to that preacher, 'Unless you've walked in the shoes of the person saying so, then don't judge unfairly.' Loving the person and not liking them for their faults and personalities is not a sin, we can love and dislike at the same time, just in the same way as God does. Love is a commandment of and from God, not only a personal choice. Sin makes people ugly, sin is of the dark realm and I don't like it, never did, never will. How many times have we loved someone deeply only to be bitterly disappointed by their actions? I loved my dear Daddy, but I did not like him for beating the other parent I had, every single day, my treasured and wonderful God-given mother. I did not like him for beating me, for making me feel useless and for telling me I was no good. He treated me like dirt from the sole of his shoe. I loved him and still do, though sometimes I wished, as a child, I was never born. I can still repeat, I loved him, but I really didn't like him at all because of his dark hooded nasty vicious and volatile evil temper.

St Kenneth's Parish Church was just up and around the top of Drive Road, close to the primary school we attended. Though the church has been demolished, the old hall building which was used for Girl Guides, Brownies and parties is still there and is now a nursery. It was there my first steps with God The Father and The Holy Spirit began. I went along to St Kenneth's as a wee Brownie and did what wee Brownies do, all sorts of tasks for your cloth badges, lots of games and activities. I was given the uniform with some badges already on as a hand-me-down from a Brownie who was moving up into Girl Guides. I was proud of my sash badges but I'm sort of bluffing here and not telling you any of the tasks I did because I can't remember which ones I did for what badges, some were for sewing and knitting, that I do remember because my mother taught me both.

I also remember the stage well because I was always on it and loved the view looking down.

My fear of heights was obliterated by the spotlights. Besides the usual Brownie songs, 'Singing in the Rain' was my stage debut, in oversized wellies and a very long trench coat. Five small Brownies twirling huge umbrellas to the shouts of, 'Watch you don't poke her eye out with that!' The choreographer was demented with us, I could tell by her countenance. No wonder, including the stems of our umbrellas, we each had three legs, two of them with left feet. At the end of the singing and dancing routine we all had to get into our positions, open up our umbrellas in perfect synchronicity, spin them around while kneeling and hiding behind them and sing as loud as we could as the sound was muffled by the brollies. Much easier said than done for primary schoolchildren. We got there in the end and, as they say, it was 'all right on the night'. We did it properly and it was a very good performance.

I loved St Kenneth's Parish Church, as I felt safe and felt as though I belonged there. It was the one place where I thought God lived and heard me in my prayers, the prayers I never once said out loud. I prayed inwardly all of the time because I had never heard anyone but the minister pray from the pulpit. St Kenneth's Parish Church was a 'must do' on a Sunday. It seemed an awfully long day, due to everything being closed, but it was more than that, it was a quiet reverent day. There was a real sense that it was indeed a Holy day no matter what religion or denomination you belonged to or supported. It was God's day and the reverence for God was always there. No one had to say it, that's just the way it was. The churches and chapels were full to bursting as the communities got together. It was a cleansing day, bath night for school (a scrub for us), ready for the new week ahead. People behaved themselves and acted differently, more relaxed and giving for one. The older generation all wore their hats, except for the men who took them off before entering into the church building. The men wore their caps throughout the week and the ladies were more inclined to wear a square folded headscarf during the week, keeping their fancy hat for Sunday. This was probably to keep the hairdo nice, or maybe the hair was needing done and the scarf hid it and showed the single curler peeking out at the front. Our mother had a few spare scarves which made arm slings for our imaginary broken arms, hanging from our necks.

The streets were almost ghostly until the afternoon, as most children went to visit their grandparents on a Sunday after church and we were no exception. Beforehand, though, anything good that was worn for church was whipped off and stashed away to keep nice. Good shoes were put away again for the following week, as were pure white socks when we had any. It never once occurred to me that we wore the same thing every Sunday because they were put away and only worn for God. After visiting our granny, I remember many a sombre, brisk walk home because The Daddy was in a foul mood and I knew we were having a very bad day.

Every Monday morning without fail, we assembled in the main hall of the school for The Lord's Prayer:

*OUR FATHER, WHICH ART IN HEAVEN,*
*HALLOWED BE THY NAME,*
*THY KINGDOM COME,*
*THY WILL BE DONE ON EARTH AS IT IS IN*
*HEAVEN.*
*GIVE US THIS DAY OUR DAILY BREAD*
*AND FORGIVE US OUR TRESPASSES*
*AS WE FORGIVE THOSE WHO TRESPASS AGAINST*
*US;*
*AND LEAD US NOT INTO TEMPTATION,*
*BUT DELIVER US FROM EVIL*
*FOR THINE IS THE KINGDOM AND THE POWER*
*AND THE GLORY*
*FOR EVER AND EVER, AMEN.*

Back in the days of the sixties, the school bell rang at four pm and we didn't get out until at least five past four, if we were good. If we were bad, we were made to sit at the front of the classroom for earache. In the winter it was dark by the time we got home, especially with the thick fog in Glasgow back then. It was so thick you couldn't tell which close was yours from a distance and at lunchtime I ran home and was mad if someone asked me to go to the shops for them. I had to do it if they were disabled or elderly, it wasn't the done thing to ignore someone's cry for assistance. It was the fact that one particular wee woman lived four flights of stairs up that bugged me, because I had to do the climb twice, once for the cash and again to take the shopping back. After months of being caught by the same old dear I was never asked again by the wummin, all because her head was thumping this day and she said she wanted me to get her a packet of Askit powders. In a fluster to get home quickly I hadn't really taken in what she had asked me to buy. Biscuit powders? 'What's biscuit powders?' I asked myself in the shop. I couldn't find biscuit powders so I used my initiative and decided to get her powder to make the biscuits. Convinced I had bought the right item I hurried back to her home. You should have seen her face when I handed her a bag of flour. She never even gave me a tip after climbing up the four flights of stairs twice as she usually did. I was glad she never asked me again because I was always the one who had to run to the shops for my mother too. I always ran because she would be waiting for whatever she needed and also so strangers wouldn't stop me on my mission. 'Run, mind,' my mother would always warn me.

We always went into Govan for the bigger shopping or to go to the pawn for some money to buy the messages, as we called them. Very rarely did we go to the pawn to redeem the items which were pawned, as money was forever short, absent rather, in our family. If The Daddy had found something to pawn, then it was as though we had won the pools (or lottery nowadays).

'Wait there,' our mother told Pannie and me as she left us standing in Paisley Road West, on the south side of Glasgow.

There was an older woman standing waiting for a bus beside us. Our mother ran over four road lanes and into the butcher's on the other side of the road. While our mother was in the butcher's, The Holy Spirit showed me a vision. I saw my mother running out of the shop and right in front of a bus that had stopped to pick up passengers. Overtaking the bus was a huge lorry. When I saw this vision, I was sick with fear and wanted to pull on the older lady's arm for help but I was too shy to do so. I was in a fearful panic. Agitated, stepping from side to side, I was hoping it wasn't true, but I knew what I had just seen. I prayed to God, 'Save my Mum, God, don't let her get knocked down, I need her with us, don't let her die.' There was no conversation between Pannie and me, as I was too focused on our mother. I watched and waited, there were no buses coming, thank God, but she was still in the butcher's. I willed her to be safe. I watched every vehicle come and go by on her side. 'Watch my mum, God,' I prayed over and over. 'Don't let her get knocked down.' Then it happened, exactly as The Holy Spirit had just shown me. A bus came along on her side of the road and stopped at the butcher's to pick up the waiting passengers. 'Oh God, help her,' I prayed with all my might. At great speed a lorry came into view and overtook the bus just as our mother rushed from the butcher's and ran in front of the bus without looking to see if anything was coming. I held my breath as she was stopped 'alive' in her tracks. God stopped our mother from being killed, or at least, very seriously injured. I was filled with the deepest gratitude and overwhelming love imaginable. I couldn't lose my dear precious mother.

I know I agreed with God that she could and should go back home to Heaven but I changed my mind, we needed her and I was keeping her. I thanked God continuously for saving my mother's life while at the same time telling Him He was not having her, she was staying with me.

I was so concerned with the wellbeing of my precious mother that I didn't give the fact that I had just had the vision any thought and accepted the vision as completely natural and normal. I loved God and, as far as I was concerned, that's who God was and that's what He did. He wanted me to come to Him alone and speak to Him, not just to think about Him. I was learning and longing for Him and He knew me, I was sure of that. I knew He was real, ministers didn't have to tell me He was real, true, forgiving and graceful. I could have a silly carry-on in church but when I was singing to The God of Heaven I was singing in reverence to The Highest and true living God.

At the age of around six years old, that was my first vision from God but it was not my first experience of God's ways. Jesus was already taking me out to play when I was fast asleep in my bed as a youngster. It was dark, night-time, and I was sound asleep in my bed, then, suddenly, I was with Jesus. I knew Jesus was chasing me as I ran as fast as my little legs could take me, down Drive Road, around Elder Park, Linthouse and Govan. Even although it was night-time and I was in my bed for sure, the street was in daylight as I squealed with laughter and tried to outrun Jesus. I'd dash through one of the closes to get out to the back so I could dodge Him but, when I got through the close, I always found the back door of the close to be locked. I laughed my wee lungs out as I banged the door with my fists but I knew I was well and truly caught. With nowhere else to go, I had no option but to turn around.

Jesus slowly walked towards me from the mouth of the close. He was beautiful and perfect, smiling with his hands held out, nearly touching the sides of the close. He was my best friend and loved me unconditionally. I laughed as I moved slowly away from the back door and crept towards Him. Staring into His eyes on the way back out, I begged, 'Don't you catch me, Jesus. Let me go past, don't catch me yet!' I squeezed against the wall as much as I could, barely getting past His hands and laughing with Him. I knew He could catch me all too easily but He let me go every single time and we did it again and again until He knew when enough was enough for me. When I woke in the morning, I was always smiling and that smile lasted for weeks as the thought of Him warmed my heart. He came and took me out to play often throughout my young years and we always played the same game, chases. I loved Jesus so much and He was the one and only true friend I could rely on. I spoke to Him often, yet when we were together we didn't talk except for me to say, 'Don't catch me yet' and 'Let me go past you.' I did nothing but laugh the whole time and that laughter had a huge impact on my soul and wellbeing as a wee girl.

The Daddy never played with me. I would have screamed the building down if he had tried. I was very afraid of him and couldn't understand his sudden change from laughter to anger, then rage. He smashed everything he thought we liked off the walls, including our cups and plates, roaring the building down. I shook in terror as I watched my mother's frightened face and became terrified for her. We didn't have photographs or photo albums, not only because of poverty, but because The Daddy burned every photograph in a ravenous fit of fury. He wiped out the memories of our poor little family. Some scattered photos escaped his clutches but I only have four photographs of myself as a child of pre-school age.

I was reminded of this incident by Pannie, because I had forgotten and repressed it. Only when she reminded me did it come back to haunt me later on and it made me break down and cry. I now remember sitting on the settee with Pannie to my left and we were sharing a blanket. The Daddy is arguing with our mum about setting fire to the house (for the insurance money?) and I scream in hysterics, 'Daddy, don't burn us! No, Daddy, no, don't burn us.'

As children, we played together a lot, as there were no clubs for us except for whatever was on at the church, If we had to pay for the activity, then I guess that's the reason we couldn't go. We collected petals from roses and other scented flowers instead to crush in water so we could make perfume with our friends, occasionally rubbing it on the close walls so the gasman would smell the nice scent when he came round to light the gas lamp. There wasn't any room in the house for toys, bikes or anything bulky. Kat had a three-wheeler bike with a red plastic seat to keep her amused, but the plastic seat was split and she had a bleeding accident in the nether regions. In contrast, we had pictures of bikes which we kept in Scrap books. My favourite Scraps were of Angels, no surprise there then. The Scraps came in various sizes and I would take mine to school to swap with my friends. Kat wasn't into Scraps, she was more likely to scrap the Scraps, tear them up. She was a bit of a tearaway, our little sister, we could ask her to do things we would not get away with because she was bolder and getting into trouble didn't faze her. Her real name was too long and colourful for us to be bothered pronouncing, with the Gaelic lilt and four syllables. In the television programme, *Catweazle* was always up to mischief and was a daft eccentric git, who was a little bit crazy and a whole lot funny. It seemed to fit sister number three so perfectly that Pannie and myself gave her the nick-name *Catweazle* because she made us laugh.

This pet name was officially used by the siblings only, everyone else called her by her proper name, though never pronouncing it correctly. For my cheek, I was referred to as Easter, Easter egg, Baxter's Soup, Baxter's Jam or Baxter's Beetroot. One of my brothers always sends me my Christmas card with 'Happy Christmas, Easter' even to this very day. I knew the hilarity would die down one day and it has. When I got married, my name changed from Baxter's Soup . . . to Scott's Soup.

From soup to eggs, which brings us to Billy. Billy was the name of the typical young Glasgow hard man who lived on the bottom of the tenement and through the wall from us, with his 'Da', as he referred to him, and his stepmother, May. He spoke rough and spat at every opportunity, which turned my stomach. I guessed May wasn't his real mother. I'd gathered that by the way he spoke to her: 'Get me a drink a watter, May, wull ye?' May did it immediately and came back to the window with the glass of water he requested. He took a look at it in detail before accepting it. 'Fill it up, wull ye, that's no' a drink,' he grunted, as if to show his authority. May did as she was told and came back with the tumbler filled to the brim and passed it through the open sash window. Cheeky git, I thought. May was a lovely meek person, clearly subservient, with her long blonde hair and angelic face. Her man was at work and Billy was hard work. She was kind, gentle, approachable and easy to talk with. No young person really knew or spoke to Billy, though, because he was tough and acted like a bully and we were a bit unsure of him.

Billy turned to me after he'd swallowed his 'watter' and asked, 'Dae ye want to go and get burds' eggs?' Innocently, I said yes and walked behind him for miles, way past Govan. Weary, I began to trail off, wondering when we would be at the end of this great expedition.

There was no fear in me, no God warning, just innocence on my part, although he was much older than I was. He climbed the trees and handed me down tiny blue speckled eggs. I was mesmerised as I gazed at how miniature they were. It was the first time I had ever seen birds' eggs so cute and tiny and I gave no thought to the time we were gone or even to the fact we were robbing the birds of their youngsters. I was about seven years old, a youngster too.

'Hey! Watch ye don't brek them,' Billy demanded as I peered into my pocket to see them again. He was high up in the trees looking down, making sure I was looking after the spoils, and spoiled they were. I had no idea they were so fragile. Unbeknown to me, there was a search party looking for us and the gentle May was frightened, beside herself with worry because I'd wandered off with Billy. My parents were furious, believing he had taken me away. They searched high and low and must have given May a hard time. On the way back I was spotted afar, straggling behind Billy. I could hear the shouting of my parents before they reached me. I was grabbed by my shoulders, off my feet, and given the beating of my life from The Daddy for going with Billy. It really hurt but what hurt more was that my mother did the same, which hurt my feelings, as I loved her. I was thrown into my bed in the recess after the beating, in order to have a good think about my actions. I learned a lot that day, for taking the eggs, I'd killed the little birds, I was told. The eggs were so fragile they shattered and were nothing but small wet crumbs in my pocket. I was like those little birds' eggs, fragile, walking on eggshells. If I had been told not to go and disobeyed the command, then I might have deserved a hand in the course of the punishment, I thought and I didn't see Billy as a stranger. The beating was the beating of all beatings. Humiliated before my little sisters and traumatised by my mother, I was used to beatings but not from my precious mother.

I was so broken I didn't get out of bed for dinner when I was informed I could now get up. Physical punishment heals, but not mental punishment. I felt like I could walk, sometimes run at great speed, many steps forward on the happiness platform, only to be pushed back to the waiting room of despair with the ticket of doom and gloom in my hand, except it was in my mind. I was well warned that when I went to church on Sunday I was to pray for what I had done and apologise to God for my behaviour. The sorrow in my heart hadn't gone away by the Sunday, as I sat on the square wicker seat sobbing throughout the service. I spoke to God inwardly and apologised for being a wretch and for taking away and destroying nature's little eggs, feeling the mother bird would have been absolutely heartbroken too when she discovered her babies had gone. It was too much of a burden to know I had murdered her tiny little chicks. In church no one asked a crying child what was wrong, no arm of comfort around the shoulders, no whispers of 'Are you all right?' I sat there, the most despicable human being on God's earth, until I felt sure I was forgiven, but I never felt that assurance.

The minister's name at St Kenneth's Parish Church was the

Reverend Thomas Low, a very nice man, as I recall, but it was the organist I had most dealings with when I was asked if I would like to join the choir. I looked forward to a Sunday morning and my sweetie from him as I got dressed in my long purple robe and pure white starched smock-like blouson. Being the smallest and youngest person in the choir, mine drowned me. The white smock draped past my knees and over the purple tunic, which was also too big, held up with both hands as we walked into the church for the beginning of the service. Both hands were needed to be clasped together under our mouths to hold our sheet music which was tucked into our thumbs. I had no option then but to use my feet to kick the tunic out so I didn't trip up. I also had to stay well away from the girl in front, as she was likely to get booted up the backside as I tried to free my feet from the purple garment. Occasionally I had to take the choir garments home to get washed and starched and that was the first time I had heard the statement 'That's a big girl's blouse', as my mother held it up against herself, asking if they didn't have a smaller one. Whenever I heard that statement from then on, I thought my mother had made it up. We walked slowly in single file from behind the organist and into the front of the church, singing:

*HOW LOVELY IS*
*THY DWELLING PLACE*
*OH LORD OF HOSTS TO ME*
*THY TABERNACLE*
*OF THY GRACE*
*HOW PLEASANT LORD THEY BE.*

The organist always prompted me to sing as loud as possible, telling me I was important because I was last and I wasn't allowed to 'Trail off'. I believed him and made sure I did it, filling my lungs before entering. When Pannie joined the choir she had to be last as she was the smallest. Not good for her. I would dig her in the side for a carry-on, then we were often scowled at by the row of old dears facing us in the pews directly opposite, who glared over to make sure we were behaving ourselves. We were such angels, not. Sometimes there would only be about three of us in the choir, at others about seven. There was a saying in Govan then that if you had a loud voice, then you had the voice of a foghorn, and that's how I learned to project my voice, foghorn-style, from the help of the ships going up (or down) the River Clyde, and by the persuasion and exhortation of the wonderful and faithful organist.

The sweetie from the dear old church organist was always the same, absolutely rotten. I ate it anyway, as sweets were in short supply in our family in the 1960's. We got sweets, most usually when we got our hands on a glass ginger bottle. This is how badly off we were, I asked neighbours for anything they didn't want and rallied up my siblings and friends until we had enough junk and had a jumble sale in the street. We didn't have anything to sell from our own house except an old paperback book and a packet of cream crackers we found in the midden. I can't believe I'm owning up to this but Hey Ho, I wasn't alone. We made the grand sum of twenty-five new pence and ran off to buy a huge plastic piggy bank to save our brand new decimal currency in from future sales. We were fascinated by the sizes of the new decimal coins, which were tiny. However, I got into trouble for acting on my entrepreneurial business idea and was warned not to do it again, and that big brand-new yellow plastic piggy bank never held so much as a single new halfpenny in all the years to come.

Before I joined the young folks' choir I was simply a regular visitor in the congregation with Pannie. On the way to church we sauntered up Drive Road and bought something from the small newsagent's named The Drive Stores and kept coins for the collection after the singing. On arriving at church, we had to be done with the huge hard penny caramel (Dainty) peeking from our lips. One Sunday morning, my mother, as usual, had no money to give us. She would more often than not give us a ginger bottle to take into The Drive Stores. The Drive Stores paper shop always put an oblong white label across their bottles, which clearly stated 'The Drive Stores', and they would only redeem the glass bottles you actually purchased from there. No messing with this chap, if that extra white oblong label was not on the front of the bottle, then you had to go elsewhere with the bottle to get your money back.

The soft drinks/ginger companies have stopped giving the deposits back on the glass bottles, which is sad, as there are still many poor children in Glasgow today. Whether begging or stealing, seeking or finding, they had made it their life's mission (just like us weans) to collect the deposits on the glass bottles. The ginger bottle companies have stripped away a long tradition and part of our national heritage. Workmen and taxi drivers were always giving children bottles and many a housewife would give them away to any children who dared to humble themselves and ask. We had a regular caller, a wee boy from across the road. He had a hard life which was evident in his vacant eyes, a poor and sad wee soul with a soft voice. Our bottles became his bottles as he faithfully chapped the door to collect them every week. His Daddy left them for another woman but would often go back to the house to see his family and terrify their mother. My heart went out to the wee soul, God Bless him. That small income from the deposit on a 'Jeggie' or 'Glass cheque' was a great income to the poor child. Now the glass bottles are lying on the sides of the streets and grass areas around Glasgow like miniature dying statues, alone and unloved, bought with a price, unredeemable because nobody wants them. That sounds familiar. I never see anyone drinking from a glass bottle these days. Like I said, so sad. However it is a sign of the economic times, needs must and all that. I feel quite emotional now, ha ha. Thank you for the memories (and cash), Barr's.

Seriously now, there we were then, with the bible in one hand and a glass ginger bottle in the other, Pannie and I, off to

St Kenneth's Parish Church, via The Drive Stores, our local and faithful paper shop, only to find, lo and behold, it was closed, shut! Horror of horrors, there was nowhere else to go with our glass bottles (Gingies) which bore the name of The Drive Stores and we didn't get our huge toffee caramel to chew on either for the road to church.

Sunday back in the 1960's was a closed day for all commercial and retailers alike and the wee shop only opened in the morning until about eleven for the newspapers, milk, rolls, ginger, painkillers, tobacco and whatever else they stocked. We daren't go back home or we would be late, so off we went to church and Sunday school with the Irn-Bru glass bottles and no penny caramel. I kid you not. After we had sung our Hymns and Psalms with the big people, along came the purple velvet bags with two handles. You know the kind, you take one handle, pop in your offering and pass the other handle to the next person. When it came to me I took the bag from the old dear next to me, placed it between my legs and tried as hard as I could to squeeze that big glass ginger bottle into the long purple pouch, totally blocking the use for other givers. The neck of the pouch was about the same width as the ginger bottle and there I was trying to force it in there for God. Horrified, with big beady bulging eyes, were the old ladies beside me, nudging me and telling me as quietly as they could that, 'It's all right, just keep it, pass the bag along!' They were frantically waving and wanting me to pass the collection bag along without a fuss, but by that time I'm up on my feet with sheer determination. trying to force the glass cheque into the collection bag. I couldn't keep it, it wasn't mine to keep, I thought, as I shot them a look of disapproval to match the one they were giving me. Once I got the bottle halfway in, I realised it was well and truly stuck. Stumped, I eventually took notice of the advice of the older ladies. I had no option then but to stand on the handles of the sacred and holy collection/offering bag to pull the bottle back out. It was stuck fast and wouldn't budge. It was God's, and I was determined, even fearful, about obeying Him, and how was Pannie supposed to get her bottle in there too? God was entitled to it and it wasn't my fault the shop was closed. Oh the deprivation! There's more . . .

When we got back home our mother said I had told lies about the shop being shut just so we could keep the bottles for ourselves. 'You should have known better,' she said as she slapped me on the back of the head for telling lies. I keep laughing myself silly as I picture the mini me trying to give God a ginger bottle and it getting stuck, it's too funny. Every time my husband sees me in fits of laughter he asks, 'What are you laughing at?' You'll find out soon!

In the 1960's we might have been poor but we did have two televisions in the same room, not many people could claim that. They were in black and white of course, huge big fat contraptions that gave an electric shock from the static when we whizzed past the screen in Bri-Nylon clothes, the material of the day then. The television with the best picture was sat on top of the other, the bottom one wearing a tablecloth to hide it. Only in Govan would someone appreciate something so much they would wrap it up in the best tablecloth. Our kitchen table donned a plastic wipeable one. The bottom television was for sound because the picture didn't work and therefore the top one showed the picture, the constantly rolling picture that is. The aerial was always placed in the area where it would best receive a picture and we were warned not to move it. I found that if I stared at the bottom of the television screen and moved my eyes very quickly to the top of the screen I could keep up with the picture by continuously rolling my eyes for a few minutes. It was very sore on the eyes, maybe good for the eye muscles though. What wasn't good for the muscles, I thought, was when I had to stand on my tiptoes and hold the television aerial up so The Daddy could watch whatever was on. I would be in agony trying to keep the aerial in exactly the same spot so the interference in the picture would stop. 'Left a bit, right a bit, higher, lower.

Staun still, wull ye?' It was pure physical and mental torture trying to hold that heavy steel aerial up.

The picture always seemed to go right at the end of a film or at a really good dramatic part, that moment when the neck was stretched to take in every word and scene of the programme. My poor neck and arm was stretched to the limit too as I tried to hold our aerial still. I knew the trouble I would get into if I didn't do as I was told but I well remember the agony and weariness of holding it because I was the oldest.

When one of the televisions would conk, out came the big old brown battered suitcases of glass-pronged telly valves to replace the duds. I remember him slapping my hand hard and telling me to get back in case I broke them. They came from the streets of Govan and were lying there because the television was already broken, obviously. We were recycling in the 1960's, big time. It was either the telly that conked due to a dud valve or the (house) meter would run out and need fed with an old shilling.

The televisions were never on before four o'clock and it generally finished around twenty past ten. When there was nothing sensible or interesting on, the television had to be switched off at The Daddy's command. No person sat and watched rubbish, as he put it. As we got older we would make sure we were in for the soap *Crossroads* at tea time though. That was always a reasonably quiet time in our family. *Crossroads* wasn't just a soap opera, it was a welcome time of peace and quiet and was a bit of sanctuary, no shouting or demanding, just silence. My favourite character was Benny, because he was sweet and innocent and picked on and I didn't like it. A friend from church, many years later, told me she loved football because her daddy was very quiet when it was on. He would be watching Celtic and her family would be in Paradise because of the peace. Her beautiful mother wasn't getting a hiding then either because they were all told to shut up so he could watch and listen to the football.

Pannie and I slept cosily together in the bed recess of our room and kitchen having the usual rants, 'She's squashing me, she's nipping me, it's no me, tell her, mum, I'm trying to get to sleep,' we griped for attention. We had to be very careful, if it was attention we wanted we would be sure to get it, but not in the way we desired. Still, tough love was better than no love at all. A cuddle would have been nice instead of the jaggy army blankets which would still itch through the pink, purple and white striped flannelette sheet. The mattress was too big for this bed recess and was slightly buckled. However, it was squashed into the space and warned, 'You will fit in there' by The Daddy.

Between the fire and the bed recess of the kitchen there was a blue tallboy with two small Perspex sliding doors and a pull-down ledge for food preparation. The bed settee, cot and armchair left no room to move, leaving a tight squeeze to reach the sink. I remember having a Rice Krispie massacre on the tallboy as the cream stopped the milk coming out from the bottle. I gave it a good thud, the wide neck of the bottle cleared and the milk shot out at great speed and splattered over the tallboy unit, bed, floor, and everywhere else, taking the Rice Krispies with it. There was nowhere else but the floor to put the whistling kettle once it had boiled on the fire, because I remember the pain of standing on it and getting burned as I fell over it, resulting in a massive blister. The pain of the boiling water was incredible, my 'stupid fault' again for tripping over it. The Daddy yelled, 'Watch where yer gaun!'

We had no lavatory (Lavvy) in this flat, hence the reason The Daddy built a bath and toilet into the back end of the only room, but this now made the back room half the size it was and it was already too small. The five of us, Maw, Paw and the three bear cubs slept in the kitchen in this tiny dwelling place, all huddled together in the one room around the fire to keep warm.

Pannie didn't like the newly built toilet area because it was dark. The 'business' therefore was done in a flowery ceramic bowl in front of the coal fire. It had a matching jug with a large handle which lived under the bed in the recess. On visiting castles and stately homes, my children laughed at having to use a plate or bowl as the toilet. We weren't posh, but was the jug not for filling the bowl to wash your hands? So where were you supposed to p . . . oh, never mind! Pannie had her very own coloured plastic potty anyway, such luxury.

On the day the bathroom/toilet was completed we were promised we would get a bath, but got sent to bed early because I undutifully informed the whole of Govan Road we were getting a bath that night and our mum was affronted. Aye, right. I bet there was no hot water. I didn't realise it at the time, but we really had no piped hot water, so how was this mother of mine going to fill the bath?, and there was no light on in there, that is, no light at all because there was nothing connected to produce light. Blaming it on me indeed. There was hardly enough hot water in the geyser to fill the sink to get washed in and to fill the hot water bottles as well. That was the two rubber hot water bottles and the brown stone one I was blessed with. Pannie owned a nice rubber one with a knitted woolly jacket. I remember those scenes well, the pulled-down bed settee with The Daddy sitting at the bottom of the bed because there was only one armchair. The coal fire blazing away and our mum sitting in her armchair. The stone hot water bottle I got was wrapped in a towel because they were roasting but every now and again the towel would slip while I was asleep and I would wake up with a massive skin blister on my leg. Sometimes it would leak if it toppled over and guess what I then got the blame of? It wisnae me! It wasn't the first time a sibling wet the bed and blamed it on the water bottle. At least we were warm and cosy, most of the time.

A geyser was on the wall above the kitchen sink for hot water, which worked very much like a kettle except it had been plumbed into the water supply and the electricity. It was a very noisy contraption and spewed steam when it got to the higher end of boiling and was regulated by a thermostat, which I don't think worked as it was supposed to. When the geyser didn't switch off immediately, the kitchen, cum bedroom, cum lounge, cum pantry, cum scullery (I'm taking the Mick now) became a sauna. It was an all singing and dancing geyser, spewing steam and banging about as though trying to get off the wall, and the noises it made, protesting about being ignored. The geyser was like The Daddy, unhappy, ranting and always boiling over.

Along with the steam from the geyser we also had a paraffin heater, which was only used in the freezing winter or when there was no coal for the fire. It was pretty potent as far as fumes went and also caused a lot of condensation dripping down the walls. Apart from the chimney and the unofficial spaces in the sash windows, I'm quite sure the ventilation wasn't that great as the smell and fumes from the paraffin was toxic. Everything in the room stank of fumes and we went to school stinking of smoke from the coal fire, which burned everything else too, the cigarettes our parents smoked and the paraffin fumes. I can still remember the television advertisement for paraffin we used to sing along to, we even sang the Esso Blue song in the school playground and everybody knew it well. It went like this:

*THEY ASKED ME HOW I KNEW,*
*IT WAS ESSO BLUE*
*I OF COURSE REPLIED,*
*WITH LOWER GRADE ONE BUYS*
*SMOKE GETS IN YOUR EYES,*
*BOOM BOOM BOOM BOOM*
*ESSO BLUE!*

Our favourite all-time advert was the one where little spacemen laughed uncontrollably in the mashed potato one. The chimpanzee tea party adverts were great family ones too and we became great imitators of the voices of the chimps and at pretending we were posh.

In the kitchen area The Daddy built up the bed recess and put stairs into the hall to get there. The bed recess in the kitchen was made into a double bed recess, floored half way up to the top area and a large window put in. Looking down, we were technically still in the kitchen so we could peek down and watch the telly until our mother put a thick curtain up to spoil the fun. The Daddy was good at building and turned the room and kitchen into a better living space but it was still far too small for our family of five, and us weans growing taller each day.

In the back garden along behind the boiler houses were the high walls we called 'Dykes'. That was where we played, circus style; walking along the wall and dreepin' doon, then swinging on the washing line as though it was a trapeze swing. The washin' pole was used for pole vaulting, until we heard the scream, 'Good God in Govan!, get ma washin' pole back where ye found it or ye'll go straight tae the bad fire, am no fur tellin' ye's wan mer time!' We held our breaths in case our mothers heard the shouts of fury and we copped it. To dodge getting caught we had already learned to sprint as we were quite athletic in those days. The game was a bogey, though when some 'Collar and Tie' from the Cooncil decided to put the steel railings back up between the concrete gardens, they were taken down for smelting during the war long before my time. Drat. This meant we'd get caught and slapped for nonsense as we weren't able to bolt through the gardens any more. I was a dab hand at squeezing myself through the 'palin's', not everybody's head fitted through them.

We thought it was hilarious when the fire brigade had to come and stretch the wrought iron in order to set some poor wean free. Well, I might not have had a big head and never needed rescuing, but then again, I was always the one who had to go and get the ball because I could fit through the palin's with ease.

I refused to climb up the dyke walls because I was afraid of heights and there were spiders on the walls which the boys would catch and pull the legs from. I never did find that funny, it was an event which left me traumatised as the boys would chase us girls and put the spiders down our tops or jackets. That fear of spiders we are not born with soon developed into arachnophobia. The Daddy magnified this fear when he handed me a shovel with a giant (tiny?) spider on it one day to put outside. The spider ran up the shovel and I ran screaming to the other end of Govan, throwing the aforementioned shovel and spider high into the air.

A good neighbour of ours screamed at her son Alec, one of our friends, to 'Get doon aff that wa' afore you fa' and brek yer neck'. He got such a fright at being caught by his maw yelling at him that he jumped out of his skin, lost his balance and fell down the other side of the dyke and broke his arm. He had a stookie (arm plaster cast) for the duration of the school summer holidays. His wee mammy had to run round the block because of the palin's, as she couldn't climb the dykes to pick her Alec up to take him to the Southern General hospital.

We had friends as neighbours, who went to different schools depending on their religion, catchment area, personal choice or whatever the reason. It mattered not whether you saw them at school, through the week or through the window, at weekends we were still the best of pals. There was one particular pal with whom I hung around, we dined together, played together and lined up together. She was my closest pal but I have to say, not my *best* pal.

The purpose of this here testimony book is to give thanks and glory to God. I don't want to name her, therefore, I'll call her 'Friend'.

Friend had a tough time growing up as she didn't live with her mother. I found this too hard to comprehend as I believed with all my heart that I couldn't live without my mother. I often asked if Friend could stay overnight on a Friday so we could play together at the weekends but this request was always answered with a strict 'No'. The only time we met then was at school.

Friend had an awful habit of blowing hot and cold and we never knew what mood she was in until we got to school. She punched me in the back one day as we were leaving a classroom and as I was at the back of the line, the teacher didn't see what happened. I have no idea what part of my anatomy she punched but I nearly blacked out, the pain was so severe I couldn't breathe. I remember closing my eyes as Friend came back to my face and growled but I never heard a word she said. I thought I was dying and Friend fled when she saw the pain reflected on my face.

Another time, she split my head wide open when she booted the toilet cubicle door in when I was sitting with my head bowed. From primary one to primary seven she manipulated and bullied me every single school day, to that final day in primary seven when she promised to kill me. She spent all afternoon circling around me like a vulture in the classroom and hissed into my ear what she was going to do to me at 4 o'clock when the bell rang. I was heart sick of it and never once answered her back. Others in the classroom were furious. 'Don't let her talk to you like that, hit her back, we'll back you up,' they all said. They were sick and tired of her behaviour too. Still, I kept my head in my jotter and quietly got on with my work. Jolting every time she walked past and punched me or stabbed her pencil into my arm. When 4 o'clock came there was a riot in the playground with yells of 'Fight, Fight, Fight.' I was sad, I didn't want this, but for the first time ever, something changed in me, as I felt a stirring in my stomach. Strangely, I wasn't afraid of her any more and I had a feeling of perfect peace as I left the classroom. There was no chance of backing out, the audience was too big and I was the star attraction for all the wrong reasons.

The crowd spilled from the pavement and covered the road. Here we go again, I thought, as I stepped out of the front gate to spot her as large as life with her jacket off, bag down, sleeves rolled up and ready to give me the 'doing' I was promised. I looked at her with pity, I didn't want to hit her but I had to, I would have got hit again by The Daddy for not belting her back, a double whammy. I stood perfectly still in the hope she would change her mind but as she lunged towards me, she was floored with just one punch and landed on her backside. I was truly sorry and tried to pick her up but her arm slid out of her cardigan as I reached out to her. She was humiliated and wouldn't allow me to help. Fight over. She upped and walked away howling. Her control diminished, she was crying on the outside and I was crying on the inside. She couldn't have been happy with her circumstances, I reasoned. Learning to cope with life's difficulties, she was venting her anger and frustration on anyone who would persevere with it. She was the school bully for all of those years and I had just decked her, and my class friends were over the moon as the giant was slain. She was still my good friend because I truly liked her but she was a tyrant no more. The next day she came into the classroom and moaned, huffed and puffed that I had torn her good cardigan from off her back, truth and lies thrown about like Dolly Mixtures. I gave her a look that closed her mouth for good. I really did like her. When she was good, she was great to be around, funny and adventurous, and I felt compassion for her because she hardly ever saw her mum and I couldn't ever imagine the thought of not having my mother. She was my friend and I constantly, every single day of my primary school life, forgave her.

The Daddy was crouched at the bottom of the hall stairs one day, crying with his face in his hands because my mother was seriously ill in hospital during a pregnancy. I felt sorry for him, things must have been really bad, I thought, if The Daddy was sobbing. My mum couldn't die, there was no option and I was baffled by his attitude, even angry too at his disbelief. This strong hard-hearted man who was good at bullying and beating my mother was crying like a defenceless baby, crumbling, yet there I was totally believing and thinking, 'No way was my mother

dying' to God. He had just let me down big time, he belted
her soul to death every day and now he needed her.

I have always said I wasn't brought up, I was belted up. If
there was one thing the teachers were very good at, it was giving
the belt. That long dark brown thick leather strap cut into three
strips was painful and I got it a lot in primary school, as did
Friend. One of the times was because a young boy walked past
the teacher's desk and bumped a pile of rulers, accidentally I
might add, which scattered over the floor. I got belted across
the hands, three times up to the wrist for telling lies apparently.
The teacher asked who dropped the rulers, I told her it was
John, John denied it and I copped it for lying. Other reasons I
got belted for was only doing ninety-nine lines instead of one
hundred. I counted the teacher's first line of the sentence along
with my own in the addition and got belted as well as still
having to rewrite the one hundred lines properly.

The boys, on the other hand (or both), could choose to do
lines or take the belt. They always took the belt as writing was
time-consuming and they had better things to do. Dropping a
crisp packet in the playground was a punishable belting offence,
running in the corridor, not covering my jotters with wallpaper,
I got belted for that and I distinctly remember eyeing up our
walls and feeling so sad and poor because our wallpaper was
pathetic and didn't match. We had none for the walls, never
mind extra for school books. Not having a pencil and so many
more stupid, trivial acts were punishable offences. To be belted
for being a child is a terrible crime, especially by teachers and
mentors who are supposed to take you under their wing and
look after you. Legalised abuse, that's all that was. I'm very sure
many an adult looks back and recoils in horror as they reflect
the punishment awarded against them for the trivial little 'crimes'
they had committed. Yet I've also heard many an adult say the
belt was the best thing schools ever had and it didn't do them
any harm. A man even told me his class of boys asked their
teacher for the belt when their hands were frozen in the winter

just so they could get their fingers warmed up. Ouch, I cannot agree as I look at primary schoolchildren today and wonder how any adult could intentionally punish and hurt them, especially when they know nothing about them, and I'm so glad this heinous act of punishment has been abolished. I cannot imagine any adult pulling out that strap on a defenceless child of primary school age. I can, however, imagine what I would do if it was my child who was on the receiving end. God gave us the children for which I, for one, am eternally grateful. No person on this earth is going to beat them up in any way, shape or form, or anybody else's child for that matter. Child abuse is a real bugbear of mine to which I shout, like any other Glesga wummin, 'Away and hit somebody yer ain size!'

I became very disillusioned and withdrawn in my youngest years and walked through a dark place asking the same questions: 'Who does love me then? What's the point in living? I don't want to be here. I hate this life! I wish I wasn't here. I wish I didn't exist.' Somehow I knew I would always exist and have a certain consciousness. I knew I couldn't truly die so I asked God to 'take me away, just let me be all alone. I don't want to take part any more, take me to a quiet dark place so I can't get into trouble. I can just watch, look on and not get involved.' I threw my arms up and begged Him to take me away. I imagined sitting above the earth and being able to see what was going on without taking part or being judged. I told God to put me there, to let me go. He, like my mother, didn't answer. Not for now anyway. I didn't have suicidal thoughts, I had no desire or notion to kill myself or die. I just wanted God to take me from the world, I'd had more than enough of it and I meant it. I imagined myself sitting on a cloud or another planet all on my own, I imagined darkness all around me and I knew I wouldn't have a body. I knew I wouldn't have to breathe because I didn't need a body and I wouldn't need food either. I had it all worked out for God but He had other plans for me. For the longest time I felt I was nothing but a burden, I lost any hope I had and couldn't envisage a future. 'Hope deferred makes the heart sick.' My little heart was sick and my emotions were slowly becoming so low that I didn't care for me any more. Home life was awful, who cared? I didn't. The Daddy was right, I was a 'useless stupid idiot'. No wonder I wanted to leave the planet, this long dreadful existence was too hard. Beaten by The Daddy, best friend and teachers. I knew God was Supernatural and could do anything and I knew He listened to me and heard me but as I brought my plan before Him, I knew He was not going to answer. I sensed the silence. I occasionally wandered off and communed with Him and waited on Him.

I didn't belong to earth, I could sense that most of all. I deeply sensed that God had a hold on me and that I craved the silence. I had to be somewhere else and desperately wanted to leave but couldn't leave my mummy alone with The Daddy. I was deeply distraught and torn in my heart.

I was on a downhill spiral filled with gloom, doom and despair and I deliberately cut back on eating because I didn't care any more. My health deteriorated from the lack of food and proper nourishment but it was also on the way down that I realised I had a tiny glimmer of power and hope. It was nothing to do with dieting, it was about self-control, I had found out how to gain some power. I managed to fight, even if it was just with food and hunger. I had to gain control or die, therefore I chose to control the non-eating path. No person could force me to eat, I thought, they could belt or hit me but not feed me. I'd stir my food into a pile and angrily stab it with the fork, becoming the dog's best friend as I slipped it under the table.

Along comes a new friend, Annie Rexia (anorexia). She slithered in like the serpent in the grass she is, hiding, waiting for any kind of invitation, and decides she will be my new best friend and move in whether I like it or not. I didn't know her but she certainly knew me from my earlier childhood and was waiting, lurking, for that right moment to pounce. A sleekit beast. I was well and truly on my own now, no cuddles, those days had long gone, so much so that I remember only once in my life ever being cuddled by my mum and I cherished it.

Annie was very much like Friend and sided with The Daddy, she only hung around to get what she wanted, the destruction of a destitute child. She deceived me with pathetic lies like 'You are ugly, fatter than your friends, useless, stupid, poor, a tramp'. Every lie was presented as the truth, which I truly believed. The real liar, Satan, is always lurking behind God. I felt deeply ashamed, worthless and alone, often taking off and wandering to nowhere in particular, mindlessly throwing one foot in front of the other, wrapped up in my own thoughts and craving the silence by escaping the raging madness of the house. I'd had enough of this manic world and I wanted to leave, I wanted to be with God, alone, to commune with Him and Jesus, whom I knew when He came to take me out to play. I presented this plan to God as bold as I could and He was to come and take me away, because I said so.

One day I headed towards Elder Park and when I got to the gate the sun split through the trees and hit the back of my eyes. I squinted and had to look away as it was so bright. The sun pierced my eyes like an electrical current, blinding me for a few seconds. As soon as the light of the electrical current came into my life, I thought the words, 'I'm going to be all right' and ran off to the boating pond with a skip in my step. I literally saw the light. God is always with me, I reasoned. Even if I feel He's not there, God is there for me. Wherever I am, The Great 'I AM' is all around and, just like playing with Jesus, I could never run or hide from God. In the silence, He showed me everyone made mistakes every day and that He loved everyone as much as He loved me. He walked with me through the park, embraced by the heat of the sun, I also felt loved and embraced by The Son. Thoughts of leaving Earth left me when I realised God was with me for sure.

I questioned myself continuously in my thoughts and even on my thoughts. Wishing I could use my voice at home without being despised. Wishing I was allowed to speak and wishing I could say something important or even valuable. I became an 'inside talker' so nobody could hear my private conversations. At least in my silence I wouldn't get into trouble with my thoughts as no one would ever know how I felt. Who would believe I was with Jesus?

*Chapter Three*

# THREE STAIRS UP

~

*MURDER MURDER POLIS THREE STAIRS UP*
*THE WUMMIN IN THE MIDDLE HOOSE*
*HUT ME WI' A CUP*
*MA HEID'S AW' BLEEDIN'*
*MA MOUTH'S AW' CUT*
*MURDER MURDER POLIS*
*THREE STAIRS UP*

That was just one of the songs we weans would sing at the top of our voices, at the hint of any trouble, especially arguments from behind closed doors or between drunk men in the streets. Except in our own abode, of course. Who would want to make The Daddy any angrier than he already was?

The first visit to our larger flat further up the drive (to number 2) was met with a combination of delight and shock. On the one hand it was huge with a large kitchen, a separate living room area, two bedrooms and a real bathroom with a toilet, bath, wash-hand basin and a big square mirror. In the lobby were the stairs that led to the attic, where a further bedroom was later fitted with a skylight window. The flat was gigantic compared to our half room and kitchen and our voices echoed as we squealed. On the other hand, we were ordered to stand well back because the bathroom had a gaping hole in the floor allowing us to see down to the flat beneath. Being three stairs up meant we had terrific views looking over to the mouth of the Clyde Tunnel, where we would often play at the walkway entrance. We were still in Linthouse but, wow, we had this great big flat with several views from the bay windows, and from the kitchen window we heard an old man sing his heart out for a coin.

The flat was on the corner of Drive Road and Govan Road. From the right side of the bay lounge window our family could see over to Elder Park, part of the boating pond and some way up Govan Road, which led to the entrance of Govan Shipbuilders. Hanging out of the other window on the left-hand side, Govan Road, we could see up to where you would walk to the Southern General Hospital, known to the Govanites as the 'Suffering General'. The Hospital has been modernised and is now 'crowned' The Queen Elizabeth University Hospital. Rather a mouthful darling, a splendid construction, still, it's known as the Southern or Suffering to the Govan folks.

From the middle window we could see the tugboats on the River Clyde go by, with a high red mast, which meant a huge boat or a magnificent ship was about to appear. Whoever spotted the mast alerted the rest of the family with the shout of 'Tugboat!' We ran to the window every single time anyone saw that long slow-moving red mast and stood in adoration and amazement to admire the passing of the most magnificent vessels only seen in films.

The bottom flat of the close was later occupied by The Daddy's brother, James (Jimmy) and our younger cousins. They had no inside toilet in their bottom tenement and had to use the one in the common close along with The Butcher, The Baker and The Candlestick maker. They had a Dunny, though, an area underneath our Aunt's flat, and we understood it was a real dark dungeon, far too manky and scary for us. There were stairs down to The Dunny but nobody could get down there for the sludge, mud and smell of faeces. When we stood in front of our Auntie's kitchen window, which faced the back court and bent down at the railings in front of her window, we could get a peek through into The Dunny below. Our eyes tried to peer past the corrugated-iron door, which was twisted, bent and stuck in the bubbling mire.

We could only imagine what was in the basement, as we never dared to venture past the few stairs which were sludge-free. The smell from The Dunny must have been horrible for our cousins, as it was directly below their window. The smell certainly curbed our enthusiasm for adventure regarding that dark place, we weren't beneath raking through the middens for 'Jeggies', but we drew the line at The Dunny. In all our years in 2 Drive Road, that Dunny was never once cleaned out and stank to High Heavens.

We had a free run of the inner square and up the top of the middens for a while because the railings were still to be put up. Despite the smell of The Dunny, the close always had a clinical odour, as it housed Simmons The Dentist, which was on the first floor. I witnessed many an adult standing at the door, shaking and in tears, terrified to ring the doorbell of The Dentist. I'd creep down the stairs slowly and sympathetically, then ring the bell for them. The problem was, I also rang the bell and ran away when nobody was there for an appointment, and I got clouted for that. I was also very afraid when I had a mouth ulcer and my mother took me down to that same dentist for a check-up, I thought they would torture me with their drill with a vengeance for being a bit of a brat. As it turned out, Mr Simmons was a civil gentleman and looked after me very well. The receptionist was lovely too, so I stopped ringing their bell and running away. See what happens when you're nice? A lovely ripple effect touched my heart and they made me nice. 'Stupid' but nice, lol.

The circular winding stairs had a banister that was great for sliding down, except for having to dodge the spikes every metre or so, and there was a huge gap over the banister to the concrete floor below. Pannie remembers a male (a debt collector) being dangled over the banister by The (very angry) Daddy because he refused to accept we had no money.

All of our neighbours were characters and left their imaginary footprint forever in my memory. Mrs Thompson lived opposite the dentist, she was one hundred years old. I had never met anyone that old before and I was shocked to the core when she died on a Christmas Day, my first experience of death. It was an awful Christmas that year because we were told to keep quiet, something else to mar the celebration of The Saviour's birthday, but peace was with us for a little while, even if it was severely solemn.

Upstairs on the second landing was another Mrs Thompson, unrelated. Opposite her was an English family, the Kennedys. At the top and opposite from us was Mrs Mann. She was good to us and would take us in and give us a biscuit when no one was at home, once in a blue moon. Out came her bible for a lecture as we sat at her table munching away on her biscuits or fruit bread and butter. She read and believed in the scriptures, telling us, 'Man shall not live by bread alone', stabbing her finger nail repeatedly into the table to emphasise the point. We nodded in agreement as we sat there out of the rain and demolished everything she put down to us. 'Mind, she would say, 'You'll go to the bad fire!' That statement was used a lot when I was a child and it always shook me up.

Our new abode was an empty big flat, due to the fact we had nothing in the way of furniture or kitchen appliances to fill it. I remember nothing of a 'flitting' because we had nothing to gather up, bearing in mind also that life was very different back then. Any gathering up or any other business was 'None of your business!' It was rude for children to butt in and ask questions of matters above our heads. Sometimes The Daddy would yell, 'Och aye the noo!' A statement which was most welcome to our ears and meant he was in quite a good mood and all was well, for that precise moment.

New floorboards were hammered together everywhere before the coverings of wax-cloth were laid throughout, as it was the cheapest floor covering available. Our parents slept on the double

bed which was freed from the tight bed recess of number 14
and placed into the first bedroom nearest the kitchen. Pannie
and Catweazle had the other bed from the upper room of the
kitchen recess, then shortly after that they had their own single
beds in the second bedroom while I got the pull-down bed
settee, in the kitchen, all to myself.

The bed settee was kept in the kitchen along with the blue
kitchen display cabinet and there were two coal fires, one in
the kitchen looking into the back garden of tarmac and the
other in the lounge with the bay windows at the far end of the
lobby. I remember the evenings when we had relatives visiting
who stayed beyond my bedtime. I was tired and crabbit at having
to wait until they left before I could get into bed. 'Is it not time
for your bed?' one of them asked as though I was invading her
territory. 'You're sitting on it!' I told her in a huff with my arms
folded and eyelids drooping. Bedtime ranged from seven until
half past eight for us and I remember I wished our guests would
hurry up and get out so I could get to my bed. I further annoyed
any guests by pulling at the candlewick bedspread which was
draped over the bed settee. I never got into trouble for that, I
expect The Daddy wanted rid of them too. The kitchen was
the hub of the home, hence the reason the bed settee was still
there for a time along with the two televisions.

The kitchen window had a cream roller blind which was
stained at the bottom from the water from the sink and
equally stained at the top from the weather elements as the
swollen sash window often jammed. A long sticky brown flypaper
dangled from the front of the window, bearing the pattern of
the unfortunate fat blue beasties which flew in and stuck to it.

The bedrooms had fibreglass curtains with huge brown and
orange square patterns which were so abstract they clashed with
the psychedelic wallpaper left by the previous owners, also with
square bold designs. I particularly remember the curtains because
they were made up with very fine soft fibres which were not
thread, as I remember pulling out the thin strands of stretchy

strips. Gazing up, I didn't like the ornate plastered designs around the tops of the walls and the plastered cement around the light bulb because spiders came and went from the wee dark hidey holes.

I learned what fibreglass was as I became detective when The Daddy was out one afternoon. In The bay-windowed living room The Daddy was assisting in the building of a boat for a mate, like you do, in the living room of your tenement building as if it's an everyday occurrence. Occasionally, I would open the door and peek in to see what was going on in there, only to be told to 'beat it!' Home alone one day, I dared to do a tour of the living room and inspected this huge perfectly built boat which lay on its side. There were a lot of rough edges on the sides of the boat, which I ran my fingers along to check if the dark grey paint was dry. There were flat strings of fluff sticking of the sides and what looked like sheets of soft fluffy thin transparent wool lying on the floor. I poked, played with and pulled at the strands and was amazed at how hard they had become on the boat, the same stuff the curtains were made of. The smell in the room was so powerful it took my breath away and I soon found out that the materials to make the boat were fibreglass and something else very strong smelling to hold it all together. The Daddy had lung problems. The last thing he needed, apart from a packet of cigarettes every day, was a room full of fibreglass and the putrid stink of the dark grey paint-on sticky stuff which was required to bond it to make it become brick-hard.

I had never heard of fibreglass, glass made in thin fine fibres you could twist and bend and make anything you wanted to, even a big boat. I didn't hang around too long for fear of getting walloped for investigating The Daddy's handiwork. The big boat disappeared not long after I'd seen it, along with The Captain's mate, never to be seen again. Big boats could be seen on the left hand of our bay window, over at the shipyard, pedal boats bobbing straight ahead, over at Elder park boating pond, and in our front room, Boaty McBoatface, a big secret grey jaggy boat christened by me after kicking it, in the 1960's

Now that I knew what fibreglass was, I wanted some, along with the sticky smelly dark grey stuff to make it hard so I could make things. My head cogs were spinning with creative ideas. A doll's house, a toy box with a lid, a secret safe, anything.

After The Captain's mate vanished, the remaining fibreglass was then perfectly sculptured to make a huge tall square bunker for under the lobby stairs which held our toys. The bunker was so big I couldn't see over it on my tiptoes and too dark to see inside it anyway. I was always the one who had to clamber up and squeeze between underneath the stairs and over the top of the jaggy bunker which was not smoothed out at the edges. When I got into the bunker, I blindly searched for the items which were wanted by my siblings and would throw the whole of the contents of the bunker over the side leaving a mountain of shoes, belts, toys, telly valves, cars, broken crayons, dolls' arms and legs, you name it, it was in the pile. That's probably another reason why the toys were broken, I'd trampled over the whole lot. I could never find anything which was requested, it was like a lucky dip, take it or leave it, or, 'like it or lump it', as our mother would always say, especially regarding our dinner. It was the same old usual junk but the fertile imaginations embraced it as a prop to enhance play.

I'd pull out whatever I wasn't standing on and throw it over the side, then I would end up getting stuck inside because there was nothing else to stand on to get me out. I had no option then but to shout on my mammy for help and when she saw the mess I had made I copped it big time. Naturally, there wasn't a sibling in sight, as they scarpered when they got what they wanted and left me all alone to take the blame for the mess, there's gratitude for you. It was hard work, this fibreglass mountaineering, and I had to decide which part of my legs I didn't want torn to shreds as I clambered in and out of the jaggy bunker. I often got into trouble for throwing the goods

overboard and making a mess, then ordered to tidy up and put
it all back, but what was a big sister supposed to do when toys
were wanted? On one attempt at a quick getaway I managed
to rip the flesh from my shin on the corner of The open
toolbox on the way out from the bunker. I have the noticeable
scar as a reminder from that deep tear to this day. Scars that
are visible are a reminder of life's stories, lest I forget. I point
to it and call it The Daddy's toolbox scar, so deep and wide it
couldn't be stitched and it bled for many days.

I don't remember if I had woken out of a sleep or not, or if
the bedroom light was just switched off by my mother, yet I
remember spiritual events with clarity. I just remember I opened
my eyes to see three of the most beautiful stunning bright shining
Angels standing at the bottom of the bed settee. The Angels
were very tall and dazzling, but easy on the eyes. As I peered
over the blankets to look down to the bottom of the bed, I
didn't see their feet. I deliberately looked and realised they were
not standing on the bed. They were erect, completely still in
the air, watching me. Naturally at first I screwed my eyes up
and pulled the blankets over my face, not so much because I
was afraid, but more because I couldn't believe what I was seeing.
Then I dared to have another peek to see if I was really was
seeing them. Every time I did this they were still there. They
were so spectacular I was unable to take my eyes off them. They
were close together and positioned in a slight semicircle, standing
erect from the bottom of the pull-down bed settee to near
enough the height of the ceiling. I saw them as magnificently
huge and grand and much taller than a human being. They
were so beautiful I concentrated on them alone and didn't even
wonder why they were there, I was just so happy they were
there. They were literally out of this world and welcoming. I
knew they weren't there to hurt me, they were there for me,
they were mine. They knew me well, better than I knew myself
and were my Angels, I knew that without being told. White
and sparkling with hints of soft glittering colours, each of them

different, with the most beautiful stunning faces I had ever seen or known in the whole of my little life.

They were in communication about me and the one on the (stage) right would often turn to face me during the silent conversation. Although I didn't know what the discussion was about, I knew they were there to guard me and to prove to me they were there at all times. I belonged to them and they were mine, they were in charge of me. They saw and knew how I felt about their presence as I lay in that big bed settee alone. I don't remember them flying off, seeing wings, or leaving, or me ignoring them to go to sleep. They were so incredible I would have watched them all night long. The next thing I remember it was morning.

I smiled all day and most of the days after that because the Angels visited me but I never told a single soul throughout my primary or secondary years at school, not until I was in my thirties at least. Even then I took some stick. Seeing Angels is personal and very natural but sharing the event with others is daunting because we then have to speak of the Supernatural, the natural which becomes Super. I loved them, though, and thought about them all the time.

The super events I now share are above our natural under-standing. Neither did I ever tell a single soul in the world of the following events, which I now share, not even to any friends or family closest to me. I didn't want to frighten anyone and, like the other testimonies I share, who would have believed me anyway? Bear in mind I had no confidence as a child and would have feared the reaction. I would have felt stupid and I certainly didn't need any more fuel to add to the 'Idiot' fire. I couldn't share everyday childhood events, how could I tell anyone this?

After sleeping on the bed settee for some time I was given a single bed of my own, which was placed in the lounge where my visions and dreams started coming along thick and fast. I am often ridiculed, mocked and laughed at for believing in God by others who don't believe. I find it harder not to believe in

Him, I've grown up with Him. I ran about playing with Jesus, which was natural as far as I was concerned. Apart from loving and wanting Jesus in my life I had no deep religious bible-thumping upbringing which was bashed into me and even although I went to church I couldn't ever remember a word the minister said. Proof of that came when our mother asked what the sermon was about every Sunday. 'God,' I candidly told her. At around that age (8yrs) I didn't tell anyone anything, not even my beautiful mother. Who would have believed a mere stupid child? I knew exactly what I was seeing and feeling then. I'm not going to spend a lot of time on this dirty dark area because it does not glorify God. He, whom you squash under your feet, is not even worthy of a mention of His name. I was not only visited by Angels, however. I must write about these events, I must explain to everyone I can that there is an evil enemy. I've seen him several times, I've even had a conversation with the dark liar via a telephone call. He is real and Hell is real.

When I was first moved into the lounge on my own, it was because the flat was being painted and decorated one room at a time after 'Boaty McBoatface' was gone, hence the shuffling around of beds. I was quite happy to be on my own as I was at peace when I wasn't having The Daddy to contend with, and it was great to have my own bed and not be kicked and thumped by another sibling pulling at the blankets and disturbing my sleep.

Night after night, on the ceiling, as I lay in my bed, I watched the swirling of what looked like small tornadoes. As they were swirling (slowly), they would swell, peak and flow, and the centre of each tornado would come down a couple of feet like a huge black pointed finger, searching, twisting menacingly, looking?, and then suck back up. It started off with one or two and then the whole ceiling was dense in a dark sort of fog as they morphed together, in smoke of black and grey, the street lights highlighting the shadows of the tornado shapes. I pulled the blankets over my face so I couldn't see. I did see though, I watched them dip and turn, swirl and swell in size, as they covered the whole ceiling in three dimensions, probably four, as it was a spiritual happening too. There was a horrible presence in the room, albeit on the ceiling, and I was scared. This horrible scene happened many times, even after I saw the Angels for the first time. I would eventually close my eyes and ignore the swirls, what I couldn't see couldn't bother me – but then I also had the most awful time with my bed moving. I'd never actually see it moving, as I was lying in it with my head covered to shut myself away from the tornado swirls, but I could feel it. I knew my bed was moving because it would tilt at awkward angles, rocking from side to side, and eventually bumped down with a dull thud, not loud enough for anyone to hear, but I heard it. God has just revealed He allowed me to witness this as other children are going through it today. The third horrible experience that happened a lot was the sense and feeling that something was walking on my bed, like an animal, a cat? We didn't have a cat. I would feel the pressure on top of my blankets. It was dreadful, starting at the bottom where my feet were and moving up, I could feel the indentations as 'The Creature' or thing moved up my bed. This experience upset me most as it was too close and I could actually feel that something was on my bed, creeping, as well as feel the bed moving. I had a sense, though, that the 'evil one' was not allowed to harm me. I knew that above all and was comforted with that knowledge. I still hated it, though, and wrapped the blankets tight around my head when I felt the movement on top of my bed. From childhood I slept with the blankets tight around my neck. No matter how warm I was, I refused to let the blankets go, my knuckles firmly clenched until I relaxed and fell asleep.

I didn't see any horror movies until I was much older. When I did see some later on in life I was astonished at the accuracy of some of the events portrayed in them. How did the writers and producers know that? Did somebody else experience what

I had experienced? Where did they get the information and ideas from? Satan, that's who! I quickly wrote the exact moment God told me that other children are seriously frightened today, they are being tormented by evil visitations in their rooms when they are alone. They cannot tell an adult for the same reasons I couldn't tell, fear of looking stupid, fear of not being believed, fear of being destroyed by the evil presence for opening up. Where do they begin? They cannot open up and explain what's going on.

I am only the messenger telling my testimony but God has let me experience these events for 'Such a time as this'. He told me that. Children are being visited by evil and are terrified.

They have entered portals and are exposed to information they should not know. Doors have opened where evil has penetrated their little souls. I did not live in the computer age and still experienced the demonic happenings which I knew nothing of.

I went back to church after backsliding, for the sake of my children. Even if I was not welcome (which I was), I had to make sure my children were brought before The Lord, who loves every child. I had no access to the internet when I was a child but I saw the evil with my own eyes. I am not the one who can solve all of the evil problems but I will expose the vile evil all day long, to save one child. God is there, He is the one who is calling and the door is open. If you cannot bring yourself to seek God, you *must* do it for your children. Too many children, even in my journey through life, have taken their lives because they are traumatised. Too many young men I knew have committed suicide. Too many youngsters are trying to change their identity, even gender, because they hate who they are. This is a lie from The Father of lies who is warping their little minds and lives. Doctors and Mental Health organisations cannot help because they have not seen or know (as I have) how evil operates.

How many of our children are mentally suffering in silence?

Ask them gently, phone Elim for advice (any Elim) or bring them to church. This is not a promotional exercise to fill chairs at church. There are no exorcisms, no shouting or waving crosses at the devil. The blood of Jesus washes everything away and it is enough, there is nothing more to be given. As I write this I have been terribly sick and hospitalised, not with just one illness, but with a raging fever, pains in my lungs, shooting pains through my head, no energy, all attacks from Satan, who is clearly trying to stop me writing, but the war against evil has already been won and the glory belongs to God who loves us to death (via Jesus). I have Angels assigned for this very reason.

On a visit to look through old photographs for this book, Pannie was shocked to her core when I told her my bed moved, then I was completely taken aback when she told me quietly that her bed moved too. I believe her, of course. Another sister was lying on her bed having a rest with her eyes closed, not sleeping. She opened her eyes to find a young girl standing at the bedroom door, beckoning her to follow her. My sister was horrified. Every time she closed her eyes tight and looked again, the little girl was still there. Naturally, my sister did not get up and follow her. Some years later a friend told me she woke up to find a little girl sitting cross-legged and smiling at her, on her dressing table. Believe and trust me, please, the youngsters who appear before you are not children! Do not follow under any circumstances. They are in disguise, not innocent, not nice (they are evil!) and certainly not of God.

When I was a newly saved Christian I thought I would share an incident with an older Christian woman. As I spoke about a little of my childhood she lowered her head, pulled her eyebrows together like a madman and growled, 'What are you talking about?' I stopped talking and realised she was not the right person to share with. Can you see why I told no other person? A 'Born Again' Christian wouldn't even listen. Many years later I did meet the right person (from Elim the first time I attended), who had witnessed exactly what I had seen and she even started the conversation, which allowed me to open up. I wrote I have seen 'him', the evil one. I will explain further on through the chapters.

Children are very vulnerable and are easier to access spiritually but God is a jealous God and He will not let any spiritual evil harm us. My experiences as a youngster were real living ones, in the flesh and in the spirit, especially when I was taken from my bed while I was fast asleep. I didn't ask for the insight but God clearly decided I was the one chosen to witness.

I am sharing with you another of the events I was actually in. As I was fast asleep I was taken from my bed and placed upon a very high hill and watched what I can only describe as flying animals of a very weird kind. I wasn't afraid because God had taken me there.

The flying beasts were hairy and gruesome with the faces of what I would now describe as gargoyles, really ugly. The flying beasts had square baskets made of wicker on their backs and inside the square baskets were other smaller beasts who had no wings, hence the reason they were hitching a ride inside the baskets. There were thousands of them swooping and flying above the land, below me. The flying beasts laughed in horror as they swooped down upon humans so the beast in the basket could pour something from a vial upon them. As a child I thought of this vial as a vase. There was great hilarity between the basket beast and the flying one. The beast in the basket was absolutely crazed with evil intent and worked closely with the despicable flyer. The vials of destruction came with spiritual contents, such as sickness, disease, bodily harm and mental torture. The contents of the vials were poured over the heads of the people running but nobody could outrun the beasts and I did not see any children in the crowd.

There was a young slim woman running and screaming with the smaller beast in the basket hanging out, pulling at her hair and dragging her along, causing her to stumble. Her hands were on her head, trying to free herself from the evil one in the basket, who was dragging her while laughing at her pain and distress. She was wearing a mauve-coloured skirt, a flesh-coloured blouse with a bold dark pattern and an opened lighter fawn cardigan, that's how long I watched her being terrified by the demons, long enough to look at what she was wearing. A thin young lady who looked respectable and well dressed in nice clothes.

The man behind her had something poured from a vial into his face that burned him and he couldn't see. He was in terrible pain and ran, stumbling, in the same direction, after the woman with his hands stretched out in front, groaning in agony. Those were the two main humans I zoned in on because they were first and I felt tremendous pity for them but there were many thousands of other humans being tortured and trying to flee from the demons, but they couldn't outrun them.

The flying demons and their sidekicks came in on the scene like hundreds of thousands of bats, making the sky black and scattered over the land in order to pour out vials of torture, sickness and diseases upon mankind. It was a real and horrible scene and I felt helpless watching the evil demons, who resembled gargoyles, torture older people at will, older than me anyway. No one could escape because the wicked flying demons were skilled and fast.

As I was watching the horrific scene from the hilltop I was suddenly startled by one of the demons, who flew swiftly before my face and stopped menacingly in front of me, as close as he could get, suspended in the air. He had no basket and stood upright before me as I was standing on the highest point of the hill. A disgusting weedy being, unclean, dark and dirty in all aspects, his intention being to harm me. I sensed he had more authority than the others as he was bigger. I was just a child but he didn't care, he 'did' children. Destroying children destroyed families forever, every day a living nightmare.

'You are not allowed to touch me,' I told him with certain pure knowledge. I communicated with thought and he

understood my thoughts and words perfectly. I had that confidence. He stared intently into my eyes as though waiting for
permission from me. None came. He was the most evil demon
and it took the biggest one to come after me, no one could
escape.

He made no attempt to touch me or even stay in my presence.
He stared into my eyes with malice, then quickly flew to the
hill opposite as soon as he received my thoughts of knowledge
and warning which I knew were of God. I was very calm as I
simply looked over at him on the other hill to my left. The
only thought I had of him as I watched him was 'You have
been put in your place and there will you stay.' Every time I
was in the same place and had the same experience, saw the
same demons hurting people, the larger demon had to stay on
the hill opposite, on my left side and all he was allowed to do
was look at me. I have since realised that the devil and demons
have some respect for God! That was the certainty I had, that
he, the demon, or it, was not allowed to touch me. With all
that went on in my bedroom as I lay down to sleep, I had the
certain knowledge that the devil and his demons were not
allowed to touch me. No matter how many times I saw the
swirls on the bedroom ceiling, felt the bed move, or felt something creepy on my bed, the dark evil enemy was not allowed
to lay one hairy demonic finger on me.

I have often thought about the poor people who were being
harmed with the contents of the vials, though. Who were they?
Who are they? I know this account is very real and powerful
and may come as a shock to some but the evil is not allowed
to touch you without God's (or your) permission. I know many
people who have been healed of cancer through prayer and I
also know some who got cancer and might argue they weren't
bitter or unforgiving. I don't even know if the people being
tortured actually saw the demons or not. They were running
and screaming because of the contents from the vials, not just
the demons themselves. The Lord God showed a little girl a

very powerful truth about the demons, sickness, disease, obedience and salvation. When we obey God, nothing can harm us. The same little girl the first primary school teacher said, 'Not you' to, God said, 'Not that one,' to the demon who intended to hurt her. God The Father fights our battles for us, that just makes me eternally grateful with everlasting humility, joy, praise and gratitude.

At the top of the wooden stairs in the lobby, there was a very small room to the right and to the left was the rest of the attic which covered the whole of the house and which wasn't floored. With the help of The Daddy's cronies, a window was put in on the roof to let daylight into the small, newly built room. A single divan just fitted in there along with a small bedside table and I was told I could have it if I wanted to. How kind, but there was no way I was going to sleep up there with the spiders and the wind howling through the rafters. I also did not want to be isolated and known as 'Esther in the attic'. I had my share of demonic dreams, visions and encounters in the room I was already in, thanks for nothing. The thought of trying to sleep up there in the cold and dark was a non-starter. I was afraid of the bogey man and was having none of it. Having now spoiled the family sleeping arrangements, I had no option but to share the second bedroom with Pannie and Catweazle. Bunk beds had to be bought so we could all get in there without too much of a squeeze.

Pannie got the bottom bunk with me commandeering the top bunk. We each had our very own grey jaggy army blankets to keep us warm, along with our soft flannelette sheets, mine with a huge hole at the bottom because it was threadbare and I stuck my foot through it. Candlewick blankets were placed on the top and no coat was required for the bed to keep us warm in the summer months. After our bedtime prayers, we three girls would 'yack' for the longest time after being sent to bed but there was safety in numbers and nothing happened when we were all together, except for the second visitation of my Angels, which I alone saw.

We arrived home from primary school one late afternoon to find there was a fully grown German Shepherd dog taking up centre stage in our kitchen, right in front of the coal fire. The new surroundings would have been quite strange for the dog but by the time we had come home it was fairly settled at The Daddy's feet. The beast stood to attention when we bounded through the door. We loved dogs and up to that point in time German Shepherds were my favourite breed but this one behaved strangely around us, having never known us. It had been found wandering in the nearby Elder Park and given a degree of care, attention and affection by The Daddy while we were at school because he liked German Shepherds too, I think. I remember him laughing his head off to my mother because he sold our dog, a German Shepherd, to someone many miles away and the dog came back three days later. He then sold it to someone else for the same money and it didn't come back. He was hoping it would because he thought it was a great income and laughingly joked about training the dog to do it for real. There would have been a lovely period of silence in the kitchen before we all bundled in after school looking for our dinner, that's assuming The Daddy was behaving himself and not beating or threatening my mother.

The Dog sat beside The Daddy on the floor all evening and I had come to the conclusion very quickly that this was not a friendly dog. Handsome it was, friendly it wasn't and I knew I was its sacrificial lamb. I tried to pretend I didn't care like my siblings who weren't the least bit interested in the dog but I sat on the chair nearest to the kitchen door, as I was afraid of it and ignored it as much as I could. It had locked its eyes on me and I felt very insecure and knew that if and when I moved, the dog was going to bite me. It was going to bite me and I needed help, I knew this without a shadow of a doubt and I needed to get away from it. How quickly can I stand up and pull the kitchen door open to flee? I wondered. The dog stared menacingly as though laughing and warning me at the same time. It became a battle of wills and I knew for sure, being a little girl, I was going to lose. Given this sure knowledge then, I had no option but to speak to The Daddy.

'Daddy, will you hold the dog?' I pleaded as calmly as I could. 'It's going to bite me.'

He was angry as he twisted his neck round to look back at me from the floor. He swore at me and basically rubbished my plea, telling me it wasn't going to bite me and looked away again. So with his assurance and wisdom (not!) I plucked up the courage to casually stand up and reach for the door handle to exit the kitchen. I didn't make it. The dog had the front of my stomach between its teeth as I screamed the house down. The Daddy shot up and battered the dog from me and threw it back into the street and I spent the rest of the evening in the Southern General Hospital, where I was wrapped in a huge bandage and given a tetanus injection.

I was frightened and needed protection and assurance. I needed him, The Daddy, the head of the family, the Captain and anchor of our destitute sinking ship, and I asked him to help me even though I didn't want to. I had to ask him for help, there was no one more able than he to protect me at that precise moment and he let me down. There was no apology, no kiss, no hug, only bad attitude and much swearing. The Daddy might even have been angry because he'd lost his new-found friend, instead he had to look after the rest of the siblings as I walked to the hospital again with my mother. I screamed as the dog held onto my stomach but I didn't dare cry when it let go. I was too afraid to cause a fuss and breach any solitary peace. I deeply craved peace, the silence in peace was priceless. I would have taken thousands of dog bites for peace. If it meant The Daddy would behave before my mother and not batter her, then I would have suffered willingly.

Despite the heartaches I still found a few, though rare, positive moments, like the time The Daddy threw his hot cup of tea full on in my face. The tea ran down my fringe and covered the sides of my hair. I sat down quickly at the table and didn't react to his anger because I didn't want him to hit my mother, so I learned to keep the peace. I stared at the wall so as to focus on something, trying to block out the violence behind my back, my little heart hurting with each manic outburst as my mother got the height and breadth of his temper, by his fists. I didn't dare move a muscle because I was frightened, that's what I got for trying to protect our mummy. The hot sweet tea touched my lips as it dripped over my eyes and down the front of my face. As it cooled and dried in my hair, it became brick-hard because of the three sugars piled into the cup. I remember clearly fingering my hard crispy locks of hair and thinking, this would make good hairspray. I sat at that kitchen table, for hours, in my own wee world wondering how I could make hairspray from sugar and hot water. My thoughts often took me into my own little world in my mind, where I could block out the animosity and atmosphere in our kitchen. I was used to squashing flowers, mainly rose petals, into a bottle of water to make perfume, now here was a great new idea, hairspray made from sugary tea. Anything to take my mind away from the harsh situation I found myself in. I was too afraid to retaliate, especially because I knew he would take his temper out on my mother all the more. I could take a 'doing' but my heart broke when he battered my precious mother.

His anger was vented at my mother early one evening just as she was getting her cape on over her nurse's uniform. He had kept her late for work as it was with his usual verbal abuse.

I thought he was going to kill her this day. He picked up the mop pail filled with filthy water and threw it all over her pure white starched apron just seconds before she was about to leave for work. She didn't make it to work that night because she was soaked through with the filthy, dirty, manky water which flowed from her face, her eyes and down her cheeks. She worked on a mental health ward, how ironic was that?

Her job wasn't very far away and an easy walk to the Southern

General but he would pile us into the car to drop her off. She would finish at 9 o'clock at night but we would all be back in the car and waiting for her at half past 8 just so The Daddy could watch her through the windows of the ward to see what she was doing, to see who she was talking to. I loved sitting in the car waiting for her too because I hated being looked after by The Daddy. The difference was, I was waiting and longing for her to come home because I missed and loved her. I wanted to try her cape on and would always touch it but she'd never allow me to as it was for her work and had to be kept in pristine condition for inspection by The Matron. I wanted to be with her at all times, just me and her, my mummy and her cape, her mantle.

One of the worst rants and beatings ever was because he didn't have the same teaspoon as before. A teaspoon? How could a beating come from something so small and so trivial as a teaspoon? That was my thought as I sat at the kitchen table and stared at the bent teaspoon he hung over the handle of the kitchen door when he threw me onto the chair. The wee teaspoon wrapped around the kitchen door knob, swaying, dangling. I stared at the teaspoon for ages in utter disbelief. Cold, sitting in my pyjamas and with morning bed hair, crying on the inside and trying to warn imminent tears, don't fall from my eyes, don't cry, staring at the swinging bent teaspoon and trying to make sense of the manic beating going on behind me.

My mother was getting abused because of you, you dirty little bastard of the devil teaspoon. Hell was in the kitchen that morning. Was it any wonder it was on my bedroom ceiling at night? He blew up in the worst anger ever. Here was My Daddy, The Daddy of three little girls and a beautiful wife, standing before us as a monster.

The Addams Family, people called us. The Daddy was Adam. My Mother had very long jet-black hair and I was often called Hester because my name was Esther and it rhymed. The coincidences were amusing, the evil angry monster in our house was real, though, and a trillion miles away from being remotely funny.

Life mellowed a little for all when the fourth member of the Baxter clan entered the brood. A boy this time, who was given the name of the first child, Adam, named after The Daddy and his father (before him). It was from then on that, as I began to grow and mature, I also began to see that all was not well in our household compared to others. The mental damage had already been done to my mother, certainly, and to us three girls, for sure. I was a cowering, unhappy wreck with no vision for the future unless it was to escape and free myself as far away as possible from my circumstances, yet I was trapped between good and evil. I could never leave my mother and I had no desire to do so. I often went out and walked alone and developed 'Actress mode', to be able to smile and laugh in the thick of mayhem to the big wide world outside, but how I looked on the outside was not how I was feeling on the inside. Of course I don't remember any of the abuse as a baby but I must have known even then. I must have jumped out of my skin as a newborn when I witnessed the shouting and swearing. I would have known fear and trembling from the womb and would probably have whimpered, cried and screamed with due cause as I was rocked to sleep.

I would have sensed my birth mother was unhappy and I would have been afraid for her and for myself. I flinched away and cringed when The Daddy came close to me, It's only natural I didn't like him, but I have said and will always say, I did love him. After all, The Daddy was My Daddy too, and most children love and look up to their Daddies. So then, The Daddy was very happy now he finally had a son, and changed dramatically, except for his manic temper.

Everyone paid homage and admired the special baby brother, who was now the apple of The Daddy's eye. He was given the name of the womb child who went back home before being delivered, stillborn. My mother had to deliver the first Adam, who was declared deceased, that's all I know. Would I have found favour in The Daddy's eyes had the first-born child survived? I didn't know and I didn't care any more. I guess life would have been very different if I had a big brother on Earth but for some strange reason I've always guessed I wouldn't have liked him any more than I liked The Daddy. I find that thought very sad as I never got to meet him but he could have been a 'chip off the old block'. Would he have been like The Daddy? Would he have bullied me too? Am I still thinking I don't have a very high opinion of the male species, who are meant to protect, guard and nurture us? Daring to agree with God when He said He 'Repented He made man' and thinking 'No wonder!' When in fact, he meant all of mankind. The ripples of hurt and disillusion waved over me constantly as a youngster. This Daddy was a fake. How could he love one child and not the other? How could he take me and Pannie into the sweet shop and buy her sweeties and not me? How could he use the same mouth to laugh with a baby and then explode vociferous lava the next?

At one point I was convinced, perhaps hoping, I was adopted and asked my mother while sitting quietly beside her in front of the roaring coal fire.

You should have seen the look of shock and horror on The Daddy's face. He looked at my mother for help before enquiring, 'Why did you ask that?' Cowering into the side of my mother's warm chair, I lowered my head and quietly mumbled to him that I was treated differently and wasn't like the rest of the family, so I just wondered. The Daddy was speechless for once in his life. Quickly keeping full control of the conversation, I also got right in there and threw in the comment about me having green eyes while everyone else's were blue or brown. I don't know what his thoughts were but I touched a huge nerve in him by telling him I was different. He knew I was different, he just used bad words to tell me so because he didn't understand me. I then pretended I was disappointed I wasn't adopted and shrugged my shoulders, closing my eyes and snuggling deeper into the smoky armchair.

So, he confirms he is My Daddy, he was never My Daddy. A Daddy is more than a blot of ink on a birth certificate. A Daddy loves all of his children. I really didn't know him as a Daddy. All I knew was that I loved him, yet I loved it most when he wasn't at home where he battered my other parent for no reason.

I had already found it was only the love and kindness of Jesus that was real. The look in His eyes, His laughter, His grace, gentleness and concern. The ache in His heart for me. He, Jesus, came for me, that brought me up and through those difficult times, thoughts and emotions. He kept me going, smiling through sorrow, pain and grief. Then, to cap it all, I learned He laid down His life for me. What other man did that? Not only was He a man but He was and is, God. I was deeply humbled. The Daddy mellowed a bit and left me alone as our new baby brother grew strong and well and was as happy as any other wee boy . . . I think, I hope.

Little Addie proudly followed The Daddy up the hall swinging his kilt while attempting to blow any kind of tune through his chanter. The Daddy wailed on his bagpipes while they both stamped their feet as hard as they could up and down the lobby to annoy the English neighbours below. I didn't have to wonder why the boy in the flat underneath wouldn't talk to me in class at school. The noise must have been horrific but they never did chap the door once to complain. They knew what The Daddy was like, they must have heard him shouting and bawling at my mother and me.

One 'good' morning I felt as free as a bird, as I playfully kicked a small ball belonging to young Addie as I ran into the kitchen. The Daddy wasn't in, the fantastic air of freedom in the house was almost tangible, with perfect peace we could all relax. As the ball bounced off the wall I slipped and fell backwards and knocked six bells out of my head. Millions of stars

swirling above me like birds, 'tweet, tweet, tweet'. The cloud
of bright sparkling stars followed me to the chair I was directed
into, around the table with Pannie, Catweazle and Addie, sometimes referred to as 'Plug'. I know we were served porridge that
morning because it looked as though I had two plates of it. As
I looked up at my mother while she was pouring in the milk
I announced, 'I've got two mummies.' 'What do you mean?' she
asked, peering into my eyes. 'I've got a mummy here and a
mummy there,' I told her, pointing my finger into space. 'I can
see two of everything,' I mumbled.

No sooner had I looked at my porridge, I was sick in my
bowl. When The Daddy came in, I was frogmarched to the
Southern General Hospital,vomiting all the way up Govan Road.
I was dragged there, gripped in my mother's hand, which I was
grateful for because I didn't know where to put my feet, given
that I had four of them and staggered all over the place.

I remember complaining I didn't want to walk and had a
great desire to lie down and go to sleep, but she yanked me
along that road at great speed, ignoring my protests to sit down.

At the hospital I was bathed in a small amount of lukewarm
water and I remember thinking there wasn't enough to cover
my legs. I 'washed' by moving my fingers on top of the water,
trying to lift it up to cover me. Voices were echoes as though
everything was a strange and fuzzy dream. I recall a distinctive
odour of some sort of medicinal liquid, lights shining on the
water, then nothing. When I came back round, I found I was
in bed. I was fine and just kept in for observation but I enjoyed
being in hospital, in a warm bed where nurses were nice to me.
I wanted to stay there forever. It was heavenly to me then, peace
and quiet with nurses looking after me, lifting my arms and
tucking me in, taking my temperature and just talking softly
throughout the night. That just goes to show you how desperate
I was for affection.

Up until the age of eleven, I cannot remember even one
instance where I was truly filled with so much joy or happiness

that I laughed genuinely (except for when Jesus came for me). When I did laugh it would have been a spiteful wicked laugh at someone else's expense. Even at that young age I was learning to become defensive, bitter, resentful, unkind, mischievous, and generally filled with so much negativity in looking forward to the new day. I genuinely cannot recall a day when I sprang out of bed excited about an event I was looking forward to and, if there was such a day, say, Christmas Day, then I knew I would still be walking on thin ice because The Daddy, The Head of the House, would make sure it went with a bang. My mother would get beaten for absolutely nothing, or for the stupidest little thing imaginable. His huge hands were constantly wrapped tight around her throat or slapping her hard across her face. One hand at a time. Slap, slap, slap, slap, giving her whiplash. She was accused of talking to everyone, men and women. She was even accused of looking at other people. This was shocking. My mother walked her whole life with her eyes looking at the ground all the time when she was outside the house. I asked her why she did this. 'Sometimes I find things,' she answered quietly. She was even accused of thinking about someone else. She was a cow, whore, bitch . . . you get the picture.

The feeling I have right now is that I would like to apologise to every family member who is deeply saddened by what they have just read. It's over, close the floodgates. Nothing can change the past, I just hope that, if there are other children needing outside help, that someone, somewhere, will help by talking with the child. As I stated at the beginning, this is my testimony and point of view from my childhood and I cannot give an account for anyone else. I don't doubt for a second that another sibling will have a totally different account by way of their own testimony and, if it's a good one with great memories, then I'm truly happy for them because people change and learn as they get older, we are not born with wisdom, it comes through life experience. That cup we imagined as we sang 'Full and running over' in Sunday school, will one day, be 'Full and running over', as we all hang on in there. The eldest child gets the roughest deal in the family. I see clearly that Pannie got treated well by way of treats and I don't ever remember her getting hit or slapped for misadventure but I still did see she was very unhappy as a child. The third child, Catweazle, seemed to get away with everything, yet she was the cheekiest. She would answer back and shout 'No!' when it suited her, even making The Daddy laugh. The fourth, a boy, could do no wrong, not only because he was the cherished one, but because he was male and was clearly wanted by The Daddy.

On looking back, The Daddy lived in a house of females before our precious little brother came along and he was absolutely livid when we had short clothes on or attempted to wander around in our nighties. The only reason our clothes were short was because they were too small. I knew this because I remember not being allowed to wander about in the kitchen with my nightie on or I would get a hard slap on the back of my leg and told to cover up. He was very critical of our clothes and was overly strict. My mother wore no make-up or even perfume, she couldn't afford make-up and wouldn't have bought herself any for fear of showing off and trying to attract the opposite sex. She wore the same old clothes and I truly don't ever remember her buying herself anything other than tights, which I got to wear occasionally. We were frequent visitors to jumble sales, where we would come out with loads of gear, kitchen utensils, books and toys, which I stole, to be honest.

There was the odd time when the door would go and someone from St Kenneth's Church would give us their cast-offs. That's what we called our clothes because they had always belonged to someone else. My socks were always at half-mast because they were too small to go to my knees. I wore black plimsolls (named Caramacs because the sole was the same colour as Caramac chocolate) until there were holes in the soles, right through until my feet bled. I remember there was a tiny amount of glass or something from the gas light in the close, which I stood on, making a patch of blood in the close every time I took a step because my soles burst and the glass pierced my skin. When one of The Daddy's sisters got married, we had borrowed shoes and clothes which had to be handed back the very next day. The one drawer we each had held everything we owned to wear, apart from the coat or jacket that was hung up in the mirrored wardrobe or on the coat stand in the hall, just our bare essentials.

I gazed on as my mother was peeling the totties at the kitchen table one afternoon. I stood opposite her, leaning on it with my arms bent to make a pillow, watching her. I loved being alone with her. After a time of silence I asked her, 'Mum, sure you don't have to eat if you don't want to?' She didn't answer me. My mum was like that, she was always deep in thought, on another planet. She would answer when she was ready, when we asked her for something, sometimes ages after you'd asked her. Even then, her answer would always be the same, 'I'll think about it,' she'd say quietly. Through time I took her answers as a 'Yes' in faith. 'Mum?' No answer. 'MUM?' 'Mum, sure if you don't want to eat, nobody can make you eat?' She lifted her head, really mad, her eyes blazing as they pierced mine and banged her wee tottie knife down on the table as she hard as she could. 'Of course you have to eat!' she yelled. 'If you don't eat you'll bloody well die!'

Wow! Straight to the point. That put an end to my inquisitive questioning. It didn't put an end to the thought though. Where on earth had the thought come from? There were no glossy magazines in our house, only big thick mail-order catalogues of amazing things we couldn't afford. They were just for daydreaming, for looking at nice things, that was all, and then the pages were used to light up the coal fire. I had never looked at a catalogue model and thought, I want to look like her, I was just a wee girl. In actual fact, I remember there were no young models in the catalogues, they were depicted as colourful drawings, it was only the adults back then who were models. I

wasn't overweight and had no desire to diet and don't ever
remember hearing the word 'diet' in our house, as our mum
was thin. Pannie was dreadfully thin, she resembled a skeleton
with skin on and we were always hungry and could eat like a
horse. We were most likely undernourished with a pinch of
malnutrition.

From out of the blue this thought came to me and began
living with me. I hated food. That was a pure basic truth, I
hated food. Food was getting the blame for the verbal abuse
because of the confrontation at the dinner table. In the scullery,
The Daddy would start or continue his verbal abuse and I wasn't
able to see my food because my eyes were tear-filled, then my
tears would spill onto my dinner plate, I detested food because
it was contaminated with my tears of hurt. Food prepared lovingly
by my mammy was nectar for my soul, but the constant battle
between hunger and my loathing for food was becoming a
mountain before me. The Daddy battered the bottle as he
splashed brown or red sauce on his dinner and I loathed the
smell. I hated sitting next to him. The brown sauce smelled
worse and it said 'Daddies' on it. It made me physically and
emotionally sick to the pit of my stomach. At the school dinner
hall the primary seven male teacher did the same and so to this
day I have confessed to a few people the same thing, I hate
food. I had no dealings with the male as a teacher, as I was in
a younger age group, except in the dinner hall. No name calling
here, just tears into the food, particularly beetroot, which stained
the cold mashed potato deep blood-red. The male teacher
towered over the tables, shouting and bawling that we couldn't
leave our seats until all of the food was eaten. Second helpings
of verbal abuse.

There was a right typical Glasgow woman who didn't stand
for his nonsense, she was the school dinner lady. She and the
other ladies didn't have time to hang about so the day was saved
by them. I don't know if they sensed I couldn't eat the food
or whether they saw me crying but they whipped the plate

away before I could say thank you. We were often hungry, yet I'd sit at home broken-hearted, crying silently into my food, as it was the only place The Daddy could get at me, which put me off my food for life. The food plus the smells made me want to vomit. My hatred of food started very early on in my childhood and I still resent it. Give thanks for it? Okay, if I must, but I won't eat it, I mused, make me! I had found the one area I could control in my life and nobody could force you to eat, I thought.

I have a distinct loathing for brown sauce, red sauce, every kind of sauce. People ask me how I know I don't like it if I've never tried it. There are more senses than that of the taste buds, I even loathe the smell. I have tasted tomato sauce as a youngster, it was all right then, nothing great. Now, because of a young lifetime of confrontation, I never ever queue up at a buffet because of the pushing, squeezing and atrocious downright bad manners and squabbling.

On a fairly recent cruise ship, where I had to balance two trays of food, one for a disabled man and one for myself, I was confronted by an irate older 'lady', I will call her. I wasn't moving fast enough for the older lady, having to balance the two trays, which were heavy. 'Are you moving or what?' she demanded. I closed my eyes for a few seconds and had to take a slow deep breath in before deliberately turning face to face in slow motion to answer her or I would have eaten her instead. 'I am filling a tray for a disabled man because he is in a wheelchair,' I told her softly but quite forthright and just a little menacingly. 'You see, I said, he can't walk or fend for himself so I am here to collect him something to eat.' She was so downright snooty and impatient, instead of understanding I was assisting someone disabled. She could have excused herself and overtaken me, that would have been fine with me, it wasn't my intention to hold everyone up. If I was only defending myself, I know I would have let it go, but I was in charge of looking after a friend and I became defensive of him.

I also take great pleasure in reminding the older generation they are years ahead of me in wisdom, knowledge and under-standing, therefore they should have more sense and patience. My favourite spiel is, 'If you want Grace, give Grace.' Food was available all day, even throughout the night if one desired. What was the big rush? A sinking ship, a siege, starvation? It's not that I have a hatred for buffets, but for arguing and fighting over food. Have it. 'Man shall not live by bread alone, but by every word that proceeds from the mouth of The Lord.'

My friend and I had a wonderful time except for the rudeness at eating times. I so appreciate being served at the dining table, which might come across as snobbery. It surely is not, it's only because I can't stand pushing, shoving and greed at a buffet, in reality, the whole confrontation thing, which is the key. The food is fine, confrontation at a buffet puts me right off. Dirty tables at self-service outlets, where people are supposed to clear their own tables makes me sick so I don't spend one penny there. The littered tables aren't the problem, it's the fact that diners think it's acceptable to leave their rubbish for others to clear away before they can eat their own food, yet I bet they found a clean table when they arrived.

I am just reminded (by God) of The Last Supper as the hurt of the nasty comments come back to stab my heart. The beau-tiful Saviour, Jesus, sat with Judas and the disciples at the Last Supper. God has just shown me in my own hurt that Jesus was hurt too as they gathered round their supper table. Someone pierced the heart of Jesus while they were eating, the one who was in charge of the money (filthy lucre), the one who smiled and planted a kiss on each cheek, the one who thought he was something and was aloof. Yet Jesus loved him tenderly. This revelation is brand-new to me and I now see I wasn't alone at the table. I hadn't seen the comparison before, thank you God. Love does hurt, but it has never hurt anyone more than it hurt Jesus. I would still much rather go without and starve than get in a bun fight over food, though.

I did meet a lovely Jewish woman a few years back, who knew me quite well then. She looked me in the eyes, pointed her finger in my face and proclaimed, 'You would love my food and you would willingly eat every bit and even ask for me for more.' I loved her words, maybe one day I will meet her again. She was laughing and downright telling me I would love her food, she made me laugh and I didn't argue with her. There was no hostility and she was promising me in a motherly way that I would be fine in her company and she would look after me and I believed her. She admitted she loved food, it was her thing, baking, cooking. rustling up new dishes, presenting her food in new ways and trying new foods excited her but most of all she loved to feed others. Her passion for food intrigued me and she loved nothing more than entertaining and feeding guests, what a woman! That was the difference here, she got it, she used food to entertain others through her hospitality, to make people feel welcome and appreciated, a true hostess, who served relationships with food and hospitality.

On reflection of my past, we children did some stupid things because we were allowed to wander and do what we wanted. I also preferred to stay away from the house of horrors as much as I could. One of my great adventures was to go to the side of the River Clyde in Govan. There was a great old pier, which was seriously falling to bits, and we would climb under and through it. If we had slipped or fallen we would have landed in the deep cold murky water of the River Clyde. The pier was filthy and rotten underneath and matted with slime and the hugest rusty nails, yet we had so much fun hiding and playing under there.

We'd gather the heaviest boulders we could find, stand at the Clydeside, throw the boulder in and count until the bubbles stopped. This showed us how deep the water was, it made no sense in feet, but we would manage to count to about twenty-four until the bubbling stopped.

Still in Govan, we went into the old tenements, which was

easy because there was nothing on the front of the closes to stop us doing so. We would enter the flats to look at the wallpaper on the walls to see if we liked it and basically because we were exploring new territory. Hand in hand, we kept our backs to the walls as we wandered around the rooms with no floors, daring to bend forward to see down to the room beneath, stretching our necks further, even to the room below that. It was such a great adventure but the truth was that the floors were the same as ours were at number 2 Drive Road, from one flat to the next. We'd get right to the edge of the hole for a peek into the flat below, not realising we could be too heavy for the remaining floorboards. We also never gave a thought to the fact that someone might be watching us go into them. There were plenty of public bars on Govan Road and Govan was not short of 'wide boys'.

We also loved to go across the road to the Clyde Tunnel walkway and sing because it echoed and, when it rained, it gave us shelter from the wind and a dry place to hide and play. We tried not to go home until just before it got dark as we were always told, 'Chap that door again and you're staying in!' We stopped playing in the tunnel when two young men from Cressie Street grabbed my cousin and sexually assaulted her. This was another one of my God experiences, knowing what was going to happen just before it did. I saw the scene unfold before my eyes as a warning and I gripped my little brother's hand and held it too tight, I wasn't letting him go. I was silently but frantically trying to work out what to do.

It was horrible, we walked towards the men with fear and trembling after being at Victoria Park. We had nowhere to run as going back the way meant going deeper into the tunnel, which could have been worse. We had no option but to go towards them as we were nearly at the beginning of the tunnel, at Govan Road end. Addie was tiny and not yet three years old. I pulled him through the railings to the cycle path and ran as fast as I could with him, pulling him off his feet. I screamed

and screamed as hard as I could, terrifying Addie. My cousin
was being attacked and I ran away with the child, not to leave
my cousin, but to get help. We didn't get far, I couldn't run
with the wee one in hand and I knew I wouldn't get anywhere
picking him up, but I couldn't leave him either. At least I could
scream and that's what I did in the fight or flight experience to
frighten them off. It's a long walk through the tunnel, especially
when you're smaller, yet we'd often do this to get to Victoria
Park for a change.

Addie told The Daddy that big boys battered our cousin, The
Daddy was a raging bull and would have damaged them severely.
My cousin told him that it was just a fight and she hit the boys
back and I said nothing, because I never spoke to The Daddy.
Many years later my cousin told me the men came from Cressie
Street across the road from us, as she could see them from the
lounge window. There is no way I could have identified them,
I didn't hang about long enough to notice what they were
wearing or figure out what they looked like anyway. That was
my first experience of a sexual encounter and I was quite
disgusted, I really didn't like men one bit. My mother played a
huge part in my thoughts too by saying she hated men. This
was understandable, she lived with one who was horrible and
was accused of being with others she didn't even know. Her
bitterness rubbed off on me and I believed her, men were very
nasty vile creatures and I didn't like or trust them one bit either.

There was a mirror above the toilet sink so we could see
ourselves as we brushed our teeth. I spent a lot of time in front
of that mirror brushing my hair and looking at myself. It wasn't
vanity, it was just that we didn't have any other mirrors, I'm
not kidding. I had not seen myself except when I caught a
glimpse of myself in a shop window. At eight years old I did
not know what I looked like properly until we got the toilet
mirror and the old wardrobe which had a full-length mirror in
the middle panel. Our family and every other family alike had
a cut-glass mirror hanging above the fireplace, but it was far too

high up for a child to gaze into and, of course, far too close to
the coal fire to try, so I didn't know what I looked like from
head to toe. There was a small mirror on the coat stand but I
toppled it once trying to see my face. If I got caught trying to
use the bed settee as a trampoline, to bounce up for a glimpse
of whatever I was trying to see I would get skelped for the
effort. The mirror above the fireplace was not in smoked glass
as some were, my parents both smoked and the mirror was
fogged with nicotine and smoke from everything that was burned
in the fire, that's the only reason the mirror was 'smoked-glass'.
Given that my mother was always in the kitchen, I didn't get
the chance or desire, I suppose, to have a look at myself.

Our toilet was the one room I could go into and lock the
door and nobody in the world could come in uninvited. I could
be on my own, whistle, sing and stay in there for peace and
quiet. It truly was a sanctuary to me, The Throne room, the
loo. I'd be in the toilet a lot, communicating by myself with
God and Jesus. Being fairly artistic, one of my favourite things
to do was to draw myself on that mirror with a wax crayon
which I got really good at. I'd stand close and very still, hardly
breathing, and sketch myself onto the mirror, rubbing in the
thick lines of my hair to add shade, curves and dimension to
my eyes, mouth and cheeks. I was fascinated that the person I
sketched was lovely, yet I didn't know if I was lovely or if the
sketch was good. It was there I discovered I could get my hand
to draw what my brain was telling me my eyes could see. I
wished I could have this artistic attack on paper because I had
an awful job trying to get the wax off quickly when someone
needed the toilet, especially when I got carried away and deeply
engrossed in the self-portrait, then frantically had to rub the
wax off with my sleeve, which smeared and left a great thick
greasy mess.

There was no central heating or constant hot running water
in this flat either. Our geyser was fitted above the sink in the
kitchen and I remember being asked to fill the pail with boiling

water. I rested the handle of the bucket on the long geyser tap but, as the bucket got heavier, it pulled the geyser from the wall, spewing boiling water everywhere. There were some things we children shouldn't have been allowed to do and this incident proves my point.

The close toilet was constantly dark as there was no electricity, so no light or switch. It was freezing cold, smelly and probably full of spiders but we wouldn't use it anyway so we didn't care. There wasn't even a toilet seat on the pan, we'd sometimes get a peek in if it had not been dutifully locked but we never went in there as a rule. It would have been so easy to fall down that huge toilet pan and get flushed away down the River Clyde never to be seen again. We often dared each other to go in and look down the pan but it was too scary. I don't know if we were scared of the dark or just scared of what was down the lavvy pan.

The butcher was one of the main ones on Govan Road who could be relied on for borrowing the toilet key from, but he always growled, 'Bring it right back!' He was handy because he was always in the shop and, when you borrowed his key, you didn't bother to lock the door afterwards, so everyone could use it at night when the butcher went home. With our cousins not having their own toilet, it had to be kept open. It was all right for the butcher to disappear after five o'clock and leave the 'no toilet' neighbours high and not dry. If you were needing to go during the night, you were basically up a gum tree without a kite! That said, no amount of persuasion was going to get us in there anyway. What if we got locked in and couldn't get out again? Death by stench from the bog and we knew the contents ended up in the Dunny round the back because of the broken waste pipes.

There was a string that held newspaper but not everyone had newspapers to leave in the toilet, as they were needed to light the fire, and newspaper didn't flush very well as it trapped air when crumpled, which everyone complained about. The toilet would get blocked and flooded and, when the toilet got flooded and overflowed, it then gushed up before it ran down and out into the common close and into the street. Well, use your imagination. This caused great hilarity among us weans and out would come the song, 'Sailing down the river in a wee brown boat'. There was a serious campaign by the neighbours, including the Dentist, to stop using the newspapers, but not everyone heeded the advice. When there was good old real toilet paper, it was in a small Izal box. This paper was slidey and jaggy and we children always pinched it for wrapping around a comb to make tunes with, which tickled our lips because of the vibration. There were no sanitary handwash gels, sprays, paper towels, or even a hint of Carbolic soap for hand washing. A long chain hung from a high-up water cistern, which was black and belched noises when disturbed. It's a good job loo blocks for the cistern weren't on the market yet, as you would have needed a very big ladder to accommodate a very small space and five hands to carry on with the task. One to hold onto the ladder, one to hold your nose, one for a torch, one to lift up the cistern lid and one to drop in the loo block. You would also need a thick mattress to land on and four legs to get you out of there as fast as they could take you after you came face to face with the spiders, each one having eight eyes. So say there were at least twenty spiders in that creepy toilet, that's one hundred and sixty eyeballs looking at you using the toilet. That's how scary I thought it was. It was a no go area for every child, no matter how desperate we were to use the toilet. There was no snib or latch on the inside of the door, meaning the key had to be used to lock yourself in for privacy. It was too traumatic to even imagine being locked in.

So then, the butcher goes to the toilet in the close for 'None of your business'. He then leaves, relieved, and bumps into every Tom, Dick, Harry and Mrs Sawdust Head, a name I had for a neighbour, because The Daddy said she had sawdust for brains, and I told her. The butcher gives his customers a good shake of the hand and chats to them for ages about the price of a fatted calf or whatever, he then gets straight back into his work of handling, sawing and chopping raw food before wrapping up your three slices of Spam. Now I'm not suggesting for one second that his hands were not sterile as he cut and quartered raw and cooked meats. I'm just saying I'm not feeling at all hungry as I tell you this. This, by the way, was the same butcher who gave me what for because I stuck up for him, the cheek!

I was in the butcher's after school with my mother and my school friend, who I have previously named 'Friend'. My friend whispered to me quietly that the butcher man was baldy, she had never seen him before. In his defence I roared at the top of my voice, 'The butcher is not baldy!' I was not popular, I can tell you. I didn't like his shop anyway, it had cows hanging up with great big hooks and sawdust all over the floor with splatters of fresh crimson blood because the heads and tails had been chopped off. People had to queue up under the drips of the bloody cows, I would call them, my mother unable to decide whether I was describing the blood from the cows or whether I was actually swearing. Her face warned me I had better be referring to the cows' blood, or else. Then over at the other counter there were birds on smaller hooks, all dead, I suppose I would have been alarmed if they were alive and flapping flyaway feathers. I was very unsure of the butcher, who killed them, I wondered? I thought I should be on my very best behaviour in his shop at all times. Another backhanded head slap from the mother who promised, 'Just you wait till I tell yer Faither.' She knew fine how to nip my naughtiness and highly strung behaviour in the bud. She wasn't going to tell My Faither at all, of course, she was a protective mother. She only said that to shut the butcher up. Me and my big mouth again. I just couldn't help myself, I was always up to something and more often than not, I got into trouble for it. Friend was appalled and didn't know where to look, she wasn't so smart with her mouth when standing in front of my mother. Then again, neither was I, most of the time.

I passed 2 Drive Road recently on a little research and had a peek into the close through the window of the main close door, and saw that the close toilet is now bricked up and painted over. When we lived at 2 Drive Road there was no such thing as a front door on the common close, never mind with an intercom. The door and intercom would have taken the fun out of chap the door and run away and playing with baws oan the wa's. People tell me they have to switch their intercoms off because they get pressed all day and night long and when they answer it, there is either nobody there or the call is not for them. It seems that the invention of the front-door intercom is nothing but a pain in the neck to most residents, so most people I know keep it switched off, meaning we have to phone or text to say we're at the door.

As one Christmas was approaching, I asked my mother if I could have a new doll, as did Pannie. I did have a wee doll with one eye, well, two at first. She had a squint, one eye was going to the shops for the messages and the other had come back with the change. Doctor Esther thought she would fix it with a Biro pen. I only wanted to straighten the eyeball but had given her deep noticeable eyeliner in the process as I dug the pen into the socket to twirl her eye in order to match the other eye. The doll's eyeball flew out and smacked me in the eyelid, causing a slight black eye to match the doll's. 'An eye for an eye' right enough. I couldn't find her eyeball as it shot away and I was blinking mad because I got hurt trying to repair her, ungrateful doll. I mean, I saved her from a jumble sale, how was that for gratitude? I was obviously not Doctor material. I also broke the only pen in the house and had to watch my parents write with just the bare inky stem, I kept quiet about that one.

On the Christmas Day Pannie and I got our dolls, she got the blonde-haired one and I got the dark-brown-haired one. I was slightly envious of hers because I thought the blonde-haired doll was nicer, like an Angel. The dolls were really big and I named mine Heather. For some silly reason, Pannie took her doll's head off and caused it to tear at the neck as she tried to get it back on. Thank God for the lock on the toilet door because The Daddy ordered me to give Pannie my new doll, Heather. Well, Heather and I had built up quite a rapport as I dressed her up and cared for her. We stayed in the toilet for hours on end and I made it crystal-clear we weren't going to be separated for anyone, we had a great life together and I kept her all to myself for many years. Pannie also got a new pram for her doll, while I got a desk and chair. In the photo you will see that I was not allowed to sit on my chair because Pannie wanted it. I dared not protest as I knew what the answer would have been by the way of a hard slap.

Various dictionaries' definition of a holiday: 'An extended period of leisure, recreation, time spent away from home travelling, a time to be free to do what you want, a rest.'

Pannie and I were awarded our first-ever holiday by Glasgow District Council in some sort of association with the Department of Education, where we were allocated between four to six weeks of residential care in the country setting of beauty, solitude and fresh air. The first of those breaks was at Fornethy Residential School. We had never been on any kind of holiday before, we had never even set foot outside of Glasgow, or seen a real live sheep or cow in the flesh. The only cow I knew was the one The Daddy called my mother. It's rude and brutal, I know, but true. I must have been about seven plus years old, making sister Pannie over five years in age. Although I remembered some traumatic events while on the first holiday at the 'Big House', I was reasonably excited to be going there year in, year out.

I remember our vests, pants, socks and clothes being labelled with our names so we wouldn't lose them. We were also given new coats. Mine was pewter-blue with a zip from the knee to neck, no collar, and two ridiculously small pockets my hands couldn't get into. Pannie's coat on the other hand was in deep red with a pure white fur collar, fur on the sleeves, and a swaying skirt, a snow-white fluffy furry hat to match the coat, and a muff. My friends roll about laughing at the muff part, the lined furry muff was to keep both hands warm and had a decorative rope for around one's neck. The three-piece coat was amazing, trendy, and made mine look dull, plus I wanted a muff. I was in a huff with no muff. All right then, enough about the muff. I did get to borrow her muff for a shot, for all of five seconds or so, before she screamed blue murder and wanted it straight back. Fearful of the assured reprisal, I immediately obeyed. What did she need a muff for? Her pockets were huge, just saying. She could have had a loan of my new coat but it would have smothered her. Hmm, there's an idea I hadn't thought of . . . Joking!

Residential schools were designed as a holiday and short retreat by the Social Services for the children of poorer or 'means-tested' families, who lived on the breadline. We were assessed as suitable to have this holiday by the nurse 'up the toon' and given the slip of paper which declared we had a clean bill of health at that present time. This slip was the declaration that there was no disease or infestation, in other words, we didn't have head lice or nits.

Mothers and children sat nervously in the waiting room, afraid of the results of their children's examinations. The whole waiting room knew the results immediately as the family exited the clinic door. Families came running out of that interview room waving the slip of paper in the air as though they had just won the lottery or got through in today's *X Factor* or *Britain's Got Talent*. Pride was important to families then, if you didn't get that slip, it was shameful, hurtful and disappointing to the children who were looking forward to getting a break. I have to say, we weren't cleared every time we appeared for our assessment, usually down to my chest sounds. Sometimes a school friend applied at the same time, and we got to go together one year when we both got the all-clear from the nurse.

The thought of leaving my mother alone with The Daddy tormented me heavily, but other than that I was up for the break. Mum, myself and Pannie caught the big orange and green double-decker Glasgow bus into the town, where we kids always rushed up the stairs so we could get to the front or the back of the bus to get a better view and so our mum could have a 'fag'. At Buchanan Street Station we got onto the single coach. I could not believe how luxurious the single-decker coach was and it even had a toilet in it, wow, a toilet on a bus! We didn't even have a toilet in our house at one time and here was a bus with a toilet in it, I had never heard of this in my life and I was absolutely amazed (and have always been since) at the talented creativity of mankind. I know, I'm easily pleased.

The luxury bus had cloth seats and matching curtains. The expensive curtains (not fibreglass) could be folded back onto wee clips, which I constantly popped as I couldn't make up my mind whether I wanted them opened or closed for the journey. The headrests on the seats were so high up you didn't know who was sitting in front of or behind you and the seats had great big pockets on each back to put things in. There were white plastic covers over the headrests of the seats and it even had a carpet on the floor, a very thick plush carpet with a design that nearly matched the seats and curtains. Again, we didn't have carpets, just old-fashioned threadbare fireplace rugs, so to see the carpet on the bus impressed the mundane life out of me. I felt like a princess being so high up, looking into the fields. The travelling part of the holiday was every bit as important as the holiday itself, as far as I was concerned, and I just loved the whole adventure.

When we arrived at the residential school some hours later, we were greeted by a sea of girls from five to nearly twelve years old who were standing still and staring at us, the new ones. From what I recall, there would have been sixty young girls accommodated altogether, a few had already left for home that day, having had their four- or six-week holiday.

All of the girls were wearing 'pinnies', an apron dress which covered their own clothes. I was watching them intently too, wondering how they got their flowery patterned dresses, did they like it here? What were their names? Where did they come from? They all looked so beautiful, yet unsmiling and very well behaved. I was soon to find out why.

We were told to go to the peg with our name on it and hang up our coats, making sure, via a warning, that we left nothing in the pockets, because woe unto us if they found out we did. We were also to hand in all personal belongings, such as earrings, watches and bangles. I got off to a bad start immediately, when the house guardian refused to believe I had no jewellery and yanked at my ears looking for the piercings made by earrings to prove I had. I also had no eatables to share with her as other girls did, which were confiscated without challenge. We were not allowed to eat sweets and chewing gum was from the devil, they informed us. We also had to declare all that was posted on to us in a parcel or letter, which was confiscated and hidden into the dark shelves of the tuck shop, basically a cupboard where your family's gifts of sweets were hidden, never to be returned. Wednesday afternoon was the only time we could visit the tuck shop, but as we had all arrived on the Wednesday, the tuck shop had already been opened and closed for the week. Parents sent on postal orders to their children so they could buy their own sweets from the tuck shop. Even then, we were told what we could and couldn't have. On leaving, the tucks were never returned to us to take home.

Next, it was off to our dormitory, which was named the 'Reekie Linn', where our newly labelled means-tested clothes were lying neatly on our beds for checking off. This was the appointed bed, where we would sleep soundly in for the duration of our holiday. The duration was unknown as we weren't informed as to whether we were staying for four weeks or six weeks, four was horrendous but that was the minimum we could stay. Prayers became 'Please God, make it four', and He always did. There was no sleeping soundly either I have to add, some poor little mite would be getting the skin taken from the back of her legs and letting everyone else know and feel her pain as she screamed her wee lungs out.

We were often woken in the middle of the night with bumps, crashes and yelling as a 'bed wetter' was discovered, most terrified likely. Children wet the bed a lot. Only God knows why, but I'm sure fear was a big factor. We had no idea of what was going on in that wee girl's family home. She probably wet the bed there too, through circumstances and fear, so how did a battering from a qualified teacher help? I ask.

Before bed we were then taken to a large bricked area, where we had a bath and hair washed and dried before being bone-combed and soaked in a powerful lotion, which nipped, stank and seriously took your breath away. I laugh at most things but picture your wee girl getting that steel bone comb dug deep into her scalp until it was grazed, no wonder the lotion nipped.

Mealtimes were in a huge dining room with the Head, Deputy Head and Teachers sitting at the long dining table, positioned so they could see us all too clearly. I have withheld their names but they can be easily found on the internet, as many other children have been abused and have written about it for all to see. Some mentally, physically and emotionally punished. All of the housemaids and dinner ladies at Fornethy smiled and got on with their jobs. I recall 'Heid the Ba' (the Head) screaming at a young member of staff, who was crying her eyes out. She was ridiculed in front of the other staff and ourselves and I felt sorry for her.

There was a large hatch in the dining room from where the food came and went, well, mostly just came, because you had to eat it, so it never went back. Again, the food was a punishment in itself and had to be swallowed and empty plates were easier to pile high. The porridge was served every two days with cereal on the alternate day. I had never seen porridge like this in my life, cold, saltless, very thin, with a skin on, and slimy,

slimy enough to thankfully swim down the backs of our throats with little effort because I hated food. My mother had no money but at least she knew how to make a decent plate of thick warm porridge. I gagged on this swill but I had to get it down my throat and keep it there, otherwise it would be slammed down onto the table at every mealtime until it was eaten. With me facing the top table of tyrants, I smiled and acted as though I enjoyed it, it was easier than getting battered by the 'Brute Force Staff', who walked like prison officers behind the chairs to scream obscenities into delicate little ears. Not that I am an expert in the nature, job description or personalities of prison officers. The only prison officers I know of are the ones who were characters in television programmes, so I have none to compare with. No children were battered or abused in those programmes. The Daddy didn't batter me as much as they did, I would have been better off at home. Even the catering staff appeared afraid, the catering ladies never ever spoke to us during mealtimes, it clearly wasn't allowed. Sometimes a couple of children (me too) would get marched to the dining room and ordered to set the tables along with the staff under the watchful eye of the house teacher who was on duty. The kitchen staff were sincere and would whisper loving motherly comments like, 'Thanks, hen' and 'All right, darling' with a twinkle in their eyes. They got on with their jobs and always seemed to be in a terrible hurry, scurrying quickly around the dining hall and back to the service area. They grabbed and threw plates, cutlery and everything else onto the huge opened hatch as though their lives depended on it. They moved very quickly, yet were as quiet as mice. The whole dining room was quiet, apart from the tapping of cutlery.

At a sitting Pannie sat sobbing into her dinner plate, with her back to the High Heid Yins at the long table. When I asked her what was wrong, she whispered to me that the girl sitting beside her had kicked her hard on her leg for nothing and it was sore. Well, I was furious so I kicked the girl back for hurting my little sister for no reason. The girl, along with Pannie, was caught crying too. I made sure she got a taste of her own medicine, but she told on me when asked why she was crying, suddenly forgetting she had just kicked my sister and had her crying too.

'Heid the Ba' hovered with a face like a bulldog chewing a bees' nest. My chair was pulled out in front of everyone with me sitting on it. She rolled up her sleeves and told everyone to pay attention and watch what happens to bullies. Even the kitchen staff were standing still when she swung her arm like a golf professional and smacked my face so hard I flew from the chair and landed on the floor. 'Get up!' she screamed. She was raging. 'Get up!' I couldn't get up, my head battered against the floor and my left ear was 'ringing'. I lay there a touch too long for her liking and there was a rush of staff. I could make out adult shoes running in front of my blurry eyes as all the children left the dining room, but I couldn't move my neck or lift my head, yet I was only concerned in case someone stood on me in the stampede of sandshoes. I didn't hear any request or command to the kitchen staff, who picked me up and placed me carefully back into my seat, sliding it under the table, where I was peered at. I didn't hear any shouting again, I seemed to be in a cloud of haze but I do remember not having to eat my food as the 'caring' teachers disappeared with the rest of the children. I intermittently heard the dinner ladies talking to each other about how terrible 'She' was, as they guided me to my bed for a lie-down, yet I don't remember getting undressed or how I got into my bed. They kept telling me, 'It's all right', not to worry, and tucked me in, their kindness comforted me and I slept soundly. When I woke up later there was someone sitting on a chair at my bedside and all was so still, very quiet and peaceful.

I think the teachers got a fright that day as they never hit me that way again. A big slipper was used on the flesh on the back of the legs, not only for being naughty, but just because they didn't like you and to hurry you along. There were no naughty girls at the residential school. There were funny ones, beautiful and talented ones, intelligent and creative ones, who all had the desire and God-given right to grow, succeed and prosper, each one somebody's wee girl. What went on at the residential school stayed there as we couldn't contact our parents to tell them we wanted to come home or tell them of the treatment we were receiving.

The walks we went on seemed to be hours long, without the use of a toilet or drink break. I suppose we wouldn't need the use of a toilet if not watered, therefore no drink for the thirst which clamped your tongue to the roof of your mouth. On many of the long walks we were to look out for the witch's leg, a long tree trunk lying at the bottom of a hill, visible from the road. Telling us all some ridiculous urban myth full of stupidity and lies about how we should not speak on passing the witch's leg, as all the other witches were watching and would be very angry. They would come and get us later on, we were told, frightening us mentally too.

There was no teaching or proper schooling during our time at Fornethy. When we were together in the classroom environment, all the teachers did was laugh and chat with each other, yelling at us if we got too loud, except when the news was on, we had to 'Shut up' and listen to it too, as they wanted to hear it. In the lounge in the evening we would be gathered for a little while before bed, where we had our supper of half a glass of milk and a digestive biscuit. For their amusement and entertainment, we had to go outside the huge lounge door, make an entrance, stand in front of them and the children and perform with a song, poetry, joke or limerick, anything which was entertaining, and it had to be good. We needed a different party piece every evening, though, we couldn't just recite 'the same old rubbish', they told us with yells of 'Get back out and put your thinking cap on.'

I sang 'Nobody's Child' (I knew how to milk that song with much emotion), 'Ten Guitars', 'Hey Big Spender', 'Three Craws Sat Upon a Wa''', 'Ten Green Bottles', 'Four Wheels on My

Wagon' and countless other songs, where everyone joined in. It was better to choose a song everyone knew, as we could sing together cheerily. It was great when everyone joined in, as we had unity and a common bond for a little while. The mutters under the teachers' breaths as we performed were never intelligible, then heads would tilt back in laughter as they left us alone in the middle of floor to get on with it. Children are great survivors and love life, always looking for more acceptance, and they thrive on praise. Give them an inch and they'll take a mile. We had a secret sense of camaraderie and I had to get up all the time, it saved my little sister from doing so. She was too quiet and would have freaked out if put on the spot. I was always fearful for her, they could pick on me all they wanted because I could take it but I couldn't let them start on my little sister. I had already learned some poetry from Elder Park Primary, This poem was performed on tiptoes, cross-eyed and acting like a drunk:

*OH THERE SHE GOES*
*OH THERE SHE GOES*
*PEERIE HEELS AND POINTED TOES*
*LOOK AT HER FEET*
*SHE THINKS SHE'S NEAT*
*BLACK STOCKINGS AND DIRTY FEET*

Ruffled up hair and playing exhausted with this one made the girls laugh:

*WHAT A CLAMOUR,*
*WHAT A FUSS,*
*GETTING ON AND OFF A BUS,*
*PUSHING, SQUEEZING, STAMPING, NUDGING,*
*NEVER WAS THERE SO MUCH BUDGING,*
*'QUICK' SAYS MOTHER, THERE'S ANOTHER,*
*FATHER ANSWERS, 'DON'T BE SILLY,*
*THAT ONE GOES TO PICCADILLY.'*

Performing our party pieces in the evenings was scary under pressure, especially as the big slipper sat beside the teachers for a wallop as we stood in front of them. This was our time and we only wanted to be accepted and loved, or at the very least liked, and we did our best to make that happen. I enjoyed performing and got more confident as I found I could make the girls laugh.

Not all of the teachers were bad, thank God. Children always supported each other with applause and merriment to keep happy, the secret was to 'Keep the heid doon and the chin up'. I could endure all things but the only time I ever felt my back getting up was when Pannie got picked on. There was no person in that place going to attack my wee sister. Although I was a child to anyone on the outside, as far as my siblings went, I was a warrior on the inside. When one of the so-called teachers was quizzing my little sister, grinning, she looked at me intermittently, knowing full well what she was doing to wind me up. Pannie, on the other hand, wasn't answering her, as she didn't know the answers. I didn't like this teacher's attitude, look or menacing tone. She turned to me and demanded, '. . . And what part of Glasgow do you think you come from?' I looked at her and felt myself grow very tall on the inside. God assisted me to answer her because I didn't think I knew the answer either and would've looked stupid to her, that's what she wanted. On the way up in this 'growing taller' episode, I remembered the postcode on our mail was written as SW1, so that's the answer I gave her. 'I don't think,' I said. 'I know, we come from the South of Glasgow, that's The Southwest of Scotland, overlooking the River Clyde at the Clyde Tunnel walkway.' She snubbed me, drew her eyes off me and cut me off by assisting Pannie in the washing of her hands by prodding her in the back to hurry up. The small, round, curly-haired so-called teacher didn't speak to me in that tone again, but she made me angry almost to the point of destruction. I only held on, kept control and waited because my wee sister was fine.

If it were not for God in the silent moments of my mind, I could have kicked off and lost control of my emotions. I would stand quietly and look at the teachers and think, You don't know me, you don't know where I've been, you don't know what I've seen. I told no one anything about my life with God. I had nothing and I was nothing, it was true, but with God there was a tiny spark of faith in Him, of hope, love, expectation, wondering, keeping my eyes and thoughts on him. He was my God. 'Are you there, God? Can you hear me, do you know what I'm thinking?' I'd always have my thoughts on Him. It didn't matter that I couldn't always hear Him because I knew He always heard me.

This holiday was the holiday from hell and we had no option but to persevere. We got the fresh air we were awarded but each year was the same, pure mental and physical torture.

A couple of the girls did manage to sneak out letters and post them when we passed a postbox but it wasn't worth it. When the parents contacted the authorities the child then got abuse when they were found out. The screaming from the High Heid Yin was a warning to others who might follow suit.

Nightly, girls would sob softly, muffled into their pillows, it was a terrible shame. We couldn't get up and speak or even whisper to each other. If you got caught you'd get beaten and no one wanted to be beaten. We all had to be brave and we made it out in one piece. It was such a fantastic relief to find out we were only staying for four weeks. The staff got away with the abuse because we were never so glad to be out of there and said nothing about our holiday to anyone, only to our friends from school who had been at Fornethy and knew the score. Now I see from reports on the internet of the horrors the others suffered, and all is not well within the Social Work Department, Glasgow District Council and the Education Department because of those years. I don't know who, if anyone, will be held to account but I do know the Word of God says, 'Be sure your sins will find you out.' I wasn't the only child battered or abused. I have heard other accounts by the witnesses themselves. Children of the sixties, seventies, before and beyond, who were in care have some sad tesimonies. One day, not too far off, there will be complaints made and registered, even another book perhaps, combining all of the residential homes and the treatment given to Glaswegian children who were sent on holiday. Glasgow certainly wasn't flourishing in the welfare of their ain folk, poor and needy children sent to residential schools because they were underprivileged.

The second residential holiday stint was the same, same place, same food, same staff, same ignorance, just a later date with Pannie and me a year or so older. The staff were older, for sure, and perhaps a little wiser. They did not physically punish me by lashing at my face this time around but they were abysmal in other ways. We endured the same long walks, with badly staved ankles as we fell awkwardly over boulders in our soft non-walking shoes, on every walk, a child was forced to walk on her twisted swollen limb.

One day we were told we were going 'in for a dip'. We were so excited, it wasn't like the staff to be good to us or treat us, so on we went on another very long walk, this time with a tiny rolled-up towel. I hadn't been 'in for a dip' before, except for a vain attempt at the paddling pool in Elder Park, which was full of smashed bottles from the drinkers at night, and I tried to imagine the secluded area where we were heading to, covered with the most beautiful trees, plants and flowers and clear spark-ling water on a flat bed of silky, shimmery rock. I even imagined there could be a waterfall where we would play beside and splash under with our hands, splattering water on each other for fun and laughing the whole time.

We walked on and on for miles by the side of the stream, desperate to stop, so long that we were too tired, and when one of the girls suggested we stop and 'Go in there?', at the pool of clear sparkly water and flat stones, just as I had imagined, the teacher demanded we 'Hurry up' and 'Move it'. 'You're not going in there,' she yelled. 'You'll dirty it!' That's what they thought of us children from Glasgow. It's one thing thinking nasty thoughts and having a nasty heart that brings forth nasty comments but to tell us all too, was hurtful. We weren't all stupid, though, and we all had a strong common bond of silence, a little nudge or wink to say all was well. They kept us walking until they found us a spot that was filthy with mud on both sides of the bank and so thick with dirt that we couldn't possibly see how deep the water was. The clear sparkly water was heaven, the dark muck hell, and they chose the latter for us.

'Get in there,' the teacher yelled. Call me naive as well as young, but I thought the fact we had no swimsuits meant we were going for a paddle, not to strip naked. This was a horrible and nasty way to treat us but that wasn't the only issue that bothered me. We could be seen clearly from the main road and some of us girls were getting older and growing in places we didn't want anyone to see and look upon. We were truly morti-fied. Tractors, with men on board obviously, could see all and would actually stop for a longer look. It wasn't as if we could swim or bathe in the muddy part of the stream, we stood in it shivering and ashamed, trying to cover our naked bodies. I still remember that deep shame and the teachers standing on the bank whispering and laughing. Sometimes the line would get crossed from being mortified to actually wanting to die on the spot. Thoughts of being dead appealed rather than stand naked for all to witness. It was a very humiliating experience. I had been to Fornethy too often and this was the very last straw. I was so ashamed I knew I would rather die than have to do that again. The staff are also to blame for destroying my confidence.

As the coach pulled away from the residential school on the long and grainy pebbles we had to pull the weeds from, we were never so glad to see the back of the place and vowed never to return. A friend, Carol, from my class in primary school, and I were peering out of the back window of the coach and were joined with others to wave goodbye to the nasty nit nurse who stood with pursed lips. She waved, we smiled and waved until the coach pulled away. We then changed our hand waves to the V sign and let her have it! She was absolutely raging and started running after the coach with her tight skirt hitched up way past her knees, which had us howling with laughter, until the driver braked and stopped the coach. 'Oh my God,' we screamed just as her raging face reached the back of the bus, just in time, the driver drove off. Phew! He who laughs last laughs longest, we still laugh at that departure. I have never been able to confess that sin to God for laughing my head off. The sight of that wicked old 'Lady' brandishing her right arm and with her skirt hitched up to run after us has me in hysterics every time I think about it. I know I shouldn't have done it but, hey ho, away ye go. Self-preservation wins, and a huge thanks to the bus driver who put his foot down and saved us.

There was a change in residential school because I refused point blank to go back to Fornethy, so the last residential holiday we went on was to Rothesay on the island of Bute. I hoped it would be better than Fornethy, it certainly couldn't be any worse, surely. This residential school was a lot smaller than Fornethy and looked over the Firth of Clyde, with much nicer scenery. We also didn't have to endure any dreadful walks for miles with a staved ankle as we were situated on the main road.

The Head of the school and other staff were terrific, except for George, the gardener. There was no verbal abuse or hitting this time round, but sexual abuse was the domineering factor for this holiday. A Haven for George. What a fantasy and reality it must have been for him, about thirty girls from the age of five to eleven. He pressed against us really hard as he grabbed us and wouldn't let go as he smothered and kissed us for at least ten minutes, that's a long time to try and hold your breath, but hold my breath I did. On running back with the vegetables, peas in the pod, we weren't asked why we took so long in coming back. I'd spend at least another five minutes spitting the saliva out of my mouth and gagging, wiping his breath away.

We were always sent on our own but other children knew what was happening, as they would stare, dying to know, 'Did George grab you?' they whispered. I must point out, it was *not* George, the son, who did this dirty deed, it was the older George, his Father.

Despite this dirty old man grabbing and pressing us with something very hard at the front of his trousers, the residential school was very good and had its own swing park, where we could play and talk unsupervised. We could see the staff watching from the window to supervise us and they were actually very nice. When we waved towards the window to them, they waved back, smiling. We in turn really liked them and one even told us she was going into Rothesay on a date. We were happy for her and told her she looked beautiful in her 'Hot Pants' as we caught her setting off for her evening out. We had more in the way of school work and art to keep us occupied and we weren't humiliated by being told to dance or sing for our supper. It was a pity we weren't sent to that residential school before, because it was a great holiday, apart from dirty sex abuser George. There was no screaming in the night from a bed wetter, who was punished for being a little scrap of humanity. There was no luke-warm, disgusting food or sloppy porridge. There were no derogatory or snide comments to our faces or behind our backs. The head teacher was a Lady and the others had dignity and respect. It was just a pity they didn't supervise us and keep a lookout for dirty George. Obviously they didn't know. Still, they let themselves and us down on that score. A big nought out of ten for that one and a 'Must do better!'

Our fourth mini holiday was a first as a family (and other relations), camping in Dunbeg in Oban, close to where our relatives lived. We popped up the hill to see Auntie Beana in Soroba, then Auntie Ivy, who both supplied us with juice and cakes. We pitched the tent on a grassy area near the water in Dunbeg and all squashed into the small tent, where I guess I had a good night's sleep, as I don't remember not having one.

The Daddy, though, was always calling the shots, commanding and demanding as usual, at the top of his voice for all to hear. 'Do this, do that, don't do this, don't do that, come here, stay away from there,' blah, blah, blah nonstop. I got into terrible trouble in front of everyone, including other campers, as usual from The Daddy when he found out I had written my name and address on a sheet of scrap paper, inserted it inside a bottle and floated it off to see where it would end up. The idea was that I might find a pen-pal so we could write to each other. That idea was slapped out of me good and proper. That was it, because of what I had done we were all told to get packed up, because we were going home. Here we go again, my stupid fault as usual, I thought, as I buried my heavy heart in my plastic bag of belongings. As we were packing up, the sun broke through and the day was beautifully hot, so we got to stay another night because of the sun, for me The Son. The bottle wasn't even my idea. My aunt, The Daddy's sister, prompted it and provided the bottle, the pen and the paper. Enough said.

We children scrambled away from The Daddy at the first opportunity to play and explore by ourselves. Up on the hill from the shore was a petrol station where we could buy sweets, but we had no money. We wandered up for a look anyway as part of our great adventure. Our eyes lit up when we saw crates of glass ginger bottles at the back of the petrol station, so we blatantly helped ourselves to the empty bottles and popped them up on the sales counter for our chosen sweets. When we had finished our supply of sweets, we did the same again for more, bringing everyone else with us.

'My, Your Daddy sure drinks a lot of ginger,' the shop assistant said. We had the feeling she was suspicious and we were about to be sussed out, so we gave it a rest. We still have a laugh at the lady lifting the bottles and taking them out to the back of the store. Off she'd totter, plonking the glass bottles into the crates. Did she not realise the crates weren't being refilled?

I still have no shame on recalling that event. I, even then, most likely had the potential of becoming a hard-and-fast criminal at a young age, thank God for Jesus. That first mini holiday with the family was also the last, as The Daddy wanted to go home and we never got to go on a family holiday again. It was a great time apart from The Daddy's bad temper, but I had learned to ignore his outbursts and he would never hit my mother in public.

Times weren't all bad or sad. Jesus came for me and took me out to play, I saw my Angels and God kept me sane, He was my hope. All that mattered was that God was there for me. He heard me, He listened, He loved me and He still does. I got, and still do get, dreams and visions, love and assurance. I also get disciplined occasionally. He whom He loves, He chastises. I was a beautiful child, not only in looks but in nature, but I could also be a very naughty and disruptive child simply because of my upbringing. I was everything a child was and should have been, simply a child.

As a child I had a strong sense of my worth through God, certainly not with The Daddy, he was my Daddy but he was not The Heavenly Father. My original intention was to write about the comparison between The Daddy and The Heavenly Father, but there is none. It would have been like describing Satan and God. There was a desperate need in my young life for tender love, care and finances. The Daddy, in his own upbringing and ignorance, just didn't know how to be a proper father and money couldn't have healed our family. It would certainly have helped immensely, but not healed, comforted or repaired our broken family unit. Many people around us were poor, it was just a simple fact of life in and around Govan at that time, though I do know we were much poorer than others. When The Daddy was in employment, we had food on the table and peace in the house, the way it was supposed to be. I remember looking at his black work jacket one morning, with a plastic coating over the shoulder area to keep his back dry, happy to see the back of him, quite literally.

Some years ago God The Father gave me a Prophecy regarding children, who are hugely important and precious to Him. I give you this prophetic word of caution, by GOD:

*'ALL CHILDREN ARE MY CHILDREN, SAITH THE LORD; MY ANGER BURNS DEEP WITHIN ME EVEN AT THE VERY THOUGHT OF HARM FROM YOUR VERY IMAGINATION, SAVE YOURSELF FROM JUDGEMENT OF SELF AND RUN VERY FAR AWAY FROM SIN REGARDING MY LITTLE ONES, STAND BACK TO THE WALL AND LET THEM PASS, SAYS THE LORD, FOR THEY ARE MORE PRECIOUS THAN YOU KNOW; TOUCH THEM NOT WITHOUT AUTHORITY, NOT EVEN TO HAND THEM SO MUCH AS A DRINK, LAY IT UPON THE TABLE AND WAIT FOR INSTRUCTION; THEY ARE MINE, ALL MINE' SAYS THE LORD. 'I HAVE EVEN TOLD MY LITTLE CHILDREN THIS, THEY HAVE KNOWN IT FROM WHEN THEY WERE BUT BABES; THEY ARE MINE, ALL MINE, AND I AM IN THEM. WHEN YOU SIN AGAINST THEM YOU SIN THRICE, AGAINST THE HOLY GOD, AGAINST MY CHILD AND AGAINST SELF. I WILL NOT CONTAIN MY ANGER. AS MUCH AS MY ANGER INFLAMES, THAT'S THE MEASURE MY CHILD WILL SPEAK OUT AGAINST YOU AND I WILL ALLOW IT. MY CHILDREN ARE PRECIOUS TO ALL AND ARE ALL MINE, AGAIN I SAY ALL MINE. EVERY HAIR ON THEIR HEADS IS COUNTED. EVERY BREATH THEY TAKE IS MEASURED. EVERY UTTERANCE IN THE SECRET PLACE OF THEIR SOUL IS RECORDED. THEY ARE MINE, ALL MINE.'*

If there was one person we could truly rely on in our primary school in Elder Park, it was the Janitor. He was like a bodyguard, confidant and agony uncle, but most of all, a friend. It wasn't

The 'Jannie's' job to look after us but he did. There was no malice in him, he never shouted angrily, just for our protection. He was up very early in the morning to heat the school for us and he would still be there long after we had gone at four o'clock. He would give us a row without blowing his top, showed mercy in the areas where we needed it and grace in the areas where we didn't deserve it. It was him I went crying to when I slipped onto a steel spike from the broken bench, hurting my knee. 'There's nothing wrong with it,' he assured me, but it was really painful. I forget his name but it doesn't matter, he was a real gem to a young child and God knows who he is. There have been very few people in my life who have been humble and quiet just like our school Jannie. Every school Jannie is the best Jannie in the whole wide world and ours was too.

Our class was lined up for our tuberculosis injection, which was the big event of the week, because the area of puncture was to be inspected a week later. There was the usual drama queen hysteria, weeping and fainting. It was alarmingly sore this jag, in the same category as the three-fingered leather strap which was viciously brought down with all the muscle the teacher could muster, and it wasn't only the belts or straps that hurt, it was the look on the owners' faces. I had learned very quickly to watch my P's and Q's whilst living in close proximity to The Daddy and his army belt. I used to hold and hide this brown leather army belt when The Daddy wasn't at home. I still remember the silver diamond-shaped studs around it, as I used to run my fingers over them before I deliberately misplaced it, usually as far down the inside of the bed settee as my wee hand could possibly push it.

This 'drama' behaviour was favourable as a get-out, an escape from reality, acting it! Whilst I was not a drama queen, the notion of being an actor lifted me from Earth to the dizzy heights of somewhere spectacular, even if just in my imagination. At this stage I just loved to learn and watch other people 'do it'. I'd watch dramas such as *Z Cars* and *Crossroads* and study the faces of the actors. I would always wonder what the characters were thinking when the camera was on another character. I would sit forward and study their faces. I wondered if they were afraid, happy, sad? Very few times did I ever see anyone who was believable, I saw them all as mechanical and they looked as though they were reading from a big roll of wallpaper, but not *Doctor Who!* He was good, I thought, mainly because he never stood still. Jon Pertwee was real and a great actor. Wait a minute! Was he not also *Catweazle?* Oh yes he was! *Doctor Who* was big in our house when the television worked. Now when I look back at old *Doctor Who* episodes, I find the scenery hilarious, yet it was believable at the time. When I saw actors adapt to other roles and spark a totally different character, I knew they were very good. There was me, glued to the television marking up every actor as though I was a critic. My mother's most-used quote towards me was, Don't act it!' with that loving slap on the back of the rubber band and ribboned ponytail. Such love! I loved my mother's love and chastening. It was a strange show of affection and sometimes I would even wind her up for a slap. I laugh when I tell my friends on reminiscing that my mother always said she was going to annihilate me. I thought it was something good and looked forward to it.

In primary school I always had a pathetic report card and would do the same as everyone else did, open it before I got to the front door, for a sneaky peek. I had to know what sort of reception this piece of paper was going to deliver, so as to know when to quickly duck. There was only ever one positive comment, which always made me smile, year after year, I was 'Good at acting'. Every other subject was pathetic. When my mother studied the report card in dismay before the five-minute lecture, I'd be so bursting with excitement, telling her there was a good comment on it, 'I was good at acting,' I tried to assure her. 'How do you know that?' she asked. 'Oh, the teacher told me,' I'd tell her sincerely. 'I'm warning you, if you don't pull your socks up you're going to be in big trouble, I'll give you acting! See you just don't act it with me!' She never ever went on about it after seeing the teacher, she must have been convinced by them.

Our Jannie looked old and tired but I didn't know he was ill as well, with TB (we were told). Later on in life and on reflection, one of my other class friends didn't look well either, she was terribly thin and was often missing, presumed sick. When we did see her she came across as 'Peely-wally'. Days after we all received our tuberculosis injections, we were comparing them. Milly and I had no significant mark or redness at all, whereas everyone else's looked really red, purple and swollen.

'Ee yuck,' we warned. 'You've got TB!' We told them to stay away from us in case we caught it. When the nurse did the rounds of examining our arms a week later, I was convinced my whole class had the disease when in fact it was the Jannie, Milly and myself who were sent for immediate medical attention. I never saw the Janitor again and Milly was admitted to hospital. When she was later released, she was unrecognisable and had gained weight after treatment. I was ordered to attend the hospital as a day patient and given medication in the way of wee white pills to take immediately until long after I had left my secondary school, with monthly hospital visits for X-rays and to discuss the shadows on my lungs. I am glad to report I am TB-free. I only have asthma, which developed later on in life due to all of the chest infections I had. I argued with my wonderful doctor until I was blue in the face, telling him I did not have asthma. He was adamant I did have it and I gave in, accepting all the medical assistance I was entitled to, which did help with my breathing.

I remember the one grand non-argument, non-fighting day in the presence of The Daddy just as we ran off to play, very happily because he was happy. We never had any of those days, they weren't the norm. We children had been playing round the back of the tenements with the bins of all things, as smoke was belching from them. Most people had coal fires then and the chimneys were always smoking as the old embers were thrown out straight into the midden, sometimes before they had died down, setting the contents of the steel bin on fire. We were poking the ashes and having a right carry-on with each other, running around with burning twigs and pieces of paper. I had been in the thick of the smoke like everyone else and had taken a deep breath, as you do when laughing, then the most excruciating pain ripped through my left lung and I felt as though I had been shot or pierced with a roasting hot arrow. That was my first ever excruciating pain in my lung. I knew I was not a well child but I was never in any pain, only fevers. I couldn't breathe in or out because of the agony. I had to get up the three flights of stairs to tell my mother I couldn't breathe because of the pain and held my breath for as long as I possibly could, crawling up the stairs. When I made it into the kitchen, I found The Daddy with his arm around my mum. I couldn't tell my mum about the pain because I didn't want to interrupt this rare and beautiful moment. Instead, I laid down on top of my bed and said nothing. I was in danger and gasping for air but said nothing so my mum could be loved by The Daddy and that was all right with me. Who would care if I died anyway? I thought. I lay still and persevered in agony as the pain slowly eased, saying nothing to keep the peace, happy my mother wasn't getting a 'doing'.

On one bitterly cold Hogmanay, as we were first-footing, I shivered violently while walking to my grandmother's house a couple of miles away, in Drumoyne. There were loads of us and I remember having a great conversation with my Auntie Isobel, The Daddy's sister, who was wearing a thick heavy fur coat. She told me she was cold too despite being well wrapped up. I suggested it might be better if the fur was on the inside, maybe it would be warmer then. My Auntie agreed with me and thought it was a great idea. This meant a lot to me because I was having a decent conversation with a grown-up who didn't rubbish my idea. She talked away with me and let me hold onto her arm, snuggling into her thick soft fur sleeve, being careful not to slip on the ice. Unlike her brother, she was kind. In the morning I was in agony with incredible pain and tightening in my chest. After weeks of treatment I got better but damage was done and, as a result. I've never shivered since that bitter night around 1968 and I go straight into hypothermia, which results in pneumonia, and because I don't shiver, I have to keep extra-warm.

On another very cold winter's day my mother sent me along the drive to borrow two bob (10 new pence) from our Auntie Isobel. With that two bob I was to nip into The Drive Stores and buy a loaf of bread. Auntie Isobel was good to us, she never let us go hungry. As I waited to cross the road in the thick snow I wiped it away underfoot and lying there covered in the white flakes was another two bob. What had made me stand there and rub my foot in the snow I don't know but we were so poor I couldn't wait to give her the two bob I found, along with the loaf of bread. I was fascinated and truly believed God put it there just for me.

It was around the same time of year when the door was answered by me to a young couple who had seen the adver-tisement in the local newsagent's for the pram that had belonged to my brother. (He was of the age when he no longer needed it.) I showed the couple the pram, which was advertised for four pounds and they quickly thrust the notes into my hand and left. Wow, I thought, they didn't hang about. When my family came back, I told my mother I'd sold the pram and handed her the four pounds. Her face was a picture, she couldn't believe I had sold the pram and got the right money for it. She was over the moon too but I thought people were very strange creatures. I guess the couple thought they would hop it quick before I changed my mind as they had got a real bargain and my mother was grateful she now had some money for her purse. I was always amazed at how God supplied our need.

I had now moved up and into the Girl Guides and I remember

that near-Christmas evening when we were taken to see *The Snow Queen* somewhere in Glasgow City Centre. I was really excited as we met outside the church on the cold dark frosty winter's night, waiting for our leaders and the coach. It was my first time in a theatre and I spoke to no one as I sat there, mesmerised by the ornate surroundings. I was having a seriously strong déjà vu, which I got an awful lot, that feeling of having been there before I saw it. We were as quiet as mice as the lights dimmed to blood-red before the curtains opened and went up before the performance. This was real! Not like the pictures. I was astounded by the stage lights of pale blue and crisp ice and it was snowing inside, on stage. How could this happen? The scenery, props and costumes as I know them now were stunning. There wasn't a lot on stage except a huge iron cage, where the Snow Queen was eventually captured and kept under lock and key but, although I was amazed, and the performance was great, the story was pants. 'Oh my!'

I thought it was boring and rubbish and distinctly told the church elders so. Well, they did ask. Out of the mouths of babes and all that.

The Snow Queen was moaning and I didn't like her. I remember telling someone she was a crabbit old witch. The show was too long and drawn out and boring and . . . I sat and analysed the performance and believe that was the night I figured I could do it better, me who knew nothing about anything. I thought the big actress, who wore a beautiful glittery dress, was a right big sourpuss. She was always grumping and groaning and nobody on the stage liked her. Neither did the audience, they were booing and hissing at her, so I didn't like her either, I decided. While I was fascinated with the surroundings, my first outing to the theatre was disappointing because it droned on and on. When I saw the show I didn't understand it and couldn't hear what was being said half the time. The show was not for children, obviously. I now know, having been trained in Theatre Production and Acting and Performance, that we should have been taken to a panto. I would have understood the script and the banter and it would have been much more fun, where we could also join in and shout back when egged on by the Dame. Strangely, I could envisage myself on the stage and on TV but I had no idea how to get there and I was never going to leave my mother alone, never, that I did know.

My artistic streak got me into bother one evening while Pannie and I were being looked after by our granny, who put us to bed. Pannie woke up when she hit the cold of the pillow. On surveying the bedroom, we found a tear in the wallpaper above the bed and decided we liked the wallpaper underneath better, so, letting rip, we stripped the lot from above the back of the bed, leaving it on top the bedspread, stour and all. Our granny stood at the bedroom door crying at the mess we had made but a huge smile from Pannie got us off the hook.

'Do you want to play at cowboys and Indians?' I asked our precious brother, because I was fed up taking him out to play with us. He was excited and shouted a big fat 'Yes!' We wore our school ties round our heads and he had on his cowboy suit, holster, gun and Sheriff's badge. It was a simple game, Big Chief, Little Chief and Miss Chief ran around the couch a few times, overpowered the cowboy and tied him up and left him on the couch. The school ties were secured tight around his wrists and ankles and a blindfold covered his eyes. We then ran to tell our mother he was sound asleep on the couch and we were going over to the park. All was well until I heard my name booming from the top floor of the open sash window for the whole of Linthouse and Govan to hear when our mum found him greetin' his eyes out. There was just no getting out without the trifle poking (in the dairy) 'Fun spoiler'.

As a child I began to have what I would call 'Precious Moments', for want of a better word, and I still have them to this very day. No one interferes when I'm having one because they don't know what's happening and I don't choose when they happen. When they happen I am disconnected from my body. I'm still on earth but I feel as though I am a Spirit rather than occupying a body. The first time I experienced it, I was playing in the garden with friends, when I became fully aware I wasn't in the usual zone. To everyone who looked at me, I was there in the garden, a child playing games such as 'Tig' and 'Hide and Seek'. My Spirit separated from my body but it stayed inside my body. When the wind blew I hit against the railings quite hard and I knew it should have hurt but I felt no pain. My laughter sounded crisper to my ears and I heard it as though I was in a tunnel of many echoes with stereo surround sound. When I also heard the others squeal and laugh, I heard them differently too, as though they were each unique and very important and I could still see them clearly. I could also see that I was looking through my spiritual eyes because everything I actually saw was so much purer, as though looking through binoculars, where everything is larger. I felt as light as a feather but was dragging my body around, which was too heavy and clumsy, like Neil Armstrong and Buzz Aldrin in their moon boots? When the wind blew my Spirit, my body had to go with it. God was blowing gently on me and I couldn't control myself.

The first time it happened I stopped playing with my friends and family and started dancing around in the Spirit, totally amazed because I was so light, yet with clumpy feet that kept me on the ground. After a while somebody noticed and I heard him say, 'What's wrong with Esther?' I didn't know at that young age I was in The Spirit because I didn't know what being 'in The Spirit' meant. I also gave the experience the name 'Rattling' and called it so because my Spirit rattled inside my body and didn't come out (until secondary school). I was acutely aware that my Spirit had precedence over my body, it was more important and had dominion over it but all everyone else could see was my body falling about as I was laughing in the fullest joy ever. I now know for sure that there is such a thing as being in The Spirit, you can remain in the shell of your body but your Spirit has full dominion where you are able and free to be with God. Only people who have truly been 'in The Spirit' will know for sure exactly what this change means. It sounds so bizarre but we are not always 'only human' on Earth. What was and is God showing me here? That I am not a body with a spirit; I AM A SPIRIT WITH A BODY. My soul (mind, will and emotions) simply stayed with my Spirit. I could now see very clearly that my body without my Spirit was nothing. It could feel no pain when I wasn't attached to it. I also saw clearly how God was able to take me from my bed to the high hill and other places when He chose for me to be with Him, it is easy for Him to do so.

## Chapter Four

# THE LIAR, THE WITCH
# AND THE WARDROBE

Bible John was the nickname of a serial killer, who was being blamed for the murders of young women in Glasgow while I was attending primary school in the 1960's.

'Here comes Bible John,' one of the younger children screamed, sending the whole of the girls' playground into mass hysteria, crushing each other as we all scrambled to get back into the main school at the same time. The front doors leading to the girls' toilets were always open but the doors leading into the actual school were closed until such times as the bell rang or one of the teachers let us in. The teachers were in a panic as they tried to calm down a school of screaming female children and investigate the incident. Our parents were informed and we were assured and reassured we were in safe hands. We were very aware of the Bible John stories from our parents and the media. Everyone knew of him and every child was afraid of him as it was believed he was close to us, as he lived in or near Govan.

Govan at that time was notorious for young men roaming the streets with open razors and I witnessed some incidents myself, though not too serious, where the glint of the long thin razor was used as a warning. One of the times I was so frightened I hid behind a tall rolled-up carpet in a carpet shop in the heart of Govan. The shop assistant locked her door as the man wielding the razor went on the rampage and told my mother it was all right, the offender wasn't coming over here. I was so frightened I thought the carpets would fall over in my effort to get behind them, then I wondered where the others would hide. The other incident was with a group of men waving their blades in a street brawl outside a local public bar, again in the heart of Govan. Our mother turned Pannie and myself around and headed away from the scene so as not to see what was going to happen next, if anything.

Bible John was 'with us' in our heads throughout primary school, as we always wondered if he was going to grab us. We all had aunties and relatives who went to the Barrowland, a huge dancehall which reopened its door on Christmas Eve in 1960, when I was four months old. The dancing at the weekends was very popular and apparently it was the place to go then, where like-minded young ladies and gentlemen dressed up for a great evening out.

When I was a wee bit older, I watched my aunties get dolled up to go to the dancing. I remember one putting baby oil on her cheap shiny red plastic knee high boots with elastic on the top and she put her thumb through the soft lining of the boot and was mad. She had to tape it on the inside to keep the torn flap in place. They also wore miniskirts, which made me cringe as I knew The Daddy wouldn't approve, but he said nothing to his sisters. On heading out, my granny's parting warning was always 'Mind now, watch out for Bible John.'

Big Marie didn't attend our school, she went to a special school on a grey bus which meant we only met at the weekend. She lived at the opposite end of our block and we could always hear her before we saw her. She truly had 'a voice like a foghorn', which was the description of the day for a loud voice. Given that we lived opposite the Clyde and heard the ships letting off steam, this seemed appropriate. Marie was built like a 'farmer's wife', a description for a big woman, even although she was a child. She was a huge child, much bigger than me. My attraction to Marie was because of her size and I knew it was better to be on her side than not, she could knock you into next week with one blow from the back of her hand. Everyone either respected her or was afraid of her. I hung about with Marie when there was no one else to play with but she never looked happy to see me, on arrival she was always looking me up and down before deciding I could hang around with her, yet never actually said I could.

One day she told us, 'Ma big sister is gonny have a baby, ma mammy saw it in her tea leaves.' I was shocked and excited and wondered how anyone could see your life at the bottom of a teacup when they had finished their tea. Back then I thought big Marie's mother was rich, making an awful lot of money reading tea leaves but I also thought she had to drink an awful lot of tea too. I imagined her mother drinking tea nonstop so she could read the leaves and I wondered if that was why Marie was such a big girl too.

Marie was a bad influence on me and would try to manipulate and encourage me to do silly things, which would get me into trouble. I could get into trouble on my own and certainly didn't need any help in that department but that was the unwritten rule, big Marie was the boss and if you didn't like it, then you couldn't be in her gang. Big Marie was wary of me. It would take her a few minutes to relax when I was in her company and I never knew why, it was as though she didn't trust me one bit and I didn't trust her one bit either. I couldn't understand why she looked me up and down too as I would smile and speak nicely to her on arrival. There was a silent battle of wills going on and I could sense it. She wanted more than friendship, she wanted control, but it wasn't on, so she never actually spoke to me personally.

When my mother had finished her cup of tea one day, I leaned over her chair behind her and casually asked her if she had pictures in her tea leaves.

'What are you talking about?' my mother asked me angrily, disapproving of such nonsense. 'Well, Marie said her big sister is going to have a baby because her mammy saw it in her tea leaves,' I explained.

'How can she see the pictures in her tea leaves?' I asked, innocently wanting to know the exact truth of the tea-leaf matter.

'I've told you before to stay away from that big lassie and I'll not tell you again, do you hear me?' my mother scolded.

It dawned on me very quickly that I shouldn't have mentioned big Marie or her maw.

'Her mother reads tea leaves for money and that's not all she does for money. I'm warning you, don't let me catch you playing with her again.'

I mumbled in agreement with my mother. Big Marie was a bully because she could throw her weight behind her but she never approached me as far as bullying went. She was a dreadful boaster' though' and I couldn't stand it. She was also a terrible liar and, in a stupid way, she caught me like a spider in a web of deceit as she fabricated her stories. She went on about how much money her family had. It was true, Marie always had great big brand-new shoes, summer and winter ones with steel toe caps, or 'segs', hammered into the heel so they could make a noise and spark when she was walking. She was proud to demonstrate this by banging her heel on the ground to spark and would point out they were good and tough for kicking someone. I was sad when I looked at her new shoes because of the ones we had to wear. I had no idea about Social Work Departments and only heard about 'means-tested' benefits from adults. Marie was entitled to everything that was going because she went on a grey bus to a special school. I didn't know what else big Marie had as I was warned never to go into her house, and that was a warning I always heeded. I could rely on big Marie to tell me what she had anyway, as it would burst out of her with much ranting and enthusiasm. She seemed to know every Tom, Dick and Harry and would bawl their names out right up Govan Road to shout hello, deafening anyone closer than four feet away. In this web of deceit I spun her the story that the footballer, Jim Baxter, was my uncle. Well, he was, in a way. The Daddy's brother (my uncle) was James Baxter, who supported Rangers, and I was proud to be a Baxter. Jim Baxter was my uncle and I always got away with it. I really didn't like to tell lies and this one wasn't a lie, it just wasn't the right Jim Baxter she was referring to.

Back to Marie, who had everything, did everything, owned everything, saw everything and was everything. I also told her Auntie Ena Baxter from the Baxter's soup empire was my auntie and she used to carry the deer over her shoulders in the freezing snow and trek hundreds of miles to make our soup. I smiled and liked this heartwarming story myself.

'She sends us presents every Christmas,' I told her. 'And she gave us a huge deer with massive antlers and big eyes and it's hanging up in our lobby,' I announced proudly, not owning up to actually getting it from a jumble sale. 'Aye! She makes sure we get hot fresh soup in the winter and she sends it to the orphans too,' I emphatically told her, making my Baxter soup auntie the best auntie in the whole wide world. A complete and disturbing lie to get one up on the boaster. Marie, in turn and not to be outdone, told me Lulu was her cousin. We were both as bad as each other, one was a liar and one was a witch. I'm staying with the wardrobe on that one. That's how we played it out against each other, the best of friendly enemies. I promised to stay away from big Marie but she let me hang around with her and her friends and I was always intrigued by her nutty lifestyle.

One day when there were loads of us, she suggested we play at Spirits. Off we went to a quieter part of the area, near a church of all places. 'Who wants to be the body?' she asked, pointing her finger and picking one by herself. I hadn't a clue what she was talking about, so I waited until she was organised. One of the girls was to lie down on the ground. 'Right,' said big bossy Marie, 'tuck two fingers under her body (from each hand) and shut your eyes.' I peeked because I was far too nosy. Marie was at the head of the girl chosen to lie down and another stood at her feet with two of us at each side of the body. 'Don't push.' she said. 'Wait until the spirit lifts.' I copied everyone else and was intrigued as I joined in. Marie began to moan some mumbo-jumbo and then we were to slowly lift the girl's body from the ground with two fingers from each hand only. I was giggling as I saw the girl was lifted up from the ground by us but when she got just past my waist height I was horrified to find she seemed to be rising on her own and was shuddering as she went higher, without any effort from my fingers, and floated up with ease. I screamed and pulled my hands away and ran backwards, then everyone, getting a fright too, pulled their hands away, screaming, causing the body of the young girl to crash to the ground from mid-air. I quickly realised I had being doing something very wicked and unholy. Marie stared with big glass-like eyes as though she was someone else. She looked evil and for a minute or so I didn't recognise her. She was totally 'Away with the fairies'. She didn't react at all when the young girl fell to the ground and was sobbing because she was dropped from mid-air and had clearly got hurt as she landed heavily on the ground. I knew Marie was bonkers when she said, 'Put the light out and stand in front of your mirror with a candle in front of your face and you will see your future husband.' Hey! That was too gross and I didn't dare do it. I saw spooks without inviting them in, I certainly wasn't going to light candles and invite them to a party, entertain and play with them.

It was also big Marie who taught me the 'Eg' language (commonly referred to as 'the egg language'), a secret language between children so parents couldn't understand what they were saying. It was very easy to pick up, so much so we became fluent within hours. All we had to do was add the 'Eg' into words according to the number of syllables they had. When a word started with a vowel, the 'Eg' would often start at the beginning of the word. For example, the word orange would be sounded as egoregange. When the word started with a consonant, the word rock would become regock, frog would become fregog and smoke would be sounded as smegoke. For a two syllable word, two 'Egs' would be added, making pencil become peginsegil, ruler would become regulegar and rubber would be pronounced regubegger. It got easier as we practised. Three 'Egs' into the three-syllable word grandmother would have to be gregandmegotheger and cauliflower would come across as cegaulegiflegower (. . . or ending flegoweger if you were posh and pronounced the words properly). Local accents and pronunciation would make a slight difference to the language. Much easier to say than write down, I have to admit. I was the first person in our house to learn the 'Eg' language and I set about teaching Pannie until she got the hang of it, and so it was that we chatted away in our own language, until I felt that familiar slap on the back of my head by our mother.

'Don't let me hear you swearing again,' she shouted. I was completely baffled at how she understood the 'Eg' language. We weren't allowed to swear at all, of course, but I thought I was being smart and my mother would never know anyway. How wrong I was on both accounts. The 'Eg' language was used in school a lot too so the teachers wouldn't know what we were talking about.

Outside of school, church and home, a lot of time was taken up with phoning 'Dial-A-Disc', which we could do for free when you rang a certain four-digit number beforehand. This secret number was passed on by telephone repair men to their children, which spread like wildfire. Every telephone call was made from a red public phone box, if and when it worked. The operator took some stick with silly questions such as:

'Is Mr Wall there?' 'No,' she would say, 'this is the operator, how can I help you?'

'Is Mrs Wall there then?' 'No this is the operator, do you want a number?'

'Are any of the Walls there?' 'No, this is the operator. There are no Walls here.'

'Well, you better get out quick then 'cos the ceiling is going to fall down!'

Pannie did this a lot, I'm innocent. Who needs me for a sister, eh? The beauty in Pannie is that she just admits her faults, throws her hands in the air and says, 'So what, mine are upfront, where are yours?' Another secret language developed years later, which included something like 'I-Y', all I remember of this language is that Polis became something like Polis-I-. The 'I-Y' language came around when Catweazle was about sixteen and able to understand it. It just goes to show how clever children really are.

I've always remembered the time we were invited to the Scottish Farmers' Christmas party in Govan. Pannie couldn't go because she was in bed, sick with a fever. It was the grandest party I had ever been to in my young life and I couldn't believe the amount of cakes, trifles, fruit juices and other goodies we were allowed to help ourselves to. We got many presents too. Scottish Farmers had just opened both their doors, stood back, smiled and told us to 'Come on in.' We freely received all we could manage to eat, drink and carry away in our little hands. That party left me always praising Scottish Farmers for giving small, poor, underprivileged kids a day in life to remember. For over fifty years I have told everyone it was the best party I had ever been to and it's still up there, on top of my happy list. At the end of the party I sheepishly went to one of the tables and asked if I could take a small cake home for my wee sister because she was in bed sick and couldn't come along. With a huge smile, I was given a square white box to fill by myself, with everything I desired for Pannie. They really blessed us in a big way. In reality it was just a standard white cake box, which probably homed about four cakes. I'm quite sure I squashed the cakes together and filled in any gaps with all of the sizeable goodies I could find. Jesus is like that, He throws open His arms and says, 'Come.' We don't have to bring a present, He owns everything anyway. 'Thank you. Scottish Farmers!' You made a wee girl very happy in 1960.

I was well used to my loving mother's slap on the back of the head but the very day I needed it she didn't do it. I had been playing with glass marbles, 'Jorries' we called them. One was rolling around my mouth like a small gobstopper (a brick-hard round sweet) and I inevitably swallowed it. It wouldn't go all the way down my throat as I gulped trying to free my airway. The small glass ball was stuck fast and I began to choke. Panic quickly overtook me because I couldn't speak to tell my mother what had happened. The Jorrie wouldn't budge up or down. I quickly ran to my mother, pointing to my throat in desperation and she said her usual, 'Don't you act it with me or you'll get thumped.' I was literally begging for it. 'Thump me then,' I tried to say. She didn't understand what I was trying to show her and I needed her to belt my back to free the marble. I was desperately trying to breathe and felt my face flush with the anxiety, my heart pumping heavily in my chest. Unable to communicate and thinking I was really done for now, I finally gave up and bent over with my face towards the floor to start the dying process in slow motion because I didn't know what else to do. The bending, though, caused the marble to pop out with a gush of air. Crying, I took the glass marble to my mother and told her I needed her to help me. I told her I was choking to death and I couldn't tell her because I couldn't breathe or talk, in tears, I told her I was dying.

She gave me the 'Hawkeye'. 'That'll teach you for putting things in your mouth that don't belong there,' she scorned. I didn't do that again, but I did 'feel lead' to chew on a pencil.

Around about this time I also remember saving an older man from getting a hiding from The Daddy as I watched myself in the mirror of a big old double wardrobe. We were at a second-hand furniture store in Govan and I was gazing into the full-length mirror of this old wardrobe, smiling. I liked what I saw, she on the other side was lovely and pure. Who said she was stupid? An idiot? Useless? A want about her? A Queerie? No, I liked who I saw. I thought she was nice. She looked kind and belonged somewhere, I knew that as I smiled at myself in my own wee world. I thought this young girl was beautiful despite what she was wearing. There were no pouts or showing off in the mirror, I just stood there still and agreed that I was not the person The Daddy said I was. It was from this moment I began to see that The Daddy was not telling the truth, because I actually accepted his comments and believed him. He even told his cronies and anyone else who listened that I was stupid. That hurt most. It was one thing for him to say I was no good but to tell the whole wide world was bang out of order. I saw the truth as I stood there. I had a 'light switched on' moment with God. I had a 'revelation moment'. It was as though God had stood me in front of that big old mirror for the very first time and opened my eyes. I don't know what else to call it except to say, 'I saw the light.' Remember too, I hadn't seen myself from head to toe before.

My thoughts were interrupted by the presence of an older man whose image overshadowed and darkened my view. He stood close behind me blocking the light, his breath parting my hair as he looked me up and down before he spoke. In the presence of The Lord, the devil is often lurking somewhere not too far off, because he only comes to kill, steal and destroy.

'You're a pretty girl, aren't you?' he asked.

I turned round quickly and with all the sincerity in my heart I replied, 'Yes.' He was towering over me but before the leering man could fire off any more questions, The Daddy was at my side, growling, 'What did he say to you?' The man moved away very quickly and I replied with shrugging shoulders, 'Nothing, he just said it was a nice day.' Liar! I saved this man from getting torn to shreds, yet he was a filthy, dirty old lech. The Daddy was a fist man, he punched first and asked questions later. No, he wasn't remotely interested in what others had to say. He punched once and walked off because there was no need to punch again.

'Blessed are the peacemakers' comes to mind as I remember that moment. All I wanted was peace. I wanted The Daddy to stop beating my mother every day. I didn't want The Daddy to give the man a 'doing', even though he was wrong. They were both wrong and yet there I was, a mere child, looking out for both of their welfares. God was in on the scene, like I said, as I saw the light because He even gave me that big old-fashioned mirrored double wardrobe to keep. He also kept it a secret too because I don't know how it got from the sale room to my bedroom. That mirror I saw the truth in was now mine to look into whenever I wanted to. I have no recall of what was inside the wardrobe throughout the years. I just remember the mirror and the secret place at the top of the wardrobe, which had an ornate, bevelled, carved pelmet around it so a hand couldn't reach or feel over the top from the floor.

The second time I saw the Angels, I was a couple of years older and in the top bunk bed, which was hard against the wall, with the big old-fashioned wardrobe placed beside the bunks. Pannie would kick my backside from the bottom bunk, all in fun, of course, they were great beds to play in when we covered the bottom one with our hanging blankets. We children would often congregate on Pannie's bunk, as it was darker and cosier, with the wardrobe keeping the light out at the pillow end. Great fun, except when I caught my hair in the hooked bed springs, which held the mattress. When I kneeled up from my bunk, I could see over the top of the old wardrobe, where I used to hide my things.

I awoke one night to see the three Angels had come back and were in the slight semicircle formation again, in front of my mirrored wardrobe this time. As before, they were communicating among themselves. When I noticed they were looking at themselves in the long mirror of the double wardrobe, I thought, 'That's my mirror.' As soon as I had that thought, the Angel nearest the bunks turned around to face me, glorious in splendour, with a bright and smiling, happy, beaming face. As

I was in the top bunk bed, I knew for certain that the Angels were definitely not standing on the ground, though they were standing firm and tall just where they were, like the first time, suspended in the fresh air. I didn't hide my face this time, as I had seen them before and I was amazed that the Angels knew my thoughts. I also wondered if the Angels could see their own reflections in the mirror. I fell asleep before they left and I didn't see those incredibly beautiful Angels ever again. I have since met the physical ones though, more on them later.

I have often told the story of seeing Angels to anyone who was remotely interested or needed to know, but you know that funny look you get from people who don't believe you? Someone asked me when telling of the incidents, 'So you've seen six Angels?' 'No,' I replied, 'I've seen three Angels twice, they were the same Angels.' I have no idea why they came to visit me or even allowed me to see them but I still told nobody until I was much older. I sometimes wonder how many times they visit and minister when we are fast asleep.

I made a confession before the family as we were gathered around the Christmas tree one Christmas Day. The Daddy had passed away by this time and I suddenly had the anointed moment to own up to the secret I had kept for over thirty years. Problem was, I could hardly tell it for laughing my head off, that's what I mean about the anointing, God helped me get it off my chest. With happy tears running down my eyes, I finally owned up to my mother.

My parents were waiting for the Christmas hamper they'd paid for all year long, with the help of an agent who took charge of the finances, weekly, and released the Christmas hamper of goodies just before the big birthday on the 25th of December. I was alone in the house, alone and hungry, as usual. I'm trying very hard to justify my actions here, so I'm appealing to you for some sympathy. I'm home alone in the big flat when the doorbell rings and the Christmas hamper arrives. The box was heaving and burst around the edges and with all the good

Christmas will in me I assisted by taking the groceries and drinks out of the box and laid them neatly on the kitchen table, scrutinising every item. The alcohol, which didn't interest me, got shoved to the far corner of the table. The tins and jars of food, shortbread and everything else were examined as I tidied the hamper out and stockpiled it neatly, deciding whether or not I liked what was in front of me. 'Good God in Govan!' I could have sworn that when I handled the heavily frosted dense fruit Christmas cake that it yelled out, 'EAT ME!' I put it down gently with both hands but I couldn't take my eyes off it. The cake was beautiful. A beautiful cake. In general, I saw beauty in everything but this cake with its frosted peaked sparkly icing and solitary plastic green fir Christmas tree, mesmerised me. Looking deep into the clear Cellophane wrapper, I imagined standing under the fir tree which was topped in snow, nothing but pure white glistening shimmering soft snow flakes. It seemed such a shame to break up the vision before me. However, a fight started in my mouth with my taste buds having a right ding-dong and set-to. A celebration of Christmas cheer was taking place in my mouth, having a party, invited by my eyes. There were no goodies like crisps or chocolate biscuits in our house, never. Hungry, starving, I couldn't help myself. I walked like a zombie, hypnotised by the glare of the sparkly icing to the kitchen drawer and came back with the wee sharp tottie knife. Before I had the chance to talk myself out of it, the wrapper was off that cake and a wedge was happily cheering my taste buds up before gleefully swimming down my throat. It was a fruit cake, not even something I would have chosen to eat, but I wasn't being judgemental at that particular moment. It was absolutely delicious, to die for, but, 'Oh God!' What had I just done? I didn't want to die right there and then, not for a wedge of Christmas cake. When I came round from my gluttonous trance, I was in a right state of panic. I had eaten the fruit cake I wasn't given permission to eat of. I tried to squash and squeeze the dense Christmas cake back into a round shape so I could cover up the missing wedge but it wouldn't go back into a circle, as it was stuck firmly to the round silver foil tray. The plastic wrapper was shredded in the opening frenzy and broken pieces of icing crumbs sat where the wedge of cake was supposed to be. The wee tottie knife in my hand was as guilty as me, covered in thick syrup and cake from the sticky fruit. My thoughts turned to the time, my family could come through that door at any moment. I was in a dreadful state of panic, caught like a girl in a whirlwind. Begging the wee tottie knife to become a wand, I ran around the kitchen table wondering what to do next. Before they came back, I ran and stuck the damaged cake on top of the big wardrobe with the Cellophane wrapping, along with the wee tottie knife, careful not to drop a solitary crumb.'

Every minute piece of evidence was hidden on top of the big old wardrobe. It would buy me some time to think about what to do next. When the family came back my serious acting and pretending, otherwise known as lying, took over. I acted really casual and didn't get involved in the discussion about the Christmas cake 'having not been sent'. I felt really bad, though, when my mum was looking for her wee tottie knife so she could peel the potatoes. I had deprived my whole family of their Christmas cake, but what's more, when they weren't in, I had to climb up on my bunk bed to get to the top of the wardrobe and finish off the evidence, every crumb, icing, pieces of fruit, the whole lot. There were loads of midnight feasts, trying to quietly demolish it without rustling the Cellophane.

The guilt hasn't gone away for that sin, every Christmas I have to buy my siblings a whole cake each. It's a good job the Angels visited before the cake was put there, I would have been mortified if they had seen it, though I know they already have, surely? When I visit the family now at the festive season, they always shout, 'Merry Christmas, quick, hide the cake!' Oh, the shame and deprivation of being 'skint'! After I confessed about eating the Christmas cake in my primary years, my mother piped up, 'I knew it was you all along.' Well, why wouldn't she, having eyes at the back of her head and being a mother?

She occasionally made us a tray of tablet and cut it into squares just before it set and gave us each a wooden spoon from the scraped out pot, quickly before it set hard, warning us not to burn our mouths. I've always wished I could make tablet the way she did but it has never worked out or set the same way. She taught me how to bake and never followed a recipe. A cup of this, two cups of that, made the baking look and smell delicious and I remembered her ways and forever followed suit.

Annie Rexia would still hang around on the baking days but because I loved the baking, I would taste it, maybe eat more than I should have. Guilt would then chap, 'Knock, knock, knock,' on my mind and shout, 'Greedy! Fat! Useless! Idiot!' when The Daddy wasn't there.

I have fitted the first interview here. There were three interviews in total. The first time I was taken from my bed for this triple event I was still at primary school, the second time was when I was at secondary school and the third time I was in my thirties:

**I was sound asleep in my bed, not even dreaming, completely sleeping like a log, dead to the world, zonked. Then suddenly I am wide awake and I find I am standing near a stage or platform with The Lord God behind me, nearer to my right ear than my left, as I slightly tilt my head back to Him as we communicate. With The Lord close to me, He shows me myself being interviewed by a male who has his back to us. There are two chairs. The male is interviewing me and the audience is on my right-hand side as I am looking on and they are quietly listening to the interview. I am looking at myself being interviewed. I know it's me, I don't have to ask who it is, although I don't know who the male interviewer is. The Lord shows me I will be interviewed and He will**

**stay with me. I got straight to the point, 'No way, God, I can't do it, send somebody else!' I was a) in my bed sleeping, b) standing in front of God and looking at myself being interviewed while c) sitting in the seat ahead of me, all at the same time. God put me back to sleep as suddenly as he took me to the interview and I remember the incident with precise and complete clarity.**

Up the next close towards the park I had a lovely neighbour who, like us, lived at the top of the building. She was a very pretty young girl by the name of Lorraine, who had a few sisters.

Lorraine was Catholic so went to a Catholic school and the Chapel was important in her life. (I only really saw her out of school in the evenings or at the weekends). Her parents were Irish and my neighbour friend went to great lengths in telling me her blood was pure deep red Irish blood and was as thick and dark as cherries. She'd pull up her sleeve to show me the veins in her arms to prove the point. It's the one thing I remember about her most of all, her pure deep red thick Irish blood in blue veins as I bent closer for a look.

One sadness I had when I was young was that I wasn't a Catholic, because I had a great desire to become a nun. I genuinely wished I was a Catholic so I could become a nun. The desire was nothing to do with actually being a Catholic, or being a nun for that matter. I wanted to serve God full time and I didn't realise we could do it just as we are. I thought God was a religious God and later learned He is A Faithful Father. God was always there for one and all but I hadn't been taught the deepest meaning of The Word. I knew He was real but I knew nothing about having to be saved by the sacrificial Lamb of God. I got a grip of the bible stories about Daniel in the lions' den and Mary and Joseph having the baby Jesus, Samson and his mighty strength, and I was fascinated, I imagined the horror of being stuck in a cage with roaring lions or in a pit of red-hot burning flames. To me, people had to endure things that made my blood curdle. These events and many other stories only caused me to look away and think, 'Thank God you were there to save them, and thank God it wasn't me.'

One Saturday my neighbour Lorraine and I were happy as we were supposed to be heading off to somewhere nice which required coppers, a handful of small change. She pushed me forward while The Daddy was working on his old car. 'Ask him,' she demanded, encouraging me forward. I tried to pluck up the courage to speak to him but my feet wouldn't move. I didn't know what to say. 'Come on,' she said, 'hurry up.' I cringed, I wanted to be able to approach him but I couldn't talk to him. I knew for certain he had no money but to me that was no problem, I would have loved him just the same without money. He always said he and my mother didn't have two pennies to rub together, he also hated money. 'I hate it,' he shouted to my mother often because he didn't have it. He was not at all sociable. I longed to be able to talk to him but I was frightened. 'I can't,' I whispered to my friend. She was really disappointed and went off on her own in a huff and not amused because I had wasted her time. I watched the back of her go until I could see her no more as she headed briskly towards the top of the park railings at the end of Drive Road. Deeply disappointed, I stood looking at the other cars, which had multitudes of small circles of dust from where the rain had splattered down throughout the night. Glasgow was very dusty then with the smoke from the coal fires. I stood there and ran my finger around the dust circles of the bonnet of a car that did not belong to us, a couple of cars up from The Daddy but he didn't see me.

My nerves were shattered around him. He wasn't the kind of Daddy I could hug or talk to. I couldn't stand being in the same room as him and I remember looking for something I needed from a small drawer in the kitchen. Fearful of an outburst, I was as quiet as a mouse. I couldn't open the drawer properly to see and I felt as though his eyes were burning into the back of my head. I knew I had to hurry up or he would start. I pulled the

drawer on the dresser out further and further and was very
nervous. I knew he was going to go off on one; any second
now, Esther, brace yourself, he's going to blow, quick, hurry up,
find it. I couldn't concentrate. How far will the drawer come
out? I wondered as I peered at the back of it, searching. BOOM!
It happened exactly the way I knew it would and I was shaking
with fear. That voice caused me to get the fright of my life
although I was expecting it. I knew it was coming, I could see
the lightning before I heard the thunder. I was shattered into
thousands of emotional little pieces. In terror I let go of the
drawer and the contents scattered everywhere. Not as fast as me,
though, I ran for my life out of the house but I was afraid to
go back home. Terrified of the outburst to come, I stayed out
wandering as long as I could. When I went back home later
nothing was said about the drawer. I don't know who picked
it up, put it back and replaced the contents. I loved him, he
was My Daddy, but I just couldn't stand him for the way he
treated me and beat my mother daily. He was ignorant. I couldn't
ask him for money, he had none. I couldn't ask him for anything,
he didn't like me. I couldn't ask, period. I was afraid of him. I
despised him but I loved him, My Daddy. He was very critical,
so much so I could put my hand on my heart and say I never
once heard him give me a compliment. When I wore white
tights, he shouted, 'Get them off, they're for prostitutes.' When
I wore black tights, it was 'Get them off, they're for funerals.' I
didn't know how to dress, not that I had much option on what
to wear anyway. I once had a black ribbon in my hair and you
would have thought I'd murdered his mother the way he went
on about it.

My auntie, his sister, gave me a pair of dark blue satin trousers. I would hold them up every day and look at them, long,
neat, silky. I loved and treasured them. I always daydreamed of
the day they would fit me and of being old enough to wear
them. I never did get to wear them because they disappeared.
I wore a pencil skirt one day with a slit up the back of the

knees, in order to walk. That's the way they are designed, otherwise you couldn't walk properly. When The Daddy saw the split, he yelled at my mother to get it sewn up as it was torn. My mother had some job explaining to him that it was bought that way and needed the slit. I might add, I had left school and was working when he commented on that skirt. If it wasn't for neighbours giving us clothes when we were younger, then we would have had nothing to wear. Again, this would have been fine if we were a family knitted together in love. Thousands of families had nothing then and we were not alone, but at least they could cuddle up with their parents and laugh at life. I had one solitary cuddle. At least I had one, some children have none.

When we were without food and hungry, my mother was able to pawn something of use. These items were not for our personal use, they were precious pawnable items. I spent many a time in the dusty wooden booth at the pawn shop in Govan. There was only room for one adult and a very small child in the booth and I would often stand further back and wait against the wall if another sibling was with us. People like us went there and begged for more money, stating they got more cash the last time they were there and arguing they were being done. I watched and heard all sorts of excuses. Sometimes they won their case and received the cash they asked for. I heard a man say he needed extra cash because his 'dug wisnae well'. His wee boy pulled on his trousers and asked him, 'Are we getting a dug?'

The Daddy had an old pocket watch on a chain, which was often pawned so we could eat, and his bagpipes were in the pawn like a yoyo. When our transistor radio and clock was missing from the mantlepiece, I knew it was pawned. Our great big Grandfather clock was pawned to stop us playing with it because we would open the glass door and fiddle with the pendulum. If anything wasn't nailed to something in our house, it was pawned. My mother had to take her own brothers' suits to the pawn on a Monday and get them back out on the Friday, pay day, ready for the weekend, she often told me. It was the done thing back then. It wasn't always that they were short of money, that's what they did for security. Nobody could steal or wear them when they were safely tucked away at the pawn shop.

I remember the look of terror on my mother's face one day when she realised she had left some of the redeemed goods on the bus. She hammered up Govan Road and caught the bus to get her things back, all of her worldly goods needed to feed us.

Sometimes my mother would get to go to the bingo hall in Govan but she hardly ever won anything. When she did win she would bring back a bottle of ginger and a fish supper. We were so happy on those nights but they were very few and far between. Sometimes it would be a bottle of Cream Soda and a box of ice-cream and she would make us an ice-cream float. When my mother didn't win, she would get hell because The Daddy was in a bad mood. While she was at the bingo, The Daddy would be pacing the floor and watching from the bay window to see who she was walking down Govan Road with. He would quiz her for hours about who she was talking to, what he said, what she said back. It was awful, he would let her go to the bingo for a wee night out, then give her the third degree when she came back. She had to bring back all of her used bingo books and show The Daddy where she was waiting on one or two numbers and we'd get to treasure the used bingo books as a keepsake. She was then banned from the bingo because he didn't trust her, unless I got to go with her. She couldn't get up to anything if I was there. I was given a pair of my mother's tights and a headscarf so as to look older than my ten years, and told to go to the bingo with her. The age limit was sixteen then. I was given a book from my mother's six-page book and joined in for the single line, double line and full house. When I won on a single line once, I nudged my mother, who shouted house, gave her membership card over and collected her winnings.

On one occasion, The Daddy came with us, along with two of his sisters. What a great night that was because it was very close to Christmas. Throughout the evening, when someone shouted 'House', they got a large box of family biscuits, as did the person on each side of the winner. We went home with no less than thirteen boxes of biscuits between us that evening but we could hear people mumbling because we got so many. When the players at each end of us won, we still got a box of biscuits and, because we were all sitting in a straight line, the biscuits piled up. They won a little money too, on single and double lines, but it was the biscuits I was delighted with. After going to the bingo for a few months, someone complained I was underage, naturally, and I wasn't allowed to play any more, but I was still allowed to accompany my mother. Surely everyone could see I was just a child still in primary school?

I remember my little brother Addie saying, 'You look nice,' as I got ready for the bingo one evening. I never forgot that compliment from such a small child and it touched my heart because my parents never ever said it. I wasn't used to compliments and I knew he meant it. I grew up well before my time and was fast becoming an adult in a child's body, feeling I had to hold it together for the sake of everyone.

From the age of eight I was babysitting a neighbour's little boy by the name of Matthew, for the whopping sum of twenty-five new pence. Tucked into his cot, he slept all evening. When I checked on him I thought he was the most perfect beautiful little baby. The Daddy volunteered me for babysitting whether I wanted to do it or not. Usually I did want to do it as it got me out of the house to watch a decent television and sit in a house with carpets in it. The neighbours would tell me to help myself to juice, which I did. I had no eating problems in anyone else's house as there was no one to hide from and no pressure to eat or else! I could take it or leave it. I also had to babysit for family members, where there was no money changing hands because they were family. I preferred the paying customers, not just for the money. They had chocolate biscuits whereas close family members had nothing too.

On a Sunday after church we were marched to Drumoyne to visit my grandmother and meet any cousins who were also there. While every one of our cousins were allowed to play, we had to sit on the couch and watch, four of us lined up, sitting perfectly with our hands on our laps. An aunt told me recently she remembers how we had to stay on the couch in military fashion unless we needed to use the toilet. Needless to say, one of the four of us always needed the toilet and it meant we could get up. Addie got away with jumping off the couch because he was the youngest. Next in line was Kat to slip from the couch to go to the toilet without asking. No sooner had one sibling come back, another would need to go. It was our way of stretching our legs and we would take our time in doing so, testing The Daddy to see how long we could get away with being up and off the couch. I never got away with it, but a big smile from one of the other siblings usually worked and, as soon as we could, we would be out in the back garden or in the street with our cousins and the other pals who stayed in Inverness Street. My granny always told The Daddy, 'That's a shame, let them out,' because she saw we hadn't the same freedom as the other grandchildren. Everyone noticed the severe discipline The Daddy administered and remained tight-lipped.

Our granny hadn't much in the way of money or food either but she would usually give us a piece with fat and sugar in it. It was disgusting but I ate it anyway because I was hungry. I remember my granny often needing a shilling for the meter when the electricity would conk. Sometimes she just sat and stared at the flickering flames of the coal fire, in peace.

We would often be there when her gas man came round to light the lamp on the landing around teatime and the poor guy was always asked if he had any money. Folk often borrowed a lot, I remember. It was always, 'Go and ask so and so if they could lend me a shilling for the meter and don't come back until you've got one.' People were generous and usually had no qualms about giving. If they didn't have it, then you couldn't get it, simple as that. I was often sent to the shop for 'Tick, where your name, date and amount owed was written in a book, to be paid at a later date. Many shops in Govan had big clear signs which stated, 'NO TICK'. Some of the signs were humorous, stating 'Don't ask, a punch in the mouth often offends', or 'Ask, don't get, Don't ask, don't want'. When the debt was paid off, the debtor's name was ticked off, usually on pay day, Friday, when the wage packets came hame with The Faither, unopened or else.

I remember The Daddy getting a severe tongue-lashing from my mother because he had opened his wage packet and bought something unnecessary and without consent. He had no business opening his wages, my mother screamed at him, and he, by the way, apologised and promised not to do it again. Every penny was accounted for in our house and that pay packet was my mother's. It was a huge household rule in many an abode, men did not open their own brown wages envelope, the wife did, or else. The men who did open their own wage packets and went home via a public bar got done in to within an inch of their lives. I saw many a man dragged from the pub by the screaming banshee of a wife on a Friday evening. That was when we started to sing 'Murder Murder Polis'. I also saw many a child seated by the door of the pub waiting for his or her Da to come out. If the mother was in for a drink too, then it was a long lonely evening for the child, sometimes sitting outside in the rain.

One of my aunts had a friend by the name of Ann McCann and we made up a song that became a playground hit, which went something like this: 'Ann McCann's goat a man, and if ye want to know his name his name is . . . Shug McGlumfer'. We would sing the song and put the name of a girl and a boy we knew of in place of Ann McCann and 'Shug McGlumfer' for playing 'Ba's oan the wa's'. We would often play balls on the walls in the closes only to get told to 'Beat it, away an' play in yer ain close'.

It is not politically correct now (and never was) to use the word 'Chinkies', but that's what our elastic bands were called then, when we knotted them together so we could put them round our ankles to play. I have no idea if the name actually had anything to do with Chinese people or not and I never wondered about it as a child. I now wonder if it has something to do with the stretched elastic band allegedly looking like Chinese eyes? Just a thought, but that's what we knew them as anyway, regardless of where the name came from. It's a small world, as they say. When I was acting in a play at the Citizens Theatre, I met a Chinese girl who is the sister of a girl I knew well. The sister told me to look out for her younger sister, Karen, at the theatre and I did. She worked in the costume department and looked after my outfits. Well, also around the same time, Karen got to do a television advertisement. The advert was about two drunk guys suggesting they go for a 'Chinky' (Chinese food) after a night out and Karen was in the advert to state this wasn't acceptable, quite right doll. The language we used as children was always innocent to us and passed down from adults who thought it was acceptable, and we were none the wiser. This was in the days when we all wanted the little 'Golliwog' pin badge we could order from the jam jars and 'Ba Bru' was the mascot on the ginger bottles from Barr's. That was our life as we knew it. At that age we dearly wanted, fought over, 'Golliwog' puppets because they were popular and if our friends had one, then we all wanted one, but we never got them. We all knew someone who had a cat named Blackie and in an odd sort of way, in order for something to be stamped out, it has to come to the surface and be presented first and that's what happened in our young lives. Though we were innocently going with the flow, there were matters such as television programmes and advertisements that are now totally unacceptable to other cultures. We have come a long way, though still not fully there, but it's the love of children who make it right and adopt friendships more easily than adults. Children accept and receive love for what it is with no strings attached, they recognise beauty in all cultures through friends and have easier access to travel than we did in the sixties. I have never heard a young child use a nasty comment to bring down someone with darker skin or a different accent but, sadly, I have heard many an adult do it.

There were always visitors at our door, like everyone else's. Someone would be selling something, brushes, encyclopedias, cigarette coupons, Co-op stamps, their own stuff, knocked-off goods or something that had fallen off the back of a lorry. I had never seen a thing fall from the back of a lorry and I used to wonder how they managed to catch it in perfect shape. How could they catch a television or a transistor (radio) from the back of a lorry without it getting broken? I used to wonder, and did the driver not know it had fallen off? Would he have not wanted it back? Given that televisions were massive then, I could only imagine a wee man's pair of legs trying to run down the street with the huge object, and thought something's not right here. We didn't get any of the goods offered but The Daddy always knew someone who was a collector and had the means to buy or barter. One of his cronies always had a few bob so that is where the goods were sent, on enquiry.

The insurance man was another weekly visitor and I'm sure there was some sort of cheque man looking for his money on a regular basis. I was often sent to the door to tell them The Daddy wasn't in, on his orders. There were times when he told us to be quiet when the bell rang. The debt collector must have heard the racket from us weans before he told us to be quiet. I got into trouble one day for telling a debt collector, 'My Daddy says my Mammy's no' in either.' The collector got the message, he wasn't getting paid and that was that.

A beautiful white poodle was brought to our house to live with us from the cat and dog home. It hid in the corner growling, shivering violently and looked frightened to death. It was taken back to the cat and dog home the next day because it snapped when we got too close, and was replaced with a black hairy mutt with dreadlocks. It had so much hair we could hardly see its eyes. It liked us, though, we could tell by its swishing tail, and it got to stay. The name of our new dog was Rags. Rags was old but he was good fun and liked to play with us and thus, he was allowed into our gang. We didn't have him for very long, though, given his age. He loved to play and belt up and down the lobby with us.

Another pet I sometimes had was a hamster. I often got to take the classroom hamster home for the weekend and was promised I was to take him over the summer holidays. When the teacher changed her mind and refused to give me the class hamster home for the duration of the summer holidays, I was heartbroken. In the end my mother bought me my own hamster for my birthday and I name him 'Hammy'. Hammy bit me a few times, just like the school hamster had done, but I'd been bitten a few times already by other little animals and was well used to it. I can only surmise they sensed I was fearful and took a swipe at me too. I had more tetanus injections than hot dinners, as the saying goes. If I wasn't bitten in the house, I'd get bitten outside by another creature. I only had Hammy for a short time before he died, and I was on my own when I took him to Elder Park for his burial. Armed with a big spoon, I dug a hole and gently laid him in it, crying my eyes out. Big Marie had me crying again when she told me a dog saw where I had buried my Hammy and ate him up. It took me ages before I found out she was telling lies. My mum assured me she wasn't even there to see any dog or she would have shouted to me, that made me happy. My Hammy was surely dead but definitely not eaten up.

When I got bitten on the finger by a fieldmouse at the park, I had to go to the Southern General, as usual, for a tetanus injection on the backside. The next day the tetanus injection looked horrific. The swelling and red mark started out the size of a thimble before spreading to the size of a saucer. I got to

stay off school for a few days but when I went back to school
I learned everybody heard I got bit on the backside by a mouse.
I never did find out if Pannie started the rumour but, to quench
it, I went round everyone showing them my invalid finger with
the tiny holes the fieldmouse had made as it tried to escape my
clutches. I let the little thing go quicker than I picked it up,
that's for sure, and it got me back, on the backside.

I knew the Southern like the back of my hand, with having
to go for chest X-rays, tetanus injections, accidents and my
mother working there. Off to the Southern we went again
then when I gashed my finger on a ginger bottle I dropped
running past the sawdust shop beside our close. The blood
flowed like a fountain, so much that I was stunned as I watched
a puddle of crimson grow deep and wide. I only panicked
when I feared I had nothing to sweep the glass up with, so
using my hands, I sliced through the vein in my wedding ring
finger. 'Leave the bottle,' women ordered when they saw me
trying to pick up every shard of glass and with nowhere to
put it, gasping at the pool of blood under me. In the hospital
my mum kept nudging me in the waiting room each time I
opened up my hand to see if the bleeding had stopped. All I
was doing was making the vein spew more, nothing could
hold it back. I was amazed at the amount of congealed blood,
it was beginning to thicken and stand up on its own. The
floor of the waiting room and the clean white gauze was satu-
rated with blood and I remember being amazed because I had
lost so much blood and never felt a thing. Once my finger
was cauterised I was able to have it stitched. After the healing
of my finger I couldn't bear the sensitivity I felt when I touched
something. Nor could I wear a ring on that finger because of
the feeling in it and I thought I would never be able to wear
a wedding ring. I couldn't stand the feeling when something
was on the scar as a horrible sensation ran up my arm when
in contact with anything and I still have that sensitive feeling
in my finger.

On the days (before the sexual assault) we walked through the Clyde Tunnel to Victoria Park, our first visit was always straight to the trees which had turned to stone. I was fascinated by them and always went to make sure they were still there, telling everyone all about them and asking if they had seen them. I loved God's planet and was fascinated by anything which was stamped with His handiwork and not made by man. I found trees to be magnificent because of their height and grandeur. They were all much older than me and my mother and even her mother. I would wrap my arms around them to hug them, telling God I loved Him for giving us the trees, grass and flowers. I hope it wasn't me who started 'tree hugging', there is no replacement for our Creator and His creation is out of this world (made in Heaven), but not to be worshipped. I could not get my head round why the trees had turned to stone, and told everyone I could about them. I'm sure my teacher and classroom friends were fed up hearing about them, as I went on about them constantly. On the subject of trees I share with you one of our daft childhood jokes:

> *Knock knock!*
> *Who's there?*
> *Theresa!*
> *Theresa who?*
> *Theresa Green!*
> *Knock knock!*
> *Who's there?*
> *Theresa!*
> *Theresa who . . . .Oh, I get it, trees are green.*
> *Naw ya bampot, trees are brown, the leaves are green.*

I often wonder who makes jokes up, they must have a great sense of humour. I know plenty who tell jokes for a living but they sometimes pinch other people's ideas. Here is one I made up as a child in the early nineteen sixties. I've heard it told back

to me and I've said, 'I made that up.' . . . I did, you know!
Needless to say, nobody believed me:

'A Scottish man, an Englishman and an Irishman have to go
traipsing through the desert, which is roasting hot and they can't
take too much stuff with them. It's agreed they will bring one
thing each, which they will share for the journey. After travelling for a long time through the sand, the Scottish man says,
'I'm hungry.' The three sit down and the Englishman shares the
food he has brought. A long time later the Englishman says,
'I'm really thirsty.' The Scottish man shares the drinks, his whisky
and water, until they've had enough. On they go again in the
blistering heat. It's too much, the heat has got to the men and,
much further on along the way, the other two say to the Irishman,
'What have you got, by the way?' 'Wait till you see this,' the
Irish guy says, and they stop for a look. They fall down on the
sand, exhausted, as the Irishman grapples at his big black bag
and pulls out a car door. 'What the . . .?' 'What are you doing
with a car door?' the other two moan in disbelief. The Irishman
says, 'Oh, we're all right here now, I brought the car door as I
knew we would be too hot and I thought I would let the
window down for some air.'

The poor Irish get it all the time, as do the Scots for being
tight or mean, but we know better . . . and I did make up that
joke . . . tell them, Lord!

At Victoria Park, one scorching Sunday afternoon, we children
were filmed for a documentary at the boating pond, which was
shown on BBC1. We knew we were being filmed but had no
idea what for, only that the cameras were zooming in on the
little sailing boats which were bobbing along. When we went
back to school on the Monday, everyone asked, 'What were you
doing in London? We saw you on the telly.' I told them I wasn't
in London, that we were actually in Victoria Park. We were so
excited and thought we were a wee bit famous but disappointed
we hadn't been able to see it on our broken down, clapped out
telly. That was my first television appearance and I had no idea

I would go on to appear in adverts later on in life. It was just a daft notion or a deep secret heart's desire.

The Daddy was a real proud man in his kilt, especially now he had a 'mini me' in his youngest, Addie, who had his own kilt and buckled shoes, which he highly polished along with his own brogues and army boots. We girls never got our shoes highly polished as we never had good ones to polish. We were taken to Clan gatherings quite a lot and I remember being at Doune Castle for some of the events. The Daddy looked handsome in his full Highland regalia, I have to give him that much credit, but that's all, not forgetting he was seen as a very different Daddy to each sibling.

One good thing about The Daddy was that he would often take us on a run to Loch Lomond when the car was working. He spent a lot of time on it to make sure it was up to speed. Well, I don't know about speed, so long as it drove there and back we would be fine. He would often give me a fright when we pulled into a lay-by as the roads were much narrower then and I was scared another car would knock us over the edge and into the water. I seemed to develop a fear of what could happen as well as what was actually happening. Through fear, being carefree in my childhood hadn't developed.

I've heard people say loads of times that they knew they were different as a child and I have to say that too. I was still a child and did the childish and childlike things children do, like lose (or find) my temper, be insolent, complain, cry and occasionally throw a hissy fit. I was not holier than thou by a long shot, but I was very spiritually aware. I knew without a shadow of a doubt that there was The God and The Devil, good and evil. I heard God's voice and was taken from my sleep many times to be with God when He wanted to show me or tell me something. I knew we were only here on earth for a short time and I knew we each had ministries and talents to fulfil and complete. I secretly knew my life and will wasn't my own. I knew I had a calling, me who fancied being a nun in order to serve God, but

I didn't know what that calling was then. I felt pulled, tugged, chosen, that is the only way I can describe it.

I walked away from primary school with my one and only prize for a national writing competition. Basically, all of the schools were given the chance to write an essay on the disposal and management of litter, which I did in my best handwriting, and came out tops. Now I could finally walk away with something other than 'Good at acting' and 'Can do better' on my report cards.

There was nothing of any value or use to pass on to my siblings when leaving the primary school, my school tie was well and truly ruined by the wash years before when the dye ran through from the boiling at 'The Bag Wash' on Govan Road, and my school uniform was already null and void. I took everything I had accumulated from primary seven and walked home with the folder under my arm, smiling at the thought of going to the great 'Scripture Union', where I would join and follow Jesus, at the high school, I presumed. Many from my class promised to go back to visit the teachers and I did too, only once, it was too soon to let them know how I was getting on.

Despite the big fight and falling out during primary seven, Friend and I readily made up and I agreed we would stay together and join a whole new class of unknowns, as two people were asked if we wouldn't mind joining another class. Friend volunteered us and it was fine with me. The summer holidays were taken up with sorting out my new High School uniform and sifting through my primary work and art in preparation for the big school, Govan High. I eagerly met back up with Friend at Govan High School in August of nineteen seventy-one and made it my mission to find out where the amazing Scripture Union meeting was.

Scripture Union wasn't to start back for a couple of weeks, I was informed, a little time to let everyone get settled in. Our primary seven teacher in Elder Park School told the class all about moving on to the secondary school and she was happy to announce we would love it. It was her who told me about Scripture Union and I was particularly eager and excited to find the class as soon as possible so I could go to it straight after lunch on a Wednesday afternoon. The teacher who took the Scripture Union class was a Christian, I was told. My primary teacher also told me proudly that the Scripture Union teacher was her best friend and I was looking forward to this event most of all as I said goodbye to the primary school forever. I loved Jesus and I wanted to learn all about Him, serve Him and be with Him forever.

By the time the summer holidays were over I was itching to get there. Finally, having found the right class, I rushed into the classroom where the meeting was held and smiled as I swept through the door, desperately eager to join in and learn. All morning long I waited for that Scripture Union class in anticipation. This is finally it, this is where I belonged, I reasoned.

I was directed to a chair without so much as a welcome or 'Hello'. There were only two other pupils in the class and Friend refused to go with me, it wasn't everyone's cup of tea. There was a deadly silence as the teacher slowly paced the floor and I thought it was the silence and serenity of the meeting and calmly relaxed with due respect. She stopped pacing the floor and looked up slowly, pointed towards me with her finger and motioned for me to come to the front of the class beside her. I had no idea what she had been discussing before I burst into the classroom as I had some difficulty in finding the class, being fairly new to the school. I slipped from my seat to the front of the desks and stood before the Christian teacher I so longed to meet, wondering what blessed happening was in store. She lifted her head in utter disgust and produced that long brown leather strap.

'You know what this is for, don't you?' she asked. I didn't know, I stood there looking at her in shock and disbelief.

'Spit it in the bin,' she demanded. I had forgotten I was eating a sweet, in my own free time I might add, but I did what she said. 'Hands out,' she spat with angry eyes and brought the belt down as hard as she could, three times on my overlapped hands.

The look on her face said it all, she hated me. She killed my soul. I was distraught, not just because of the belt, or eating (Annie Rexia also saying, 'I told you so!'), but because I thought she was a Christian. I looked up to her, she was my lifeline to God, Jesus and Heaven. How could she do this to me? Does Jesus not love me any more? Jesus hates me! From that day on I bowed my head and turned away from Him with shame and couldn't believe He had left me. I accepted she was His representative and His servant. I went back to Scripture Union a couple of times after that, hoping, praying, I might be forgiven for eating that one sweet but she wouldn't speak to me, as though I was invisible. I really did try but there was no love, no peace offering, no forgiveness for the massive crime of eating when I wasn't supposed to. Eating, that disgusting crime, got to me again. I felt so unloved and unwanted. I'd been abused by The Daddy physically and mentally from birth, abused by my best friend all through primary school and now, at the grand young age of eleven, abused by the one teacher I thought would guide me through the path of life with Jesus. For six long weeks during the school holidays, I believed my life would change for the better as I yearned after My Jesus, who came for me when I was little and took me out to play. I knew I was getting a new school, new friends, new clothes, new life, new education, but all I wanted and needed was Jesus. My primary teacher lied to me, I thought. What was wrong with me that people thought it was okay to use me as a personal punchbag? No wonder I was 'twisted' just like The Daddy said. I guessed I was not wanted by God after all, I believed I wasn't good enough to be loved. I knew I wasn't good enough anyway, there was no getting away from that fact. What a huge blow that was, a massive letdown, shattered, where was I to go from here? I didn't want to be a nun any more anyway, I reasoned.

Who wanted me? Nobody. How could somebody who loved God hate me?

There was talk of us leaving Glasgow and I so desperately wished it was true because I didn't want to be in Glasgow any more. I wasn't sure where I wanted to be but Govan High's Scripture Union teacher destroyed me and it wasn't the dream I had hoped for after all. Someone in Pannie's class in primary school had already left to live in Inveraray and we were told we would be living a good bit away from Inveraray, we were just waiting for the news to move, we were told, but I didn't really believe it.

Was it a plane? A helicopter? From the earliest age I can remember until my late teens, around nineteen seventy-nine, I had the same dream where I was being watched by an intelligence on Earth. While it was true I hadn't seen an aeroplane close up, because I had never been on one, I knew a plane couldn't hover or sit still in space like a helicopter. I also knew the small craft were not helicopters because they had no huge swirling blades and anyway, they couldn't be as close together as these smaller craft were. They came to the window in a matter of seconds and sat there, all knowing, all seeing and looking for me. They found me and I had nowhere to hide, as I got up to flee I knew they were staring. In the dreams I always got up to run out of the room when I first saw them coming but it was too late, I knew they had already caught sight of me. They found me and knew I was at home. Sometimes there would just be one aircraft, at other times there could be up to five all lined up together. I hadn't done anything wrong but the intelligence operators of the machines where watching me at all times and I knew it was pointless trying to hide.

When I saw 'drones' on the television one day, I knew that's what I saw more than fifty years ago, in the dreams. The drones have eyes, I knew that in the dream because they were too small to hold an adult, yet I knew I was seen, as they have video and photography equipment. At the time of seeing the drones I had no idea that someone, government, or any other agency was operating them from another building or from the ground.

They are remote-controlled pilotless aircraft that can (and will) be used for surveillance, even by private companies, as they are not under any restricted licence. They are silent too, it's not everyone who looks up to see if they are being filmed or watched by a strange entity. The drones are fully equipped with sensors, navigation systems, Global positioning systems (GPS), and can be navigated autonomously. What does it mean for us? Basically, you can run, but you can't hide. Our mobile phones have a tracking device, as have some cars. On social media our phones can 'ping' and tell the whole world where we are at any moment. People I know well go on holiday and the first message they send out is, 'I'M AT THE AIRPORT!', telling everyone they are on holiday and leaving their houses free to burgle.

That was the meaning of the dreams I saw even before drones and mobile phones were invented. If you think you're not being controlled now, it won't be long until you realise you are, then the next step is to actually own you. 'For this reason, I'm out.'

One of the first statements I told everyone when I became a Christian in nineteen eighty-two was that we would all have to have a microchip inserted into our hand or head. No one answered, 'Cool!' Most ranted, 'They're not putting a microchip in me!' Others told me not to be so stupid, it will never happen, despite countries having already done it and passed the microchip in trials. People have come a lot further on in knowledge.

'Yes, I know all about that,' they say. 'I think it's a great idea. No one can steal from your bank account because the chip is in your hand.' The chip is an ownership of Satan.

Often, I was fast asleep but suddenly found myself standing on a platform of thick concrete levitating at the top of a deep hole. The concrete was wobbly and I didn't like it, looking to God and telling Him I was scared. By thought I knew I was perfectly safe and He was not going to let harm come to me.

At first the holes were the size of large cellars and at other times so dark and deep I couldn't see to the bottom as I bent over carefully to peer inside. Each hole was different every time I was taken and shown them. I had no idea where I was as I concentrated on what God was allowing me to see but I would gasp at the enormity of the situation. Neither did I know why the hole was there, only that the ground had collapsed and that the earth was disappearing randomly and quickly under my feet. My young life was awful in the flesh and I hated it but God often came for me now that I was too old to be running around and playing chases with Jesus. It's only recently that I realised God was placing me on top of 'sink holes'. If only I had the courage to speak out and tell everyone about God, Jesus and The Holy Spirit. I had zero confidence among people and saw that God Himself was teaching me and showing me what was happening on the Earth, a confirmation that this was not our permanent home.

## Chapter Five

# IN LOVE WITH LIFE

⌒⟶

I had only been at Govan High School for just under three months when we moved away near to Lochgilphead in Argyll. This time, the only residential schools I saw from then on were the ones I saw from the outside, as in Achnamara. I was now to become a local, living in the fresh air of the country. From what I remember, The Daddy was to start a new job with The Forestry Commission in Argyll, that was the reason we were allocated a house owned by The Forestry Commission.

We travelled to Argyll and viewed Port Ann first because The Daddy had been given the keys to The Forestry Commission house at number thirteen. It was bare except for many spiders, and in need of decoration. Otherwise it was a semi-detached with its own gardens and driveway. There was the fantastic smell of burning logs, peat and coal lingering in the air and a weird big contraption in the kitchen known as a Rayburn, which was very old. I have since always loved the smell of a log-burning chimney, which reminds me of Port Ann.

Port Ann was built in a circle of sixteen houses looking into what is known as the Bullring. A short lane to the top took us onto a small field with one goalpost and a strong well-constructed see-saw and a garage for a neighbour's car. There was nothing else but the forest and a large wooden structure which was the forest-fire lookout platform.

We then drove to Kilmartin, fourteen miles further on towards and beyond the town of Lochgilphead. We stood outside the second house for a viewing only, as The Daddy did not have the keys for it. It was a lovely little village but I had already fallen totally in love with Port Ann and demanded that we live there, so then, Port Ann was chosen as the designated abode. As if The Daddy ever listened to a word I said, but God was clearly in on this agreement. It didn't stop me in becoming vociferous, though, and saying I really loved it there.

I was twelve years old when I was left alone in our new house with some of our belongings. There were no curtains up and I was cold with no heat, nor did I have any television or even a radio for company. The family had driven back to Glasgow, leaving me alone in the house overnight, in order to bring back the rest of their belongings. I stood and looked out of the bare window a lot, which I think the neighbour across the lane spotted. She came over to ask if I was all right and when I told her I was alone, in she came, rolled up her sleeves and gutted out the Rayburn. I stood back and watched as she used her bare hands to sweep up, then provided coal and lit the Rayburn, which clunked into life, pipes banging around the house as the water heated up.

I forget the name of the wonderful neighbour who lived opposite us. She lived with her elderly mother and had a huge, overweight white West Highland Scottish Terrier, which grunted heavily and rocked from side to side as it attempted to walk. Our neighbour explained about the other half of the Rayburn having an oven and how it would provide hot water for the toilet and kitchen. She then took me over to her house, where I got washed and fed with some supper before she led me to the spare room, where there was a huge single bed that was very old and high, ornate, and beautifully made up with pure white fresh linen. I loved the bed. It was a bed only seen in castles, palaces or stately homes, absolute luxury, and too good for the likes of me, I thought as I nodded off. I slept soundly in peace and quiet for the first time in my life. Nothing spooky or creepy lived in Port Ann, or so I thought. I hadn't seen the wildlife yet, from the smallest to the largest of God's creatures.

The flat, which had no floors in the bathroom and kitchen, was sold, giving my parents a small cash windfall many months later. There wasn't much in the way of furniture to collect, except for the beds and table and chairs, which we needed, and I never saw the blue kitchen unit, the huge fibreglass bunker or my wardrobe with the mirror in the middle ever again. There was nothing of mine to bring back except for Heather (my big doll) but she never arrived with the furniture. I didn't need her but I always wondered what had happened to her and her baby clothes I so carefully kept pressed in my big drawer. My Heather was better dressed than me, that I made sure of. By this point we had an old Cairn terrier by the name of Sandy, we loved him so much and I couldn't wait for him to arrive to take him for a walk and discover Loch Fyne and the surrounding areas. I knew Sandy would love it, the new smells and fresh air would do him the world of good, I reasoned, as he was never allowed out on his own because we lived in a flat.

I daydreamed no end while I was alone in our amazing new house with its own gardens. The windows were much smaller than the ones I was used to in Drive Road and I thought they were quaint, just like a doll's house windows. The spiders on the windows outside the back bedroom were in colour and completely different from the Glasgow spiders. The Glasgow spiders had tiny bead bodies with long legs all around but the spiders I was now looking at were black, red and orange. I was so glad they were on the outside as I peered through the pane for a closer look. Then, oh my God! What a fright I got! I saw a Danny longlegs that was as big as a bird, as it hit the window and fluttered for ages behind the glass. I was astounded as I saw how thick its body was and I could clearly see veins of fabulous colours in its wings, I was scared, shocked and mesmerised at the same time. I thought my family would never believe it when I told them about the huge Danny longlegs, well! They are in for the shock of their lives, I beamed, happy to be the bearer of this frightful but astonishing good news, I had also better warn them never to open the windows either, I mused. I was to learn later that this amazing creepy flying creature was a Dragonfly.

The following day my neighbour took me into Lochgilphead, where I was to go and wander around the town while she did her shopping and I was to meet her outside the chemist, but I was too afraid to wander away in case I lost sight of her. Her act of kindness has forever left a glow in me. She lit our fire and her kindness lit up my life, what a marvellous neighbour.

The small village of Port Ann had nothing but fabulous neighbours. Murdo, a neighbour in the Bullring (the circle) would tell us to go to his freezer and take as much fish as we wanted as he became friendly with The Daddy, giving him tips on fishing. We had a few fish suppers from Murdo's freezer, courtesy of Loch Fyne. The Daddy never ever had any real true friends he socialised with, as far as I knew, so these new friends and neighbours had a great impact on his life. He always spoke very highly of them. On reflection, I don't think The Daddy was ever loved or shown any affection, which must have been difficult for him (growing up). That would explain his disturbing and manic behaviour. He didn't know how to behave socially. He didn't know how to receive praise and when he did, it floored him. Murdo would take The Daddy onto Loch Fyne for fishing trips and sort of took him under his wing. Pannie got to go out in the boat and close to the small island beyond the Blue Rocks. The Daddy never asked me. I would sit on the Blue Rocks by myself many a time and wish I was over at that small island, maybe one day. Yes, I would love that, I thought, but I never did get over there. I'd sit there for the longest time, smiling and wondering who lived over the other side of the water.

Mrs McCloud, Murdo's wife, became good friends with my mother and I overheard them talking a few times when she was giving my mother advice regarding The Daddy's mental health. I still didn't realise at this age (twelve) that he was, in actual fact, mentally ill as he hadn't been to any hospital and I never heard anything in relation to his mental wellbeing.

All of the neighbours in Port Ann were kind and friendly. There was someone for everybody to confide in, each member of our family had a friend in Port Ann who was also in their class at School and 'Crusher' (Eileen Kennedy) was in my class. There were no shops in Port Ann and it was never referred to as a village, just sixteen houses in a circle. No house had a telephone, there was one at the bottom of the road but it never worked when it rained as all you would hear was a crackle. This was very inconvenient in an emergency unless you had a good mode of transport, as we found out one day with Pannie getting knocked down on the main road, as she did a figure eight on her bike. Everybody asked how she was. 'She's fine,' I stated. 'She's in the Argyll and Bute hospital.' Morag, who was in my class and from Furnace, nudged me and whispered, 'That's the Mental Hospital!' 'She's mental anyway,' I said for a laugh. I was supposed to say, 'The Mid Argyll'. I became too busy enjoying my new life and didn't have much illness apart from the occasional fever, and my lungs benefitted tremendously from the clean fresh air. Still, I always had my regular white pill medication to take daily and had to attend the hospital monthly for my usual X-rays but that was all, not one single attendance for accidents, believe it or not. The hospital was right next to the school and was easy to get to just in case there was an accident. I should have been there for a head injury, I guess, and because of the 'Out of body' experience I had, which I will elaborate on soon, but my love for life got in the way.

I would often wander off alone with my new little Cairn terrier dog, Corrie, another addition to the family, and spend hours just walking up long winding forestry roads, letting the dog roam free. I was at peace and ecstatically happy for the first time in my life.

One afternoon, on turning a bend on a forestry track, I was alarmed when I looked up and saw the most magnificent stag standing before me. The size of its enormous antlers took my breath away. It stood its ground in majestic form, staring back while Corrie ran up to it, barking her head off. I couldn't move a muscle and tried to call Corrie back through clenched teeth but she wasn't having any of it. The stag looked down at Corrie as if to 'tut' as she ran around snapping at its ankles. Undaunted, the stag slowly sauntered off without a care in the world.

On another walk I came across two dead adders, which are highly venomous. I don't know what I thought I would do with them but they had lovely skin and I could make something. I picked them up, threw them over my shoulder and hung them over the washing line when I got home until I decided what my next plan was. What a telling-off I got from everyone. 'Don't you know they might just be stunned?' adults asked me. I was informed that one of the wee girls in Port Ann had already been bitten on the ankle by the feared adders that freely slithered around us. I didn't do that again but I did cause a right stramash when I yelled there was an adder under the wooden lookout in the forest, which turned out to be a bicycle tyre. The adult men were armed with sticks, knives and all sorts to catch it, warning us to keep well back out of the way. As we had to make our own entertainment, we would join in to play football, where we were totally useless against the male species. A hard crack on the head by Peter put an end to that when I could hardly see or even hear properly one evening. I managed to make the short distance home, a couple of houses away and lay on my bed, not telling a soul. When I woke up in the morning I was still fully dressed. I had concussion again and kept it to myself, not wanting to cause a fuss. I didn't see 'two mummies' this time because I could hardly see at all and the strange vision cleared. We didn't play football very often. It was usually a game of Kick-The-Can or a climb onto the 'Lookout' for a chat. Unfortunately the lookout platform had had enough of our weight and collapsed in slow motion, thank God, because there were younger children playing underneath it at the time. They had managed to get out and away from the direction it was falling in.

The phone box became a source of amusement one day when Eileen helped me in my naughty cunning plan. We called all of the children who were out playing and decided we were going to see how many people we could cram inside the red telephone box for the *Guinness Book of Records*. No such thing was true but they all fell for it big time. I had been getting small jokes and tricks delivered from a mail-order distribution catalogue, and ordered stink bombs. They were in little glass tubes, which had to be stood on to be broken. The problem was in trying to break one in the phone box without giving the game away. We told our gang to squeeze into the phone box and I managed to break the glass vial, then Eileen and I held the door tight shut for as long as we could. It was a very naughty thing to do to our loved ones and friends but it was hilarious. I might as well own up and tell whom it may or may not concern that it was me who dropped the foul stink bomb in school, yep!

I am sitting here typing, in tears and howling with laughter as I think of the naughty things I did. Larry the Lamb, our dog, is trying to get on my knee because I'm happy and he wants to join in. I clapped my hands so loud while laughing that the guinea pig, Buttons, got a fright. He jumped high into the air and scampered into his house, causing the cage door to fall.

My mother always told me I would cause trouble in an empty house, but it's her I'm trying to write about. Taking a deep breath. She was sitting in front of the coal fire, minding her own business by reading the newspaper I brought in for her from down the street during my lunch break at school. I had one stink bomb left and it was burning a hole in my pocket, so to speak. I was also bored. I was boring! You cannot be bored if you're not boring, someone once told me. I needed to creatively invent something to do to keep me occupied. Unfortunately no one else was around, so my own deeply cherished wonderful mother was the intended target. I stood on the tiled hearth and messed around, poking the fire coals, hitting the poker on the grate to cover the breaking of the glass vial, but all I was doing was getting on her nerves and she told me to 'Beat it'. She wasn't paying me any attention and I felt wholly justified in my actions. Right! That's it, I thought, she's getting it! I stood on the fragile vial and cracked it before I scarpered faster than lightning. Sparks flew and so did she, I can still hear the echo from her voice as she boomed she was going to kill me, Oh God! No wonder I had sore lungs, I laughed them all out.

When I fell out of the tree over the fence at the bottom of the garden and landed flat on my back from a bit of a height, Eileen ran to get my mother shouting, 'Mrs Baxter, Esther fell out of the tree and she's hurt!' My mother looked over the fence to see me sprawled on my back and bellowed, 'If you don't get up out of there, I'm gonny pan your face in!' I quite liked my face as it was so up I got without delay and got back up the tree out of her way. My mother sure taught me faith, lol. At least I was overcoming my fear of heights, I just forgot to hold on tight. Tough love was better than no love. I loved her so much it was hard to annoy her but when I did, I would always get right back under her loving, caring and protective wing. Tough love nurtured me to wise up.

Back in Glasgow it was very easy to play at chap the door and run away, but not in Port Ann, due to the fact that most of the houses were in a circle, so all the neighbours had to do was look out of the window to see who was at the door. There could be no mischief, but once, when it was getting dark and most curtains and blinds were closed, we decided to play chap the door and run away anyway, so we sent Kat up to a neighbour's path. We had a bit of a time egging her on to do it and she finally accepted the challenge after some persuasion. She chapped the neighbour's door and we promised we were holding the gate open for her, so she believed, but when she went to run down the path and out of the gate we held it shut tight. She turned back quickly, not knowing what to do, and went back to the door as it was opening and stammered, 'My Daddy said can he get a loan of your bicycle pump?' We were hiding and rolling about with laughter. Kat had to be commended on her quick thinking but we didn't dare do it again, we didn't want to fall out with our neighbours, or get slapped.

At Halloween I met 'The Handsome One' of Port Ann while Eileen took me around the houses, guising. I didn't have a costume to wear, so improvising, I borrowed one of The Daddy's old boiler suits, stuck on a wig, dirted my face and attempted to present myself as an oily motor mechanic. When 'The Handsome One' answered the door I stood star-struck, just smiling from ear to ear and staring into his beautiful eyes. He was even better-looking than Donny Osmond. I don't even recall if he gave us anything as a treat and we certainly didn't trick him, he was too handsome for childish pranks. Eileen gave me a nudge back to earth and my airy head flew round the rest of the houses that evening like a faerie in drag. I was quick to learn that the Handsome One had many admirers and was well out of my league. At the age of thirteen years and two months I set eyes on my first crush, I was in love with life.

For some daft reason, Ailean next door, our neighbour at number fourteen, decided that after borrowing our chip pan with the fat content included, she would bang on her wall and we could bang back in reply. I thought it was a daft idea, but as always, I aimed to please. 'Ok,' I said, thinking she was off her head, 'You go first.' She did, bang, bang, bang. I replied, bang, bang, bang. She did it again and I replied. Again and again we banged our living-room walls. She looked at me very sheepishly the next morning as we gathered for the school bus and told me her daddy was absolutely furious at me banging on the wall. He had come in from work earlier than usual and heard the banging on the wall. Angry, he joined in by banging back and I thought it was Ailean and carried on using the wall as a drumming post, with pots and pans. What a carry-on. It's not as if we couldn't contact each other, all we had to do was open our bedroom windows to have a chat. So Mr Cunningham, wherever you are, it was not my daft idea, and your youngest daughter, Ailean, started it, though admittedly, I didn't need much encouragement to join in on the ridiculous wall-beating task. Drum roll . . . Just another daft story that has been passed down throughout the years with a little titter.

We would venture through adder pathways to get to the Blue Rocks, where we would sit by Loch Fyne and sometimes go for a swim or just dip our feet. A longer walk to the left took us to Otter Ferry, where I would often saunter on my own with Corrie. There really was nothing else to do but go for long walks, even in the rain, which I loved and still love to this day. People in Glasgow are always moaning and constantly complain about the weather . . . I genuinely love it. It may come as a shock to some people, but we are waterproof. There are worse things in life to complain about. I know I annoy some people by disagreeing with them but come on, raindrops? The truth is, friend, you annoy yourself and me into the bargain with your moaning. Those watery little droplets can produce the most beautiful rainbows. Get a hat, umbrella, hoodie, plastic bag, scarf or whatever, better still, get a life, get in love with life. Get your wellies or walking boots on and go for a hike in Argyll.

Working as a carer has left me quite unresponsive to petty complaints. I have held the hands and heads of the dying until they have passed on and left this Earth, singing hymns to them and telling them about The Lord Jesus. I have massaged people who lay prostrate and could not respond except for groaning sounds. I visit people who are totally disabled and have to be spoon-fed. I wash and cleanse the bottoms of both genders and all ages. I wipe snot from the faces of the disabled. I constantly shower naked people. I have been bitten, scratched, spat on, sat on, kicked, nipped, punched, slapped, had my hair pulled out by the roots, had a gun popped full on in my ear, all be it fake, but loud and painful to the ear-drum, grabbed by perverts, abused mentally, subjected to sexually explicit comments, called a liar and a thief. I've had my coat and uniform torn and been totally humiliated in public places while doing my job, by mental health sufferers and those with Dementia, Alzheimer's and Parkinson's. Would you like to swap places with somebody who can't get out? Reflect in silence. Your action causes a reaction and I'm not the person who likes to listen to the drips and dribbles of nonsense. The rain falls on the just and on the unjust, says The Lord. Anyway, anointed rant over. I needed to get away from the house and the rain was the very least of my horrendous problems. I often watch the 'rain fall' only to find it's spiritual and not the actual wet stuff.

I would go for long walks up forestry track roads on both sides of the A830, past a derelict cottage with a steel roof in the middle of nowhere and by the ruins of an old cottage at the other side of the road, opposite Otter Ferry.

The cold winter nights were very long and dark all too soon and the highlight of the week in Port Ann was the visit of Lipton's grocery van, which came on a Thursday night, as late as ten forty pm but by the time it got to Port Ann the van was practically empty unless you had a grocery order put in from the previous week. In Glasgow the sound of the chimes of an ice-cream van is nothing but a pest when they chime after nine o'clock at night, with the shops now open twenty-four hours a day, there is no excitement at their arrival. We don't have ice-cream vans where we live but when I heard one in Darnley while I was working as a carer, I asked, 'Is that an ice-cream van I hear? How common,' I stated. My client burst out laughing at my cheeky comment. I loved to make this young man laugh. I was no stranger to the ice-cream van when my children were growing up because they wanted to go to it every time they heard it. In Port Ann the weekly visit from Lipton's van was special because we had no shops. It was also exciting to see what was in the van and to meet and greet the driver.

The postman, Colin, would also be around from about three to four pm with the mail. Many years later we met up with him as a relative due to a newborn. Naturally, being a postman, he knew the names and addresses of many a family but I didn't remember him.

Our school friends from Inveraray didn't see daylight in the winter except at the weekends as it was dark when they left for school and dark by the time they got home again. We got on the Furnace bus to get to school. If we missed that school bus, then the Inveraray school bus could take us to school, as it always came about ten minutes after the Furnace school bus. If not, there was the local passenger transport which passed at nine but there were no buses every hour where we lived. The buses arrived at nine, twelve, three, and a later one at around six pm, going in to Lochgilphead.

We had got into the bad habit of thumbing a lift when we needed to get to Lochgilphead and home again to Port Ann but usually the locals would pick us up. We depended on them and were grateful for the lifts to and fro but I got a fright one day when I was trying to get back to Port Ann. A driver travelling in the opposite direction from me screeched his brakes hard and did a quick turn to my side of the road and demanded I 'Get in', I calmly said, 'No,' and didn't move. He drove off and I was given a lift by a neighbour, thanks to God.

The Daddy caused me great humiliation with his old banger cars. He got the bus to Glasgow with my mother one day and drove back with what I can only describe as a blue, hand-painted, clapped-out, rusty, oversized, antiquated sardine can, proudly announcing he paid twelve pounds for it at the motor auction. The banger broke down and who should stop to help but one of my schoolteachers, Mr Milne. I was beetroot-red, I wanted the ground to swallow me up. Have you ever seen the movie, *Uncle Buck*? Well, that affronted niece was me. That car backfired and had the town of Lochgilphead turning heads for all the wrong reasons. The *'Clampetts'* looked rich next to us. The Daddy stripped that car down in the driveway of our house and asked me if I wanted to help him and learn how to fix cars. I flatly refused and ran off. I felt bad later about saying 'No', as he was changing, but then, so was I. He was trying to communicate by sort of holding out an olive branch in the shape of a spanner but by then I couldn't reach out and take it. I had no interest in old cars and I still couldn't talk to him, we were truly alien to each other.

I couldn't forget the hurtful things he had said and done and he was still the same man I knew, I lived with him. I was broken by his actions and suffered physically by not eating and mentally by his rejection and temper. My confidence was null and void and I didn't know how to behave socially, just like him. It pains me to write this but the adults who knew me at that stage of my life will confirm this. I was painfully shy and felt worthless, even certain schoolteachers at Lochgilphead constantly told me I was nothing, but I never said I was anyone special. Having lung problems and needing air, I yawned a lot in the classroom. The verbal abuse I got for yawning from the history teacher was shocking. Seriously, I got hell for drawing in air. Done and dusted now. That was another thing, the number of times teachers banged their chalky duster on my desk in primary school and threw it at our heads was unforgivable. No wonder children developed asthma, tiny airways caked in chalk to accompany the soot, stour, fibreglass, freezing fog and liquid paraffin was not healthy.

I wished, years later, that I had taken up The Daddy's offer to learn car maintenance but I did learn to change my own wheels, oil, water, wipers and bulbs, plus jump-starting, towing with reversing, assisting to replace a prop-shaft on a Volvo (several times), mending my own exhaust, and so much more. I also passed my driving test the first time and have never had one penalty point or endorsement on my licence in my lifetime of driving. A lot of that is down to The Daddy, as I observed him while he was driving, so he did some good, in a strange way. His mental health, however, continued to suffer and became exposed when his mother died. She was the only grandparent

I knew, the others had passed away before I was born, or when I was tiny, I don't know. I have never seen a photograph of my maternal grandparents, because they were burned in a fit of fury.

When our parents went to Glasgow at the weekends it was down to me to look after the siblings. Needless to say, we would get up to all sorts of deeds, good and bad. On one of those such Saturdays, I decided I would make tablet, but we had no vanilla essence. Having no shops nearby, I couldn't get it and we didn't dare ask a neighbour if we could borrow. I cannot remember if I had followed a recipe or not but I loved baking and set about making toffee instead. The toffee didn't take too long and it worked out fantastic with the right consistency, and I got it cut into large squares before it set and hardened. The squares didn't assist in the breaking up of the toffee when it set, so out came the hammer to smash it into all shapes and sizes. Pannie recently informed me she stole huge chunks to give away, around our friends. I laughed and told her I hadn't noticed. That was what the toffee was made for, eating! I truly loved to feed other people and, if they enjoyed it as Pannie said, then it makes me happy. The toffee was delicious and was gone by the time our parents got back. I must have followed a recipe because I remember thinking I would make it again one day.

Home alone on another weekend, it must have been raining as we all stayed indoors and did indoor activities like putting the fire poker through one of The Daddy's old Bakelite 78 rpm records to make fruit bowls, at least that's what we decided to call them. We had great fun watching the records melt into fruit bowl shapes over the coal fire. As we all had shots each to see who could make the best fruit bowls, we must have melted a good few of his old 78 rpm records. Then of course we had to burn the evidence on the basis we had no fruit for the invented bowls, or something like that. We moved on to crisp packets and held them over the burning coals until they became tiny as they shrivelled up. We were fascinated as we tried it with everything and anything, making things 'crispy', as our brother

Addie called it. When our parents came home and asked what we were up to, Addie eagerly piped up, 'We were making Crispies.' Uh oh! I could feel a slap heading his way. 'Rice Krispie cakes,' I jumped in with, throwing myself on top of him before he let the cat out of the bag. We did a lot of things we weren't supposed to do but I can confirm none of us put a cat or any other animal in any bag. Addie, definitely yes, a cat, not so.

Lochgilphead High School also had the primary school attached, which meant we all went on the same school bus. Addie, the youngest, and Kat went to the primary. One of my friends' mother was the teacher of Addie and she told me her mother would say, 'Oh no, here comes A damn Baxter.' It made me laugh (sorry, Irene, I had to use it, lol). The teachers were fantastic and we didn't have to address the males as Sir all the time. In Govan High it was 'Sir' at all times and they wore their long black swishing gowns with bell sleeves. There was a tremendous air and grace, yet authority, when the black cloaks floated by us, we would automatically get into the side of the corridor to let them go on and had to be extremely respectful. It wasn't so much the person who commanded the authority, it was the black gown, which floated as the air swept the garment up. Lochgilphead High School was much more informal and relaxed and we could even wear trousers or a kilt if we so desired due to the cold weather and longer distances to and from school. I was amazed, our health and welfare was respected, and it made a huge difference to my life, as I was often feverish. There were no hard and fast uniform rules as our wellbeing and welfare came first.

I became the editor of the school magazine named 'GAB' (Girls and Boys), which was great fun, as I had to find news, interview and invent a crossword. It was heavily handwritten and produced through sheets of carbon paper, which was tough, and sold for the grand sum of 2p.

Mr White, a teacher at Lochgilphead, took me aside one day.

'Esther,' he said, 'I have to tell you this, you haven't a snowball's chance in hell of passing your maths exam.' I thanked him very much for realising I was struggling and for telling me the truth I already knew. I didn't do numbers. Arithmetic was one of the exams I passed later on, at night school, where I went with some friends just for something to do in the winter. I only got a 2 in the result but it was better than the D, E or F I received when I was at Lochgilphead High School.

Maths was a nightmare for me. Mr Logie caught me staring out of the window and asked me what I was looking at. 'I'm thinking,' I told him with my chin resting in my hand. 'Thinking,' he said, walking up and down the front of the class with his hands tucked into the back of his trousers. 'Yes, thinking's very good for you, keep it up,' he replied, so I did and kept looking out of the window. I was thinking I hated maths with a passion and I so desperately wanted to run away from his class.

I occasionally asked Mr Logie if I could leave the class to go and practise cross-country running and he kindly agreed. What was the point of keeping me in the class to carve on my desk with a compass? I could understand the basics of square roots but when alphabet and pies (pi) were added to numbers I just saw a plate of alphabet and number spaghetti. I really believed I was number-dyslexic and couldn't comprehend it. Nor did I want to, because I didn't have a mathematical brain. Despite this, I have a great memory for recalling phone numbers, area codes, registration plates, tax, national insurance, bank details, you name it, I can fire numbers off so easily without having to search for them, except on the very rare occasion when I am stressed and suddenly lose all memory just when it comes to keying in my four-digit PIN number at the front of a busy queue, we've all been there, I think.

Theresa, a friend I met later on through church, explained to me that maths was where everything is in order and fits perfectly into place. 'Like keeping your shoes all neatly in their own boxes so you know where they are,' she said. She switched a light on in my head and I sort of got it but the truth was, I still didn't like it and felt it was too late to start trying, but it made good sense. I am pleased to tell you I am a little further on and can calculate my own tax returns. I don't like it and it drives me crazy, but at least I can do it.

My very favourite subjects in school were English and Art. I loathed cooking, simply because I hated food. I got better as I was growing up because I had mouths to feed and that alone set me on the right track most of the time. People still saw through me, though. I'd pressure people to eat up, and provide more than was normal, because I thoroughly enjoyed feeding others. Not all was lost. I loved baking because I had a sweet tooth but I would always tell people I had already eaten earlier and couldn't possibly eat another thing.

Dressmaking was great but I made a mess of sewing the hem on another student's skirt project, which put me off. It was a skill that came in useful later on in theatre, though, because I was creative. I also gave Miss Gilchrist a tough time when I first started her class. Miss Gilchrist took both cookery and sewing classes, where I discovered a huge magnet and asked Morag what it was for. 'For picking up the pins that fall on the floor,' she enlightened me. I constantly dropped the pins on the floor so I could pick them up with the magnet for my own amusement, fascinated by the way the pins dangled from each other at the tips. Miss Gilchrist said I was going to be trouble, so I was. My sense of humour occasionally got me into trouble, like the time she called out, 'If anyone wants felt [for sewing] come into the cupboard.' My untamed sense of humour running riot again, because I thought it was funny. I didn't let her forget it until I met her at the post office on the corner of Locgilphead's town one day when there was no school on and we stood chatting for ages. I realised with that one-to-one conversation that she was a genuine lovely little lady and she didn't once mention my odd scatty behaviour. From that moment on I behaved in her class and did really well. Thanks to her, I am still a whizz kid on the sewing machine, making theatrical costumes and altering clothes for disabled people by adding invisible zips into seams so they can get their arms through without breaking them. There were no opportunities that I knew of for drama classes as such. There was a mention of them in English class but they didn't materialise in school, therefore I didn't go and, if there was a drama club around, I would sure love to have gone. I had zero confidence but was desperate to act, perhaps be someone else instead of me.

Despite my hilarity, I had serious self-worth issues and was afraid to eat in front of anyone in the dinner hall because of the behaviour at our dinner table, and I was actually afraid of some foods. I didn't have to see the food, smells began to turn my stomach. Occasionally I would go in to the dining hall for chips but something happened to the fryer and the chips stopped being served throughout my whole journey at school. There was nothing to entice me back to the dinner hall and I never ate there again. I chose to go down the street as we called it, at lunch-time, where I would buy mints instead of food. I would rush out of the house in the morning with no breakfast and have no lunch. The dinner at tea-time wasn't enough to sustain me and I finally collapsed in the street on one of my lunch breaks while visiting one of The Daddy's friends, who worked as a driver with a bakery. I could hear Janette faintly calling my name as I lay flat out in the rain, which bounced lightly off my face. I was too weak and roasting hot and welcomed the cold wet droplets, which were cooling me down. After some time of resting on the ground I managed to get up, but I was completely and utterly exhausted.

Janette got a fright and told me she was shouting my name over and over. She got me back to school and left me in the medical room, where I slept all afternoon. In a panic she came back at four o'clock and got me onto the school bus home. Another time, I was just about to hit the floor again when we were standing in the choir on the school stage. I distinctly remember wishing we didn't have to sing that same song over and over again, it was making me feel awful. I tried for the longest time to stay on my feet, but I saw deep red as though I was looking at my own blood on the inside of me and felt my head swimming around and again, I was very hot. Miss Menzies spotted me swaying and asked if I was all right. I said 'No' just before I collapsed. Morag was asked to help me from the stage but I stumbled and nearly fell down the stairs on the way out. I only remember being assisted to a bench to sit down before I fell down. Still not a soul noticed I wasn't eating properly, except Annie Rexia who had come from Glasgow to Lochgilphead.

From that first day when 'Annie' visited at aged eight, I was on a very slow starvation journey. I was reasonably happy, in fact I was happier than I had ever been, I was in love with life at Lochgilphead High School, but emotionally I was in a fight, with food. Then there was all the social rubbish of being non-confident and scared of how I acted, spoke and looked, which took its tight grip on me. I had also developed the perfectionist trait which stayed for many years, one of Annie's uninvited friends obviously. I had to do everything perfectly, I would straighten, smooth, tweak and wipe. If someone touched the page of a book I was reading, I had to wipe away their unseen finger prints, meaning it was all in my head. I was in my late thirties when I lost it one day when putting a can back onto the shelf of my kitchen cupboard. I was convinced I hadn't put it back properly and turned and went back to fix it, making sure it sat on top of the other can properly and faced the front to match the other cupboard contents, it looked fine as I closed the cupboard door and walked away, uneasy, still not satisfied, I turned, went back again and 'tweaked' it. The fourth time I turned and went back to look at the position of the can, I stood still with my arm outstretched to touch it again. I had had enough of this torture and screamed at myself out loud to, 'Leave it!' and walked away defiantly. From that moment on I would deliberately mess things up and walk away. I was sick to the back teeth of being told (in my head) what to do and being told I was no good. The years of my life I have wasted on listening to the devil's lies were gone. I had to stop this crazy perfectionist trait and I finally broke it by disobeying myself and disobeying the one who was manipulating me. I hated being controlled, especially by a force of dim-witted evil. In my mind I thoroughly believed I had to be perfect to be loved but when I also believed God wanted me to be perfect too, it became harder to break habits. Jesus says in the sermon on the mount, 'Be you perfect even as I am perfect,' (Matthew 5, verse 48). By my very nature I was a perfectionist (apparently), being born in August, cataloguing me in the cosmic diary as a Virgo, a perfectionist. The self-control I had found earlier was warped, I had been deceived. Nobody was perfect, yet we were to be perfect. I didn't understand. It took years of prayer, love and hearing God's Word that untangled the web of lies I was cocooned in. Be ye 'Complete' was the real message. I was complete through Jesus but not yet perfect. From then on I became much more abstract in my thinking which has helped immensely, thinking and acting outside my brain box. I was learning to be me, through Him.

At primary school we were taught to stay within the lines when learning to write and in colouring in, which I could do perfectly. Perfection was a prison and hung around with Annie and they were not my friends, that is not the kind of perfection God was talking about. I'm still not perfect but I am real and true to myself and God. I decided to let go and let God. I taught myself to go over the lines if I wanted to, to become abstract, to reach out, to mess up, to go beyond my vision, to think outside the box, to openly disagree with people when I had my own opinion, to speak up for myself and start fighting (I think I may have gone too far the other way but so what?). It's my life, I thought, not anyone else's.

On that note I share with you an incident I watched while

sitting in my car at my local shopping centre, the Avenue at Newton Mearns. It was a gloriously hot summer's day and I had the car windows down, when I watched an old frail couple cross from the car park to go towards the centre.

'Button up your jacket,' the old lady scolded her husband as she grabbed him by the sleeve. He pulled away from her, stripped off his jacket in defiance and swung it over and round about his head before throwing it to the ground, singing at the top of his voice, 'It's my life, It's my life and I'll do what I want.' He then started dancing on the small lined pedestrian crossing, doing his own jitterbugger thing. His wife was furious at him for his display but he made me laugh until my belly ached. I didn't know them and they both might even have passed away by now, as I reckon they were in their late eighties or early nineties. He was a star and I have never forgotten his antics. He did exactly what he wanted to do without a care in the world because it was his life, even in defiance of his bossy little wife, God bless them both.

The minibus from Lochgair Church would pick us up on Sunday morning and even if no-one else was going, I always went. I remember there was no organ to accompany us in our hymns, I can't remember if there was no organist or if the organ wasn't working. On that tuneless note, I cannot recall one sermon or word from all the years of attending church at Lochgair. It was very nice and I wanted to go on my own accord but there was nothing there, I know, I looked and didn't find. I only kept it going as par for the course and learned a lot of the hymns that I still remember today, but I learned nothing else. My soul (mind, will and emotions) was hungry and not fed. Having felt that, I was the happiest I had ever been in my young life and didn't spend too much time seeking God because of the Scripture Union incident. The Daddy was still the same Daddy with his negative comments, and the yearning for God was still there as I questioned life, but I sort of reasoned that if God wanted me, He knew where I was. God was the invisible friend who wouldn't speak to me, not yet anyway. We had no Scripture Union at Lochgilphead High School and the visiting school minister was a grouch. I wasn't being judgemental, I saw him as a person who I didn't think was a Christian and if he was a Christian, then I certainly didn't want to be one. I was happy working, learning and growing and still had a huge sincere smile when I went on my long walks alone with my little dog, Corrie.

When looking through my old single and long-playing vinyl records one day, I smiled at the fact I have scribbled EB loves AS on them. God, even then, had me put my husband's initials on them. I met my first boyfriend at Lochgilphead High School but I was terrified when Pannie found out. She ran straight to The Daddy and told him I had a boyfriend. Sure enough the interrogation started and I had a hard time of it. Pannie, though, got away with murder. She was the unofficial news reporter of the family, telling all. Yet she herself, the little madam, came home sporting a huge lovebite on her neck and when asked what it was, she told her sweet Daddy she fell down the stairs, and what's worse, he actually believed her.

The boyfriend and I met during school intervals and stood in a corner of the school, snogging. When the Technical Teacher, whom the girls didn't get, caught us smooching one day. I got sent to the PE Teacher for punishment. The boyfriend got the belt but the Technical Teacher, being a gentleman, refused to punish me and sent me instead to the PE Teacher, who dutifully and playfully kicked me up the backside and told me to go away.

On my one and only visit to the boyfriend's home in Achnamara, I met his family. He took me to his bedroom along with his friend, who stayed in Achnamara, but before my boyfriend could shout, 'No!', I had jumped hard on his bed for a seat and heard the most awful crash. He looked at me in shock before getting down on his knees to peek under his bed at the smashed glass display cabinet where he placed his proud collection of all sizes of eggs. Oops, what was it with me and birds' eggs? I was mortified, it had taken him years to build up his display. Needless to say, he didn't ask me back to his house, due to the lack of transport, I gather, not the fact I scrambled his birds' eggs.

All was well as a teenager, until the new intake of first years came in on the scene and my boyfriend spotted the Julie one. Julie's brother, Thomas, was in my class at school and was a right laugh, he'd always distract me. You would be wrong for thinking it was the other way round but no, he distracted me. He would whisper, 'Esther, Esther,' until I turned round to see what he wanted and have me in fits of giggles by doing or showing me something silly. It got to my ears that the boyfriend had dumped me and was now 'wowing' Julie. I was shattered. Julie and I had our own words and falling-out spats, but the first time I saw her I thought she was gorgeous and I could clearly see why my first boyfriend had eyes for her. Over a week later the boyfriend changed his mind and decided I was the one after all, but he had killed me inside by his cheating and I didn't heal from the rejection. I later learned that it was Julie who told him to 'Do one!' He also started getting too familiar and developed wandering hands, which I wasn't ready for. I was getting really annoyed with him trying it on and at one point I grabbed his roaming hand and severely twisted his previously broken wrist. I didn't mean to hurt him but his face was a picture of torment. Well, I had warned him one time too many and he wasn't listening. I hadn't just hurt his wrist, his feelings took a pummelling too.

Achnamaric Romeo decided he would come along to Port Ann one Saturday so we could be together for the day to discuss our relationship. I had no idea what was to be discussed but I felt terribly uneasy as the hours went by. He still hadn't been to my house and I wasn't inviting him in to meet the parents, no way, so we had nowhere to go. Throughout the Friday night I was deeply troubled in my soul but eventually fell asleep. When I woke up during the night, God told me to '**End the friendship**

**quickly**'. That's what God told me to do, with no explanation. I wasn't to see or be with my boyfriend any more. He was travelling all the way from Achnamara to Port Ann to be told it was over and I couldn't phone him to tell him not to come, so it was with a heavy heart that I had to wait until he arrived. When he did arrive, I met him at the mouth of Port Ann and we sat on the tiny bridge with the stream running under it, on the main road. Before he got his chance to enlighten me or make any decisions about the day, I told him I couldn't see him any more. Gutted, I was breaking my heart and I could hardly talk for sobbing. 'Why?' he kept asking me. 'Is there someone else?' 'No, there isn't,' I assured him, and I didn't know why, so I couldn't explain why. I knew what I was to do but I wasn't told why. I was obeying God but I couldn't tell the boyfriend that. He wouldn't understand. I didn't understand 'why' either but the God who saved my mother from being killed by a truck was asking me to do something very simple. I had to obey God's will, even when it made me cry, I was going to obey Him, and did.

The boyfriend put his arm around me as we cried together and he pleaded with me not to break us up, but I had to stay strong and stick to The Heavenly Father's will. I watched through blurry eyes as the boyfriend walked back up the road, crying, and I was crying too because I had just hurt him. When I got back to my bedroom, I bawled buckets of tears but I also felt a huge sense of relief at having obeyed God, even although I had just told my first love it was over. It was a sore one and I was desperately heartbroken, alone and 'empty'.

Imagine how Abraham felt when he was told to take his little son Isaac to be sacrificed on the altar, he must have been broken inside. It has to be done. When God asks you to do something, it is for a very good reason and there's no point in questioning Him. Afterwards I noticed a total sense of freedom. I wasn't bound or held by any male influence. I belonged to God and Him alone. Perhaps that was the reason. I was so upset I couldn't go back to school for a week as I couldn't face seeing the boyfriend again. While I was still grieving, my little dog Corrie was knocked down and killed. I didn't even have her to cuddle. I dug a hole in the garden and buried her. Grief overwhelmed me. I thanked God for her little life and told Him how much I loved her. She went with me on every long walk, my companion for when I was thinking and looking for God. How much more alone could I get? I was completely shattered and emptied from the inside, out, that's the only description I have to give. When I was pulled into the office at school for being off, I told them it was because my dog died, but it wasn't just the death of the dog which had sent me into lock-down. I needed time out, it was the perfect time to be silent before God because He had to separate me from all distractions. I needed to be alone, I needed God. I needed guidance in areas where there was no counselling. I needed a heart to heart and there was nobody else there. I eventually learned that counselling came from the silent times with God, He was and is the real Mighty Counsellor. He knew where I was all the time. He stripped me back to the bare essentials of my heart and there was nothing else in there that I wanted, needed or desired. He broke me and emptied me out as though I was a clay jar and commanded my full attention.

It was shortly after that, I don't remember how, but Julie and I became the best of friends and hung about together in Ardrishaig. We were always howling with laughter and I knew from the very beginning I really liked her. She was nuts, in a pleasant and proper young madam sort of way. She had the great knack of pulling faces and coming away with the most ridiculous obscure statements that had me in fits of laughter. If she didn't like a boy she told him so straight to his face, leaving no stone unturned in the assassination of his character, in the nicest possible way, of course. Her tongue was as sharp as a knife and I used to fall about laughing at her honesty. See, I knew I liked her and the rapport we had was great.

We never went off anywhere drinking and smoking or anything like that. We couldn't, everybody knew everybody and their great-granny. Gossip flew into history, even before it was revealed. Not that it mattered, because if we did get into mischief (we didn't!), it was none of anyone's business. We were young and innocent and enjoyed chatting, but most of all, laughing, and boy oh boy, how we laughed.

We hung about and chatted with locals and any newcomers. Newcomers were easy to spot, they were gullible and nice. One of the locals who was a bit older, offered to give us a fun ride on his motorbike. Julie went first and came back in no more than five minutes, just a wee spin up the road and back, as there was no spare helmet. When it was my turn on the back of the bike, he yelled, 'There's the police!' He revved up and flew into a tiny opening which was a labyrinth of hedges, thorns, brambles and stinging jaggy nettles that tore my legs to shreds as I was wearing denim shorts. Julie was in kinks laughing but at the same time she was going to throttle the guy for zooming off with me, so kind. Julie was a brilliant friend and another great person who made me smile and laugh for a little while longer, bless her. She was 'The One.' She made me laugh more than the boyfriend, God took her from my boyfriend and gave her to me, so bizarre you couldn't make it up.

Just as before, while I was still attending Lochgilphead Secondary School, I was taken away again by The Lord for the second time regarding this event:

**I was sound asleep again and found myself standing at, or on the same stage I had been on before, with God behind me. I was in my bed sleeping, standing before God and looking at myself being interviewed, all at the same time. I was being interviewed by the man who had his back to me and I couldn't see his face, I still don't know who he is. I could see myself full on and knew it was myself I was looking at. The audience was to my**

**right, further away than God. I knew I was being inter-
viewed and I wondered later if it was because I was an
actress. God told me He would be with me. I wasn't as
brash with God this time and I didn't flatly refuse to do
it. This time I said, 'God, I can't do it, please send
somebody else.' Back to bed He put me, where I was
remained fast asleep.**

I had no confidence whatsoever, I was frightened. I couldn't
even begin to imagine myself taking on this task. Being an actress
was okay, you pretended to be someone else, I thought, but not
being interviewed in front of an audience. I had come on a bit
further from saying, 'No way, God', though, and I still hadn't
imagined I would be an actress, I wasn't leaving my mother.

My mother started work in the Lochgair Hotel as a kitchen
assistant and I followed shortly after to work on the dishwasher
machine. On a Saturday I helped out in the kitchen and have
never forgotten being handed a whole lettuce by a neighbour
from Port Ann, who also worked in the kitchen. She was always
very critical and seemed to be carrying a whole plate of chips
on her shoulders, normally we'd just say she has a chip on her
shoulder, no, this woman had a plateful on hers. When my
mother wasn't on my shift, the neighbour would say my hair
was awful, she'd criticise my nails and just regularly nag, nag,
nag, depending on her mood swings. I've always said my neighbours were lovely but sometimes their invisible halos would slip
or fall off. I had no doubt people spoke about me behind my
back. I heard them, I was poor, not deaf. Anyway, she handed
me this lettuce and told me to go and wash it. I did as I was
asked and came back with it. Bear in mind this was my first
job. 'What's this?' she shouted. 'The lettuce,' I innocently told
her. 'You asked me to wash it and I did.' 'Am I supposed to
plop it whole on the customer's plate?' she scolded. 'Take the
leaves off and wash them individually,' she demanded, refusing
to take it back from me.

Well, blow me down, I thought. How was I to know I was to strip it down and wash each leaf separately, she never said so. She was much older than me and should had shown me what to do, I thought. It's called training and I was her (very) underage teenage apprentice. I know I did stupid things through ignorance but that's what adults are to do, train us, I thought. I'm not thick, I can do it, I can peel the leaves from a lettuce and wash them. I knew teenagers were hard work but adults don't help themselves either sometimes. It would have been so easy to explain the task. All of these amusing thoughts ran through my head at the stainless steel sink as I lifted each leaf and shook it like a doll's outfit. Take lettuce to sink. Peel leaves off and thoroughly rinse under cold water. Shake excess water off and place gently into the colander. Transfer to bowl. Take it back to Mrs Greetin' Face.

I smiled nicely as I gave her it back but that smile was not a mirror image of my thoughts, I have to confess. It's not hard, adults, to bless, train and nurture teenagers and little ones. You will find that in later years they will give you the glory for that assistance and remember you with much love and affection. I remember how much I craved guidance, love and a kind word, it really went a long way, and that's why I've written so much about my teachers, it was their job to help me grow. My adult life would be a reflection of their ministry and vocation. To be fair, Lochgilphead School Teachers had the difficult job of undoing all of the damage that had been done in my earlier years and I'm pleased to state that they did well. I wasn't the best student but they fine-tuned me into becoming the best adult. Despite the continuous chants of 'Glamour girl, here comes the Actress, look at her, she's nothing but an Actress!' prophesying unknowingly, into my life.

Where are we? Right, back to the Lochgair Hotel, three miles from Port Ann on the A83.

In the summertime we would have university students working at the hotel and have them over at our house for a wee drink and music, it was great fun. The students who worked in the bar, kitchen and reception were much older than me, and richer, kind and friendly. I loved getting to hear about their lives, where they came from and what they were studying. I was very interested and fascinated by their visions and brains. They came across as brilliant academically and way out of my league. I loved their energy and passion for life. They were studying hard, working and having a ball at the same time. They were completely free to live the lives they wanted to and I felt, even then, I could never leave my family to seek my own will, I knew I could never be like the students. I couldn't just fly off and do what I wanted to do. I admired their lives and freedom but, while I thought it was fantastic, it was their amazing journey, not mine, and that's why I loved to hear about their lives and adventures.

One of the male students was really taken with Port Ann, he thought it was a terrific place to live and enquired as to what I do there in my spare time. I informed him I loved to go for long walks alone, pick hazelnuts and go to the Blue Rocks amongst other things.

'I'd really love to go there,' he said. 'Would you mind if I walked with you one Sunday afternoon, a stroll along the beach?'

'Yes,' The Daddy piped up before I could draw breath to answer. I was livid because he answered for me and because he said yes, I would. I didn't want to go for a walk with this guy. He was lovely, he really was, but he wasn't stepping out anywhere with me.

'Eh, no,' I said bluntly, bowing my head, and gave no reason.

'Go out with the boy,' The Daddy coaxed, giving me his full permission. I looked at him with steely eyes. 'I said no!'

'Oh, why not?' the Cheery guy laughed. 'Just a nice walk down the beach, just a walk, that's all.' The Daddy was sitting there telling him I would go to the beach with him while I'm drawing him spears instead of daggers. I was so embarrassed by being put on the spot.

'I don't want to go a walk with anyone, I like being on my own, so I'm not going, get it?'

The Daddy was stunned and a bit embarrassed as I shot him down in front of his new-found friends.

'Well, that's all right,' the student said. 'There's no harm in asking.'

'So don't ask again,' I told them both. 'It's my life,' I pointed out, 'and I'll do what I want.'

I was working now and The Daddy had lost the little girl he seemed not to want. I often wondered if he was angry with me because he had lost his first-born child, Adam. Did he ever get counselling, did he want to show him how to fix cars? I felt sad for him. My parents must have been heartbroken when they lost their first baby. Again, life never pans out the way we imagine, that's for sure.

After I worked at Lochgair Hotel for a couple of years, I got the sack for not turning up to work and going to the pictures instead. At the same time I had knocked back the owner's son, who wanted to take me out again to the pictures. I was always positive the sacking was due to the fact I declined the son's offer of the second date. We had been to the picture house the week before but I had promised a friend I would go with her. I was disappointed to lose my job, especially because I had real money for the first time in my life.

A girl in my sister Pannie's class had parents who owned the Royal Hotel in Ardrishaig and I was given a job there to work at functions at the weekend. It was great to be part of the marriage receptions and enjoy the celebrations of the couples who were starting their married lives together and meet their families and friends. Many were local but they came from all over the Highlands and Islands North of Scotland and across the water, from Ireland. Oh how the Irish party, like no other nation, except for Scotland, of course.

Many came from abroad and it was amazing when I was allowed by the owners and the wedding party to be allowed to stay and join in with the celebrations. That's what I call being 'happy at your work'. It doesn't seem like work when you're enjoying yourself. The kitchen area was a great place to relax and have dinner and tea before work started.

Pannie's friend, Fiona, and her parents were smashing too. It also left me amazed when I saw how the parents of others treated their youngsters. I had never had a celebration birthday party, but then, I'd never had more than one cuddle. When other parents were kind to me I was overawed, and I really saw the love in other family homes, which only highlighted how poor we were, not just financially. There are other ways to be poor, such as poor in Spirit. I also saw another side of some friends who had lovely parents, but they spoke to them with audacity and cheek. For all we were poor, I never once took it out on my parents. I was embarrassed loads of times, sorry even, but never resentful. I would go over to my neighbours in Port Ann one night a week to give magazines and to stare at their coloured television. We still had a black and white television and I couldn't get away with the amazing colour of the programmes. I would sit and stare at the TV. Then, there was the peace. To observe a family who respected each other was phenomenal and that's when I realised our family unit was very far from normal.

I also started working at the Argyll Arms Hotel in Ardrishaig, which took up most of my time after school and at the weekends. This job was actually more than work, particularly as an older member of staff would just stand with her arms folded, telling me what to do. She did an awful lot of talking without actually saying anything useful, and not a lot of physical movement either. Stupid and fearful me would do as I was told, 'Stupid is as stupid does'.

I actually remember feeling like Cinderella one morning as I was cleaning out the cinders of the fireplace with her leaning right over my back to make sure I was doing it properly. I think the bar may have been a bit unstable as she was always holding it up while gossiping about someone or other. I just got on with my jobs and did what I was told while she supervised, a lot. The only time she uncrossed her arms was to point at what I was to do next, which was somewhere amongst this little lot:

Get up very early in the morning while others sleep,
Straight down to the lounge and gut out the coal fire/hearth,
Empty cinders from the coal fire outside back door, incase still hot,
Pack inside of fire with newspapers, kindling, firelighters and coal,
    light it,
Polish around fireplace, bring in logs and coal for side, refill
    buckets,
Wipe down all of back seating areas,
Put last night's used glasses behind, into the bar sink,
Clean and polish tables, turn upside down and place on long
    cleaned seats,
Brush down chairs and place on top of tables,
Vacuum all of the lounge carpet,
Clean the glass doors from fingerprints of grease,
Take all (very heavy) tables and chairs back down,
Set out cutlery, placemats, glasses, menus, condiments, and fold
    napkins,
Go to bar next door and sweep the floor,
Wash and polish the beer stains from the top of the bar,
Mop the floor,
Clean the bar door glass,
Upper hall, spray floor and swish with the buffing machine,
Clean the stairs,
Vacuum the rest of the hall carpet,
Clean both sides of the inside door,
Sweep/mop between the doors,
Clean both sides of the outside door,
Clean both male and female toilets,
Clean all mirrors and pictures.

Then get a cup of tea and something to eat, as by the time I'd finished that lot, the breakfast cook was up, another 'nippy sweetie'. She always got out of the wrong side of the bed and burned my ears with complaints as she sided with my mentor, who supervised my work. For all the work I did, I would only have a slice of toast with bacon and a cup of tea. There wasn't time to sit and have a full-on breakfast and I felt uneasy, I felt I would have been the one taking liberties. When I had been fed and watered I was then off to the back of the kitchen to prepare all of the salads into old ice-cream containers and other square plastic tubs and lay them freshly done on the cold stainless steel table. Untrained, with the use of the large sharp spinning mechanical slicer with no protective guard, I would carry on working by:

Shredding the iceberg lettuce thinly with slicer for one tub,
Slice the tomatoes by hand for another,
Slice onions thinly using the machine,
Fill a tub with small pickled onions, another with olives,
Slice boiled eggs when cooled with the little hand slicer as
    required,
Make up egg mayonnaise,
'Fan'-cut the gherkins,
Slice all of the cucumber very thinly using the large whirring
    machine,
Grate a tub of cheese,
Butter bread and rolls,
Make little round butters using two wooden carved slats (for the
    soup and rolls),
Polish plates for above salads,
And spoons for service,
Cut up various fruits for fruit salad to accompany the ice-cream,
Whip up double cream,
Clean up, wash up, take customer orders, take staff orders, run,
    run, run, and smile.

'Did she tell you to do that?' The 'folded arms' one would ask, referring to the Proprietor. Then, secretly, the Proprietor would ask me what the 'folded-arms' one said about her and she would be mad at her when I told her. It was awful being caught between two older female adults who heckled me for information. They sat and drank together, they could just have asked each other. That's why I, Cinders, just bowed my head and got on with it. Yet I will say that when the two of them were together they probably spoke about me. I also will say, if I had to choose a winner between the two ladies, the Proprietor wins hands up. She let me stay in the hotel, gave me a hot toddy with brandy when I had a nasty cold and fever and shared her cream eggs with me. All Mrs 'Folded-arms' gave me was cheek and a headache.

I have never shared with anyone about how hard and long I worked at the Argyll Arms Hotel but I have always known full well I would somehow write it all down one day, remembering exactly as I have just done, long before I knew I was going to write a book, I ran the events over and over in my quiet head. I worked upstairs too when there was a function on, making up sandwiches, vol au vents and nibbles, collecting and washing glasses and cleaning up after the allocated function.

Once a week, the Handsome One would take us to the community hall at Minard for a game of badminton. There wasn't much else to do and if he wasn't a team player, a good sport, then my life would have been even poorer. That's what I mean when I say money couldn't have helped our broken family, the Handsome One made my life so much richer in other ways.

Mandy (whose dad was the projectionist at the pictures) came from Furnace and was originally in the year above me at school. Through illness, appendicitis, from what I remember being told, Mandy was put into my year to complete her studies. From the moment we got together until we left school she was a pure 'scream' (her words). We laughed uncontrollably behind our

books in Mr Proudfoot's geography class and he always threatened to split us up. We sincerely promised not to do it again
but we couldn't keep that promise. He would just shake his head
as if to say, 'What's the point?'

Dear Mr Proudfoot got us to remember the order in which
way 'Stalagmites' and 'Stalactites' went by reminding us 'Tights
come down', which had us laughing again. It did help me
remember and I've used it to describe the bloody ceiling, later
on. I had no idea life could be so rewarding and people so
beautiful. All I needed was to be shown real, pure love. All of
the laughter I'd missed out on as a child was now concentrated
in my young teenage years and I missed Lochgilphead School,
my neighbours and my friends dreadfully when I left. Seriously,
for as long as twenty years I dreamt I was still at school and in
Port Ann and was always in my school uniform. The primary
school years were the worst years of my young life and the
secondary, without a shadow of a doubt, were the best. There
were a few ignoramuses in the school who were bullies and I
got beaten up on my first visit to the youth club, leaving me
on the ground in despair, which meant I couldn't go back.
There are always people who will talk and snigger behind your
back but, in reality, they are the poor souls. Still, I have always
told people about Lochgilphead and made it plain I had been
to the best school in the world, not forgetting they were also
the best-looking.

I kept the next holiday for now as Mandy and her family
took me to Butlin's in Ayr for a week. This was my best holiday
ever during my schooldays.

We dressed up to the nines every evening and wandered to
discos, dances and competitions, where Mandy outshone
everyone. She was very pretty and her daddy would say proudly,
'Look, not a bit of make-up on her face!' Parents are so embar-
rassing, but right most of the time. It was a fantastic holiday
and all down to Mandy for inviting me. We left school and
eventually lost touch but I always vowed that if I had a boy I

would call him Christopher after her brother and if I had a girl I was going to name her Amanda after my very funny, sweet, talented and gorgeous friend, (Who is now a famous TV presenter and 'Acts' too).

Well, I had my boy and surely did call him Christopher, but when my lovely little girl was born I couldn't possibly name her Amanda, that's not who she was. I lay there and stared at her sleeping and knew Amanda wasn't her name and I couldn't make it suit her if I tried.

Here I go again, at the back of my mind always lies a joke. I only heard this recently but I had heard it years before and forgot it, about the guy who takes his girlfriend home to meet his parents and his dad is slightly deaf. The dad asks the young lady her name but he doesn't hear her answer. After asking the girl her name a few times, her boyfriend gets really annoyed, goes over to his dad and shouts slowly into his ear, 'It's a man, Da!' It never fails to make me laugh.

My Out of Body Experience (OBE) happened as I left school at 4 pm. I didn't speak about it for many years because it was not normal to leave your body, was it? When my body separated from my spirit as a child, it did not leave. I was in the spirit but 'rattling' inside my body, as I have explained earlier. As far as I was aware my heart was sound and well, it was my lungs that were problematic. It wasn't long before the OBE event that I suffered tremendous pain in my left lung in my Modern Studies class at School.

Our whole class were having a great laugh with the teacher, about something daft probably, I don't remember. I took in a huge gasp of air during the laughter and felt something like a hot sword pierce my left lung again. I stopped laughing as soon as the pain shot through me and lowered my face onto the top of the desk, unable to breath in or out, exactly the same pain as I had had when I was in primary school and I didn't tell my mother because she was being loved. Not a soul noticed I was in pain in all the camaraderie. I have never ever breathed in that deep again for fear of the same pain. By this time, I was in fourth year and soon due to leave at the summer holidays to head on to Oban High School. I didn't know what I wanted to do when I left school. I only knew my life wasn't my own, Anyway, to be seen to be doing something towards my career I filled in an application to join the Police.

As part of the process I had to go and have my eyes tested, which gave me the 20/20 result towards the requirements for entry, perfect eyesight. An officer came up to the school, where I had an interview and a short written test, which was fairly routine and I didn't think I did too badly, there were no difficult maths equations anyway. I didn't want to go to London, though, let alone anywhere in England, and I didn't really think any doctors' reports regarding my lungs would have done my imaginary career any favours. Never mind, my eyes were perfect. Not only were they perfect, I didn't need reading glasses until I was in my late forties, much to everyone's amazement. I imagined being in the Police and I believed I would have been good at the job but I knew it was just one silly pipe dream to run off and seek my own will. I certainly had no ambitions to be an actress. Again, I just thought I would be good at it, that was all. What I did know for sure was that my mother needed my help and I was never going to leave her. God had placed that desire deep within me and I readily accepted it.

Well, here's a gift for you. I can only try and describe the event in my limitations, but get this, you are in for a real treat when it's your turn.

**It was a gloriously warm sunny late afternoon, just after four pm, when I left school for the day and walked down the main street to make headway towards Ardrishaig for my evening shift at the Argyll Arms Hotel. I crossed the road at the post office, walked by the public toilets and proceeded to walk alongside the grass at the head of Loch Fyne. Every other person was now behind me**

as I walked away from the front of the small quaint town.

The school bus to Ardrishaig was always busy and I had plenty of time to get to the hotel before half five so I just slowly sauntered along, enjoying the heat of the sun.

As I lived in Port Ann I was not entitled or permitted to travel on the Ardrishaig school bus and didn't enquire. My schoolbag was quite heavy as I lifted it up to throw it over my shoulder and, when doing so, I commented to my inner self, 'I am really happy.' As soon as I thought those words I noticed the grass began to change and stretch towards me. It was already pristine and well kept but it started behaving differently. The grass was already as green as grass can be, obviously, to me anyway, but it got greener and greener, the green that it was became brighter and purer. Aware something was happening, I slowed down until I stood still and observed it. I began to see each blade as a piece of grass in its own right. Each and every single blade stretched up and was alive. The grass was living and stretched up as if to greet and acknowledge me, the grass knew I was there.

Now, I've just told you my eyesight was perfect, the optician tested my eyes and the police took the report of evidence away as part of my application form. The grass became a vivid green I can't describe, a green I had never witnessed before. This green I was fascinated with does not exist on earth. Not a green with life and breath and intelligence and knowing in it. The grass was interested in me as though it could see me, it knew I was there, it loved me and welcomed me, reaching straight up as though to embrace or touch me, reaching towards me as if to say, 'Hello, you.'

The grass morphed into a true state of reality that I had never recognised before and I couldn't stand on it this time, I had no desire to do so as it was way too precious. After I had looked at the indescribable green grass for a while in astonishment, I lifted my head up and looked out towards Ardrishaig to where I was heading but I didn't see a thing.

There was no land, no road, trees, hills, No Ardrishaig! Nothing. I just saw HEAVEN. Putting the word 'just' with 'Heaven' in the same sentence shouldn't work, but it does, in that Heaven is so profoundly beautiful compared to everywhere else. When I looked back down I saw the pure living greenest grass again. There was no dirt on or in the grass, it was alive, Heavenly grass, on Earth. I'm aware I keep going on about the grass but if you've not had the experience then you've not seen the grass for real! This grass was alive and had intelligence, it was intelligence. I lifted my eyes back up and looked out again towards Ardrishaig, but still, I saw only Heaven. This area of Heaven had no horizon because there is no beginning and no end, that was the first thing I noticed as I wondered where the ground met the sky. There would naturally (I imagined) have been a line of engagement between them both but the light that was on the ground was the same light all over, in fact, at this part I was seeing, I didn't see the ground. Yet Heaven is a real place, more real than Earth but I don't have the mentality or words to explain what I experienced and saw.

There was light, crystal-clear light, forever and ever, so everlasting I couldn't see to the end, also because there is no end. The light is the most amazing bright, white, shining, clear, transparent and eternal light, yet it didn't hurt my eyes. The light is much brighter, clearer and greater than the light on earth. I was able to look clearly forever and because forever has no time, it has no end.

I was aware, as I was looking straight ahead in the

surrounding light, that I was not to turn my head around to the right, where The Almighty one was, behind me. I knew if I turned around I would be staying in Heaven. This information was pure knowledge.

I was completely overwhelmed by LOVE, PEACE and JOY. In those three I was whole, I was healed, I was back home to where I came from and where I belonged. Now I was Happy! Totally and divinely, 'In love with life'.

When I looked back down to the beautiful green grass again, I was alarmed to see I was leaving Lochgilphead and leaving the Earth, even although it was literally straight into Heaven. My legs were on the earth and my head was in Heaven. My (flesh) legs started to give way and buckle underneath me as my inner Spirit feet went past the inside of my knees and my hands were up to my shoulders. I was overly tall and saw the ground from the height I now was.

I quickly looked over to the left side of Loch Fyne, which I could now see because I wanted to and followed the outline to Port Ann. Of course, I couldn't see Port Ann, it was too far away, but I was seeing Heaven and was part in it. As I tried to look to Port Ann, I thought how my parents would be absolutely devastated if I left them and I didn't need or want them to be traumatised.

I said to God, 'I can't leave them,' I also said, 'No, I'm a sinner, I'm not coming.'

At that I tightened my Spirit hands into fists and pushed them down back into my body as hard as I could and then bent my arms up as though putting my body back on, like a coat. I realised my legs were collapsing beneath me because my Spirit was exiting and was above my knees. When I pulled myself back into my body, I was staggering all over the place because my knees had already bent and I was on the way down to the ground,

**the pavement. Anyone watching would have thought I was drunk. I straightened myself up and continued to walk along the road, towards Ardrishaig.**

'OH MY GOD! Was I having a silent heart attack?' I didn't feel any pain. Was I dying? I was leaving the Earth. God would have let me stay (in Heaven). I couldn't stay. My mother and family needed me.

As I carried on walking, one of my schoolteachers stopped to give me a lift to Ardrishaig, immediately after I straightened up from my wobble. I didn't thumb a lift, he just stopped the car to give me a lift because he knew me well. I cannot even remember which teacher it was, either Mr Morrison or Mr Logie. I got into his car and couldn't speak. I was stunned. I always tell people I cannot remember what I had for my dinner the night before but, with each spiritual encounter, I can recall every single minute infinite detail as though it had just happened and because it is real and true. I have great clarity on spiritual experiences as earthly ones are dulled. We cannot hear music or see colours properly, everything is so muffled and glazed to our ears and eyes on our planet, Earth, even with perfect eyesight and hearing.

I kept staring at my teacher because I needed to talk to him but he was looking ahead at the road in front, in his own thoughts. What would I say anyway? 'Excuse me, sir? I think I was just dying there, y'know, before you picked me up.' I didn't know how to tell him something I had never experienced before. It's not every day you nearly fly off to Heaven. I looked out of his front windscreen too, then back at him, for ages, thinking, you have no idea where I have just been. I also wondered what he thought as I kept looking at him but words would not come out of my mouth. Where would I begin? Mention the grass? He would have probably thought I was smoking it.

I knew I was different, I knew it! The close exit from Earth had a profound effect on me.

God spoke to me (not vocally), telling me not to turn around. My physical senses altered too, my eyesight changed in that I was now bothered by Earth's artificial lights. Even years later and right up to this present day, driving in the dark is difficult as the beams from the bright lights hurt my eyes, yet Heaven's light is more powerful, brighter, but bearable, your eyes are opened and you can really see.

Noise pollution was much worse, unbearable, I could hear sounds on Earth no one else could hear. I could close my eyes when I was bothered with the light but the hearing was intolerable because the sounds weren't just coming from the outside and into my ears. The sounds could filter past my eardrum as though coming from the inside out too. I could hear bees and wasps that were miles away, the very deep low humming sound which alarmed me and caused me to panic because I was afraid of being stung, due to having asthma and allergies. I heard music in the wind, I would hear music when it wasn't possible to hear music, such as swimming under water away from everything.

Later on in years, even recently, I would try to turn my car CD player off when it wasn't even on. On one particular day when the music wasn't on, (I checked it umpteen times), I heard the music of several choirs singing at the same time. I could hear individual choirs and soloists. It's mind-blowing. I tried to pinpoint where in the car it was coming from but it's as if someone is sitting on my shoulders, singing just for me. I have grabbed people and shaken them. 'Listen!' I tell them. 'Just shut up, be quiet and listen!' I have fought with people until they believed me, hanging on to them, ordering them to hear. Out of every person I've asked and held on to throughout those years, only two people have heard the music, because I physically held on to them and demanded they listen until they heard what I hear.

My parents and siblings had now moved to Oban while I stayed on in Ardrishaig at the Argyll Arms Hotel, working during the summer holidays and meeting Julie for a gander. There were some new summer season staff at the hotel, who would insist on going to the local dance hall for a disco, ceilidh, or whatever was on and I would get dragged along with them, quite literally. 'They won't let me in,' I'd plead. They wouldn't take no for an answer. One of them stuffed my bra with tights to make me look older and plastered me with make-up and lipstick and gave me a handbag full of hairbrushes, hairspray and perfume.

I got talking to a sailor who was boarding at the hotel. He knew I was under-age but the proprietors looked after me and wouldn't allow me to drink or stay in the lounge after a certain time. He was a fine guy, very nice, and went along to the village hall and offered to buy me a drink. 'I don't drink,' I'd told him often enough but he informed me he was drinking dark rum and Coke and that it was nice. He talked me into trying one and I agreed. 'Cheers,' he said, as he handed me a glass. Having no airs, graces or decorum, I took a big gulp and swallowed half of the alcoholic drink, trying to be all smart, sophisticated and grown up. I nearly passed out as I tried to catch my breath when the alcohol bounced off my throat, nasal passages and brain. He fell about laughing at my first attempt with alchohol. I slammed it on the bar and told him I didn't like it and not to waste his money. He was was a friend, was, until he tried to liquidate me to death by deadly Dark Rum.

I also met a handsome guy who was a dead ringer for the singer Gilbert O'Sullivan, we got chatting and I agreed to meet him the following Saturday. He was a fisherman, and would hire a taxi from Campbeltown to Ardrishaig and have the taxi-driver wait all evening for him to take him home again.

I met him about three times and quite liked him, until I spotted him from across the road one Saturday when he clearly didn't see me. There he was in the middle of the road waving his arms, drunk and shouting like a big daft bampot. 'Hmm, I thought, fisherman or not, you're not the catch I thought you were.'

As it was very cold and with nowhere to go, there was nothing to do at the weekend unless there was a dance on at the village hall. Also, given that I was underage, we couldn't go into any lounges, public bars or even hotels as everyone knew everyone, and everyone would know I was underage. Mr Fishy would ask me to sit in the back of the taxi with him but, with the driver having a good peek from the rear-view mirror, I felt awkward and intimidated. I also felt God telling me he wasn't the one and I had the good sense to say goodbye to Mr Fishy Campbeltown before God told me to do it and I stopped dating him.

By the time I got to Oban, my family had settled into their flat and The Daddy had taken a serious turn for the worse mentally, crying all the time. He broke down one day as I put a jacket on our little sister, intending on taking her out to the park. He asked me not to put the jacket on her. Was it the jacket that bothered him? I was so confused, the jacket went on regardless and we got away from him. Losing his mother, my grandmother, had tipped him over the edge and we all suffered through his suffering. The hardest part was not knowing how to help him and I couldn't cope with his crying, it distressed me too much.

I was going into fifth year at Oban High School and found some jobs at a local hotel working at wedding functions again and part time in the fish factory on the pier, scrubbing prawns for Young's at the weekend. I hated Oban, it stank of a putrid odour from the whisky factory, which was hard for me to stomach. I stank of fish too, my whole life began to stink.

The smell would be in my nostrils all day and make me want to retch and throw up. I still tell people my educational life was marred by smell, except for Lochgilphead, my favourite dearest green place (Sorry Glasgow, Lochgilphead is The Dearest Green Place in my life, the grass is greener).

The eternal stench at Govan Road came from the sewage works right next to the Southern General Hospital. Who in their right mind builds a hospital next door to a sewage plant? In the summer the smell was filthy, well, it was faeces, bad enough on a cold day but in the heat it was dreadful. It still stinks but not as bad as it did in the sixties. My life stank, literally.

I related this stinky story to an old lady as I told her I was writing a book, and happened to mention the sewage works. She told me her husband, Bill, worked there (at the sewage plant) in the sixties and it was stinking right enough. She went on to say that he dropped his jacket into the sewage pit and tried to drag it out. His friend tried to stop him, yelling, 'You don't want it back after it landing in there, leave it.' Bill replied, 'Naw, am no wantin' ma jacket, it's ma pieces in my pocket ah want!' I told her I couldn't allow her story to go unread.

I was totally excluded from the family as far as The Daddy was concerned and I would go to work to get out of the house and away from problems I couldn't handle. He'd take off on family outings without me, I wasn't surprised but I was deflated and still a bit sad all the same. At least he was getting back to his old self, I reasoned. I did not want to see a grown man cry and not be able to help. He didn't want me there anyway and I knew it.

Uncle David, my Mother's brother, paid us a visit one teatime. He worked in haulage and was in Oban doing a drop-off, and came up for tea and a rest before heading back to Glasgow. I was in the kitchen baking fruit loaves, scones and apple pies. I wouldn't eat them but I loved baking for others. Uncle David popped his head into the kitchen to say hello and eye up the baking. He got his tea and a good plate of eats.

'Who made them?' he asked me. I told him I did.

Going into the lounge, he lifted his plate of baking high towards The Daddy and commented, 'I thought you said she was useless.' Well, you could have blown me down, I knew what The Daddy thought about me but did he have to go and tell my aunts, uncles, cousins and anybody else he spoke to, that I was useless? Stupid? I was so hurt, I groaned, I was paying my way while he was out of work. I went around that kitchen and slammed everything about, smacking utensils and bowls off the walls and into the sink. I was not a happy bunny and made up my mind right there and then to show him just who was stupid and useless. His words, actions and presence destroyed me, my dreams and ambitions, my confidence, and he was still at it, still hurting me, still proclaiming to one and all I was useless.

The family dimension was changing dramatically due to all of us growing up and finding new friendships, relationships and events. This meant we were often outside and away from The Daddy, who was off work and on the sick. As we lived in a flat now, there was no garden to sit out in but there were parks and great walks. Compared to Port Ann, Oban seemed like City. I met some new friends through work and had a lovely time with one in particular. She was older than me and had not long left Oban High School. We met at the weekends to hang around, all dressed up looking for a gig. I was always the one sent into the off-licence because of my height for our weekly one can of lager (shared) before we went into the Corran Halls where there was a band on.

My sisters had found their own friends too and were getting on well. Little sis was still too small for nursery, though, and most of my time was taken up with looking after her, which was a real joy.

As the Out of Body Experience was still as fresh in my head, I thought about it every day, all day. I would go over the event on my own with so many questions. Why did you let me see right into Heaven, God? How come I hear music? Where are you? What do you want me to do? Where do you want me to go? My whole life, will and emotions were in and with God. I eventually became a real party pooper because I now wasn't interested in drinking or going out to the dancing, I found the nightlife incredibly dull. I ditched a date because I wasn't inter-ested. We had already met up and he was eagerly looking forward to our next night out. I just couldn't go and had to tell the guy it wasn't on. Again I was stuck for words, I didn't know why. I told him there was nothing wrong with him, it was me. I was shocked to see him outside my front door kissing the next-door neighbour a few weeks later.

Bingo night was a favourite of my mother's and I went with her on the one night her neighbour friend couldn't make it. We girls never ever fought but there had been some stupid argumentative spat of words between myself and Pannie over nothing much, and I went to slap her because she was goading me and doing my head in. She had a large pair of scissors which I didn't notice in her hand, she lifted her hand up automatically to protect herself as I aimed a swipe at her. The scissors were opened and stabbed into my arm, muscle and veins at the exact position of the scissor legs, causing horrendous pain. It put an end to our silly argument and she didn't mean to hurt me, I had basically done it to myself out of frustration and anger. The pain was so bad I had to hold my arm up with my other hand for about three weeks. The muscle in my arm had been pierced, causing pain so bad I felt ill. It became clear later on that I was supposed to stay at home. No one else was at home with The Daddy except for baby sister, who was now a toddler.

'**GO HOME**,' I kept hearing as I sat in the bingo hall with my mother. I wasn't playing bingo, the agony in my arm was making me feel ill and, no matter which way I sat, I couldn't get comfortable. There wasn't much to see on my arm either, just two puncture holes and a bit of swelling, but I felt as though my muscle had been chopped into three parts. Although the pain was atrocious, it didn't distract me from the words I was hearing and I knew I needed to go home. I had the same feeling on leaving the house but, after the spat with Pannie, I went out. '**GO HOME**,' God said clearly. I looked at my Mother and said nothing. I'll just wait until she's finished, I thought. The urge to go home, though, was deafening in my soul but I didn't want to go home and leave my mother alone and I knew as the bingo hadn't finished, my mother wouldn't have wanted to leave then. I wanted to wait and bring my mother back up the road. If she was going to see something terrible, I wanted to be with her. What on earth has happened? I wondered. I was sick with worry. What has happened to our little sister, what has The Daddy done? Oh God, I thought, I can't do this, help us. I knew deep within me something awful had happened, God was not telling me to go home for nothing. Finally, carrying my throbbing arm and feeling nauseous, I quickened my steps up the road trying not to panic. I remember the dreadful strong silence between my mother and me as I pretended nothing was wrong. There was no point in hoping nothing was wrong because I knew it was bad and I was right. I had heard God's voice clearly.

Even before we were halfway home, I could see the pale flashings of blue lights above the tops of the buildings, lighting up the sky. We're coming, we're coming, I thought, heartsick and struggling with my arm. I only wanted to see my baby sister, that was all.

She was trembling in her urine as she had wet the settee in fear. The sliding lounge window above her head was opened wide by The Daddy and the room was freezing from the cold night air. He threw himself from the three-storey high flat and climbed over the wire fence and sat on the railway line waiting for the ten o'clock Oban to Glasgow train. A neighbour who had seen him pass their window below saved his life by calling the police. If they'd had their curtains or blinds closed, no-one would have seen him falling or sitting there on the dark track. I was never so glad to see my little sister and grabbed her, never to let her go again. Now she'll understand why I love her so much. I was committed to her and The Daddy was committed to hospital.

The Daddy got the help he needed and had a network of support surrounding him to help him cope with the depression on top of his other factors in mental illness. He appeared fine

for a while, giving no cause for concern. In a strange way I felt
taller than his illness, taller than him, stronger than him. I couldn't
buckle under his whims or the little authority he had.

Once The Daddy got treatment for a few months we moved
back to Glasgow. It meant leaving all of our friends behind but
it wasn't too far away and many visited and stayed with us
throughout the years. I met and said goodbye to Irene (Leckie)
as we were leaving and brought my new 'friend' with me on
the day we left, I grabbed her and didn't let her go for about
ten years. As Pannie said goodbye to her friend, her friend's
mother gave me a cup of tea which I drank sitting in her garden,
quietly.

I watched what I thought was her mother's dog raiding the
bin. I called out to her mother and told her the dog was eating
rubbish from the bin. 'I'll kill it!' her mother screamed, shooing
it away. It came sneaking back with a glint in its eye, wagging
its tail, only to get more verbal. I totally fell in love with this
skinny Border Collie. 'I'm going to put by boot up its backside,'
she shouted, telling me it was a stray. I lifted my hairy new
(stray) friend up for a kiss and cuddle but I couldn't leave without
her, I felt she was mine.

'Can I bring her with me?' The piercing reply from The
Daddy was 'No!' I ignored him and nestled up with my stray
dog for the journey.

'If that thing's sick in the back it's hitting the road,' The Daddy
informed me.

He did it before when I was a little girl holding onto our
beloved black dog. The Daddy opened the car door and threw
her out to wander the street while I looked back and wondered
where she would go. I was heartbroken. I stared out of the back
window until we were gone. It traumatised me, as I feared what
would happen to her. I loved and missed her. It wasn't going
to happen ever again, I promised.

No sooner had the words fired out of The Daddy's mouth
when the unthinkable happened, she spewed. 'I've got it, it's all

right, I've cleaned it,' I promised, groping in the dark to grab anything I could use as a rag.

I was right about Shepa, she played a huge part in our family and was meant for me, an amazing gift from God, which I dearly treasured. She pushed my arms out of the way when I sat bent over with my face in my hands, crying, I was never allowed to sit that way. I wasn't even allowed to be sad, she wouldn't let me, as though God Himself intervened. She was intelligent and understood every word I said to her and her obedience was phenomenal. She looked after little sis too by walking her to school, sitting there all day waiting for her to come out and walking her home again. She got up on her hind legs to look in the classroom window at Burnbrae Primary School and the teacher then allowed her to come into the classroom to sit at little sister's feet if it was raining. I loved that dog more than life, she was truly given by God.

I needed her and God gave me her as a friend and companion, and what a companion she was. God has given me three dogs that have been great companions. The first one was Shepa, the best ever, I could not have picked a more beautiful loving-natured dog if I had searched the whole world over for her.

The second one He gave me was a Yorkshire terrier. I was watching it go off its tiny head in a neighbour's car and thought, 'Wow! Look at that little whippersnapper.' I didn't think it was friendly at all but the neighbour explained to me that her brother was out working all day and he couldn't look after it. She asked me to take it and I agreed. We called him Ben and had an amazing time with him, the cheeky little thing made us laugh no end.

The third dog God gave me was lying on a seat in our church charity shop. People laugh when I tell them I got him in a charity shop but it's true, only I didn't pay for him. The woman who was looking after him was sick with a blood disorder (cancer) and couldn't look after him any more. She explained he was brought over from Australia by her daughter and was very needy and insecure. She wasn't wrong. His name was Junior but we changed it to Larry because he looks like a lamb. He is a Bichon, who is very lazy, so lazy we have to carry him home if we take him for a walk. Again, he is a treasure and brings us much joy. God has given me the secret desires of my heart and knows full well what is good for me, all free too.

## Chapter Six

# *THE BURNING BUSH*

⤜⤚

I mentioned already that someone came over to our house in Port Ann and kindly lit the fire for us, the best neighbour ever. Well, not to be outdone in grace and neighbourly love, someone lit the fire for us in Glasgow too. We arrived at our allocated home in Priesthill on the south side of Glasgow and what an almighty shock we got. Our intended house had been deliberately set on fire by the local hoodlums during the night and all that stood were the bare bricks. No roof, chimney, doors, nothing! The hedges, rose bushes and grass were burned and blackened. There was no voice coming from the burned bush, God didn't say a thing as I stood and surveyed the squalor before my eyes.

I had a young man (Uzie) in stitches telling him this story and he thought I was making it up, but it's true. We can look back and laugh but it certainly wasn't funny at the time. We ended up getting another house close by in the crescent instead but my heart sank to the soles of my feet. The second house was horrible, cold, dark and damp with red painted stone floors. There were polystyrene tiles barely hanging from the ceilings, the bathroom had been painted with dark blue gloss paint and the kitchen was a howler. What a culture shock! Compared to the one that had been burned, though, it was a palace, and beggars can't be choosers.

My mother was from Househillwood, close to Priesthill, which was a very desirable area when she was a child but this house was a midden, with no windows or doors. Fibreglass sheets were removed as the workmen replaced the glass in the windows and put two doors up. Not new ones, I have to say, but we needed doors and the letterbox was fitted on a later day. The wind howled up the hall through the rectangle hole in the door with a haunting welcome of its own.

I could make it sound nicer perhaps by letting you know it was a semi-detached and the garden had a stream running through it with man-made stepping stones. Above a stream, normally, one would build a quaint bridge over running water, but not in Priesthill. It was covered by tar in a vain attempt to hide the water but every now and then the tarmac would collapse, naturally. We would have some job trying to keep our feet dry as the water rushed up and out from the underground stream below, which was racing to the nearby Brock burn.

As we were given this house in an emergency, we had to move into the abode as seen, with no carpets, curtains, heating, gas or electricity, the kind of goods that are necessary. There weren't even any curtain rails above the windows so we could quickly hang curtains up, or sheets even. To our dismay there weren't any light bulbs either so we could see what we were doing when it got dark, and darkness wasn't too far away, given that we got there after four o'clock. I had to take a lead role in an awful lot of the organising, then there were mouths to feed and beds to build. Where on earth was I to start? As I stood still, the sight of the squalor made me want to crawl into that small sink hole at the side of the house and disappear forever. How could people live like this? I protested and asked myself, feeling destitute.

We were told the previous tenants kicked up a real stink with the City Council because the bedrooms at the side and back of the house were riddled with dampness and causing havoc with her children, who had asthma. With the torrent of water cascading down by the side of the house, it would have been easy to surmise that this had something to do with the dampness. However, in the front and side bedroom there were bird droppings and feathers all over the floor, mingled with birdseed and droppings from the pigeons (doo's), which were shooed away. The cupboard was full of birdseed bags and urine sludge. Being an emergency, the City Council hadn't yet been in to clean the house. It was beyond filthy and The Daddy's chest was really bad. Bird droppings are dangerous to those with chest problems. It was hard and long work but we had started to turn a house into a home and things got a bit easier. We had just left a brand-new build in Oban with two toilets for a shelter in the ghetto. What another bleak dismal dark day that was.

We had some really nice neighbours close by though, and my mother found a good friend in our next-door neighbours, a lovely caring family named the Converys. They were very like us in ages and we each paired off and had fun in our years ahead.

I needed a job quickly as The Daddy was on long-term sickness benefit and mum had to look after him. He was pathetically ill, mentally. I got the phone book out and looked up hotels in Glasgow. I only phoned one and explained I had just moved to Glasgow and was wondering if they were looking for any staff in the kitchen or for waitressing. Apart from scrubbing prawns in Oban, catering was all I had experience in. The manager asked me to come in on the Friday for an interview. I did and got a waitressing job there and then and started work on the Monday. You could do that then, leave a job on a Friday and start a new one on a Monday. The *Evening Times* newspaper was always plastered in jobs and they were easy to come by. I couldn't be too choosy, though, and I knew my life was with my mother and The Daddy.

I found the hotel (the Royal Stuart) easily, it was owned by a huge record company. The hotel sits beside the River Clyde and opposite toilets that were actually open to the public. Split shifts were a pain in the backside, as a lot of time was wasted hanging around in the afternoon after lunch, too much time to waste, wondering if The Daddy was all right. As there was hardly any time to get home and back again for work, I would often just spend the day in the city centre shopping. The younger family siblings loved to see what I came home with, as the goods I bought were always for them.

The staff at the hotel were a great bunch, there were not that many of us, so quite family-orientated. We got on really well and had a great laugh. From a Monday to the Friday we would do a roaring trade in business lunches, from twelve until two thirty, and we got to know a lot of regulars who had luncheon vouchers. One of our regular customers was known to us as Mister 'I'll have your pleasure', because that's what he always said when his starter and main course was finished and we asked him what he fancied for dessert. I used to stand there and think, 'Oh no you won't!' The older staff would nudge me forward to get his dessert order because they didn't want to but neither did I. He was such a really nice man too, we'd just be having a carry-on.

The hotel was poorly decorated, with threadbare carpets and holes covered by huge rugs, and in dire need of a makeover, although it was spotlessly clean. I was told one of the older and quite posh waitresses, Betty, tripped over the tired old faded carpet while she was carrying a tray that contained cream, and fell flat on her face. Not one bit funny, poor soul, but she wore a noticeable wig as her hair was terribly thin. She was a real lady as ladies go, prim, proper, polite, but overly pleasant. She was always immaculately dressed and walked tall leading with her nose, she wasn't 'stuck-up', that was just her persona. She landed flat on her face after tripping over one of the holes and managed to keep the silver tray in the air above her head, supported by her bent elbows. Her wig flew off and her head was absolutely covered in the cream, which continued to drip blobs on her thin hair as she lay horizontal. The waitress who told me was crying with laughter. 'She didn't move a muscle either, she lay there in shock until she was rescued,' she told me. I never ever let on I was told the story of her hair-raising day, of course. I always felt protective of her. I could imagine her lying there with her crème de la crème hairdo, waiting for a knight in shining armour to lift her up.

I was also told of another incident where Betty put her big best foot forward, again. When the late Princess Magareeta stayed at the hotel (not her real name. When I discovered there were hundreds of things I couldn't write in a book I had to go through all of the chapters to change names.), Betty went with the head housekeeper, Helen, to look at the wonderful array of outfits belonging to the Princess, which were hanging up. Just for a quick peek, of course, no one would ever know. Betty told me this story herself, what a hoot she was. Here was the bold Betty, giving her opinions on the royal dress outfits as she examined them one by one. Flicking through the expensive garments, she voiced her opinions, 'I wouldn't wear that,' she stuffily proclaimed and was caught red-handed by the regal Princess herself, who politely replied, 'I wouldn't normally wear it either,' smiling. Oops! Glad it was before my time.

Betty was always the same, she came across as strait-laced but we knew her as having a great dry wit about her. The staff there took me under their wings and looked after me by making me laugh, they were a real good workforce and a credit to the bosses, whoever they were, as we never saw them.

We also had a handsome Italian head waiter named Sergio, whose wife gave birth to their first child, a daughter. His wife brought their newborn baby in for us to see. She was beautiful with a whole head of thick jet-black hair just like her parents. Sergio was proud of his little gem as he paraded her around the restaurant for all staff and customers to admire. We each took a turn of holding little Angela and told Sergio we were keeping her. He was a strict family man and had a great way with the public. The look of love into his wife's eyes said it all, he was gloriously happy with his life and family.

Sergio's speciality was throwing the utensils around while preparing the feasts of the flambé, firing up the flames with alcohol, at the table, which the guests loved. He was a real man's man and we ladies would laugh at his antics because we couldn't include him in any of our girl talk. We did try. 'Get out of here,' he would rant. 'Do not you talk to me like that about woman's dresses, I am a man, I come here from my wife, she talk all day about clothes, now to listen to you all day, yap, yap, yap!' He would let off steam in his Italian accent and broken English. We would imitate him lovingly and he would tell us we were 'crazy'. He'd throw his hands towards Heaven, asking, 'Why, God? Why? You put me in here with them, you torture me, they crazy, the lot of them!' He meant it too but he was a delightful man with a great sense of humour and the rapport we had was special. He treated us with great respect and, despite us winding him up, he was very protective and gentlemanly.

None of us ever had a disagreement. On the contrary, one of the waitresses, Eileen, was ill one night with severe stomach pains and we couldn't help her except to phone her husband, who came to collect her.

The cashier at the front of the restaurant was called Maureen and she was the daughter of one of the waitresses, whose name I forget. Maureen couldn't leave her post at the front door so we'd bring her a cup of tea or coffee and something to eat. Her mother was as mad as a brush. She was the one who pushed me out to get Mr 'I'll have your pleasures' order all of the time. We worked together most days and had a good laugh at life.

No one wanted to hang around too late, especially when the kitchen was closed, and we had buses to catch. Maureen's mother would get agitated when people didn't move it after their evening meal. She would hover around the table clearing everything but the table legs. 'Can I get you anything else?' she'd politely ask. 'Another coffee? Another drink? A TAXI!'

Patty was a waitress who worked during the day in an office for a businessman who poached her, 'stolen', she always said with a cheeky laugh and a wink, from her previous employer with the promise of more money. She was a big girl. She had us all in fits of laughter one night when her jet-black T-shirt began to develop huge white circles of clouds and plumes of dust every time she moved. We could hardly make each other out for the plumes of 'after-shower powder'. She had run home when she had finished her office job, jumped into the shower and then got into her black waitressing clothes, but not before she had emptied half a tin of this powder down her bra. It got worse when she started banging at her chest like a gorilla in order to get rid of the white powder, in front of the customers too. She looked like a gigantic powder puff. Patty was our secret weapon for pulling in the tips, with her huge assets, and her smile of course.

The Head Chef, Danny, was always immaculately dressed in his whites and was a great and attentive chef. The others were greasy-haired bikers. Nothing wrong with being a biker, or greasy-haired for that matter, but they were dirty verbally too. Their smutty innuendoes used to drive me nuts, especially when I was too busy and they were mucking about. I was often humiliated when they asked which manager was in for dinner because they stood on his raw steak before cooking it. I was too afraid to tell them to stop it or tell the manager what they had done. I can't even believe I'm telling you this but that's what they did. I had no confidence, I wasn't just meek, I was weak. I was frightened of men, frightened of confrontation, frightened of everything and anything. I would turn bright red and could feel my face burning like a hot poker if anyone looked at me longer than they should have.

The other chefs were disgusting except for the pastry chef, Jimmy, he was a gem, especially when we asked for a wee bit of ice-cream for lunch or dinner. 'Of course you can, hen, you're entitled to it,' he would say as he slapped the bowl to overloading with every kind of ice-cream, sorbet, fruits, cream, sprinkles, cherries and anything else that would fit on top.

Neil and Helen worked the room service and we'd always meet them in the kitchen. Neil would often fall out with Jimmy or vice versa, and what a screaming match that would be, with anything from ladles to sprinkles flying through the blue air. Never when Head Chef Danny was there, though, they were the best-behaved staff then. We would stay in the hotel if the weather was bad, watch television, have dinner, tea and biscuits, whatever we wanted.

I remember a big jolly businessman who visited a lot. He was always in the kitchen with the chef and he gave me the following advice with his finger pointed in my face, on the stairwell one day, 'When you get married, get married to the person who makes you laugh.' I never forgot that advice and, sure enough, the man I married makes me laugh. His jokes and ad-libs range from funny to corny but most of the time he jokes about something. He has a positive outlook on life and is cheery most of the time. Credit where credit is due, because I've met others who were not so funny, they just thought they were. There were takers, moaners, users, abusers and wasters. It was particularly important for me to have faith in the male sex because my opinions up to that stage weren't highly favourable, given the life I'd lived. I only saw men as downright selfish, a totally different species from the female. It didn't take long for me to figure out that men were indeed only after one thing and when they realised that one thing wasn't available, then they'd move on, usually leaving and muttering something degrading. So then the feeling became mutual. They weren't getting what I had and not one of them had anything precious to keep me even remotely interested. A personality would have been a start, I reckoned.

Without a personality was the window cleaner who was often at the hotel and must have hated his job. All I got out of him was that I was sitting on a gold mine and he couldn't understand why I was working at the hotel and not making good use of my fleshy assets. Every single time he came in, he said the same thing. What a smutty manky creep, I thought, my mother was right about men.

Another of our guests was an older lady from Texas, who was holidaying in Scotland on her own. I thought she was remarkable for taking off and holidaying wherever and whenever she felt like it. I thought she was so brave and I remember thinking at that time that I would never have gone to another country on my own. Well, I had never been outside Scotland. She came across as a bit strange and eccentric but I was fascinated by her. I was astounded by the fact that she had to be finished with her meal early as she had to phone home to speak to her dog every night, which I thought was hilarious. I used to go home and tell my younger siblings stories about my day at work and they were always ready to hear how the other half lived. I was always a great story-teller, I just used my imagination to invent the most funny, crazy and ridiculous stories to amuse my siblings, I don't know if they believed the one about the woman phoning from Glasgow to Texas to speak to her dog but it was absolutely true. By the way, she didn't just speak to her dog. She had to raise her voice so the dog could hear her and so could the rest of the guests at the hotel. A funny vivacious wee lady.

Stars came and went often at the hotel, as it was owned by the record company EMI, but there were much nicer hotels in Glasgow by then. One of the head turners I encountered was the old man himself, who owned a popular brand of jeans. He was very small and thin and was strutting around, in his own brand of jeans, of course. He asked me if I knew who he was and when I told him I didn't, he kindly informed me. I would never have known, I just knew he must have been very rich and important, as he was followed by the most amazing 'leggy' models, all wearing the same brand of jeans. He was nothing to look at but he sure felt and looked good with his entourage of beauties at his side. They were all beautiful, kind and warm-hearted, don't you just love nice people?

Other guests we had were from a huge clothing company for children, which also had child models, who stayed at the hotel a few times too, and they melted my heart with their big eyes and sweetness. They were tiny child models for the clothing company Ladybird, who were accompanied by chaperones and when we served them, they'd reply, 'Thank you very kindly.' Their manners were fabulous to behold. Not only were they beautiful on the eye but they were beautiful little people. I've met people throughout my life who have been every bit as beautiful until they've opened their mouths, what a let-down to themselves. On the other hand, I have met people who were not so 'fair in the face', yet they have been the salt of the earth. Every time, though, it has been a complete surprise when I thought I knew someone by their appearance, only to be proved wrong when they spoke. Never judging people by their faces or expressions is as true as The Word says because we know nothing about them.

Quite often there would be a function on at the hotel. This is where I met The 'little star', as she fronted one of the wedding bands. On this particular evening it was her big night for the television documentary on BBC1 that threw her into the lime-light. I served her pudding before she went on to be filmed throughout the evening, sago or semolina, something like that. That's the beauty of speaking to the chef, he will get you anything that's not on the menu provided you give him plenty of time to do so. Still a student at the Academy of Music and Drama, our little star was very quiet and nervous. She was really tiny and I remember loving her dress as it had a neat waist, as I did then. This little songbird had a huge voice and we enjoyed listening to her belt out songs such as 'Spanish Eyes' and 'The Last Waltz'. I've always had a soft spot for our native songbird and I tell people all the time, 'I was there when it happened.' Good for her and great for us, except she left us and went to live in America and we hardly heard from her for a long time. I still have her first long-playing record and even a record player to play it on too.

The hotel was a great place to work and left me with many happy memories. The record company eventually sold it on to a private family and it wasn't the same after they left us. It was still quite good but most of the staff left and I did too, so that was the end of an era. We'd still go back to The Vinters bar next door, which was our local meeting den, for a catch-up. The staff looked after us well and when a place treats you well it's like a second home. I was needed at my first home more often, though, and I felt increasingly uncomfortable when I wasn't there, as my mother was struggling with looking after The Daddy, who would get up, turning night into day. I felt bound in a huge way to be close by at all times and often silently went about my daily business with my thoughts still towards The God I needed. If I had any ambitions they were well and truly already buried, not dead, just buried. I needed to be there to look after my mother and young family, who took off in different directions in the twinkling of an eye. The Daddy was housebound and had stopped eating due to his mouth becoming inflamed and blistered, also because he didn't want to eat. He'd have cups of tea and fluids but more often than not, they'd lie cold at his feet. He would sleep all day on the settee and would only communicate when he wanted to, but the fire in his eyes had long gone out. We felt frightened because he was a high risk on the suicide scale and tried to take his life again by swallowing all of his medication. He had been sectioned a few times, which meant I was a permanent baby-sitter when I wasn't working. My heart was broken again the day I watched him being led down the hall to by two Community Practice Nurses, to be committed. He seemed to jolt, not walk, as I watched him being taken away.

He would interact with the younger family but was very quiet when I was around. I was in a profound predicament, I was always on some sort of a diet or non-eating phase, wouldn't eat, now I had The Daddy who couldn't eat. I always remembered the incident at the kitchen table with my mother when she was peeling the potatoes and wondered where the thought had come from, I wondered about it for years. 'Sure if you don't want to eat, you don't have to?' I now found myself looking at a mirror image of my eating habits and naturally began coaxing The Daddy to eat, as he was far too thin for a grown man. In a sort of sowing and reaping way, his behaviour towards me caused my eating problems and now he was going through the same dilemma. I tried all sorts of food, custard, ice-cream and cakes, the kind of foods which might tempt someone to break a diet. I still couldn't get The Daddy to eat enough of them to sustain him. I often wondered if he wouldn't accept it from 'stupid' me? When we turned our backs on him for even a short time, he would give the cakes, biscuits, crisps and sweets away. He wanted to please younger members of the family and he would always put them before himself. The younger members of the family, not realising how thin and weak The Daddy was getting, would naturally take what they were given and eat it because it pleased them and him. The Daddy was always telling everyone to look after the younger ones because they meant the world to him and he was too ill to do it himself.

My next job was with a furrier's as a model, which gave me my nights off as I finished at around five pm. The job was so dreary if there were no buyers booked, as it was my job to strut about modelling fur, leather, suede coats and jackets. It was there I learned about the different animal skins such as Coney and Borg. Wearing animal skins and furs was becoming increasingly unpopular and I began to feel uneasy in doing my job, due to comments and fear of reprisals from activist groups. The management would receive hate mail and just bin it. I also began to question my loyalty as I loved animals and I realised that, if it offended other people, then it was easier not to flaunt the business in their faces. I had also begun to look at the garments and think, this used to be a cute little rabbit. Well, that got into my head and upset me so, needless to say, the job only lasted a year or so. I was frightened I'd be attacked because I worked at the furrier's in Ingram street, especially as I paraded the garments for sale. I was also scared they'd all fall on top of me again, as the rails that held them were dreadfully unsafe. They had already fallen on top of me countless times, imagine being killed by the skins of deceased animals. I thought there was a sort of 'serves you right' omen about it. The modelling job wasn't for me, as it was far too boring and I left to join one of the best department stores in Glasgow, working for the management team.

It sounds quite good but I was only serving them food and drink. I was warned *never* to discuss what was said at the private table, so with that in mind I never did. The warning came from the head waitress, who interviewed me. That was clearly understood and I did as I was told. She had a daughter, though, who worked in another department and when one of the other waitresses overheard the managers discussing her, the mother bombarded me for information. She was the one who told me never to utter a word the managers said at the table but she gave me a hard time because she wanted every detail they said about her daughter. Talk about being caught between the devil and the deep blue sea. I had been there before, in Ardrishaig. Again though, I met some great new friends.

One of the waitresses, who was a great help, was Isa. Her husband was very ill, the other staff said and, unlike some of the 'stuck-up' waitresses, who came from Drumchapel or Easterhouse, she was a truly humble soul. I really felt for her and there was a quiet mother-and-daughter sort of relationship around her. She was a builder, a comforter and a help despite her own heartaches. The other waitresses were as hard as nails and thought they were something, walking with their noses in the air, but not Isa. She spotted how they treated me and saw I was really down in the dumps one day. I can't remember how the conversation came about but I muttered to her casually, 'It doesn't matter, Jesus loves me.' She stopped me in my tracks and replied, 'He does, hen, he really does.' She made me smile and left the peace of God stirred up in my heart. Isa wasn't like the other waitresses, she had sorrows at home just like me but she still took the time to give me the love and confirmation of Jesus.

She loved Jesus too. She must have wanted Him, needed Him. When she spoke about Him, her eyes sparkled and her statement was genuinely filled with much deep love.

Within the managers of all of the heads of departments, there were two Christians apparently, so I was told, because believe me, I would never had known. I found the one who was a true Christian, he was full of light. He was an American and he had Jesus for sure. I could see Jesus in his eyes, by his words and actions. He lived the Christian life, you just know when you meet someone with Jesus, they light up other people's lives too. Naturally, he was well-mannered, warm and kind and I was drawn to him. I loved Jesus but I still didn't have the relationship with Him I knew I should have and I didn't know how to get it. I just knew I wanted Him back so much. Isn't it amazing how God took a guy all the way from America to Scotland to light up my life? The manager never mentioned Jesus once, he didn't have to, that didn't matter, I sort of found Him again in this manager, like seeing the love of your life from a distance before you are actually introduced.

Now, on the other guy, I couldn't have met someone ruder than he was. He was a Christian too, I was told, but I didn't believe it. He was so very handsome and tall, a fine specimen of a man, but he could have passed as Satan quicker than a Christian, a deception Satan still uses, his beauty. I dutifully brought this 'Christian' manager a bowl of ice-cream and a silver teaspoon. They had their own cutlery, as was the usual custom at this huge department store.

'What am I supposed to do with that?' he boomed for every Tom, Dick and Harry to witness. He held the teaspoon in the air and I turned beetroot-red. I didn't know what he was talking about and became flustered, what was wrong? I wondered. 'Well?' he bellowed, again for everyone to hear, but I didn't understand the problem. I finally came to the conclusion he wanted a bigger spoon, could he not just have asked me for one? He got me into a great deal of trouble with staff because of a teaspoon, something so little and pathetic as a tiny teaspoon. I had been there before too, what was it with men and teaspoons? Big mouth, ha ha. I can laugh now, again, because I don't stand for that nonsense from grown adults. Nor do I feel any guilt by announcing the manager as having a big mouth because he clearly did in more ways than one. I have grown from that cowardly shy little person who was mortified and pathetically frightened at every situation to the one who now has the mind of Christ. I don't stand for 'Oh woe is me' pity parties. By the way, I also served his very 'good' friend, who was a well-known children's entertainer and was a regular on television most of my young life in a cartoon sort of adventure. On the programme you could have your birthday announced and send in a picture or a painting. Oh, man alive! What a shock I got when I encountered him in real life. His television partner, a dog, was lovely, though.

Apart from a few delinquents, the department store was a nice place to work and we always got our lunch before Joe Public, if we wanted any. We also got a great staff discount on any goods, even across the road at the smaller 'sister' store. It was great to be able to browse. I also had a friend at the larger department store, at an 'in-shop', downstairs, who worked on the ground-floor level and who would give me her samples in make-up as she worked in one of the make-up and perfume in-store counters. I was quite well off given that I couldn't resist the clothing departments. I had bought an expensive dress from one of the in-store shops one day when the American manager's daughter accidentally soaked her clothing in the kitchen. I insisted she wear the brand-new dress because she had nothing to change into. She looked amazing in it and took it home, bringing it back another day. I was delighted to let her have it and her American daddy was blown away at my generosity, but I just willingly shared what I had, that was all. That was all because of his Jesus, His love is infectious. Nobody shared Jesus with me though.

The days always went by quickly at work in the restaurant and I'd meet my cousin for a refreshment at the city's plush fish bar/restaurant after work. She loved to wander around the departments while waiting for me to finish, then she'd quiz me relentlessly about the managers. She liked the look of some of the younger managers, but then, everyone did. They certainly were not short of admirers. Sometimes the staff would get together after work for a night out, which was good fun, although I hardly ever went.

On one occasion at work I was accused by the waitresses of having an affair with one of the men at work and threatened with 'You just wait 'till his wife finds out'. I was angry with them and demanded to know who 'allegedly' saw us together sitting cosy in the public bar. I was furious and went straight away and collected the man by the arm, with whom I was allegedly seen getting cosy and stood him in front of the waitresses. I got them to repeat what they accused me of in front of him and he was furious too. I could have left the liars to have their day and allow them to accuse me but I went home every evening to heartbreak and had enough on my plate without accusations, sneers and lies at work and had to stick up for myself. If he was seen in a public bar with another female, fair enough, but it certainly wasn't with me, I told them. None of the waitresses would own up and tell me who it was who 'saw us', because they didn't see us at all. Oddly enough, there was a young girl who worked in the kitchen who was dating an older married man, nothing was was said about those two, given that he was triple her age. People are predators, having two eyes in the front of the face just like animals, and seek to devour anyone who seems weaker, just like Satan.

It's nothing short of bullying to pick on a younger or meeker member of society and I was slowly but surely gaining the confidence to whip back verbally. There was a place in my abdomen that was growing spiritually, like a baby that was invisible but getting bigger and stronger each day. The viper waitresses with forked tongues were silenced. They didn't apologise but at least their mouths were slammed shut when they realised I wasn't taking heed of their nonsense any longer and their whispers and silences, on approach, stopped.

On the rare occasions when I did go out with the staff, we would invite anybody and everybody along who wanted to join us and I felt I had to ask the in-house plumber along, after what I'd done to him in the kitchen. It was really busy as per usual and I was in running mode, collecting orders from the customers and taking back dirty dishes. While this was going on, the in-house plumber was underneath the sink and had taken the S-bend off to unblock it. With the used remains of the teapot in hand, I started happily chatting away to the plumber by bending down to look at him under the sink as I poured out the remains of the teapot down the plughole as casual as you like, splattering him full on in the face. He banged his head on the sink on the way up from the shock of the warm tea. I got a fright because I realised I'd just burned and half drowned him. While still holding onto the teapot in the panic, I tried to help him and smacked him with it. It was so true, the guy was wriggling all over the place, the poor soul. Well, I was always told I was stupid but how could I now prove I wasn't? I always wonder how he tells the story. I bet my name has been mud ever since. It just didn't dawn on me that I couldn't use the sink while he was unblocking it. It still makes me laugh to this day, what a terrible thing to do to someone. He got burned, thumped and clunked one after the other, and that was me being nice.

## Chapter Seven

# LONG DARK BLOODY NIGHTS

*e~~~~~~~~~>*

On a later journey home from work, the bus had just got to the National Savings Bank on Barrhead Road, not far from the old Pollok Centre, when the blue lights of an ambulance lit up the sky and I got the familiar punch in my gut. I knew then without a shadow of a doubt that the ambulance was heading to my house. In comparison with the ambulance, the bus seemed to be crawling along. I was devastated as my eyes followed the lights of the ambulance at every turn, even up to where I lived. I willed the driver to hurry up as I peered, heartsick, out of the window. When it got to my stop I was already up on my feet to jump off and run down and round to my house. The front of the house lit with many blue lights from the ambulances and several police cars.

I ran through the police in a daze, as though in a dream, and I had 'no sound'. When I saw the two gigantic clots of blood on the toilet floor I thought my mother had lost her babies. I peered down for a closer look but I could only see the massive clumps of thick congealed blood. As I lifted my eyes I saw the four walls in the bathroom as crimson with blood raining down as though someone had thrown buckets of blood all over them. The ceiling had lumps of congealed blood oozing and forming points that dripped like bloody stalactites until they thickened and could drip no more. In the bath was the deepest red water imaginable, it looked like a bath of blood. The blood was in gallons, it seemed, not pints, there was far too much. In slow motion I turned to see my mother's belly was huge and realised she still carried her babies. My baby sister, where was she? How many people were in our house? Too many. Too many questions filled my head at the same time but the smallest one was 'Why?' That was all I kept saying as I wandered around in a haze of slow motion, 'Why?'

I walked aimlessly between rooms, not knowing why, where to go or what to do, completely shocked, still no sounds. Multitudes of emergency services vehicle lights dazzled my eyes as they lit up the hall. Police in the house, all over, and when I wanted to go by them, I slowly lifted my hand and moved them out of the way and they let me. When I was at my work all I thought about was my family. I worried myself sick, hoping and praying they would be just fine without me, but not this night. I knew it. I knew I had to be at home. God was always right, my family needed me. I still don't know who cleaned the toilet, my mother's not here to confirm and I cannot remember, all I remember is the blood. Far too much blood, huge clumps set like a jelly. I thought no one could possibly lose that amount of blood and live.

My mother told me and the police she had made The Daddy a cup of tea while he took a bath. She kept calling to him that his tea was getting cold and he answered her in his normal casual voice, telling her calmly he was just coming, that he'd be out in a minute. He was cutting his arms and neck, not straight across, but long ways, up and down his arms and veins, which is why there was so much blood loss. It was also harder for the medics to stop the flow of blood because of the way he had cut himself. He never said anything to my mother about what he was doing, it was all in silence, and he was leaving all of us that night. He had intended leaving us before, this time he did, for a short time only. God had other plans, though, and saved his life through the work of the paramedics and surgeons, who fought for him several times as his life ebbed away. The paramedics also saved my mother from being arrested because they witnessed The Daddy say, 'I'm sorry, Emily. I'm sorry', as they quickly left with him to flee to the hospital. The Daddy was sectioned again under the Mental Health Act, until he healed physically, in Glasgow's Leverndale Hospital. Emotionally, he never recovered but, with psychiatric help, he was stabilised and began a new chapter in his life with the birth of his twin boys just weeks later, whom he adored. He had a reason to live now, to look at two helpless baby boys.

My poor mother must have hated her life. I felt I could never leave her to seek my own life and knew I was to stay at home. My mother was forty-one years of age when she fell pregnant with twins, she thought she was going through the change of life but she popped out two boys first. That was a huge shock to everyone, especially me as baby sister was always that, the baby of the family. Pannie was also married by this time and was pregnant too, that's why the siblings were a bit of a shock. The newborn boys were to become uncles when they were just months old. Pannie followed in my mother's footsteps and got married to her sweetheart when she was just sixteen, to get out of the house, she always told us.

After a year or so, the family were doing well, with the twins growing up and my mother finding a bit of a social life with our next-door neighbour, Vi, short for Violet. My mother and Vi were great together and were always laughing at something. It was good to see my mother happy, so good that I thought I'd take off and get a job away for the summer of nineteen eighty and ended up going to a large hotel on the outskirts of Inverness.

I started waitressing and lived in the sort of 'barracks'-type rooms close to the hotel. They were just chalets of single or double rooms within a corridor of gaps held together with steel doorways and laminated partitions, which were gapped and open-aired at various points, where the wind howled violently on a good day. I shared a room with a girl from Lewis. I met newcomers, Pauline and Mandy from down south and Patrisha from Wishaw, who was cheekily called 'Pishy Trishy fae Wishy' by the live-in housekeeper.

The first of the barrack bedrooms was the largest and was the hovel where we would all meet after work in the evening for a get-together, but mostly we would pop into the bar and listen to the band. Iona from reception was the lead singer's girlfriend. The lead singer was hobbling about, I remember, because he had accidentally run a lawnmower over his toes. Ouch! When we weren't in the bar, as I stated, we would be in the hovel with a few others.

Pauline and Mandy occupied the hovel and their family owned a hotel. They were also working as waitresses so they should have known better, but they didn't care. You see, they'd all go out and pick 'magic mushrooms'. I was told they were magic and I just took their word for it. They then put them into the small teapots belonging to the hotel kitchen. Conveniently, they had a portable gas stove burner in the bedroom, where they heated the mushrooms in the teapot and inhaled the contents. That was fine with me, they also smoked 'weed' and 'green', whatever that was. I didn't know then, I just thought the 'green' didn't look very green, and as for the weed? It looked like a squashed beef cube to me. I didn't take any of that stuff but I was never above anybody or snobbish about anybody else's bizarre leisure activities. Pals were pals as far as I was concerned, each to their own. Except when it came to serving breakfast to the hotel guests in the morning, that is. It drove me mad when I couldn't find the small teapots for one or two guests. Of course, I knew where the teapots were and when we did manage to get our hands back on them for the guests, the inside of the teapots were burned and stained by the boiling of the 'magic mushrooms'. No matter how much I tried to scrub the teapots, there were always mushroom designs and stuck mushrooms at the bottom of the pots. It's no wonder everyone was so laid back and cheery at breakfast-time. Except for me, I have to say. I was always up to high doh searching for the small teapots.

I knew God had told me not to go to Inverness but I shrugged

Him off. The intense gnawing away at my soul haunted me daily, even hourly, and I was so sorry for seeking my own will instead of His will. All I did was think about my mother and family and worry about how they were coping without me. I bitterly regretted it in the years ahead. How could I leave my mother, who needed me at home? I thought I was downright selfish and had no peace within me. On a journey back to Glasgow for a weekend, I was disturbed when I saw the amount of weight my mother had lost in my absence. After a long weekend, a bit of catch-up and partying with a few of my friends, I decided I was coming back home to Glasgow to stay, especially as I had met a nice handsome young man by the name of Eddie. I should have stayed at home even then, but I went back to Inverness to collect my worldly goods and put my work's notice in. There were always new staff who arrived on a weekly basis and many didn't stay for more than a couple of weeks, as though they were just there for a holiday.

One of the waitresses greeted me as I bounded into the kitchen for something. 'There's the new guy, Peter,' she said, motioning over with her head, past the steel tables. I looked over to where she was talking about and when I saw him, I felt the most almighty punch in my inner gut from God, the strongest I had ever felt. This Peter was deep in conversation with another man. I immediately knew I didn't like him and took the deep punch as a crystal-clear warning from God to stay away from him.

'Right then,' I said to the waitress and got on with my job. I had been made up to supervisor very quickly and had loads to do. The restaurant manager, Jim, thought he was in with a romantic chance and promoted me but I felt very uncomfortable. I owed him nothing and had to let him down gently but bluntly, which, I have to say, he didn't take too kindly to.

The rejection made him angry, which only confirmed I should leave. Jim stayed in the hotel itself, as did the new guy, Peter, I was informed. There was no reason on earth for me to dislike

Peter, as I'd never met him before in my life and he had a Glaswegian accent like mine, so we could easily have got talking. I was a nice person, even naive and gullible, and would have spoken to anyone without God's intervening warning punch in my abdomen.

At a function we were allowed to attend, we sat up at the back of the ballroom where I could see Peter leaning on the bar chatting away with another guy. I had become strangely afraid when leaving the hovel to get to my own room just a few doors away. I had the awful eerie feeling that someone could jump into the corridor from the outside, because the old barracks had slots of entrances and exits where there were no doors attached and there was only a very dim corridor light, which made the darkness of the hotel grounds almost tangible.

The only other time I saw this Peter was when I hurried into the kitchen to find him warning the chef, 'If you ever talk to me like that again, I'll take your ******* head off your shoulders!' He towered over the chef and maybe my presence stopped the chef from getting knocked out. They both looked in my direction when I entered. Alarmed, I turned quickly and pretending I had forgotten something and shot right back out. I didn't see Peter again, thank God. I don't know who left the hotel first but I thought that was the last time I would clap eyes on him. I have to go forward thirty years or so to finish this chapter off as I don't want to delve too deep into it anyway. *Good God in Govan* has been written to thank and praise God for His love, mercy and grace, for protecting me in times of danger, for speaking to and with me, for taking me away to be with Him and for allowing me to see visions and have dreams, not to belittle or judge another human being of their sin, even The Daddy.

On watching *Crimewatch* one evening, I saw the police reconstruction television programme appealing for the missing years of a murderer by the name of Peter, surname withheld, as the case is still open. It was the same man who was at the hotel in

Inverness and I could have been dead if it were not for God and his loving 'punch'. I would have spoken to the murderer and I too would have seen him as a charmer. The rest would have been history, and another dreadful time for my mother. I also felt it would have been my own fault for disobeying God because I left my mother while she needed me.

God gives me punches as warnings, right inside my stomach, from the inside out. That was the strongest punch God ever gave me and even to this present time in my life he has never warned me as clearly as that day when he did it in the kitchen of the Drumossie Hotel in Inverness. I have so much to be thankful for, even in my sin (missing the mark) God has looked after me and kept me safe.

I had taken some photographs while I was working at the hotel. One was of a young girl by the name of Elaine, who came from Culloden. Cars that were parked in front of the hotel could not be traced by their number plates for reasons I don't know and people who worked at the hotel denied it, perhaps because they were on benefits. End of that story.

I arrived back in Glasgow to stay, and enjoyed being off work for a few weeks before going to the Albany Hotel, where I met Jane, a waitress I became friendly with. There was no solid romantic hero in my life. I really did like Eddie, but unfortunately Eddie liked everyone and I saw straight through him when I watched him play with the button on my cousin's blouse. He was known as 'Fast Eddie' for reasons I never found out, except he was rather fast when he spotted a pretty face. He smoked dope, or was it me who was dopey about him? I had met up with him on the weekend break from Inverness and didn't see him until many months later. We bumped into each other a few times. Sometimes my heart skipped a beat, at others, confused, I bowed my head and bolted. I loathed cheats and didn't trust men at all.

I got fed up with the long disco nights and early mornings as we waited for a taxi outside Central Station in the rain and

I thought, 'There has got to be more to life than this.' I really didn't enjoy anywhere with ridiculously loud music. Trying to hold a conversation where communication was blasted by hundreds of decibels was impossible. Smiling away with a drink in the hand and pretending to hear what the other person had said was intolerable. Then there was the sore feet, because we always had to have new clothes and shoes for the weekend and, of course, the shoes or sandals would nip and hurt. I would always end up with a 'howler', as my cousin stated, 'I don't fancy yours much.' I didn't fancy hers much either but did she have to run away and leave me with her latest nip's awful pal?

I went home with a dog one night, or I should say, in the wee small hours of the morning. I mean a real dog by the way, not a man. I had gone to the flat of a guy my cousin fancied and I was left sitting alone in the lounge with his friend. We had nothing in common as usual and I wanted to go home. He kindly walked me out so I could jump in a taxi and it was then that I saw a dog lying on the road, which had been hit by a vehicle and was in desperate need of help. I waved a taxi down, dragged the dog into it and took it home. I got me a 'lumber' after all. The dog was taken care of by People's Dispensary of Sick Animals and was fine.

On a visit to the doctor's for my usual monthly chest examination, the doctor noticed I had lost a lot of weight. I told him I was fine because I was just dieting again, but now I was eating normally. He said I was a little underweight and asked how long I had been dieting for. The truth was, my diet was always appalling but sometimes I would go overboard and eat very little for months on end, but I would usually sort myself out when I got too hungry. The doctor asked me about my menstrual cycle and I casually informed him I didn't have one. I hadn't ovulated for a few years and I didn't care because it wasn't important to me. The doctor asked me if I could be pregnant and I laughed and replied in all honesty, 'No, I haven't done anything to get pregnant.' It was a true statement, as far as I was concerned, my last short romance with Eddie had been six months previous and there was no other on the scene.

He referred me to a well-woman clinic to find out why my cycle wasn't flowing as it should but I knew it was because I wasn't eating properly. I read the magazines about dieting and knew the calorific value in everything. I had the light downy hair on my face just below my cheek-bones known as lanugo and I knew I had amenorrhoea but I certainly wasn't telling my doctor anything he didn't need to know where my relationship with food was concerned. I had the most amazing profesional and personal doctor, but I still wouldn't open up to him. He made me smile by asking things like 'What's up with you now?'

I was sent on to the Royal Samaritan Hospital for Women, on the south side of Glasgow for an examination, as they were the experts in gynaecology. I couldn't be bothered with all the questions I thought they might ask me about food, and nearly didn't attend, believing there was nothing wrong with me. I did turn up for my appointment, though, and the first thing they did as routine was a pregnancy test. I didn't give the pregnancy test a second thought as I waited for the next phase of any examination. I was absolutely stunned when I was informed I was pregnant, so stunned I told the nurse it wasn't true. 'It's not my result,' I told her, it's someone else's, and I honestly believed what I was telling the professionals. She informed me that not only was I indeed pregnant, I was over six months gone and in ten weeks I was going to have a baby. She gave me a piece of paper for my doctor but I can't even remember what it stated. It was probably the due delivery date or something.

I walked out of that hospital in heightened shock, in a state of total disbelief, and walked over wet cement. I ate little enough to sustain myself, how could a baby be fed? I wondered.

There was a worker in a boiler suit on his knees, who had part cordoned off an area of pavement and rolled a design into the cement with a spiked roller. It was only when I realised I was splashing through his wet cement that I looked down to see the forlorn look of dismay on his face as he sat up straight. My face must have been a picture too because he didn't say a single word.

A baby? I cannot possibly be having a baby, I thought, as I ran my hand over my perfectly flat stomach and tiny waist but it was easy for me to cast my mind back to the weekend of partying, because there was no other male involved. From a stick insect, I blew up like a balloon overnight as I let go of all dieting, now I had a good reason to eat properly.

Fast forward, my sibling twins were now about two years old when I was back at work, at the Albany Hotel. Across the road, looking out of the huge windows of the Carvery, we could see the landscape of the red-light district. I met new friends at the hotel, one of them a lady from Malaysia, whose name was Lita. She lived quite close to me and we would walk to our respective buses together via Central Station. I was heavily pregnant with my first child by then and waddled like a duck on ice. Little Lita, at four foot something, and I would be walking home by the red-light district and we'd get stopped every night and asked, 'How much?' What a sight we must have looked together, laughing and trying to run for our buses.

The bus would take forever, as drunks scattered their change all over the floor, 'singing like a Linty', and holding the queue up. If I got on the bus too late, it would be full of revellers and comedians going to the dancing at the Plaza Ballroom from the pubs, and I'd sit there staring out of the window and wondering why nobody sat beside me. On the other hand, if I got on the bus too early, it would be empty with not a soul in the downstairs area except for me, tired and weary and exhausted at times from the long hard day's work. So who do you suppose would get on the bus while I had my eyes closed and minding my own business? The city drunk with a twinkle in his eye and a song in his heart. Every seat was empty except for mine and the bus driver's. The drunk would get on the bus and 'clock' me. He would then stagger from side to side with his finger pointed at me, serenading me with alcohol breath and slobber. Here we go, I'd think, and sure enough, even with every seat empty, he'd plank himself right beside me, telling me how gorgeous I was, as though I was one of his family or he'd known me all of my life. It never failed, if the bus was packed, nobody would sit beside me and if it was empty, I'd get a friend. In retrospect, he was just an all-singing, all-dancing, happy drunk. I was just too tired to join in, there were worse kinds of people in Glasgow.

All was well as far as life was going, until I got off the bus after work late one night and saw three young men sitting on the wall at the school railings of St Robert's Primary School. I was given another strong punch by God and knew I was in danger. They were sitting almost opposite my house, just a little further up. I didn't know them. I might have known of them in hearing their names but I had never had any dealings with them and I certainly couldn't put a face to a name. I knew they were up to no good, though, by sitting in wait with nothing better to do. It's not fair to judge people but on this occasion the revelation punch came from God. I could see their heads moving from side to side, so I knew they were talking to each other and watched them lift their heads up for a look. I put my head down and tried to pretend I wasn't interested but at the same time my eyes darted around me in fear, trying to quickly think of what I could do in this emergency. The orange street lights were on and the area was quite dull. The row of shops to my right-hand side were closed, as it was about ten forty-five at night. As I passed the gates of the houses to the left, I wondered frantically where I could run for help. I had to pray quickly. I needed God's help right there and then, so I prayed under my breath, 'God, keep them on the wall until I get past.' I begged God, over and over, 'Keep them on the wall', as I had to walk straight towards the guys to get into my house. My legs became so weak with fear I thought they were going to buckle under me and give me away. 'Keep them on the wall, Lord, keep them on the wall,' I groaned, pleaded, begged, demanded and commanded. I didn't need to be a rocket scientist to know I couldn't fight them off, and there was nobody to help me. I was shattered, physically and emotionally, and totally defenceless. It was so hard to act casual when my legs and heart were having convulsions within me and my only help was God. I kept walking towards them and got so close I could easily speak to them quietly if I wanted to. They were not interested in small talk, though. I looked at them square on, with only God on my mind and in my heart and when I finally got to the corner, all they had to do was jump off the wall onto the pavement, 'Keep them on the wall, God, I muttered, keep them on the wall.' I felt I forced God with my will to keep them on that wall. As soon as I had to turn the corner, right in front of the guys, I quickly turned and ran, screaming at the top of my voice, 'DAD!', as the guys jumped off the wall to grab me, running like lions after prey, and I've never ran so fast in all of my life.

Thank God our steel gate was open, because I belted through and slammed it backwards to give me a chance to escape their clutches. As I practically crashed through our front door, which was unlocked, the guys stopped and one shouted, 'Ha ha, we wurny chaisin' you anyhow!' Of course they weren't. I just imagined God had punched me deep in my abdomen and warned me I was in danger of being attacked. I imagined the guys ran after me, I even imagined I had a daddy who could fight and defend me to the end. The Daddy was too sick to swat a fly but they didn't know that. It was the Heavenly Father who saved me.

That is not the end of this testimony either. When I told my younger sister Pannie I was writing a book, I told her it was about God, Jesus, The Holy Spirit, and the Angels I had seen. I told her I was writing stories about the times God had saved me from danger, such as the time I got off the bus and came face to face with the three guys who were going to attack me.

Pannie's eyes widened with horror as she turned ashen-white and asked me who the guys were. I told her I didn't know and testified how I had to pray for my life as I knew without a shadow of a doubt I was going to be attacked.

It turned out her best friend was gang-raped by the guys, who roamed around the area where we lived in ghastly Priesthill. It was horrendous, I worked day and night and didn't know who was hanging about. Glue sniffers, one with a newborn baby in a pram had a can of glue at the baby's pillow. Sniffing glue and hairspray were the cheap demon drug of the day then. That was the first time I heard about the gang-rape incident, as it was never reported to the police. I was deeply shocked and truly didn't know this story. I did know I was in for the beating of my life, though, perhaps brutal rape was on their minds, I don't know. How horrific. They know who they are and I deeply rebuke them, even in their future lives.

Pannie's friend and I tried on clothes and I gave her some of mine, some to borrow and others to keep. We chatted away but I never knew. I remember thinking she looked sad when were talking one day but I had no idea she'd been through that horrific ordeal. I remember seeing her hurt, sad expressions and sensed something was wrong but didn't know what or why. I now wish she had felt she could open up to me and talk about it, that hurt too. What kind of a friend was I to her when she did not have the confidence to share her nightmare with me? I still bow my head in shame and wish I could have reversed the clock for her to keep her safe, the way God keeps me safe. Priesthill was an awful place to be alone in at any time, full of thugs, glue-sniffers and housebreakers but it was the same in every area that ended in Hill. Priesthill, Blackhill, Nitshill, Cranhill, Govanhill, and so on.

Well, there you are family and friends, there's the reason why I loathe red sauce. The night I saw the blood crying from the bathroom walls and ceiling left a permanent reminder of The Daddy. Blood, red sauce, brown sauce (at the dinner table), tears in food as a little girl, it's all the same to me. I'm not damaged now but I was for years. Now maybe some of you will stop joking and confronting me with a bottle of the stuff. I don't fear it, I don't have a phobia, I just don't like it. Stop chasing me around and shaking bottles, it's gross. Stop sticking it in front of my nose, honestly, stop asking me if I would taste it for a million pounds because one day I might say 'Yes'. I don't like any kind of sauce and I don't want to like it. What does it matter when the world is destined for fire? When people are destined for Hell? My loathing of sauce isn't going to change anything. It wasn't only the sauce I didn't like, it was the lumps. Huge lumps of blood on the toilet floor, oozing from the ceiling. It is over, finished . . . and I still don't like sauce, deal with it, I won't perish through lack of 'Bloody' sauce!

It took me more than thirty years to realise I was deeply affected by the attempted suicide that lonely night in the bathroom. I often dreamt my teeth had broken and fallen out and my mouth was filled with blood, and woke up because I wouldn't swallow, only to find my mouth full of saliva. The dreams were truly awful, I dreamt my hair was soaking from being in the bath, to find it was actually soaking with sweat. Some of us had dreadful nightmares for years. I also developed a fear of the bath in my dreams, which became a reality when awake. I always dreamt that when I stepped into a bath the ceramics would shatter into shards, which gashed my legs into deep pieces, spewing blood from my veins as it quickly turned the clear bath water the deepest red. So in the waking hours I was afraid to get into a bath, it was fine once I actually got in and sat down quickly but, psychologically, I hadn't related the nightmares to the reality of doing so. I was also afraid of standing in a shower that was over a bath. A wet room or boxed-in shower on its own was fine, so I couldn't understand what was wrong with me. It was only when I was speaking to a Christian friend from Elim over a coffee one day that I got the revelation of the dreams and put the incident away forever. I hadn't realised the fear of the bath I dreamt about lingered because of the attempted suicide. The Daddy was still alive and the bad dreams and nightmares had become daymares with no relief day or night.

There were terrible hard times for the other siblings too and there was no counselling. All of the siblings except for the twins (who weren't born) are so deeply and emotionally traumatised that I'm not allowed to mention their names in this book. We haven't spoken of our childhood. One morning, even years later, my mother told me the police and CID were at our house in the middle of the night, dozens of them surrounded the house.

In terror, our younger brother, Addie, ran all the way round to my aunt's at three o'clock in the morning in his underpants and bare feet, terrified, and battered her door to tell her The Daddy had chopped us up and hung us from the radiators. It wasn't true but my aunt thought it was obviously and called the police immediately. I, being heavily pregnant at the time, slept soundly as the police shone their torches all around to make sure we were safe. It was a terrible time emotionally for all of us. It was no wonder my mother took to drinking heavily after the twins were born. That was me now a babysitter to two toddlers who were the young uncles of my newborn child too.

Dark days became long dark nights, even in the summer, as I listened out for The Daddy, who was up, not doing anything but going to the toilet or lighting up his tobacco. I never knew what to listen out for. Movement meant he was alive. He was awake, alone with his thoughts, and I was awake, alone with my thoughts, listening out for him, praying for him. He needed to be saved from himself and we needed to keep him safe. All the while, getting on with life, school, shopping, birthdays, Christmases, going to work, and all else life throws at you. The constant fear of never knowing when the suicide monster was visiting The Daddy. He was quiet, he said nothing all day, never an inkling about what he was going to do or what he was thinking. I would lie in bed listening, in silence, listening for nothing, listening for what might happen. Listening, Listening for what?, or who?, listening for the suicide monster, listening for the evil which visited me every night before I went to sleep, listening in case death was visiting. Wondering what was going to happen next, alarmed, fearful, unhappy, sobbing, panicking, afraid to sleep in case . . . shh.

## Chapter Eight

# ALL WORK AND NO PLAY

⸏⸏⸏

When I returned to the Albany after the birth of my gorgeous baby boy, I met up with Jane, who was the same age as me. We bonded immediately as though we had known each other for years. Jane had the most amazing long hair, blondish, with thick soft natural curls. Her skin was smooth, pale and flawless, she was tall and thin but very dipsy, or as we say in Glasgow, pure Dolly, as in Dolly Dimple (simple). She wasn't simple, though, she just had a purity about her that was intriguing, but sometimes when you spoke to her she would just stand there staring with a smile. The lights were on but no one was in there, seriously, she was totally vacant at times. Her smile and innocence drew you in and I couldn't help feeling she was vulnerable. She was another Farrah Fawcett, drop-dead gorgeous, but she didn't know it, realise it or play on it. Her Angel-like purity had an amazing effect on everyone. Not much make-up sense, though. Her eyes were always caked with light blue eye shadow and her lipstick was too dark for her complexion. She didn't need any make-up, it just made her look silly, and she didn't need any help in that department. Who needs me for a friend? I'll tell you the truth, no problem. Could I be describing myself here? Is that the way The Daddy saw me? Is that why Jane and I bonded so well, two peas in a pod? I wish I had her hair.

The trouble with Jane was that she was a complete magnet for the opposite sex despite being married with two beautiful little girls. She didn't have the sense, like me, to tell men where to get off. She would flap her eyelashes and she drove me mad when she told me who smiled at her next as she perceived it as an invitation, so terrible problems arose at work when the restaurant manager, who was also married to a lovely nurse apparently, showered Jane with affection. If ever anyone wanted his cake, eat it, and still have it, it was him. The Dolly part of Jane meant she just lapped it up like a happy little puppy. I felt fiercely protective of her, as she had previously confided in me that she was unhappy in her marriage, and I felt she was far too easily led. The restaurant manager loathed the fact I was getting in the way of his worldly desires because I begged Jane not to go and meet him as he asked, 'What benefit would that do?' I asked her. I pleaded with her but she said she was only going to talk with him. From then on I wasn't informed of any secret liaison, as I didn't agree with it, and I didn't ask. I valued our friendship and it wasn't my place to become her judge. Nevertheless, I'd still give her my tuppenceworth and tried to steer her in the right direction.

I've had my share of proposals and not all of them for marriage, I can tell you. I always had this notion that some guy would come up and just straight out ask me to marry him, then I spoiled it when it happened in the restaurant of the huge department store. He walked up to me and asked me the straight simple question without even knowing me, we hadn't even spoken previously. 'Will you marry me?' he asked, right out of the blue. I stammered, 'No, I can't because . . .' He put his finger on my lips and said, 'No excuses, just yes or no?' I looked at him, embarrassed and replied, 'No.' 'That's fine,' he said. 'That's all I wanted to know.' It's really weird how your imagination of thoughts and fears come to pass.

Okay, so, as usual, I didn't dislike the restaurant manager, I just didn't respect him. He made such a great big fat pompous fuss when his priest came to dine that it annoyed me. Treating him like a king, royalty, and it made me mad because he was a hypocrite. I also knew my friend Jane well, she always confided in me and shared her fears and concerns, especially when she

took an overdose of medication because she couldn't cope with
the events in her life, her husband's attitude, and some other
incidents that overwhelmed her. She was a bit like myself in
many ways, she didn't get the respect she deserved and felt like
a 'no one'. The last thing she needed was this manager character
messing her around but I felt powerless to stop it. I was a friend,
an ear, a help, a comforter, a confidante, but despite all that I
nearly lost her one day when one of the trainee managers told
her, 'Oh, just keep taking the tablets,' quite sarcastically when
she didn't understand what he was asking her to do in the way
of a task. She blew up and I had some job telling her that I
had never told a soul about her overdose, it was just a figure of
speech the trainee manager was using. I then pulled the young
manager up later and told him to watch his mouth. He didn't
know she had taken an overdose and had innocently put his
foot in it. That was the only reason I had to tell him and explain
the fragile situation, but Jane thought I was gossiping about her
and I had to try and keep her together. I didn't want to lose
her.

Everyone finds out your sleazy sneaky secrets one day, for
sure, but they weren't going to find them out from me, even
although I didn't approve. The whole hotel knew about the affair,
they weren't blind. Back then there were three ways of communication: telephone, telegram and tell-a-woman. Women aren't
blind, they could see the doey eyes of Jane as she watched the
manager's every move, the little whispers, the not-so-secret touch
by way of the hand on the shoulder when having a word, his
cheeky subtle winks and bashful smiles.

Our relationships with the manager had become unworkable
and unprofessional because of his lust. There are many times
I've heard waitresses say, 'Oh I could write a book,' and so they
could, here's the one I've done, though it's not about the life
of a waitress. I'm sure one day a waitress will put pen to paper
when she thinks there is a book inside of her and that book
will be a cracker. I would read it, even add to it by way of

diverse stories. So much laughter, tears, horrors, revelations and scandals. Oh yes, between us we've got a hit there. With a reflection on the lives of the staff, customers, clients and suppliers, there could even be a soap opera better that what's showing on television these days, with every soap copying each other. That was why we were always warned never to discuss what we saw or heard while we were going about our business. Not because of client confidentiality, but because of the sin and debauchery that hung around hotels, often exposed and heightened by drugs and alcohol.

The drug used in the hotel was 'speed' and was provided by one of the chefs for ten pounds per small bag. The carvery waitresses needed it in order to keep up with their work of running to and fro quickly as it was an 'eat it and beat it' dining experience. The turnaround for each sitting was forty-five minutes and all had to be fed and watered well within this time limit. The hangers-on were politely moved to the lounge to finish whatever their tipple was.

At the hotel with us worked an old waitress, who could run like a cheetah, when she wasn't drunk, that is. Most times she would zoom in to work quite tipsy, but the problem was, she would also drink the leftovers from the bottles of wine, and the actual glasses with the dregs left by customers got necked too. Her work station was a large tiled area for the waitresses to go and work behind. Only two waitresses could use this space and it was a well-known fact she was one of them. This was where she lined up all of the glasses of whisky, brandy, vodka, wine and everything else with even a hint of alcohol, such as a Rum Baba or a sherry trifle dessert. In the end she would pour the already mixed spirits into one glass and down the lot. Woe unto any of us who took away leftover alcohol to be dumped in the kitchen, regardless of whether they came from her customers or ours. As the night went on we had to all muck in and help her to do her tables, sending her down to the toilet and shower area to sober up so she didn't get fired.

The waitresses were treasures. Many an irate and ungrateful manager would shout, 'You can get waitresses off the street.' 'That's true,' one waitress shouted back. 'You can also get prostitutes off the street.' That would clamp the managers up because we knew the score. We knew all too well, they would come into the hotel with their torn tights and sit and have dinner with their business clients. The waitresses had an answer for everything and everyone and they weren't afraid to shove back when pushed. '. . . And their manners are a hell of a lot better than that of certain managers,' one went on to say.

I used to feel heart-sorry for the street girls, as they were plied with alcohol, and I wanted to pull them out of their seats, hug them and tell them not to do it. The businessmen disgusted me, then there was the wife back at home who didn't know. Wedding ring missing? We had banter with the ladies of the night quite often as we finished work and headed home, sometimes just saying, 'Good night,' as we passed. The wedding ring, which was usually taken off and left in the room by the punter, was taken as a trophy and a punishment for cheating on the ladies left behind at home, the night girls told us.

Another lively waitress, who joined us in the evening was Ivy from Pollok, she got sacked for stealing small pots of preserves. Who told on her?, I wondered. We never got searched. She always had the longest nails in Glasgow, ridiculously long for a waitress. She told us she had got on the bus one day and proceeded to give the bus driver her fare, when one of her false nails fell off into the bus driver's hand and she stabbed him with her other nails trying to get it back. We were dismayed we weren't going to see her again, her banter was great. It was fine to take goods home, so long as the customer and manager signed them off. I was given a beautiful gold and silver striped watch from a customer, which I wore for many years.

A new girl from Canada, who was staying in Glasgow with her policeman boyfriend, joined us. She laughed at my name and decided it was easier to call me Easter, so that's what I was called, says she, always smiling and laughing. It was lovely to hear she came from Canada and loved Scotland and I always wonder how people from the past are getting on.

I'm reminded of the three Americans I served when I was very heavily pregnant. I couldn't carry so much on the tray with my bump and had to do extra journeys, which tired me out. The Americans, two males and one female, never looked at me once. It was in the Carvery, so they basically served themselves. I only got their starters, drink orders, cleared away their plates and served them dessert. They weren't rude, they just totally ignored me, not a hello, good evening, thank you, goodbye, nothing. Even when I said goodnight as they left, they didn't smile or respond. On clearing away their plates I was stunned to find a ten-pound note under one of the plates. On the other hand, you could bend over backwards and go far beyond the call of duty for customers, give them more dessert than they were entitled to because they asked, and then get zilch, or even a complaint, for your efforts.

On the upper level, I met a tiny little girl by the name of Leanna, that's what I'm calling my little famous songster chicken. She sat there on her own while her manager, chaperone or whoever he was, piled up his plate at the Carvery. As I had no other customers, I went over and spoke to the tiny songbird. She wore a small chiffon cream-coloured dress and I noticed her underskirt was falling down and off her. We had a few private words and I asked her if she was all right, to which she meekly smiled and replied, 'Yes.' I lifted my eyes over to the small bald overweight man who was with her and wrinkled my nose cheekily, which made her laugh. It was just one of those precious moments in a lifetime when you have a fleeting rapport with another person. She was everyone's little darling when she found fame and opportunity knocked on her door. I often recall her sweet face and smile and she reminded me that no one knows you, they think they know you but we know nothing about each other. We don't know each other's thoughts, heartaches, tears on pillows, fears, nothing, we really don't know anything about anyone. Anyway, we had an amazing one-to-one in a brief moment of time, which has lasted forever, and we hardly even spoke. She left me with a smile, I hope she remembered my wrinkled-up nose and smiled too.

I wanted the older man to stay away so we could have a longer chat, as I felt we connected, me in an older sister sort of way but it didn't happen. I thought about our meeting for years and wished we could have had that deeper chat. Sleekit Annie R had befriended her too and eventually stole our little songbird away from Earth and deprived us all of her music. I was deeply saddened and thought of her often as lonely. She needed me and I needed her. I needed and wanted to help her because I understood her, but she was gone all too soon.

I met many famous people through my work but I never once asked for an autograph, they were just people at the end of the day, like me. There were silly stories, like taking pillow cases home and framing hair strands left on them. The stars weren't big in my life, even when they were hugely famous. I hadn't the time or will for partying with anyone. I just wanted to do my job and get back home to make sure my family were safe. No one could compare to Jesus. He was/is my true star and I couldn't see past Him. I had an Out of Body Experience, had seen Heaven and had been out to play with Jesus. There is none higher than Him. There is not one famous person in this world who can turn my head, because I know we are all the same. We all have to give an account for our talents and not hide them. Some people I know who are talented are too afraid to develop and share their talents. My little Leanna was hugely talented but she flew away to Heaven and I never got that wish to talk to her again. That's another long-playing record I've kept to this day, what a truly fabulous little star.

We weren't allowed to ask private questions of our customers or comment on apparel, we were just there to do what was expected of us, so I was in turmoil one evening when a businessman who always came in during the day with his friend, invited me to have a drink after work one evening. He was moving out of the Carvery and into the lounge after his evening meal, with his multitudes of clubbers and friends who had just dined with him. He had a girlfriend who was American and he always proudly boasted he brought her back to Scotland but his friend was single and it was him who gave me the gold and silver watch, after much protesting. They were our 'Ain folk', high flyers, and spent a small fortune every day. One of them owned the disco (so he said) on the River Clyde waterfront close to the statue of Saint Enoch. Saint Enoch was a woman by the way, I always thought Saint Enoch was a man, for some strange reason, obviously because no one enlightened me on that fact, so I'm telling you, in case you thought the same. We could have a bit of banter with the customers in the afternoons. As long as we were making wine and spirit sales we were fine. Money talks, as they say. There was no fraternising whatsoever, though, says the married restaurant manager who was doing a sneaky with Jane. This customer wanted, demanded and commanded I be allowed to join them after work one evening and there were chauffeurs to take us home regardless of whether we drank or not. I kept saying I couldn't, not just because I didn't want to but because it wasn't allowed by the hotel bosses and restaurant manager. I got out of the overnight trip by way of his helicopter because my lovely friend and next-door neighbour Kathleen, wouldn't go. At one point I was up for it but I'm glad Kathleen had her head screwed on and declined the offer.

The business client argued profusely that I be allowed to accompany his crowd after a huge sitting where much food was eaten and much more alcohol consumed. He bought wine and champagne at astronomical prices and that was his reason for demanding I be allowed to join the company. I didn't know where to look. The restaurant manager was absolutely furious but when the businessman snapped his fingers and reminded him how much money he spent at the establishment, the manager had no choice but to back down. All I could do was stand there and shrug my shoulders with an 'It's not up to me' attitude. I got one over on the manager but it wasn't my intention. I had no interest in going to flash parties because I worked long and hard, and I was always too tired by the time I got home, given that there would be loads of duties to carry out there too. I just watched with humility as the manager was brought down a peg or two for putting me down and giving me more work, while presenting Jane with bottles of wine each week for the highest percentage of wine sales.

Jane only worked at night and the afternoon guests didn't drink as much as the evening ones, as they were usually in with clients. I pointed this out at a staff meeting, much to the restaurant manager's annoyance, where his face turned bright red when I announced he always gives the weekly wine prize to Jane, yet she did the fewest hours. He didn't look too comfortable beside the other managers when I told him the percentage factor wasn't working for us as a team and the full time staff were penalised. There were other tasks to do during the day, such as cleaning and replenishing, whereas the staff at night walked in with everything sorted for them and this was a bit of a slap in the face to the full-time staff. The presentation of the weekly wine bottle prize was duly stopped. No love lost there then, except that Jane left the hotel due to difficulties at home. It wasn't long after her that I left too but I sure missed Jane and had no way of contacting her. There were no mobile phones, Facebook or other social media sources to keep in touch as we have now and we drifted apart until God brought us back together years later.

## Chapter Nine

# GOD MEETS ME IN THE TOWN

I moved into my own flat and thought it would be great to be able to leave my shampoo and products down and be able to find them where I left them. Everything I owned was used, moved or taken. That was the norm in the house with youngsters and teenagers. I could clear my own dishes away and not return to find the kitchen like a bombsite, or the toilet looking as though the whole street used it. I got into decorating the flat the way we wanted it and little Christopher had his own bedroom. Having said that, I had my younger siblings and nephews who stayed over and it often resembled a children's nursery with sheets draped over furniture to make tents and dens with chairs.

As I reported earlier, my hearing had become much more acute after my Out of Body Experience and I heard all sorts of sounds that I hadn't been aware of before, such as music, voices (talking), bells, ships' horns, bees, wasps, and various sounds I couldn't understand. It would be so easy to say, 'Ah, but your dad was schizophrenic and he heard voices that weren't there, yet he heard them.' I certainly wasn't schizophrenic and hadn't heard the sounds before my Out of Body Experience.

Scientists say that people who had a Near Death or Out of Body Experience were ill and the images they saw of Heaven were a figment of their imagination because 'their brain was dying'. My brain didn't die and I was not ill. 'They were unconscious,' they say. I was fully conscious and standing up when I noticed Lochgilphead's front grass become greener, I was perfectly wide awake and had just had my eyes tested and they were perfect, 20/20 vision. I've heard all of the scientific reasons for saying people did not see or go to Heaven. 'It's the last gasp of the dying brain as blood flow slows before the heart simply stops beating'.'Oxygen levels fall and the brain fires off one last electrical impulse,' they say.

I will admit I don't believe a certain lady who says there is no Hell. Satan will be thrown into it in due course. I wasn't shown Hell but I was also taken out of my body to stand at the Great White Throne, where I saw the very God himself sitting on His throne to my right hand. He lifted me up so I could watch my life review. It's true no one can see God and live, that's why God took me out of my body while it rested in bed. I repeat, I was not unwell, I was standing up, looking down on the grass for the longest time, then looking out to crystal-clear Heaven. My body did slowly start slumping to the ground as my Spirit was leaving because the body, by itself, would have had no life in it.

We are a SPIRIT, which is alive, we have a SOUL (mind, will and emotions) and we live in a BODY. When the SPIRIT leaves the body, the SOUL (mind, will and emotions) has to go with it. It blows me away when intelligent adults will not humble themselves and speak to The Lord God Almighty. Why not? Are they afraid? Something to hide? Like Adam and Eve in the beautiful garden, hiding because they had sinned and found they were naked, which didn't upset them beforehand. God loves us so deeply and He wants us to have that relationship again but we must choose.

There was a story in Glasgow about a wee boy who told the bus driver and all the gaffers to 'just let the tyres down on the bus' when it got stuck under a bridge. The inspectors stood around scratching their heads while the wee boy was pulling on their jackets. They ignored him, treating him as a pest, until one finally took notice of him, even if just to get rid of him. They walked around the bus and wondered, could it be true, could it happen? Then they tried it and it worked. One bus was free because a little voice in the wilderness wouldn't give in. The moral of this story is the same, God always using the little nobodies on earth to tell you the true stories and there's hardly one person taking the information on board.

Transistor radios were the sound system of the day when I was born, known to all as the 'tranny', much more modern than the cumbersome radiogram, which couldn't be taken outside to hold up to your ears. Our tranny usually took pride of place at the end of the mantlepiece above the roaring coal fire and the antique wooden clock with its wind-up happy face always sat in the centre of the mantle with the key tucked in behind it.

Pannie had her own tranny, which had a built in tape recorder, a real modern up-to-date piece of technical electrical equipment, which could work off the mains switch or battery. I laugh out loud when I think of the technology we have today in comparison. It was in the early seventies and without fail, on a Sunday, Pannie would record the top twenty pop music from her transistor radio straight onto her cassette tape recorder so she could listen to it all week. I thought she was the 'cool chick' of the family back then because she knew what was in the pop charts and could sing all of the songs, she knew much more about pop music than I did because I wasn't particularly interested in that type of music. If I liked a song I'd buy it on a 45 rpm single and play it to death on the record player.

I was just a Donny fan, others at Lochgilphead High School preferred David Cassidy and some liked Rod Stewart. Our mother told everyone she did not remember what colour my bedroom carpet was because she hadn't seen it for ages, it was strewn with Donny Osmond long-playing records, LPs for short. She was never allowed to move them, I knew exactly where I had put them and I would do it myself, not on the day she requested, of course, because I was still using them. This scattered teenage filing system worked fine for me. It was the same with my wallpaper, every single square millimetre was accounted for with a poster or article about Donny Osmond and his other family members. I was going to marry Donny Osmond, along with millions of other fans, I was the one. I even imagined I would become a Mormon too because I loved Donny so much, but Jesus had other plans. How I was going to find Donny was a problem I needn't have concerned myself about . . . yeah, and I still have a few of his old long-playing records too.

The first single I bought which was not a Donny Osmond one was 'Hello Summertime'. The record player was my favourite mode of playing tunes before I got up to date with the cassette recorder. Cassette tapes were much smaller than the huge fat eight-tracks which went into the car stereo. Along with old crooners, I heard the Morse code a lot on the tranny. It could be heard easily, especially if it was in between stations. I also heard it on the car radio a lot as a child so I was well aware of the sounds. DOT DOT DASH DASH DOT: I hadn't a clue what it meant, I just knew it to hear. It didn't bother me in the least, as a matter of a fact I quite liked it at first. I always tried to guess what the communication was. 'That's it, you lot, off to bed early tonight with no tea. Esther can stay up late with toffee ice-cream and cream soda' to the beat sounds. My little imagination could run amok with these secret messages, giving me my heart's desires for my own amusement. From the age of about six years old it was normal and easy to hear the Morse code sounds, as they would often interrupt the airways as I heard them in Glasgow in the early nineteen sixties. I heard them clearly in the seventies too as we travelled from Glasgow to Argyll, where we lived in quite close proximity to a huge pylon. Whether that had something to do with picking up the Morse code I don't know but I'd mostly only hear it through the transistor or radio and in the car.

I could walk into the space where I could hear the Morse code with my natural ears and walk out again. If it was in the car I could get the car radio turned off, it wasn't a problem then. It became a dreadful debilitating problem after my Out of Body Experience, when I noticed I was picking up the Morse code in my head. Again, it was fine for a few years but when I moved into the flat on the top of a valley, I could hear it constantly.

There were pylons everywhere beneath and around me but again, I didn't know if they were the cause of the problem. Throughout the day, when I was at work away from the house, I was fine but the moment I went home I could hear the sounds of DOT and DASH at all times. When I went to bed it was so much worse, desperately loud and clear. The more tired or exhausted I was, the louder it would sound, like a continuous beating drum in stereo between both ears. It never let up as I tried to sleep.

My hearing was ultrasensitive but I felt as though my brain was a transmitter or transformer, picking up the Morse code. I then wished I knew all about the Morse code, so I could tap out the messages I was receiving to prove I was getting them, to find out what they meant. Like a constant dripping tap, I was tortured for six and a half years. I had a nervous breakdown one night and pulled every single electrical device plug from its socket, including the fridge and freezer. I couldn't take it any more. When I was satisfied there was no power going through any wires in the house I threw myself back into bed, weeping, but I still heard the DOT DOT DASH DOT DOT DASH DOT and I had no idea on how to get it to stop. Who could I tell?

I eventually sat in the chair opposite my doctor and looked at him, stalling, because I felt so stupid, I couldn't find the right words to say and I ended up blurting out, 'I hear the Morse code all the time, especially at night, and it's driving me crazy.'

'I can't take it any more,' I told him. Naturally, with my embarrassment and him not knowing what to make of my statement, there was a long awkward pause. It sounded like such a weird statement to make right out of the blue. Nothing more was said by either of us and, when he changed the subject, I was quite relieved. He was the first person I had ever told. If you can't confide in your doctor, then who can you talk to? Every other person would think you were totally crazy, mentally defective, or perhaps schizophrenic, like The Daddy. I wasn't crazy, only mad because the noise of the Morse code was doing my head in.

There were other sounds too but they weren't intrusive or didn't last as long as the six and a half years I had to endure every night with the Morse code. Later on I was picturing the strange look on my doctor's face when I told him I heard the Morse code and realised I was totally alone with this huge problem. I'm glad I can't see your faces as you read this. What a bizarre thing to have to share but surely I'm not the only person in the whole wide world who picks up or receives airwave sounds after an Out of Body Experience. I can't be the only person in the world to have heard the Morse code without an external solid device. I am unique, I know, but not that unique! I only want one other person to tell me that they do too. Someone else, somewhere, must know what I'm going on about here. I don't work in any military or army and I don't know how to use the Morse code or decipher it. It caused me nothing but grief and sleepless nights for far too long and it became a very destructive enemy.

On the very first night I moved house away from the top of the valley, I cried when I lay down to sleep, 'I can't hear the Morse code any more!' That was my first pure night's sleep without the dotting and dashing pounding between my eardrums, so I figured out that the area where the last house was situated (on top of the valley) was the problem.

It wasn't me going crazy, I could pick up the Morse code when I lived in the house at the top of the valley but not in the house at the bottom of the valley. How could that happen? I don't normally use the word 'hate' but I hated the Morse code, it made me ill and I couldn't tell anyone. Who would have believed such a ridiculous story? It is so true and I still hate it.

My mother played for a women's darts team between Nitshill and Darnley and would meet in the Nia Roo public inn with her team-mates for a practice or a competition. Sometimes the competitions would be held in another bar or club some distance away. The Nia Roo means 'Oor ain', as I discovered when she was sitting in front of the mirror one evening doing her hair. I spotted the reflection of her pale blue sweatshirt in the mirror. I was asked to stand in occasionally when the numbers were down in the team as the ladies played all over Glasgow. Sometimes we played, sometimes we supported, but mostly we sat and chatted.

In the summer, team members went on holiday as was the norm, leaving the team quite short of players. They met up once a week at least for practice or social sessions, competitions, heats, sandwiches and of course, a light refreshment with a little alcohol (a swally). The evenings were always enjoyable, especially if the team won. It was a whole lot safer than being in the ladies' football team where I was a member. I didn't stay in the football team long enough to consider it enjoyable as a sport or a leisurely event. You would have thought a ladies' football team would have played against other like-minded ladies' teams, right? Wrong! Our games were against huge muscular policemen, well over six feet tall. I would curl up into a fur ball screaming, 'Get away from me!' when they charged with their studded boots. I also waved to my team members warning them not to pass me the ball or else I was going to 'do them in' regardless of whether the police were there or not. Most times in life I have been a team player but in the ladies' football team I certainly was not and didn't last very long in the club. The police smashed us in goals, there really was no need for that behaviour, just a bunch of 'Heid the ba's'! Nice to get them back, Whoop! Whoop! Seriously, away and kick somebody yer ain size, lol. Bless their big nylon socks.

It's no surprise to those around me that I eventually fell away from the so-called friends in the darts team because they ripped me off big time. They ran a money menage, a saving scheme where you paid a small sum of money weekly for twenty weeks. We were given or chose, by the way of a draw, a date when you would collect the lump sum. I had taken two turns and received the dates of Christmas and the following New Year week, which I was very pleased with. Most people welcome extra income at that time of the year and it was a great way to save every week. That was Christmas and the New Year taken care of, I thought.

Just shortly before I was due both my menage turns, the people who had already had their turns and their cash in hand stopped paying their dues into the scheme. I knew what was happening here, I wasn't going to get my money for Christmas or for the New Year, yet I was still expected to put into the pot. When I called at the door of the organizer, who had taken extra money as security for mishaps, I found I was standing before a very heavily pregnant lady, who was crying because of all the stress put upon her by her unfaithful so-called friends. Quite often, betrayal and the holder of the purse go hand in hand. She had taken extra money from each person as security and got to keep it. However, with regret about the situation I apologised to the woman and assured her I wouldn't be back to bother her again, and had to say goodbye to the money I wasn't going to receive. I couldn't bear to see her so upset, though I had to tell her I now wasn't paying, because no one else was. How much of a mug was I to be? That money, four hundred pounds in total, was for my two year old's Christmas. I was totally disgusted with the women (not all of them – if the cap fits!) and left the ladies' darts team with no respect for them because of their greed and dishonesty.

Not all was lost, though. Just before I decided I wasn't going back to the darts team, I was sat beside the daughter of one of the team players and we chatted away all evening. She was an

extra, a stand-in like me, surplus to requirements in case any
members didn't show up. We got on like a house on fire and
spoke as though we'd known each other for years. She told me
she was leaving Glasgow to join a band, as she was learning the
bass guitar. We got on so well on that first night of meeting,
the one and only time we saw each other, that we swapped
addresses and promised to write to each other, which we did
for a while. In one of her letters she asked me what I would
like to do in life. As I lay upon my bed writing to her I stopped
for a good think, but I really didn't have to think much about
what I wanted, I already knew. I was very honest and wrote, 'I
don't know if you can understand this or not, but I really love
Jesus, I want to find him and serve him. I've felt that calling
and known it all my life and now's the time. I don't like this
world and what it has to offer.' I went on to tell her what I
knew, about the dreams, visions, visitations, words of knowledge
and all else Godly. I just told her the truth as I experienced it
and that I felt a life without Jesus wasn't a life at all, just a totally
meaningless existence. As I poured my heart out to her she
didn't rubbish my thoughts or put me down the way some
people did. I explained to her I always felt chosen and different
from other people, a calling which wouldn't go away. As I
thought about God and His love and grace while I was writing,
I began to cry and couldn't see the page through my tears.
Sobbing, I slipped off of my bed, onto my knees and poured
out the following prayer:

'Dear God, I'm so sorry, God, I'm so sorry. I hate my life.
If you are there, God, if you are really there and you can hear
me, if you are really real and if Jesus Christ did die on the cross
for my sins, and if I need Him to be saved, then I ask Him to
come into my life. I don't want anybody else, just you. I'm not
coming to look for you in churches or chapels or Jehovah's
Witnesses or Mormons or the Transcendental Meditation I saw
advertised on the subway, or any other people or building, in
case I don't find the real you. I'm asking you to come to me,

you come into my heart. You find me, Jesus. If you really are God and Jesus died on the cross for me, then prove it, you come to me, come and find me, God.'

I sobbed my heart out uncontrollably as I surrendered to God there and then on my knees at the bottom of my bed.

'I'm a sinner, God. I need you, you've always been with me, helped me, protected me, loved me, cared for me, watched me, known me, wanted me and now I want you, I need My Daddy . . . You, only you, The Real God, The Living God of The Bible who is The WORD.'

I made it crystal-clear that God was to come to me as proof that He was the real, true, living God because I wouldn't trust anyone or anything other than Him. The God that was The Creator and owner of the Universe, of The Bible, The WORD, was to come to me to prove He was the true, one and only God.

I knew there were counterfeits, liars and deceivers and I didn't want to be deceived. I met the demons when I was on the high hill, where Satan flew before my face and I knew he was able to pass as a being of light. I wasn't taking any chances, I wanted my Daddy God and He was to come and find me because I trusted nobody and refused to put my trust in anyone.

After finally pouring out my heart to Him, I was silent. I was overcome with the most awesome presence of peace and quiet in my soul.

I knew He heard my cries, He poured himself out over me like an oil flowing on the inside of me, and that would have been enough, I had finally found Him, He came. As I knelt in a slump at the side of my bed, He wrapped me up with himself. The Most High God comforted every part of my being and wiped away my tears.

After all of my younger years of searching, wondering, hoping and even talking about The Lord God of the Universe, singing the Christmas songs, dressing up with funny home-made hats at Easter, singing in the choir with the long purple frock and white blouse, whispering to Him in the park, groaning, looking up at the stars and so on, He came to meet me. The Lord God of Israel, The World, The Universe, Heaven, came to my house right there and then and melted Himself over me like a warm running ointment. He wrapped me up and stayed with me. I was the happiest I had felt for a long time. In oil form, I felt Him from the very top of my head to the toes on my feet, on the inside.

I went to bed smiling and very relaxed that evening and realised, for the first time in my life, as far back as I can remember, I didn't have the bed covers wrapped tightly around my neck. I was always frightened of what was going on in my bedroom, with the swirls, the bed moving and something creepy on my bed, and used to tuck myself in far too tight, but not that night. The bedclothes were loosely on my shoulders and not wrapped tightly around my neck. That fact in itself was a huge testimony of my salvation just for me, from The Father. God was with me. The fear that had gripped me every single night of my life since I was a child fled! It ran away, gone, completely and utterly vanished without a fight.

I wasn't aware of any evil presence, it was as though the whole room was washed clean. I was profoundly aware of the presence of God.

I lived frightened, fear gripped me in many ways. I was afraid of people, the devil and his demons most of all when I was alone, afraid to eat and even afraid of voicing an opinion. If someone banged into me in a supermarket I would apologise to them for being in the way. I was afraid of everything, even myself. I was afraid of being ill because my family depended on me and if I was sick, then their world would fall apart. I kept pain to myself. That very night, though, the fear fled so fast I didn't even know it had taken flight, that was the first sign I experienced of the power of God, along with a 'knowing' He heard me. I had no fear and in its place I had real love and peace. I knew I was deeply and intensely loved and that love was poured into my being.

The next day I had to jump into the city centre for a quick errand, to renew my Transcard for travel on the buses. I was always served by a beautiful smiling woman with blonde hair piled high up on her head and I deliberately went to her window because of her smile. She was serene and gracious and I was very drawn to her. She made me feel welcome by asking how I was even although she didn't know me. If I had to describe an Angel in human form, it would have been her I would have chosen because of her smile. I knew nothing about her at all, she was just a lovely motherly lady I felt a bond with. I felt, in a funny way, she knew me, she understood me, she got me and I got my Transcard.

Still buzzing from the experience with God, I was heading towards the sunlight and didn't recognise the young lady who was coming towards me and nearly walked by her. She called out my name. It was Jane, pushing her baby buggy, with her youngest daughter in it.

I hadn't seen her for ages and still hadn't met her two little girls up to this point. She looked absolutely stunning, fresh and new. There was something different about her, apart from the fact she wasn't wearing the silly blue eye shadow she always wore. Her hair was longer and fuller and even more blonde than I remembered. The ends of her hair appeared soft, light, feathery, translucent, and shone into the sun as though almost invisible. Her face was full of light and radiance. What I'm trying to tell you is that she looked pure, angelic, Holy, but I knew her so I knew I wasn't standing in front of an Angel. She didn't look like that the last time I saw her, although I did admit she was lovely anyway, but not like this. She looked like she had just come straight from the Throne of God. She had a radiance and a beauty that took my breath away and now I was the one standing and looking bemused, or Dolly Dimple!

I had had my encounter with God just the night before and I specifically told Him, for sure, that He was to come and find me. Jane had no idea what had happened to me the night before and I didn't tell her anything. We exchanged pleasantries after the shock of meeting each other. 'Where are you going?' I asked her. 'Home,' she said, 'I've just been to buy a bible,' she told me and pointed to the rectangular box sitting in the hood of the buggy. She went on to state that she went along to an outdoor tent campaign and gave her life to God by accepting Jesus as her Saviour. She told me the story of Nicodemus and explained that we must be 'Born Again,' even telling me that Nicodemus didn't understand what Born Again was, given that we were already born once in our mother's womb. She explained how we needed to be Born Again in The Spirit because our first birth was of water. I got it. I finally understood what it meant to be brought back and bought back, to God, through Jesus the Saviour. Every word she told me struck a chord within my heart. I saw her, saved, the likeness of God, that's why she looked so pure and beautiful. I nearly fell at her feet, the glare of the glory on her was so powerful.

'Can I see it?' I asked her, pointing to her bible. She let me open the box, separate the white tissue paper and lift out her big brand-new dark blue King James Bible. I held it as though it was a small 'Ark of The Covenant'. I loved it, I just stood there in the morning glory of the sun and held it as though it was a brand-new baby, The Word of God. I held The Word in my hands. The Word became flesh and dwelt among us, I was holding God, THE WORD, He came and met me the very next morning just as I commanded! I stood and looked at it and saw that there was a real true living God. He heard me, He was in my hands. I said, told him, I wasn't going to look for Him, He was to come to me and He did and there He was, THE WORD. Not a soul in the world knew what it meant for me to be holding this new bible and I never did tell Jane what had happened the night before. This is it, this is my testimony to her.

Jane invited me to church on the Wednesday evening at the Christian Friendship Centre in Dennistoun in Glasgow and I immediately said I would go. I was in a daze, totally in love with Jesus. Despite sort of knowing Him before as a child, I was now an adult with a totally different relationship. He was My Daddy before, now He Was/Is Everything, Brother, Teacher, Listener, Helper and The Great I AM. He had come to me the night before, when I was crying on the floor by my bed. He met me the next day in the town and there was so much more to come. I loved Him, Oh God, how I loved Him and DO still love Him.

If my heart was dancing from the night before, it was now leaping somersaults. I was already bursting out of my skin telling people about God and I wasn't even officially saved. I hadn't confessed with my mouth and believed in my heart publicly.

Jane warned me sternly that Satan, the devil, would use every dirty filthy cunning trick in the book to stop me coming to the Wednesday evening meeting and she was right. Nevertheless, I wasn't afraid of him any more. He, the fallen angel, Lucifer, didn't stop me going to that service, I had waited far too long for this life-changing moment. I turned up with my little son after getting two buses to Dennistoun for the service. I learned some bright and fresh 'Happy Clappy' songs before The Word was preached by the pastor, Johnny Morrison. After that there was an altar call, where we were asked if anyone would like to give their heart to Jesus and my hand shot up. I was in Heaven on Earth. I met my first new family in Christ and I'd just only begun to live the life I'd always wanted, without fear of condemnation and with all freedom. My young son was also right at home in the church and found plenty of friends, uncles and aunties and even childminders. We were invited to stay over often with many of the churchgoers and often stayed with Anna, the prophetess, but cheekily named Anna Banana by Christopher. He settled in so casually that he'd often go to the fridge, pull the door open and ask, 'What have you got for eating?', which made Anna laugh so much. She said she loved his faith, believing as a child that he would get something nice to eat. Everyone was truly amazing, we knew we belonged there and it wasn't long before seven of us piled in, filling a row of seats.

After I had been 'saved' on the Wednesday evening, it took us two buses to get home and then a bit of a walk, before we climbed the long winding road up the hill to get home. It was tiring on little Christopher's legs, 'Won't be long now,' I assured him as I pulled him up the hill by the hand to the top of the valley. It was a lovely warm night and nearly eleven o'clock and there was no one else on the street at this time. The huge bright full moon seemed to be smiling down on us as we made our way home after the fantastic evening. Beside the moon there was a very large star or light. My first thought was that it was a star, naturally. It sat beside the left side (stage left) of the moon and it looked as though the moon had a full stop fitted perfectly beside it. I had never seen a star so close to the moon before, never had I even seen a star so large and bright either. The full moon was spectacular in its own glory as we climbed the steep hill, taking us closer. I kept watching the moon as I was walking up the hill because I was fascinated by its brightness, and something else, the 'star' got even brighter and larger and it started to move towards us. I stared at the star as it was on its way down, thinking I must have been mistaken, because it was now moving. It could be a plane, helicopter, or an unidentified flying object, but there was no sound, so I knew it wasn't an aircraft of any kind. I was absolutely puzzled as to what it actually was as it came closer and closer.

Two men now appeared from out of a close, opposite to where we were walking, I now knew wee Christopher and I weren't alone. The two men, though, couldn't see the great light in the sky, as they were both bent over with their faces looking to the ground, because they were doing a 'moonlight', moving furniture at night so no one sees them. One of the men had a single bed over his back and the other had the mattress, which was flapping away on his back, behind him. Both men were stooped to the ground as they walked with their eyes on the pavement, as though God had timed this event perfectly. I thought the men would look up and see the light but they were too busy with their flitting. The men were there so I wouldn't feel alone and scared but they weren't supposed to see this light either, I thought to myself. Brighter and brighter it shone as it seemed to be coming down in slow motion, yet it couldn't have, because it was beside the moon when I first saw it. I knew it would have been thousands of miles away from our Earth. The huge brilliant light could have been either behind or in front but it looked still looked as though it was beside the moon like a full stop, that's what I saw. There it was, this bright light, travelling at a terrific speed towards me.

My heart beat faster as I wondered what God was doing. I had my child with me, what was going to happen? The light came straight down from its place beside the moon and was nearly upon us by the time we got to the top of the hill. When it got to the roof of the house opposite mine I grabbed little Christopher up, held him tight and ran to the flat, telling God I just wanted to watch it from the window. I ran away from the light. I didn't want to fall down as though dead from a powerful God experience while I had a child to care for. Sadly, the light wasn't there when I ran into the flat and looked out of the window. I was desperately disappointed but I thanked God for showing me the light the night I got saved.

God came into my room at night, when I cried out for Him, and overwhelmed me. He met with me the very next morning in the city centre when I told Him I wanted Him to come Himself, then met me again as a light on the night I gave my heart to him. I regretted running away from Him but He could have got me if He'd wanted to, He was proving He was real, The real God, The God who became flesh and dwelt among us, The Jesus Christ who laid His life down for us as a sacrifice because we needed Him, I needed Him and He was there. I told Him I wouldn't go and look for Him and He wasn't offended. He said, 'Behold, I stand at the door and knock, if anyone hears my voice I will come in and sup with him and he with Me.' (Revelation 3, v 20)

When my uncle, my mother's brother, learned I had received Jesus and had become a Christian, he laughed, 'So you've seen the light then?' How little you know, I thought. 'Yes,' I told him, 'I really did see the light.' That's not unusual for God, that's what He does. He did it before when Jesus was born by sending a great bright light to guide the three shepherds, He did it with Saul, the persecutor who became Paul and He did it for me. Seek Him, ask Him, and He will do it for you.

I have spoken to God at great length about running away from the light. I've told Him I regretted running away. I also told Him if He ever did that again I would still run away! God fills me with laughter, just like Jesus, who came and took me out to play. There is a huge difference between things happening in the Spirit and things happening in the flesh. Jesus is easy on the eye in the Spirit, completely natural, but in the flesh our bodies can die as we 'fall down as though dead' from an encounter with God. I wasn't filled with fear when I was in the Spirit with God, yet I was when in the flesh. I was able to look the demons right in the eyes in the Spirit when I was a child. The difference between the flesh and the Spirit is universal, the flesh belonging to the world as dust, but in the Spirit we are whole and beautifully made up.

Jane called me the next day after the Wednesday meeting to find out how I was getting on. She told me she was amazed I had even gone to church and got saved so eagerly. I was amazed I had met her in the town that morning after not having seen her for ages and held 'The Word' of God in my hands. She admitted she was afraid to tell me she was a Christian in case I laughed. She judged me so wrong. We must never judge whether we believe someone should hear the good news of The Gospel or not, we are only assigned the job of opening our mouths and telling others about how good and loving our Heavenly

Father is. He is a good, good Father who came to our defence and laid His life down as a sacrifice for us. My earthly Daddy was ill and millions of people need their real Heavenly Daddy, it is not up to us who gets saved or not. God had set us up together, that's why we met in the town the very next day when we hadn't seen each other for a long time. I liked her before she became a Christian, now she was a real special friend who followed Jesus and not any man, except for her husband. She had found the real purpose in her life and spoke to everyone she met, about Jesus. Her new life was every bit as infectious as mine and we witnessed together at work, always, drawing crowds where people called out, 'Come and hear this!'

She asked how I was getting on and I babbled on about getting Jesus, about the church, the people, about the steeple, actually we didn't have a steeple but I was so happy and full on I couldn't shut up. I went on and on about how much I enjoyed my experience although I didn't tell her about the light from beside the moon. Some experiences are so mind-blowing you can't share them, she might have laughed at me, though probably not. It was too soon to tell anyone something I didn't under-stand, until now, and don't bother asking me because I still don't understand, just smile and get your own relationship going with The Heavenly Father! Then when you tell me something about The Amazing God I will smile, take everything in and love Him all the more for saving you. My testimony about God, Jesus and The Holy Spirit is true. I wouldn't dare write about God, Jesus and The Holy Spirit and lie.

Here was Jane's next step in her walk with Jesus. She told me she had hands laid on her and was prayed over to receive The Holy Spirit. 'What's that about?' I asked her, hardly waiting for the answer. She told me our bodies were the temple of God (The Holy Spirit) and He would come and live in us and give us Himself as a comforter and a helper. The Holy Spirit would then give us utterance so we could speak in tongues, another language, which is Godly. A language no one else would know or be able to learn except by the anointing of The Holy Spirit. Before she had even finished what she was telling me about The Holy Spirit I told her I wanted that. 'I want The Holy Spirit living inside of me, I want to speak in other tongues, I want that Heavenly language.' Jane told me it was too soon, I'd only just got saved. Too soon? I thought, after all those years, I don't think so! I've ached for Jesus all of my life, He's not getting away now, I'll never let him go, never! Then there was talk of baptism by water. What? Where? When? How? I had so many questions that Pastor Morrison and Anna kept going into fits of laughter at me because I wanted everything 'right now'. If they had it from God The Father, then I wanted it too. Like the little primary schoolkid, there I was with my sleeve rolled up to the neck for some of what others were getting. I didn't just want what they had, I wanted more than them.

Anna, the prophetess, took me under her wing and always spoke so gently and softly, she took her time in prayer and eased me quietly into The Word. She gave me a bible but I wanted my very own and went to the same Christian bookshop where Jane had bought hers and I bought the exact same bible she bought. That bible eventually fell apart with use, I'm glad to say. I would have been disappointed in myself if it looked as though it was never used, like my other one. Anna showed me where Matthew, Mark, Luke and John were in the bible and encouraged me to start reading from there because that was the milk of The Word and I would understand it. She told me to pray before reading it and God would help me and open up my heart to what The Word was saying and meaning. I read it every moment I could, right through to the book of Revelation, I was spiritually starving. Then read it over again. When I got to the book of Revelation I would gasp in shock as I understood the signs of the times we were living in and realised we were truly living in the last days. The events of the world lined up perfectly with His Word, OH MY GOD! I had been to The Great White Throne and stood with the multitudes dressed in white. I was reading about events God had shown me as a child. I realised then that God was with me all the time and He really did hear me. What's more, He really did see me and look out for me. He sent me Angels to guide and protect me. He gave me visions and dreams, it was all there. The Word (bible) was (and is) true and alive.

'No, no!' Anna kept saying, and laughing along with Pastor Morrison. 'Keep to the milk of The Word, you're not ready for the meat of The Word yet,' but I would take my bible and shove it under the pastor's nose, asking, 'But have you seen this?' I had just found the book of Revelation so amazing because of what God had already allowed me to see and I couldn't stop telling people what was in there. I thought Jane was clever when she told me the story of Nicodemus needing to become born again, but I was on fire. Anna then explained the Psalms but I had already read them and Job, Ruth, and Esther, of course, being the same name as myself. I kept reading that bible, The Living Word, then looking up as though I was reading the great book in the film *The NeverEnding Story*, with Jesus saying, just 'Call my name.' I'd slam the bible shut and shout, 'No way, God! Eyes on wheels?' I was fascinated by the historic events of thousands falling and dying in one day, creatures with four faces, many hands and eyes. Paul speaking in tongues more than us all, really? I would show him!

The pastor was amazing. He gave me a book explaining the long gap of millions of years at the beginning of the bible when I asked him about the prehistoric monsters. 'If God created the earth and rested on the seventh day and we can count right up to today's date and the Earth is so old, then how come there were giant creatures on the Earth and . . .' I never gave Pastor Morrison a minute's peace. God also bore witness to my Spirit. I got it, Satan needed to go somewhere when he was thrown out of Heaven for his pride. He fell to Earth and caused mayhem for millions of years. God renewed and fashioned the Earth for us, making it spectacular in beauty, and created a garden, in

Eden. The huge gap of millions of years was in the first few verses of Genesis and I recognised it as I counted the years.

The pastor gave me books on the subjects I asked about because he was exhausted with my questions, I think, and questions they were, too deep for the normal new-saved baby Christian, but he always gave me the answers I was looking for. I still didn't get the eyes on wheels thing though, so I just asked The Heavenly Father. Still waiting for that answer, I might add. I WILL GET IT, LORD! I ask him constantly about the eyes on wheels and just like the way I used to ask my mummy when I was a wee girl, I say, 'Lord, let me see your other eyes'

Jane phoned me with the great news that she was finally filled with The Holy Spirit and was now speaking in other tongues. She had seen a billboard while she was travelling on the bus and the caption read, 'Open your mouth.' She had desperately been waiting for God to do it for her and knew that God was telling her to open her own mouth and He would fill it, so she did. 'What? The Holy God of the whole Universe came on a Glasgow bus to allow you to be filled with His Spirit and give you the gift of tongues? On a Glasgow bus? Are you kidding me?' She went very quiet and I sensed I'd probably dented her confidence. 'I'm sorry,' I told her. 'why shouldn't He come on a Glasgow bus? The buses are His, I'm just jealous. I want to speak in tongues too but it's not happening,' I confessed to Jane. Jane and I had the sort relationship where we could be really honest with each other. After our conversation, off I went talking to God, still overwhelmed.

'On a Glasgow bus, Lord? You went on the bus to give Jane yourself and gave her the gift of tongues, why not me? I want to speak in tongues,' I complained.

Everywhere I went, all day and night, I moaned to God about the same thing. 'I want to be filled with The Holy Spirit and speak in other tongues. Why can't I?'

Anna had already laid hands on me and told me to open my mouth and start speaking but I was too shy to do it. I'd stand all day long practising with my mouth open like a daftie, but not actually uttering any words, so obviously I wasn't speaking in the God-given language, because I wouldn't actually say anything, then I'd wonder why nothing was coming out. God would give me the gift but He was teaching me a lesson at the same time, that my faith needed an action. I would have to do something to get what He was going to give me.

Little Christopher was tucked up in his cabin bed sound asleep and I could't get to sleep for thinking about God. I wanted Him to live in and through me and I wanted to speak in other tongues. As I lay in bed quietly, a huge loud sound came from my oesophagus, which sounded like the voice of an older man. It was rich and deep and made me jump as I was nodding off. I had finally decided it was time to sleep but God had other plans, He was going to give me what I wanted before I nodded off. As I tried to sleep and shut the world off, the voice came again from much further down, much louder and deeper than the first time, and lasted longer. I was startled again, 'What was that and where did it come from?' I asked myself. Still, I rolled over wondering, and decided I was still going to go to sleep. The third time it happened it was like a lion's roar from the pit of my abdomen. I sat upright and said 'All right, God, I'll do it, I've got it, I've got the gift of tongues now,' and I did. I opened my mouth and started speaking the words God gave me because I knew if I didn't He would keep this up, and that's how I spoke in other tongues from then on. I was too afraid to speak in tongues in case I was doing it of my own volition and making up my own words. I was also afraid I would be blaspheming Him or saying something I shouldn't, because I am very good at that! I had said to God that if He did it, then I would know the gift was truly from Him and it was. That sound that came out of my mouth was like a roaring lion. All I had to do was actually speak and God would refine it. Thank you, Holy Spirit.

As I had a day job, I did some evening work as a jobbing waitress. Once you did a couple of shifts and the manager saw you were good, he wouldn't let you go. I was supposed to start at eleven am this particular day and was told the job finished in the wee small hours the next morning. I was raring to go except for the sore head I had when I woke up. By the time I got ready and left for work my head was splitting. As I stood up to get off the bus in the town centre, I prayed a silent prayer within myself, something simple like, 'God, my head is too sore and I've got to work all day until late. I won't be able to do it if it gets any worse. Can you heal me, please?' As soon as I finished talking to Him in my thoughts, I felt a warm glow come from the top (inside) of my head and run down past my eyes and face as though someone had poured warm oil over me, thicker than the salvation oil. It was beautiful, I actually felt it for real and as it washed down me it washed the headache away. I had never felt it before and I've never felt it since and I was completely pain-free to carry on working.

We set out the tables for a massive 'Gentlemen's cigar night', where a comedian was to perform later on. At around six o'clock we were ready for the onslaught, when the restaurant manager approached me and told me to tuck my cross away under my blouse because it would offend the guests. That very day the beautiful God had earlier healed me of a pounding headache and the Satanic one wanted my cross hidden. I never argued with anyone but I wouldn't allow him to pick on me as he threw his weight around and squared up to the restaurant manager with a Holy boldness.

'That cross is just a symbol, a reminder that Jesus laid his life down for you. I don't care who it offends. Did anybody care when their offences were laid on Jesus on the cross?' I got torn right into him. 'Don't you even go there, mister, because I'll tell you a few home truths about the cross,' I told him as he walked backwards, trying to get away from me, and don't ever talk to me like that again, do you hear me? Knocking my pan in all day while you just walk about in circles shouting and bawling and throwing your arms and your weight about!'

Who was this person I was becoming? Who had just raised her voice and said all that? I actually stopped in my tracks and thought God, where did that come from? It wasn't like me, so I walked away and got on with my work, when I noticed the other waitresses were smiling. I didn't know them that well and I think they thought I was a quiet girl. Well, I was really but not where God was concerned. The restaurant manager was snapping his fingers and calling the shots all day, which was fine to begin with, but he really was getting under our feet, grating on us slowly and was dampening our personalities with his dark mood swings. When the rush hour of serving started, he was at it again, flicking a white service towel at the queue of waitresses as we got into a single line to take plates back into the kitchen. 'Hurry up, hurry up!' he shouted in front of the seven hundred plus guests. 'You're last!' he informed the waitress at the back. It was hilarious when we all turned back to see who was last and listened to her speech. At the top of her voice she boomed for all of the guests to hear, 'You just listen here to me, son. I'm gonny tell you this, it's a fact of life that in a queue anywhere, somebody will always be last. If it's no me that's last, it'll be somebody else, 'cos that's how a queue works. Now you've just wasted my time and everybody else's wi yer moaning. If you want tae help us, away and sit in a corner oot the road, 'cos we're aw sick ae looking at ye.' It was brilliant. This arrogant restaurant manager who thought he was something was trying to put down grown women who had worked all their days in hotels and they weren't having it. I actually said to someone foreign recently that Glasgow women will either kiss you or kick you but they will still look after you.

After the dinner was done and dusted, we got sent out for a couple of hours while the comedian cracked his dirty jokes. Unfortunately we heard a lot of them, because the guests demanded their drinks by the bottles. We couldn't keep our ears closed and I found the comedian had crossed the line with his filth when he mentioned children in his jokes. I lifted my head high and told whoever was interested that the comedian was disgusting and many agreed. I was never a prude but he was just plain filthy and bang out of order.

By the time our shift was finished, it was five thirty in the morning and the restaurant manager begged us to stay on and serve at the breakfast shift, which would have finished at eleven am. Needless to say, he was told he was 'on to plums' and we all left to catch the early-morning buses home. We had been on our feet from eleven am, which would have meant we would have been working for over twenty-four hours nonstop, and I mean nonstop.

## Chapter Ten

# THE BAPTISM

Not too long after I began attending the Christian Friendship Centre, I was instructed and taught the reasons for my baptism, because I kept harping on about it. I wanted it all. If Jesus had purple hair, I would have followed his trend. I was never baptised or christened as a child and I couldn't wait to wash the old me away, and longed to be standing in the presence of God as I was being cleansed in my choice of white clothes. The baptism was arranged to be done in a shallower part of the River Clyde, nearer the Erskine Bridge, on a dull, reasonably nice day. It wasn't raining, put it that way.

We couldn't have any family or friends to accompany us for the special ceremony, only church members, because a few of us were getting baptised and we were all squeezed into the available church cars for our Journey. It was an amazing life-changing event, even although the River Clyde was very cold. We had to get changed in the back of the car to get our baptismal garments on, which was difficult, given that there were three of us in the back seat of the car clambering for leg room. There was already another person in the passenger seat of the car and it was the same for the men who were in the other cars.

We had a singsong of praise and worship, followed by the service, as we stood on the water's edge, before going deeper in to be baptised one by one, cheering and applauding as each brand-new man and woman surfaced from their baptism. We were chittering away as we found It freezing cold. We then had to stand dripping wet until everyone was baptised, trying to keep cosy with the towel we were handed and smiling from ear to ear because we were now 'A new Creation'. I knew I was soaking wet but I actually wondered if I looked brand-new, because I truly believed I was, all sins washed away forever. Just like a wedding, photographs were taken by the nominated car drivers to capture the precious moments, although none of us hung around posing for several group photos.

Pastor Morrison lost one of his sandals in the silt of the River Clyde, which caused me to buckle up in laughter. I didn't find trying to get stripped and dried in the back of the car too amusing, though. We were so cold we were drying each other's limbs because we couldn't feel our own, what a hoot. Despite the cold, it was a great day with the rest of the fellowship, and another experience with God, which we had all been looking forward too, especially me.

We laughed about our baptisms even years later, as we told new Christians about getting baptised in the River Clyde and about the pastor losing his sandal, which he never did find. There were other stories of folk who had surfaced from their baptisms to find they had toilet paper in their hair. It was good to laugh and soften the blow for the new believers of the future, who might encounter the same fate. My personal recommendation would be that the church takes a holiday in a very hot country and does the baptisms there, but impatient Esther wouldn't have wanted to wait that long. I was now a brand-new person, with every sin I had ever committed forgiven and washed away, never to be brought up again.

My sin wasn't massive on the grand scheme of things. There were no shootings, lootings, anarchy, carjacking, computer hacking or dog snatching (maybe I did take someone's dog from Oban, I forgot about that), but sin was still sin nevertheless. That dirty look, gossiping, cheating, stealing, lying, anger, you name it, I did it. Okay, I didn't murder anyone but I still knew deep down that I was a sinner and needed to be forgiven. Sin is sin, end of. I refused to let go and leave my body for that very reason when I said, 'I'm not coming, I'm a sinner.' We only needed to break one commandment, the lying one was as deep as the 'Shall not kill' one.

A chance to start a brand-new life after having become a brand-new person seemed too good to good to true, but that's how it is. Most of us have said, 'If only we could turn the clock back and make amends.' Well, here was the perfect opportunity to do just that. I had to pinch myself to make sure I wasn't dreaming. I knew God was good but my tiny imagination could never fathom the depth of His love, goodness, mercy and grace.

Jane and her husband were another family who often had little Christopher and me back for dinner on a Sunday afternoon to save us going all the way home. The evening service began at seven thirty, with the choir an hour before. There was no time really for travelling home and then back to church on a Sunday bus service. There was certainly no shortage of hospitality at the church, someone always made sure we were looked after.

The lead singer of praise and worship was absolutely amazing, so anointed and filled to the very top of her being with God (Holy Spirit). She went on later to produce a compact disc which has been played hundreds of times in our car and home, named *The Four Seasons*. It really is a terrific CD. It was Aileen who introduced me to the latest in Christian CDs but hers became my favourite as the music goes. I was always blessed and loved the praise and worship most of all. It was a fantastic time to sing to God and show him how much I loved and appreciated him.

Sharon Morrison, the pastor's daughter, would take Christopher to stay overnight when I had something important to do and once took him under her wing while I went on the first holiday with the church. Sharon laughed when I told her Christopher had a bag of sweets and I wanted one. I was trying to be diplomatic about him giving me one of the sweets of his own accord, so I said to him, 'I love sharing, don't you?' 'Yes, I love her as well,' he replied'.

Angela Morrison was no blood relation to the others. She was very sporty with long blonde hair, and was a breath of fresh air. Friends with Violet May, who was a constant giggler. Angela would grab little Chris a lot and swing him around the church, she was his pal. She also took the Sunday school and invested a lot of her time in pastoral care of the younger children, who looked up to her. This gave us a chance to stay in church to hear the word of God without distraction while the little ones did their own thing.

Anna, the prophetess was well versed in the bible and in life experience. There was never a moment or time she wouldn't devote in prayer or give a book to you for your growth and, like the pastor, loved answering questions, no matter how trivial they were. One of her ministries was the 'Source of Light' bible-study books, which were to be read and filled in on the gaps of the questions and answers pages. Certificates were awarded after each course of around six completed books. It was a great educational format sent to Anna from America and she was the sole source for Scotland at that time. Anna allowed me to help her with that ministry until I had got used to it, then allowed me to do it full-time. To keep a watchful eye on me, she would hold on to the studies and certificates until I was up to speed with the administration side of them, then I got to take charge of that ministry. Everyone loved the courses and a huge number of certificates were allocated to new believers for their devotion and their growth.

From America, there was a family who came to settle in Glasgow to assist Pastor Morrison in the ministry at the Christian Friendship Centre for a while. Eventually, for unknown reasons, they fell out with Pastor Morrison and left to do their own thing. Pastor Morrison often invited guest speakers. One was 'Drunken Duncan', who was drunk on The Holy Spirit. Drunken Duncan always refused the assistance of a microphone because he had a huge powerful booming voice. He told us a terrific testimony of the time he commanded a dead dog to come to life in the street. The dog had taken a fit and dropped down dead but Duncan got right in there with his booming voice and commanded the dog to get up. A gathering crowd were laughing at him and telling God that he was praying for the dog with comments like, 'Oh, my God, he's praying for the dug!' Some were even ignorantly shouting 'In the name of Jesus!' That made Drunken Duncan gather all the more faith as he rebuked them and he didn't give in. The laughing and mocking crowd were astounded when the dog got up and ran away from them. I loved Drunken Duncan's visits. He always had a terrific story or testimony to tell, and did a great prison ministry. Who better to do that than a professional?

Another visitor I recall went by the name of Norman. He was a teacher who was very quietly spoken and meek. Besides being older, he seemed frail at times and moved very slowly. He told us his wife was unwell and I thought he was amazing for ministering to us despite her not being well at home. He said The Holy Spirit was looking after his wife while he carried out his work for God. He was an amazing teacher, not only did I take in and understand every word he said, I got hold of his tapes and listened to his teachings many times over throughout the years. He was the complete opposite of Drunken Duncan and I spoke highly of them both in years further on. Both were truly God-gifted and God-sent.

Besides tithing (giving ten percent of our income), there were events in the church we did quarterly, such as the 'All-in-All', where we gave up our whole week's income and trusted God to meet our needs during that time. I couldn't do the 'All-in-All', I kept telling the pastor because at that time I wasn't working, with Christopher being so young. I only received thirty-eight pounds per week and that was including the family allowance. The pastor wanted me to put it in at some point and just trust God, test Him to see what would happen. I agreed I would one day, and the pastor told me not to save up for that day, but to do it exactly as it should be done.

Well, while I was shopping in Nitshill one afternoon, I was astounded to find forty pounds lying in front of the counter of the paper shop, two brand-new twenty-pound notes. There had been reports of a robbery flying through the air that day but that was all I knew, gossip really. I picked up the forty pounds and put it into my pocket. I didn't hand the forty pounds to the cashier because I didn't think it was his as he was on the other side of the counter. I felt if I gave it to him, it would never have been handed over to the rightful owner, therefore, I took it straight down to the police station, where it was documented. That way the person who lost it would surely get their money back. I took the thin slip of paper given as proof that it had been handed in and I tucked it away into the back of my purse and forgot all about it. The money wasn't mine to keep and, if I had lost it, then I knew for sure it would have meant an awful lot to me to get it back, having a little mouth to feed. I often went without food for myself. I was used to it and was good at it, fasting often.

Three months after finding the forty pounds went by, which just so happened to be the week of the 'All-in-All', as the pastor kept reminding us, I braced myself and put the whole of the thirty-eight pounds I had into the offering at the Wednesday-evening service and trusted God, not having a clue as to where the money was going to come from. I had completely forgotten about finding the forty pounds months earlier. On the Thursday morning I was searching deep in my purse for a postage stamp and came across a thin folded scrap of paper. It was the one I had received from the police when I handed in the found forty pounds. The paper stated that, if no one claimed it, then I could have it back. I wondered, nobody would just forget about losing forty pounds, surely? It was worth a lot more back then. I thought I would go down to the police station for something to do and find out anyway, as I had my Transcard for travelling, so that's what we did, little Christopher and I. I handed the police officer the pink folded slip and he disappeared with it.

When he came back, he gave me an envelope with the two new twenty-pound notes and smiled. On the week I had put in my all of thirty-eight pounds, I collected the forty pounds the next morning for my honesty, the other two pounds would have covered my bus fare, had I not already purchased a monthly Transcard. How's that for God's perfect timing? Wait until you read about tithing a (toy) car, my friend scorned and humiliated me no end about it.

We could spend the whole three days in the church 'upper room', which was carpeted and comfortable, when we were fasting, then breaking the fast, we would have supper together, which would bring us out of it. I would join in as often as I could but I went a whole lot further with my first forty-day fast. I never told a soul, not even the pastor, as he told us to tell no one on earth when we were fasting, so only God knew. He also told us to make sure we were praying as there was no point in fasting without prayer. I had three very small liquid meal replacements a day to keep my strength up and spent the time with The Lord at every available opportunity, reading no magazines or watching the television. At busy times, I would be thinking about Him, praying inwardly, speaking or singing in tongues.

When I went to the church early on one Sunday morning, still on the fast, Anna, the prophetess, opened the huge bolted side door and stood staring at me. I stepped forward to go in but she didn't move out of the way. I looked up at her and smiled, still she didn't move. I was then looking at her, thinking she was being a bit weird because she wasn't moving out of the way to let me in. Eventually she did move so Christopher and I could get past her. She bolted the door again behind her and told me she could see an aura, a light all around my body. She said I was glowing and that's why she didn't let me in, because she was astounded by the light surrounding me and had never seen it on anyone before. She explained I looked like The Ready Brek kid on the advertisement for cereal, who shone because he was filled with his warm breakfast. I told her then, it must be the glory of God because I was fasting, and we discussed what I was fasting and praying for. I didn't go into too much detail, it was a private and personal choice to seek The Lord God on my own, as I was growing spiritually. Word then gets around faster than the fast.

When the American pastor found out I was fasting for the forty days, he drew me an awful look from my face to my feet as though in disgust and asked rudely, '. . . and what are you fasting for?' I was hurt by his attitude and he left soon after, though it was nothing to do with me, thankfully. I felt I needed words of encouragement at church, how sad is it when you are walking with God and a pastor puts you down? He never smiled, neither did his wife nor his children, never. As a matter of fact, they were very grumpy for Christ-like folks. Well, I was just 'an idiot', The Daddy said, wasn't I, why would God listen to me?

Yet He did. Despite that, I still had admiration for the Americans who joined us and I was genuinely interested in them. He walked into my church, my home, and spoke to me like a slithery serpent, as I constantly prayed and begged God for the salvation of my mother and The Daddy. No matter, I continued my forty-day fast and prayed for the Americans also.

Another visitor to the church really hurt my heart. I hadn't realised how much I respected him until I had 'His dream'. The visitors consisted of Mr, Mrs and their beautiful daughter. He would preach and we'd have a fantastic time in fellowship afterwards with them. In short and without condemnation, judgement or name-dropping, the visiting pastor dropped his guard from Satan and befriended a much younger member of the church, who was near enough the same age as his daughter. It has happened before, and no doubt will happen again, when the armour of God has slipped for the one who steps out of line. He had an affair with the young member of our church and it became a terrible time for all concerned, the visiting pastor blaming her for being the seductress and him getting blamed for being a pastor who should have known better. It was a terribly sad time for the church, as though the affair had taken place in our own household, yet I didn't think I was judging him, I was just emotionally hurt at his betrayal, because I loved that visiting family, and now it was all torn apart on so many sides. That was the trouble, I still loved them and it hurt all round. I felt hurt for his wife and daughter and, needless to say, we didn't see them again, as they had to stop visiting our church and the offending ripples stayed with me for a long, long time.

I had a dream one night long after they left, where the pastor who committed adultery was slowly walking towards me with his arms held straight out like a cross and he was sobbing. He was naked and pathetic, his manhood had been cut off and the stitches in its place were in the shape of a cross. I looked at his groin and saw it very clearly. I cried and apologised because he was crying. 'Esther, what more can I do? What more do you want me to do?' he asked. His heart was breaking and I woke up sobbing. He doesn't even know I had this dream, he doesn't know how much he hurt me and the church, or does he? It was his dream.

I didn't know I was judging him, I just felt so grieved because I loved, trusted and looked up to him. Men of the world had affairs but not men of God, surely, I told myself. I trusted church and believers to have their eyes solely on God The Father and I was let down. I don't think the young girl got off lightly either. When someone breaks your heart, God has to repair it and it can take an awful long time to heal, leaving scars.

I met the visiting pastor years later at a different church I attended and he didn't recognise me. He had no idea who I was and my current pastor had no idea I had already met him when I was a new Christian. I didn't speak to the visiting pastor because I didn't feel led to. He was much older and looked awfully tired, frail and alone and there was no beautiful wife or daughter by his side. So sad. Thankfully, he had repented and was still on the go for God.

Remember that lovely woman I used to meet at the Transcard centre, the one who looked so angelic and was always asking me how I was? Well, get this, there was a family at the church of four sisters and one of the sisters was about my age. We became friends and I was invited up one weekend to stay over with her. All of the girls had dark hair so I would never have guessed in a million years that the pure blonde lady was, in actual fact, their mother! It's no wonder I felt such a bond with her when I went to purchase my Transcard and would only go to her cubicle. I got to know her for real and her hospitality was marvellous. It's amazing how you don't know someone but God puts that person on your heart. My new church friends' own mother was the Transcard Lady who looked after me and smiled throughout all of the dark years when my heart was heavy and she eventually gave her heart to Jesus as well.

There was another beautiful blonde girl who appeared at the Christian Friendship Centre by the name of Jackie whose hair was way down to her waist. She was sweet and sociable. She really did look like an angel and behaved like one too. She told me she was always in trouble with the police before she came to accept Jesus into her life. Every time she got a new pair of trainers, she had a great urge to smash a police-office window or do something very bad in front of the police so they would chase her. She had to prove to herself that she could still outrun them, but even when she did outrun them, they would always catch up with her later on at her house. She was well known to the police for this behaviour. When the police finally nabbed her, they wouldn't handcuff her, they held her by the hand to the wagon. She was too cute and, looking at her, you would never have guessed she was a wee rascal before she accepted Jesus into her heart. I know I shouldn't laugh but to picture her fleeing in new trainers and with gorgeous long blonde hair flying in the wind gets me every time.

Another live wire, Andy, who was on fire for God, told me he used to break into houses and I told him I didn't believe him. He was telling me his testimony (just like I'm telling you) and I was saying, 'Get away, I don't believe that.' When God changes people's hearts and lives, you can't see the dirty dark past in them, they really are new creations. Andy took a shine to Christopher and considered himself daddy material, and was quite upset when I told him no thanks. 'But you'll grow to love me,' he said. 'No thanks' was final, I couldn't. I could love him with the love of Jesus in my heart but not with intimacy, not me, the love of my life was my little Christopher. God had my husband planned, I told him. There were other offers in the church, there's nothing wrong with that, plenty of young men looking for a wife, but I could not see past Jesus.

Pastor Morrison was terrible at matchmaking but he would always try anyway. I'm sure he would have loved us all to have a church wedding and dearly wanted to marry us off.

He was trying to set me up with a newcomer because he was single, obviously, and because he had two semi-detached cottages, each with four bedrooms and three acres of garden. 'No!', Pastor Morrison, I complained. We became very good friends and that's how it stayed.

Another guy in the church kept going to the pastor and telling him that God said he was to marry his daughter, Sharon. Sharon was affronted but Pastor Morrison, her daddy, just told him, 'When God tells me you can marry her, then you can.' He then used to kid Sharon on that one day God would tell him. The guy got fed up waiting and went round all of the females in the church telling us that God told him he was to marry us, not all at the same time though. We would walk away mumbling, 'God, don't you dare.'

One Sunday morning Christopher was very happily sitting in a small room just off the big church hall with a child younger than him, and Angela was popping her head in to make sure they were fine. We could hear them constantly giggling and came to the conclusion that all was well, until I was bothered about the silence a bit later on, a mother's intuition and all that. I was uncomfortable with this particular silence and kept nodding over to Angela to go and have a peep in the door to see what they were up to, but she smiled and waved over, telling me they were fine. I wasn't convinced but Angela kept giving me the thumbs up, as she could hear them in the adjoining room. At the end of the service we went into the room to fetch them, as it was tea, sandwich and juice time. In that wee room we could hardly see the two little boys for a mountain of coloured tissue paper and party hats. How they managed to get the Christmas crackers down from the top shelf I do not know but every box was opened and every cracker was torn apart for the toy inside, hundreds of them. I stared up at that top shelf in total disbelief. There were no ladders or chairs. How did they manage it? No wonder I was on the edge of my seat. How on earth did they get them? I aways wondered, but I never found out. It was a colourful sight, though, and they had a cracker of a time.

The children were allowed to be children but sometimes the adults were the biggest kids around and we had some bellyaching laughter together. A visit to the island of Mull was our first short trip away. Jane, her friend, the pastor and I only went for the last three of the seven days. The assistant pastor, Danny, and the rest of the crew had well settled in to the camp, which consisted of an old barn with bunk beds, which sat close to a cottage, where we got fed. The daily duties and chores, such as collecting firewood and cleaning out the makeshift toilet, were already evenly divided between them before we arrived. Danny was a laugh and a half and could pull some ridiculous and obscure faces, which had us howling. We laughed constantly, much to the annoyance of one of the older generation, Margaret with the funny accent for one, who young Christopher would imitate. It didn't matter how many times I told Christopher not to do it, he loved her accent a bit too much and would holler and repeat whatever she said at the top of his voice. Danny was of no help at all, I have to say. If there was any real mischief around, Danny was there under the pretence of rebuking it while winking with his eye and stating, 'Beware of the winker.'

The pastor drove Jane, her friend, whom I met for the first time, and me to the island of Mull. Jane told the pastor she had to be back for her husband's dinner at six o'clock, but we soon realised it was almost five o'clock and we weren't even halfway there. Jane was not a happy bunny and grumbled the rest of the way there, aided and agreed with by her friend. The pastor told Jane to chill out and enjoy the journey but she moaned and groaned the rest of the way, the pastor pointing out in no uncertain terms that she had chosen to come along. For the last leg of the journey we had to be driven by a tractor and a muddy trailer, with us perched up on the back for a couple of miles. I was the only one on the back of the trailer suitably dressed for the adventure. Jane was wearing high heels and a pencil skirt and her friend was not much better dressed for the occasion. The pastor got to sit on the tractor with the driver, away from the moaning minnies.

The mucky trailer bounced and threw us all over the place as it negotiated the potholes, some as big as craters. Jane did not shut up and let go when she realised by then that not only would we not be back for her husband's dinner, we were staying over for three nights. On another deep troublesome treacherous hole, the trailer bounced us sky-high, throwing us into mid-air and off the trailer. I managed to come down to the ground by landing on my feet, Jane went head-first into a boggy ditch and her friend got a softer landing in the ditch, right on top of Jane. I had never seen the pastor laugh so much as he lifted his hands up and told us it was God dealing with us in the order of our complaints. It was too funny, except for poor Jane.

The pastor got to stay in the warm cottage with the owners and we stayed in the bunk beds in the old barn with many spiders, where I was given a top bunk, our coats and jackets thrown on top of the beds to keep us extra-warm. The guys' sleeping area was in the other side of the barn, where through the cold bricked walls you could hear everything. There were no carpets, something that didn't faze me, and a bare light bulb swinging in the air, the old rickety half-doors could close, and that was it. The toilet, which was out and round the back of the barn beside the logs, was basically an old tin bucket along with a cold tap on the wall for hand washing. We got toast cooked on a long blackened fork at the fire of the main house before we had a time of praise, worship and prayer and then turning in for a good sleep. I was in my Father's house with my spiritual brothers and sisters, pressed up against the fire for a heat, just like it was when I was a little girl. The difference was my Heavenly Father loved me. I closed my eyes and relived my childhood, God made everything good again for His little child, me.

On the first morning of our stay, after a wash and breakfast, we were gathered together in the fresh air to discuss the day's canoeing activities. Danny came running, shouting, 'Esther, Esther, come here quick 'til I show you something.' 'What is it?' I asked, delighted he wanted to share this secret discovery with me. 'Look!' he said. 'Shh, don't make a sound,' as he was standing with an empty plastic carton. 'Come closer,' he whispered as he took me nearer to the barn and stood in the doorway. 'Are you ready?' he asked, and I nodded. 'Watch this.' He dropped some pebbles into the plastic carton and rattled it really loud before he gave it to me to hold while grabbing onto my sleeve. 'Keep shaking it,' he said. From all over the hills, crevices, nooks and crannies of the rocks, goats clamoured and headed straight for me, because that's what you did when it was feeding time. He laughed his head off at the boys' end and I had nowhere to go, frantically looking to get into the barn, but he was holding the door tight shut. (Remember I did this to my wee sister at 'chap the door and run away' in Port Ann.) I only just made it into the other barn before I was butted senseless, clambering up to the top of the first bunk bed after throwing the plastic tub with the pebbles into the air (like the shovel with the spider). Danny was laughing his head off and my heart was pumping in somersaults. I had to pay him back, I thought. He'll keep, I mused, as I considered a cunning plan to get him back. I was in cahoots with Violet May and couldn't tell too many people what we were up to, but Danny (the assistant pastor!) had to be paid back for his mischief.

After a little thought we collected the biggest clump of stinking soggy seaweed we could find and set out to find Danny's bunk bed. We had a problem trying to locate which bunk was his, and came to the conclusion it the one with his bible on top of it. We put the soggy seaweed carefully between the sheets and laughed all day at the thought of Danny mangling his toes in it. After supper, a heat at the peat fire and the prayer meeting, we couldn't stop smiling, daring not to have eye contact in case we started laughing, hiding our faces and keeping our heads down as though in fervent prayer, but inside we were rocking with laughter. Our bunks were shaking as we waited for the moment Danny's feet touched the seaweed, crushing our faces on our pillows to hold back the long due laughter.

There was an uproar next door with screaming but it wasn't Danny who screamed, it was Jim, who was a quiet gentle guy who never did anything wrong. Danny was up shouting at the top of his voice, 'In the name of JESUS I rebuke you right now. Devil, come out of that bed NOW!' We were crying sore with laughter. To make matters worse, or even funnier, Margaret with the funny accent kept repeating, 'You don't know you're born, you don't know you're born,' as she disapproved of the nonsense. She didn't even know what had happened but she disapproved anyway, which started us off again. It was hilarious, and what did that statement even mean? We went about for the next few days telling each other, 'You don't know you're born!' Our ribs and cheeks ached constantly with laughter throughout our holiday to the point where I was bent double, holding my sore sides. 'Good God in Mull' too!

Some of the group climbed over the hill and walked for miles to report that the most amazing golden sandy beach was situated on the other side and I wished I had gone with them to see it. The barn owners told us the beach is so exclusive that the Queen visits by helicopter.

We canoed, collected wood for the fire later on and cut peat to dry from the peat bog, which was fascinating when we were told that no one had ever seen that piece of peat on the Earth, it was there long before Jesus came to Earth, untouched by humans, and we got to take it apart in slices. I was in awe of the thought of being the first person ever who dug up that peat, which had lain untouched by any other human.

We prepared dinner for the evening and did tasks as a team but, most of all, we laughed and laughed and had the best time ever. My breakfast of cornflakes and goat's milk straight from the goat, was snatched by one of the guys because I stared at it for too long. I couldn't get my head round tasting the lukewarm milk and needed to counsel myself, talk myself into trying it and give thanks for it but, before I could make up my mind, it was down someone else's neck. Everyone was ravenous, with the fresh air building up whopping appetites.

Ian, another truly meek and virtuous guy, had brought a Mars bar from Glasgow and laid it on the centre of the table. That Mars bar had a price tag of ten pounds on it, as offers were put in to have it. There were no shops for many miles and that bumpy dirt road would have to be negotiated again, twice, en route to anywhere. The female host of the cottage canoed to farms for the eggs and milk, never chocolate. If there was any strife in our camp at all, it was down to the Mars bar, because it went missing, and I was mad because it was chocolate and no one should ever deprive a woman of chocolate. It's an unwritten rule amongst women at a certain time of the month in any camp, chocolate must be available. When I protested about the missing chocolate having been stolen, Ian remarked it was all right, whoever took it was welcome to it. I could almost see the room turning into a murder mystery over a Mars bar. 'I give it to the person of my own free will,' he quietly announced, but I was still mad at the person who had pinched it. I don't even know if I was mad because I wanted chocolate or because someone had taken advantage of Ian. I bet it was Danny boy up to his tricks again. We never did find the culprit or the missing Mars bar, and there was no comment from him.

Danny boy had a great personality but the best part of his character was his sense of humour. He was a bit of a leader, a ringleader! On our ski trip to Aviemore, we went ice-skating one night and I thought we were just doing a sort of bonding, team-playing bit again when he called us together for a game. I should have known fine well that if Danny was in the thick of it, there mischief was too. Up to that point we were skating by ourselves and trying not to fall, me in particular. I was taking baby steps because I'd never skated before and I didn't like heights, I liked my feet firmly on the ground. Eventually we came together and held hands as Danny suggested. The guys were in on this prank, as they decided they would do one male, one female, in the line-up so they could hold onto us very tight. To make matters worse, I was at the end of the line. We skated together fine for the first few minutes before they started their cunning plan of swinging us around the ice, from the centre, at great speed and, because I was last, I had much further to go, right into the barriers with a crash, bang and wallop as we all were flattened.

Oh, the good old days. There was the time I brought a sledge along for Christopher and the snow was so thick it caved in over him like a mini-avalanche. No one can say church is boring and if it is, perhaps you are in the wrong church. It's not all laughter, though. There are times when someone is going through a tough time or has lost a family member. There are no words to bring people back, but there is great hope and

comfort and Jesus is Lord of all. Our holiday to Salou was painful
for me as we landed. It was my first holiday abroad, my first
flight experience. My ears were extremely sore and my head
was splitting from the high altitude of the flight and the roasting
hot temperature in Spain. No one had warned me of the
'yawning' exercises I should do, or to simply chew a sweet on
the plane when ascending and descending. As the headache got
worse, I pleaded with everyone and anyone to get me painkillers
as soon as possible but there was no pharmacy close by. The
pastor, being a man of God, kept telling me to pray for healing
but I was in agony and couldn't focus. I walked around with
my head in my hands, then I was as sick as a dog. I didn't get
any painkillers until bedtime, then I had a good night's sleep.
Everyone was too excited to get going to explore the surrounding
area, the beach was fantastic and Danny wasn't with us, Hallelujah.
Actually we missed Danny, but not too much. At least we didn't
have to watch our backs and look out for tricks all the time. It
was a terrific holiday with great sun and rest.

We all had to take a turn of sharing The Word each night
for a few hours before being let loose to the bar for a soft drink.
It was a great learning curve sitting with our group and speaking
out what The Lord God had given each of us during the day.
The whole day was peaceful for the person giving the sermon
and my quiet time took me all day, as I tried to conceive what
God was giving me to say, then I went back to very first thing
God had said to me in the morning. Pastor Morrison really
encouraged us after we spoke and enjoyed all our parts in the
services. It was peaceful, like living in Heaven on Earth. I was
amazed with things that normal holidaymakers abroad take for
granted, like slipping my sandals off to stand on the sand, which
was impossible. You would have thought I had just stood on
burning coals the way I danced about trying to get my feet back
off the roasting sand. Everything that was steel seemed to practically take a layer of skin from my fingers and the tap water
was not for drinking. Still, it was a great holiday, it amazed me

that we could jump on a plane for a couple of hours and literally follow the sun.

Our holiday in Tunisia was beautiful but not as hot this time,
though definitely hotter than Glasgow. The hotel was awesome
and the staff very attentive, but still, we couldn't go outside the
hotel without being followed by the local men. There were only
two women on that holiday and we still got followed when we
had bodyguards. We needed Danny there to protect us – can't
live with him, can't live without him. Little Christopher made
himself useful in assisting the gardener, by getting under his feet,
no doubt, but the gardener couldn't speak English to tell him
to go away. He plucked weeds and played with the huge watering
hose, soaking everyone and everything around. Christopher also
befriended the local kittens, much to the annoyance of the
mother cat, who slashed him across the chest with her dirty
claws. He had the scars for a while as a reminder not to go near
them again.

On a quick outing with our chaperones one day, we tried to
purchase some milk outside of the hotel for the pastor. Anything
a pastor wants or needs, you get it as though you're doing it
for Jesus. We have no idea what was in the small bottle but it
did not resemble milk. On the way back to the hotel we watched
a very old man dressed from head to toe in black hobbling
towards us and we discussed quietly between ourselves how old
and tired he looked, walking at a snail's pace. His head was
facing down to the ground as we passed, with his arms behind
his back as though using them to support himself. He looked
so infirm. When we passed him by and looked back in compassion and sadness at the old soul, we were astonished to see he
was actually swinging a huge curved machete behind his bent
back. That was another reason why it was unsafe to wander
from the hotel. The pastor was aware of the dangers of being
in Tunisia and we were a bit apprehensive and stayed close beside
each other. There was nowhere else to go but to the pastor's
room, where we spent the evening praying and in The Word.

The pastor had repeatedly warned us to stay close together, which we did. Two weeks after flying home, a young lady from Glasgow lost half of her leg in a bomb explosion in one of the bars we were in, close to the hotel. That's how scary it was.

More often than not, it's the tiny little things that mean a whole lot to me and speak volumes in God's company. I was looking through my young son's top drawer for a pair of socks one morning. In the sock drawer I pulled one pair out after another and stretched them. 'Too small,' I said, and placed them on top of his unit. I did this a total of six times until I found a pair that would fit. 'I need to get you some new socks,' I told him. When we were fed, watered and dressed, we went for a walk round to my mother's, Christopher's granny. The first thing my mother said when I entered the house was 'I got Christopher some pairs of socks.' I looked into the bag. His granny had only gone and bought six new pairs of socks the day before and had them there waiting for us. God says, 'Even before they finish praying to me, I will answer their prayers.' (Isaiah 65, v 24)

Another time, I looked at a lovely denim dress that I really wanted. It was long with a neat waist, but was far too expensive. After holding it up for a moment, I decided food was more important and put the dress back on the rail, disappointed. Some days later, I had to go to the house where my mother worked, to give the lady a hand, as my mother was unwell. It just so happened to be the day the woman was doing a clear-out of her wardrobe. The outfits she was keeping were thrown on her bed and the others into a black bag for a charity shop. She held up a brand-new long denim dress and looked at it to decide whether to keep it or not. It was much nicer than the one I had been looking at and more expensive too. She looked me up and down and said, 'Here, that will fit you.' A new long denim dress with the label attached, which was three times the price of the one I had been looking at. God really does supply our every need according to his riches and glory, and gives us our hearts' desires too.

I took on a part-time job in a pub in Shawlands at night and at the weekends, simply so I could walk across the road to the driving school on the opposite corner to book and pay for my lessons. The pub has Mary Queen of Scots' handprints above the door, I've been told. Not so, I can tell you. The handprints above the door are astronomically huge. When I was involved with the Glasgow Museums, I handled one of Mary's rings and it is so tiny I couldn't even get it on my pinkie.

Before I started working in the pub, I was given a warning by a friend, Helen, who told me the manager was a terrible sex pest and she warned me not to get over-friendly with him. I didn't like his manner, so stayed out of his way and got on with my job. There was also another man there, who worked at the local primary school in Shawlands, and he also worked in the bar part-time. One day, when the pub closed in the afternoon, the men closed the outer pub doors as I went into the office to get my jacket. They both came into the office and the schoolteacher held the door closed with his back against it, arms folded. It was obvious to me they had misadventure on their minds and I was afraid. As I went to get out, I sensed they had other plans and was quizzed about matters that were none of their business. I didn't know what to do. There I was trapped in an office with two older 'big' men and I knew they had bad intentions. I looked down at the manager who was sitting, grinning and grilling me. I had no idea how to get myself out of the situation, and realised Helen wasn't wrong about this guy. I tried to stay calm and told him I was a friend of Helen and she had told me all about him. She had only told me he was a creep and a sex pest but he wasn't to know that. The manager was startled and sat up straighter and nodded to the teacher to move out of the way. I have no idea what the statement meant to him but he was now startled and let me go. Last chance saloon. I didn't go back to that job, nor did I give a reason, they knew the reason. The alleged sex pest was a married man, I don't know about the teacher, but I can't believe he got away with working in the local primary school. Names withheld, lucky them.

I continued with my driving lessons but the instructor would totally mess about. I love to laugh and have fun but I wasn't taking driving lessons for a joke or a joy ride. After twenty lessons, bearing in mind I only got thirty-five to forty minutes of the hour I had paid for each time, I wasn't happy with this so-called British driving school. I got shot of them and booked with a private one-man band. I told him about the instructor wasting my time and made it clear I just wanted to pass my test, I didn't have money to burn like rubber. I booked double lessons with my second instructor because I wasn't paying for an hour and only getting forty minutes. The travel time the instructors took from my money wasn't my problem, I told him. I was only with the second instructor for a few weeks when he informed me blandly he had booked me in for my test. He never uttered one word out of line. It was 'Turn left here, turn right there.' He was a superb instructor and I passed my test the first time. I could hear The Daddy prompting my mother, 'Ask her if she passed' as I swanned around the house, because I was making them wait. When she did ask, I waved my piece of paper in the air and said of course I passed. I was so happy to have passed, every young driver is. My parents needed a driver and now they had one, and the other siblings caught up later.

We did a lot together as a church, and Christopher and I attended seven days a week. I worked there and we practically lived there during the day and only went home at night to sleep and change. Pastor Morrison bought us our first car, a Toyota Corolla, which was old but looked fine with its tinted windows and leather bucket seats. Christopher loved it and was in charge of the radio. Shoes off, feet resting on the dashboard and his little arm swaying out of the window was his usual pose. The car didn't start in the rain, though, not for anybody, not even with prayer. I knew fine well how to drive, tow a trailer and a huge caravan, as I often did, and I was a dab hand at reversing the caravan into neat spaces. As the church had a pool of cars, the pastor didn't have a problem with giving us a car but occasionally he'd give me a lone of a car I just didn't know how to operate, like the car that kept repeating 'Stand away from the car, you are too close, stand away from the car.' Christopher thought this was hilarious and would give it a hug to hear it speak. This car had a cockpit, not a dashboard, and it didn't have a miles to the gallon ratio, it was gallons to the mile, a real big beauty but so thirsty. I refused to drive it because it attracted too much attention in Nitshill. Crowds gathered at the voice of the car so as to provoke it into some kind of action. To me it was just a car. If it got me from A to B, then that's all I was concerned about. I was a bit scared in case I pressed the ejector seat button, though, and sent Christopher flying up to Heaven before his time. Another car we got to drive was a Peugeot 504. I had hidden a huge hairy rubber spider in the middle of the steering wheel column while I was playing with Christopher. I wonder who found that? I hope he found Jesus first. He probably had a heart attack when dismantling the car for any repair that required the removal of the steering column.

The only problem with having the car was that I had to run people home and, more often than not, they lived in the opposite direction from the south side of Glasgow. The pastor was a very generous and kind man who laughed a lot, usually at his own jokes, but he'd laugh so much he had us laughing too. Throughout the years, though, we had heard all of the jokes loads of times and our laughter became smiles, but the pastor still threw his head back and laughed as though the story had just happened. He had the joy of The Lord, which was very infectious, and he loved praising God.

Shane was a nice guy I used to chat to when I was younger and still going to the local pub, when I went with friends to listen to the resident band. When I became a born-again Christian, I stopped going to the pub, but I would still see him often in the street. There was no romance between us, he was just easy to talk to. One day when I bumped into him, I was telling him about church, Jesus and all the trimmings, and told him how great it was, and also witnessed to him about the need for salvation. He listened intently and I invited him to church. He was genuinely interested, so it seemed at the time, and I had no reason to doubt him. He said 'Yes' and I arranged for someone to look after little Chris while I drove all the way back from whichever house I was at to pick him up but he was never there. I don't know how many times I wasted fuel and time by going to get him, then I'd wait for ages in case he was just late. 'Sorry,' he said when I found him weeks later, and he would agree to go the following Sunday. Again and again, I went all the way back to get him and take him to church and bring him home again but he never showed face. I told him I didn't want to give up on him and it didn't matter about how many times I came for him, but I also told him firmly that he couldn't treat God with contempt and disrespect like that. 'I come all that way for you so you don't have to walk or get two buses,' I said. 'It would be better for you to say you don't want to go rather than say "Yes" and not show up.' I warned him that, if he played mind games, then one day he wouldn't be able to go because 'Now' is the day of salvation, and something could happen to him. He wholeheartedly agreed with me and promised he would go on Sunday, yet again. I had been there so many times before but I couldn't not go and get him, as I had promised, and had to keep my word. He wasn't there. He never did come to church. Shortly after I prophesied the warning to him, he walked into a lift when the doors opened, believing it had stopped at the floor he was on, but it hadn't and he plummeted way down in a dreadful accident, breaking both of his legs as he fell to a great depth. I read about it in the local newspaper. To this day I've never seen Shane again. I hope he does give his life to Jesus, the seed was well sown there.

I hadn't realised I had prophesied into Shane's life until I remembered I had also spoken into John's life too. It was the very same scenario really, I told John all about Jesus just like I told everyone else and invited him along to church too. He had been dating the sister of one of my good friends and he was easy to get on with. He too said he would come to church and I went back for him straight after Sunday dinner, so I could get him to the evening service. Time after time he wouldn't be at the designated spot where we had arranged the pick-up. Still, I waited for as long as I could and then drove back to church in time for the service, with nobody with me. Walking in alone to the service, shrugging my shoulders, was always a downer, that was another soul who hadn't registered for Heaven, I thought. When I met John, I told him that Jesus was waiting and knocking on the door for him to answer and I also told him that, if he didn't make his mind up about accepting Jesus, Satan wasn't very far away. If he didn't give his life to Jesus then he was not protected in his sinful life. I told him it wasn't a problem to drive him to church, to save him trying to get there on his own, and he seemed genuinely interested, even promising he'd be there at the arranged time for the next, and the next and the next evening service. He didn't turn up and I told him if he didn't keep his word, then one day he wouldn't be able to come to church. I warned him not to take the chance of putting salvation off, as he never knew the minute when his life would change and he again agreed, saying I was right. He let himself and me down again, then I heard the story of his down-fall very quickly, through my friends and the media, that John went to answer his door, not realising there was a gun sticking through his letterbox. His leg was blown off at the knee. I was shocked, so shocked that I thought I'd better stop telling people that, if they didn't go to church, then they wouldn't be able to go. I hadn't realised I was prophesying.

On a Saturday we 'can-collected' in the city centre in aid of the old folks' lunch club and Christmas parties. It was a very humbling experience. If you ever need to find out what humility is, then that's the very way to go about it, do can-collecting for charity. The pastor thought he would brighten up our day once by hiring costumes for us and I ended up with the pure-white heavy snowman suit. It was quite cold in the morning but by the afternoon it was an absolute roaster of a day and I was sweltering in the huge white cotton wool suit. I felt like a complete prat, as my face was beetroot-red because of the heat. A snowman? I was a puddle inside. Still, sometimes businessmen would put ten pounds in the tin. I thought they were fabulous but I remember one freezing cold rainy day in the winter, when our hands were as cold as ice and I couldn't stand outside for a moment longer. Raymond, the church member with the two semi-detached cottages, and I decided to shelter in a tearoom for a good hour. 'Oh help,' I said, after sitting in the tearoom for ages. 'We need to get back out there.' We hardly had any coins in our cans so we went to the bank and asked for a pound bag of pennies each to put in our own cans. We felt guilty for skiving and had to make our cans heavier.

Our can-collection donations always did what it said on the tin and the money went towards the lunch club which provided a meal for senior citizens, and many older men without a good woman at their backs got a heat and a three-course meal. I could tell by the way they wolfed it down they were hungry. It was a shame to see people in need and I was glad of every coin that fed them. I want to say a huge thank-you to the Glasgow businessmen and everyone else who put money into our cans. I can put my hand on my heart and tell you that the money did stay in Glasgow and it did indeed feed the pensioners in Dennistoun, as I said. Thanks a million to all of you kind hearts everywhere, you know who you are, God bless you.

The Christmas parties were great and we had a smashing time entertaining the old-age pensioners after their meals. Danny and I disagreed over who was to be the compere. It was my idea first but he jumped on the bandwagon and stole it. 'He did, you know, Lord!' I ended up giving in and letting him do it and sang 'The Banks of the Ohio' instead. Jane sang 'Puppet

on a String' and young Margaret did some Highland dancing.
Aileen sang, leading us all in a sing-a-long. There was plenty
of food and gifts for all, a great celebration with Jesus at the
top billing. Christian Friendship Centre was my first church,
my first family, my introduction to the Father, Son and Holy
Spirit, and we loved going there. I eventually took my baby
sister, my twin brothers and two nephews too, which filled up
a pew, or chairs rather, but 'pew' rhymed better. There was
certainly no shortage of children, love and laughter at Christian
Friendship Centre, that's for sure.

My youngest sister even got her own identity badge for can-
collecting and did very well, even getting a job in the church.
The rest of the boys were a lot younger but they all got on
really well. My only fear, and it was a stupid fear really, was that
one of the children would be sick in the church, not just sick,
but have an episode of projectile vomiting over the person sitting
in front. I know it was a silly thing to imagine but the thought
horrified me. I would sit and perspire in church, even at the
thought of such a horrible event. I actually dreaded this happening
because children are easily excitable and can't hold it in. It came
straight out of Job 3, v 25: 'What I feared has come upon me,
what I dreaded has happened.'

Well, one of the boys did exactly that. One of my little
nephews bent forward first and, without warning, the poor
person in front got splattered. The whole church gasped in
horror and Pastor Morrison stopped speaking The Word of God.
I ran away, to be honest. Everyone thought I had run to get a
bucket of cleaning materials but I had scarpered right to the
back door. I wasn't cleaning that up. I don't know if the fear
caused it to happen or if it was a prophetic word of knowledge
coming to pass but 'come to pass' it did and I didn't fear it any
more. It was done and gone, just like me. Another tale I laugh
out loud at when I'm trying to get to sleep.

A new guy appeared in church and after a few weeks he
started bringing in his guitar and playing it down at the front

row of the church, right in front of us. He settled in nicely, never missed a service, minding his own business and strumming away to the songs of The Lord. He was a cheery chap, happy and contented, learning the songs as he went along. Lovely, I thought, this new guy is so on fire for The Lord. He was very young and quite quiet and came to church immaculately dressed in a pristine suit, collar and tie. While the pastor was preaching and all was oh so quiet as we were intently listening, out of the blue the young man sitting in front of us slapped himself hard right across his face at lightning speed. Well, that was me, falling off my seat with laughter, especially when Christopher started imitating him by doing the same thing and shouting, 'Pyong Yong Yong.' I couldn't stop thinking about how hard he had hit himself, perhaps to stay awake.

After the praise and worship we would hear the announcements and then The Word of God. Sorry God, but The Word could be very tiring to the ears if it wasn't spoken with enthusiasm (which comes from the Greek word *enthous* and means 'possesed by God'). It was all too easy to become sleepy, very sleepy. The whole church was nodding off at this particular service as the pastor's voice became a hypnotic drone that sent us off to noddyland. He droned to the point where some people were snoring and we'd all smile as we turned round to see where the noise was coming from. Another time I was so tired I could feel myself nodding off. I clenched my eyes as tightly as I could, then relaxed, trying every trick in the book I could find to stay awake. I tried to fight it but my head was begging to go south as it got heavier and heavier, it didn't care so long as it got a sleep. I got sleepy, sleepier and just before my head fell off my shoulders, I jumped into the air and shouted, 'AMEN!'

'Amen?' the pastor asked with a quizzical look on his face. 'Jesus!' I thought as I sat up straight, what had I just shouted Amen to? Looking around, other eyes asked the same thing. I just shrugged, faced the front and started paying attention again now I was wide awake. I never did find out what the pastor was preaching about or what I had shouted Amen to, but I didn't care because I didn't hear him anyway. Silly little things still make me laugh out loud, a lot.

I've got low blood pressure. If the pastor's droning, I'm liable to nod off. Preach it properly, Pastor, keep us on our toes. The older generation and young babies are the first to nod off. I found it particularly hard when I was in the praise band, which is hard work, giving every atom in my being for the ministry. The anointing makes it an easy yoke to bear but, when I sat down to partake in 'The body and blood of Christ' (bread and cordial), it wouldn't be too long before I wished I was back down in my bed for another good rest, or sleep probably.

Whole families would come to church. There was Jack Hunter for one, sons Paul and Ian, and Mum, whose name will not come to my memory, Netta, Nettie? Something like that. I used to tell Ian he reminded me so much of Jesus, he was meek and gentle and put everyone before himself. He spoke quietly but firmly and always attracted people round about him and his family. They were all beautiful, that's what God had turned them into, 'His image', and I used to pray that one day I could go to church and have my whole family there, not for me, but saved, that was all I wanted, salvation for everyone. Jack's family were all saved and I used to tell them, 'I wish my family would come too.' I felt hurt and deeply disappointed because they weren't there. I managed to get all of the children to church and even got The Daddy there, just once. The Daddy by this time was very ill, fragile and thin. Pastor Morrison led him to The Lord and he accepted Jesus Christ into his heart. **My Daddy was saved!**

Before he died, I went to my twin brothers and told them their Daddy wasn't going to be here much longer and they should visit him with this in mind. The relationship between us was still that of an unspoken one except for 'Yes' and 'No' when I asked him if he wanted a cup of tea. He was pathetically broken mentally and physically, and who do you suppose had to look after him? Yes, it was me. I still loved him deeply and his disposition tore at my heart. He didn't appear to love me but I cared not a jot for any emotional baggage or past time reflections regarding hurt by this time. He didn't know love, he'd never met love, so never loved the way God loves. I had Jesus and I was to love My Daddy and that's just what I did as I looked after him. He brought a smile to my face one day when I caught him playing with my little girl, Sarah, his grand-daughter. He always had time for the children, and they, being children, were never judgemental. The grandchildren would clamber up and onto his knee, whether he liked it or not. They loved with the pure childish and childlike God love that accepted everybody. He was showing Sarah how to do something with her hands and rhyming off:

*'There's the church, There's the steeple*
*Open the doors, And see all the wee people.'*

Sarah made him do it again and again. He seemed to perk up before he went home to Heaven and delighted in the innocence of a toddler who would stand before him and make him enter-tain her. She had no preconceptions, feelings of anger or judgement. She would just climb up onto his knee when she wanted to and put her arms around his neck. My Daddy loved her, I could see it when he held her. He threw himself on top of her high pram when the ceiling collapsed because of a harsh winter and covered her with his body. He laid his life down for her. We were the ones who probably loved him the most, as we yearned for love in return, but Jesus was there to heal our hearts. He loved us so much he laid down his life for us, only to get spat on, sneered at, abused, hated and unrated. The sacrificial, perfect, no-sin God, who became flesh and died for us, with all the love in the Universe. Love hurts so bad sometimes, but it's better for love to hurt than for hate to deceive, lie and imitate.

My Daddy didn't attend church and I didn't care about that

because he was too ill. I placed a blanket over him and tucked him in while he was asleep on the settee one day as God told me he was going to take him home soon. On the day we found he had died in his sleep, the medicine cabinet fell from the kitchen wall and was caught as it landed on younger sis. I told her to leave it and I would clear it up, sending her off to the Christian Friendship Centre where she was working. It was a perfectly good day, we thought, and our mother went off to the shopping centre for her messages. At that point we weren't aware there was a death in the family until about 11am because it wasn't unusual for our Daddy to get up whenever he wanted to, as he turned night into day anyway. He always said he wanted to pass away the way his father went, in his sleep. It was three days after his birthday on August the sixth he died and he hadn't the strength or will to open his gifts, which lay on the top of the settee.

A friend who was staying with us had her Christian music blaring away from the bedroom while she dried her hair and Auntie Mary (our Daddy's sister) was making tea. God had taken me out of the house the night before and I stayed with a friend. While staying with the friend, I didn't feel too good and I asked if I could go for a lie-down. The pain shooting down my left arm was really uncomfortable but I wasn't overly concerned about my heart despite the Out of Body Experience I had years earlier. I had no idea then that The Lord was showing me our Daddy was having a heart attack. It didn't last long. I fell asleep unplanned, I think he did too, as the pain was gone when I woke up. I got up very early in the morning and took Sarah back home. There was no response from The Daddy when he was asked if he would like a cup of tea. When I went in to check on him, he had gone and I knew The Holy Spirit was in the house with us that day, as He was with me while our Daddy was dying during the night. I had previously agreed we would look after someone's dog while they were on holiday and I couldn't back out as they had already left for abroad. The in-laws of the family point-blank refused to take the dog, even when I explained our Dad had died in his bed and was still in the house. We had no option but to keep the promise of dog-sitting with Boomer, who had a huge lampshade on. Boomer would get up and try and go into the kitchen from the lounge but his huge lampshade got stuck on the door, which made us laugh, because he just stood there until someone got up and moved him away. We were always saying, 'Will someone help Boomer again? He's stuck!' We laughed a lot through the dark days of our loss because of Boomer, as he literally kept us on our toes.

I thought I was fine, I cried a lot and I suppose the grief knocked six bells out of me. When the doctor came to sign off the death certificate, the police, who were standing outside the door all day, finally went away. As our Daddy died in the house, it was just a formality that had to take place. We went to Govan police station, where I received the death certificate, and we left, well, the rest did, they got back down the stairs, but my legs wouldn't go down. I couldn't understand it, I got up the stairs all right but I didn't seem to have any going-down genes. Try as I might, I couldn't get my legs to bend and everyone else was so busy chatting to the police that I was left behind. I had to turn around to go down backwards. Again it made me laugh. There was something beautiful in the tears accompanied with laughter, like a healing ointment. God had wrapped me up again in Him. My Daddy was saved, led by Pastor Morrison, and for that I was so grateful, I loved him deeply. Life with Jesus is all about Love, mercy and forgiveness. There was no baptism for The Daddy because he was too ill but he accepted Jesus and that was the only thing I wished for, that my Daddy would be saved.

## Chapter Eleven

# LIFE IS A PEACH

I have told this story a good few times because it still amazes me. Although it's a horrible one, I quite like to see people pulling faces. Eve in the Garden of Eden comes to mind when I think of this story and I have to admit I was in the frame of mind for disobeying God when I heard Him. I wanted to do my own thing, particularly because I didn't understand why.

One day I held in my hand the most amazing, large delicious-looking peach I had ever seen in my life and it felt perfect, exactly ripe and ready for eating. After inspecting its beauty and perfection, I put it to my mouth to bite it but, just before my teeth sank into it, God gave me that familiar punch in the gut and said very clearly,

**'DON'T EAT THAT PEACH!'** I thought I had never seen one that delicious-looking and I was hungry, I went all out to disobey God and got set to take a bite again, then stopped. While inspecting it, I started with the questions towards God: 'Why not? Why can I not eat the peach?' Every time I went to bite it, I stopped and had a good look at it. It was beyond perfect but I was also a bit scared of disobeying God. I had one eye on the peach and one on the sky, thinking, 'Pie in the sky when you die.'

God won. Out of curiosity I took the peach to the kitchen and got a large knife out and halved it in two. To my absolute horror, out fell the hugest crawly beastie I had ever seen in my life, with a hundred legs, though I didn't stand still to count them. It was very long, slinky, shiny and black, yuck. God knows

I was already squeamish as far as my food was concerned, I cannot even begin to imagine what would have happened if I had eaten that peach to the centre, expecting a stone. There was no stone in the peach and I have always wondered how the giant beastie got inside the beautiful peach. I mean, how? Just HOW? I might have said 'No' to God but I'm so glad I changed my mind and obeyed him. God, I had no idea you were protecting me by taking something good away, thanks a million!

A simple little story here about taking my rubbish bin bag out to the larger bin container downstairs. As I wrapped and tied the full kitchen bin bag of refuse for disposal downstairs to the back of the garden, I was given the familiar punch inside my abdomen, gentle though.

God also said, '**TAKE CARE AT THE BIN STORE.**'

What on earth was going to happen at the bin store? I thought. The huge bin couldn't fall, it was far too big and was set behind steel doors. I was baffled as I made my way downstairs, perhaps there were neds hanging about, someone untrustworthy, I didn't know. It was dark and stinky inside, as you would expect a bin store to be. I didn't get too close or enter, bearing in mind how God had just warned me. Full of the brave faith pills, God's pill-Gospil!, holding my breath I pulled the heavy steel door fully back in order to throw the bag in. There was a horrific wail, screech, and this big black hairy beast jumped out of the top of the bin and wrapped itself around my face before hitting the ground and scrambling away. Although God had just warned me beforehand, I still got the fright of my life. Someone had shut or deliberately put a cat in the bin store and it wasn't best pleased (neither was I). 'Okay, God, thanks for that."He who sits in the Heavens shall laugh!"' I know where I get my sense of humour from.

'**STAY AWAY FROM THE LIGHT.**' The Lord said, so why did I go ahead and carry on? Our ceiling light bulb blew and shattered, sending the glass from the bulb blowing out everywhere and only leaving the metal connection part still engaged in the light fitting. I cleared the glass from the shattered bulb up from the carpet and surrounding area. On close inspection I could see the shattered bulb holder wouldn't come out by hand, so off I went to find something to prise it out with. Brace yourself at my stupidity and don't try this at home, or anywhere for that matter. I made sure the lounge light was switched off at the wall as I dragged the stepladders through, along with a pair of scissors. You did not, I hear you think. I did! Up on top of the ladders I grabbed hold of that light connection and stuck the scissors into it to try and poke the metal part of the bulb out, happy the light switch was off. I thought that would do. As the steel scissors connected with the light fitting the boom was terrific and I got down that ladder far quicker than I went up, I can tell you. Only then did I realise how stupid I had been as one of the scissor legs had a hole in it, phew . . . SHOCKING! I never even felt a thing, God, but I did learn a thing . . . to do as I am told. 'Thank you, Father.' To obey is better than to sacrifice. The Lord God still had a lot to teach me, and I still had a lot to learn. I learned to do exactly what I am told.

Rush hour always started in our house very early in the morning, not only in the chaotic traffic. The usual Mummy things were taking place, like getting the children fed and dressed for their schools, getting the dog walked and getting ready for my work after blow-drying my hair were the order of the morning. I had already cleaned the kitchen and mopped the floor, and had left the mop bucket water sitting, as the dirty water was to go outside when I was on my way out. A smaller portable mirror was propped up on the kitchen unit so I could blow-dry my hair there and do another twenty-odd things at the same time, like yell, 'Brush your teeth,' 'Get your packed lunch out of the fridge,' while I held it opened with my foot and so on, you get the picture. Face made up, hair nearly dried, I put the blowing, vibrating hairdryer on the unit while I brushed my long hair through a bit before finishing it off. The hairdrier hummed as it vibrated along the kitchen unit top, fell off and headed for the mop pail full of water. I automatically went to grab the hairdryer as it proceeded to land in the mop pail of water but, before my hand got a chance to grab onto it, it was hit away! The warning was there too, of course, but there wasn't anyone close to me as I went to grab the hairdryer. Not only was The Holy Spirit punching me, the Angels were hitting me now. Thank you, Father God. I would have given myself a free perm, but I would also have been dead without your intervention and wouldn't have been able to tell the story.

'**BEWARE OF THE DOG**.' I dutifully obeyed when I got this punch because I had already had my fair share of dog bites and scars on my body as a testimony. I was having a quick visit to my friend's house for a word before getting the bus to work, mobile phones weren't on the go then and she didn't have a house phone, so I was popping in to tell her I would see her later on in the evening when I had finished work. When I got to her house, though, her neighbour from the downstairs house was in the garden with her beautiful well-built black-and-tan, long-haired German Shepherd, a fine and handsome beast. As I put my hand on the gate to go in, it was then The Lord told me to '**BEWARE OF THE DOG**'. Enlightened with this information, I asked the neighbour, who was in the garden having a cigarette and waiting on her dog to do its business, if she wouldn't mind holding the dog by the collar until I got in and went upstairs to my friend's house as both main doors were side by side. I just wanted to have a quick chat and I was in a hurry, I told her. The downstairs 'lady' declined my request with a form of industrial language, informing me emphatically that her fully grown hound did not bite. Yeah right, how did it eat its dinner then? Suck it? I'm joking. It wasn't funny at the time. I heard The Lord God right and acted upon His knowledge and wisdom. I don't know if I was more scared of being bitten by the dog or its owner and I had been there before. Just like the last time, I took her sound advice with a deep breath and casually walked in, closed the gate behind me, and up the path I went with the feeling I was the dog's sacrificial lamb. I didn't look at the dog as I headed for the door, so as not to provoke it in any way. The beast leapt like a lion and tore the sleeve of my brand new blue shiny jacket to ribbons as it bit right through to the bone of my left arm. The pain ripped through my whole body. My arm was warm, wet and sticky as the blood poured down the inside of my sleeve and out of the cuff, saturating my white work blouse. To make matters worse, the owner grabbed her dog by the collar and tried to tear its teeth away from my arm, making the dog rip away more of my jacket and tear at the flesh on my arm, which was even more painful. She finally managed to free her beloved pet and marched it indoors, slamming her front door. I was in shock and my friend wasn't even at home. The neighbour downstairs was then furious because I went to the police. I had to have stitches, a tetanus injection, and couldn't go to work for a week because of her dog, and she was mad? Not only did she not offer to contribute towards my wages or new jacket, she didn't even come back out to offer me so much as a sticking plaster to stop the flow of blood. I had to walk all the way down to the police station, where they wrapped my arm up, before heading off to the hospital. They offered to drive me there but I decided to get the bus. I left the matter in The Lord God's hands. I didn't want anything to do with my friend's neighbour, her dog or her family, and I stopped visiting, meeting her at other places instead. I later learned from my friend that the dog which 'didn't bite' savaged the woman's husband when he walked in late one night and crept in with the hood of his jacket still up. I hold my tongue, thoughts and hands to Heaven.

Twin number two (Robbie) had a terrible plague of warts over both of his hands as a youngster. The warts had warts, they were thick and bulgy and I didn't want to hold his hand, but you can't treat a child badly or make him feel self-conscious because of a disease or affliction. My mother gave him a row for constantly biting his fingers and nails and she told him he was going to the doctor's sooner rather than later. On a Friday afternoon she took him to the doctor, who agreed his hands were a total mess, and told my mother to take him to the clinic first thing on Monday morning. There they would start burning the warts off and treat his cracked and bleeding sores where he had been picking. It was another one of those quick off-the-cuff prayers that was said for the healing of his hands and I promised Robbie they would be better in no time. On the Monday morning he was taken off to the clinic, where he lifted up his perfect little hands with not a spot or blemish on them, not even any scar tissue to suggest there was ever anything wrong. Between the Friday afternoon and the Monday morning, no one even noticed the warts were gone. They had totally disappeared.

I'm on a huge boat gripping tightly onto the handrail. I notice the sky is bright blue when I look up but the turbulent waters demand I get back under the sea. My stomach is heaving every time the vessel sinks as low as it can get before it is thrown violently to the skyline again on the crest of each wave. Every time the vessel goes to the depths of the raging sea, my stomach goes with it. I am sick and frightened and cannot let go. As the side of the vessel gurgles beneath the waves, I feel fear, failure, torture, death . . . and I'm soaking wet. I dare not let go of the slippery rail, it's the only thing I have to save me. Under it goes again, my face battered by the swishing, growling and grabbing of the water, trying to prise my fingers from the rail. 'I can't hold on any more,' I scream inside as the deep darkness holds me under the water for the umpteenth time. Nor can I hold my breath any longer because, each time the vessel drags me under the water, it takes longer, deliberately I feel, to come back up. I don't see evil, but I 'know' it, I can sense it, to the left of me. Somehow I know it's standing there, silently watching on its own, like a cat toying with a mouse, frightening it before the kill. It's watching me as though it has nothing to do with the situation but I sense the presence of darkness looking on. I can drown in life's problems all on my own, 'it' reasons. It will just stand back and watch me die because I cannot breathe, my lungs will fail me and asthma will get the blame, not Satan. I sense he has brought me here. He can't touch me but he has interfered with a chink in the armour and managed to get me on my own. He says nothing, he simply stands quietly, arms folded, watches and waits, with pleasure, until I die.

'Oh God, not again,' I plead inwardly as the huge boat smashes against the water's surface. This is not the 'peak and flow' of a vessel in a violent storm. The storm was my storm and made just for me, the evil buccaneer aiming to destroy and bury treasure. The boat deliberately dips menacingly with one purpose, death, but I somehow know it won't completely sink. How do I know it won't sink? I don't know how I know that. It can't sink or I will die. Like the dream where you are jumping down the stairs and you never reach the bottom or you die. Like jumping off a cliff, you never reach the bottom or you die. Everyone knows that, except the people who have reached the bottom and have been unable to confirm it because they are dead. I'm not ready to die, it's not my time. I just need to hold on the tightest I have ever held on to life and hold my breath but it's too hard. I am more than half drowned, I am too exhausted to fight. Nobody knows to help me or save me.

Once more, the vessel takes a leap from the skyline and smashes into the water to get rid of me for good. It gurgles, slowly and deliberately, knowing I am fighting for my life, but I hold on, fingers pained with cramp.

Holding my very last breath for far too long, the vessel does something it hasn't done before in the deep, it completely tilts and rolls underneath the water, it turns upside down and stays there and is going to sink. My long hair sways softly away from my face and all is getting calmer. The blue sky is above and I'm at peace. So this is death then. I knew it was death, I knew the vessel couldn't sink or the end would come.

I see the light in the darkness of the deep getting brighter and the evil presence backing off. There was nothing else to happen then but to relax my fingers. It was the end, I couldn't hold my breath any more and I slowly let the last of my air go. The peace was beautiful. In the brighter light under the water was total peace, and GOD. It wouldn't have mattered if I was to die, God was there by His Holy Spirit. The evil had to back off when The Holy Spirit came. I thought of nothing but letting go and letting God take full control. In the light of His presence the vessel is moved very slightly and slowly and is set in motion towards the upright position.

In the twinkling of an eye I am back in my bed, absolutely soaking wet from the perspiration of the nightmare and gasping for the air that was stolen. I sit up and cry but I am still alive to take care of my family. With God's help I begin to live, life is a peach.

On another seriously turbulent night's sleep I had a terrible dream in which God was telling me He was taking my mother home. I was wrestling with God and I told Him He wasn't taking my mother home, I still needed her and I told Him, 'You are not having her, not yet, I need her!' I kept reasoning with Him and I wouldn't budge or change my mind. I was sobbing in the dream, yet it was so real and lasted for quite a long time, simply because I wouldn't back down and give in. I could feel the power struggle and I couldn't give in or let her go. For me the dream became a nightmare and I woke up. When I woke up I sat up in bed and realised I was actually breaking my heart and my pillow was soaked with my tears. I prayed there and then and told God the dream was horrible and I shook my head, saying, 'No, God, You can't have her, she's mine.' I lay back down with a heavy heart and still refused to give my mother back. I knew I had told Him she could go back to Heaven but I couldn't let her go and I wasn't about to change my mind. I fell asleep again as it was still dark and early in the morning. I was back with God for round two of the discussion, the continuation of the dream where God was telling me my mother was due to go back to Heaven. Again I wrestled with Him in the dream and I refused to let my mother go. I couldn't let go. I told Him, 'She has to stay here, I need her.' I promised Him He could have her but not yet. I wasn't ready to be on my own, with all of the children being so young. 'God, you can't have her, it's not debatable, I need her with me.' I argued with Him, there was no way I could agree to what He was telling me, and I woke up again. still sobbing. and prayed, 'No, God, I said No! You're not having her yet, she has to stay a little while longer.'

My prayer and wrestling with God The Father could be construed as cheek or downright audacity. I saw it as having a relationship with The God/Daddy in Heaven. I just couldn't let my mother go back or I would die, I told Him. I desperately needed her. There was no talking to my earthly daddy but I could talk to, and with, my Heavenly Father. I have always feared The Lord, The Heavenly Daddy, but I respect Him and I trust Him, there is a love blood bond (through the cross) which works both ways. Still, He was *not* having my mother.

He never hurts me physically, emotionally or mentally. I'm not afraid to approach Him to talk to and with Him. I'm not afraid to bring forth my good reasons and requests, and talk to Him regarding my heart's desires. He looks out for me and protects me and in turn I deeply love Him because of the kind of Daddy He is. He loves me so much. I become as a child when speaking to The Holy of Holies. That's how I speak to Him because we are related, He is my Father. The Heavenly Father loves it when His children dig their heels in and bring forth their good causes, He takes great delight in our faith attitude. He loves to see and hear us acting like Him because we belong to Him. He sees our personality and growing character, and sees us accepting that He is the true and only God. He says, 'That's my boy/girl/child/beloved.' We love it when we see God working in us, He loves it when He sees us working in and for Him. Like Father, like son. Like Father, like daughter.

We are allowed to say 'No.' It's more than likely we will see His point of view and realise He is always right and He will bring us round to the truth of His ways. Have you ever seen a little child in distress and disagreeing with his or her parent? We are no different, we are His little ones and He allows us to communicate in any fashion.

God didn't take my mother home then, He let me keep her. Had I told her this story when she was alive, she would have been really mad at me. She had already told me about the slap on the face she gave the doctor when he brought her back from near dying as she gave birth. She told me she didn't want to come back and warned the doctor, 'Never do that again!' Sometimes I am right, loads of times I am wrong, but God The Father is always the same, loving and kind, and He deeply cares. He is a loving, caring Father and cares deeply about us.

*Early photo which survived the fire, aged 3,*
*taken at Craigton Cemetery*

*A young Esther*

*Me (Esther) and Pannie*

Out of the four photos I find of me,
my eyes are closed in two.

*Swirls on the ceiling, bed moved and something walked on top of my bed in this flat.*

*2 Drive Road was bought for the sum of £500, payable at £34 a month along with a second-class stamp. £500 for a kitchen, bathroom, two bedrooms, large lounge and an upstairs small bedroom with a skylight. I was eight and a half years old when the flat was purchased and it was there that I saw my three Angels twice, the first time in the kitchen and the second time in the second bedroom.*

*When we moved to Port Ann in Argyll, I never saw the evils or my Angels again.*
*In Lochgilphead, though, I saw Heaven as I was leaving my body.*

ENTRY 15/2/69.

Code No. MR. D.  G.Y.3/6

Name  MRS. G.B.BAXTER.

Rent
Rates
PURCHASE PRICE
£500.

| DUE | DATE OF PAYMENT | No. | R/P | PURCHASE PRICE | AMT. PAID | AMT. O/S |
|---|---|---|---|---|---|---|
| 1969 FEB. 28 | DEPOSIT £100 PAID DIRECT TO URIE & MACRAE | | | 500.0.0 | | 400.0.0 |
| MAR. 28 | | 73,900 | 400.0.0 | | 32.0.0 | 366.0.0  C |
| APR. 28 | | 73,900 | 366.0.0 | | 28.0.0 | 338.0.0  C |
| MAY 28 | 4561 PAID MAY 1969 | | 338.-- | | £34.-- | £304 |
| JUN. 28 | 4604 18th June 1969 | 304 | | | £34 | £270 |
| JUL. 28 | 4464 18th July 1969 | 270 | | | £34 | £236 |

Who wouldn't love to pay £500 nowadays for a two-bedroomed flat? But would you if it had spooks?

I see The Daddy has added his name, my mother must have had the buying power and he would have been upset his name wasn't included.

My mummy and The Daddy.
I think I took the photo.

*Pannie and Esther (me)*
*'Happy' Christmas at 2 Drive road.*

Check us out with our school pinafores on, on Christmas Day. Pannie is sitting on my chair with her new dolly. Our dolls are bigger than the Christmas tree The Christmas lights were frosted Santa and Snowman heads, which tasted horrible. How do I know that? I tasted them! When they were switched off, of course. Children taste things, maybe I was just so hungry, who knows, I tasted them anyway and they were salty and gritty, that I do remember. Tinsel (thin strands of metallic coloured foil) is draped over the tree for added effect. Effect of what, I don't know, but it is there.

If this photo depicts our happiness on a Christmas Day, it only goes on to relate how fraught our daily living was and how terrified and miserable we were, growing up with a family member harbouring a mental illness.

It was in that kitchen the German Shepherd bit my stomach as I tried to get the door open. It was there that The Daddy threw his hot tea in my face when I tried to stop him hitting my mummy and it was in there that I saw the Angels the first time. It was also in this kitchen I stole the Christmas cake (because I was hungry) and had to hide it on top of the big old-fashioned mirrored wardrobe, to finish it off. I chose not to repair the damaged photo because we were damaged, daily.

*At Doune Castle.*

*Kat is perched beneath the wishing well which was also deep and water-filled (with a grate over it) as Pannie contemplates making a wish with her as currency. They do love each other really. When I said we were poor, I meant it. I am wearing my school blazer on a day out to one of the Clan gatherings, along with a non-tartan cheap wrap-over skirt meant to resemble a kilt.*

*The Daddy in his 'rigout'.*

*Me (Esther), young Addie and the very innocent-looking 'Catweazle', who brought the Irn-Bru bottle down on his shin for not moving fast enough to give her a drink.*

*Irn-Bru was made from 'Steel', you know, no wonder it hurt so much.*

*Baby sis on my knee and Corrie in the background at Port Ann.*

*I left Port Ann not long after this photo was taken and was 'leaving' for Heaven too, the day I had the Out of Body Experience when the grass changed to its true colour.*

*I left my heart and my love behind in Port Ann for a long, long time.*

*Esther, Aged 15 (While at Oban High School)*

*'Stupid, Useless, Fat and Ugly' (allegedly). The wicked enemy is a liar.*

*Note: only my mouth is smiling and it's clearly fake. I can still feel the pain in her heart by looking at her sad eyes. Also note the lollipop look; when the head appears too big for a skinny body, one of the telltale signs of being too thin.*

*Note to self: Fat? Ugly? Stupid and useless? And you believed it? Look what life, lies and Annie R (Rexia) did to you. Perfection came along to live and lie to you but 'Perfect Love' (Jesus) casts out all fear.*

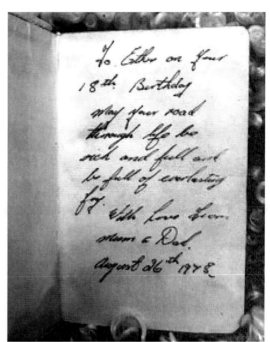

*The little white Bible I asked my Mother for when she asked me what I would like for my eighteenth birthday.*

*Who asks for a bible, I ask you? But that's all I wanted.*

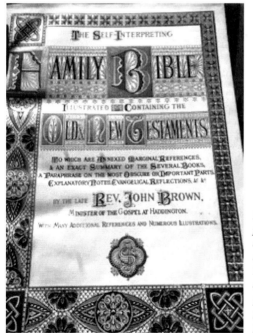

*Many years later I asked God for a present from Him as Christmas was coming up, to search my deepest heart and give me a secret heart's desire. I had totally forgotten about wanting a great big old church bible.*

*Minutes later, He gave me this great big old family bible, which no one knew I secretly desired.*

*The wee man (Christopher) was not overly impressed by Santa.*

*Perhaps that's why he trashed hundreds of Christmas crackers looking for a better present.*

*Little Christopher with our very first car, which Pastor Morrison bought us.*

*Our first church was at the Christian Friendship Centre in Dennistoun.*

*In all the years I went there, my husband worked as a manager in a supermarket around the corner, right under my nose, though I didn't know it and didn't find him until thirty years later.*

*Having a great time at Christian Friendship Centre's Christmas party
for the elderly in the community.*

*All thanks to the fine folks who donated for this cause to take place in the city's Dennistoun.
Thanks a million for your support. Can-collecting was often very cold and humbling.*

*Baby 'Kitchen Girl'*

*Miss you so much* ♥

*My friend took her own life because of
the distress and nightmare of Quarrier's.*

## Chapter Twelve

# THE BACKSLIDER

Having left the Christian Friendship Centre after the death of my Daddy, I fell away from going to church for close to five years. During that time I also eventually turned away from The Most High God, The Lord Jesus Christ and The Holy Spirit, which broke my heart. I deliberately broke my own heart and relationship with The Godhead I had been searching for from when I was a little girl. I certainly didn't stop loving Him and, on reflection, I'm even glad it hurt like hell so as to show me where I truly belonged. Having a second dip into the life that was so unattractive only confirmed what I already knew, it was still grossly unattractive. The exact time it took me to realise I had made the biggest mistake of my entire life was seven days, one week, that's all, one was indeed weak.

A man I had previously dated and turned away from looked more attractive years later under Satan's pathetic lying eyes. Satan was, and is, a snake, a charmer and a stalker. I knew he was around here and there, but it had never bothered me in the slightest because I didn't heed him and I recognised when he was close by. After the seven days I was caught between the devil and the deep blue sea, unable to walk or cross any divide to get back to God because I knew I wasn't worthy. I was deeply ashamed and couldn't look to my Father God for comfort.

Now I realised I was, again, stupid, useless, an idiot, and no good to anyone. I really was like Eve in the Garden of Eden this time as I hid my face but I couldn't hide my shame. I was unable to approach God. I couldn't even pray. I covered my head with my hands and rocked and groaned. I had crucified my Jesus and taken part with the sinful crowd who shouted, 'Crucify Him.' I was a despicable wretch who deserved nothing, and I was dying inside and had allowed Satan to take over the abuse when my Daddy died.

On reflection, I was having a Daddy versus God experience, where I now loved my Daddy as purely and honestly as was commanded to, without reservation. The complete opposite had happened with the two Fathers and turned my life and perceptions upside down. I now found I was unable to approach the Heavenly Father to communicate with because of my actions and had no words to describe the despicable me I had become, just for a taste of the world.

I could only love my Daddy as much as I did because someone had to die. He died and Jesus died (for our sins). I saw, felt for and had compassion for people when I understood they were every bit as vulnerable and broken as me. I allowed myself to be manipulated by Satan, who took over the role of my Daddy, assisting me to believe I deserved this life, to believe I was useless, but God was showing me I wasn't created to be abused.

From the womb I was terrified and the control ruined and thwarted my development as a child. I was allowing Satan to walk in and continue the abuse and take over where my Daddy left off. I was allowing him to destroy my soul and I clung to life on the big boat because I was, without words, allowing him to destroy me. He was killing me because I let him. He stood back with his arms folded and watched me struggle with life because I had no faith, because I had no fight in me. I was battered up and I had to learn to fight back.

There is none other who has the infinite knowledge of creation and the talent of creativity in order to perfect and change the mistakes we make. Creation designed to naturally bend and mend itself because it was told to by the Creator. Everything obeys, everything except sin.

My God-given Earth Daddy was hurt by his circle of life.

That included his own upbringing with his Daddy, which wasn't an easy life. He was poor in spirit too. He was hurt, belted physically, hungry, wretched, poor and uneducated. His father was illiterate, I was informed. He had no shoes. I had shoes – they might not have fitted, and they hurt my toes awfully, but at least I had shoes. His world and destiny exploded in creative bursts when he met his beautiful darling wife, my mother, stealing her away from her own father and marrying her on her sixteenth birthday. Only through time did I learn some facts from his siblings, which raised my eyebrows and humbled my heart.

My soul ached in despair. I couldn't talk to my Heavenly Father because I had deliberately turned away, my shame burning my whole body and mind. My own free will was snared and I fell for it, just like some of our ancestors in the bible. I understood how and why they stumbled and fell too, by deceit, listening to lies, a haughty spirit, boredom, tiredness, laziness and everything else that can be labelled a chink in armour. I had nowhere to fall before I accepted Jesus into my heart because I was already at rock bottom. To die to self when 'born again' is the ultimate redemption calling. There is nothing higher, nothing more to ask for, nothing more to be given, it isn't just 'Finished', as He gave us life more abundantly, a new beginning. It was a brand-new day, which was the first of eternity. I had completely and totally fallen in love with the one I had waited all of my life for, then ruined it through deception. All of the blessings we have been promised; a mansion in Heaven, healing, perfection, love, joy, peace, streets of gold, amazing feasts, a crown of the most priceless jewels, which we would gladly lay at His feet, and the love of our lives, Jesus, were lost. All far too beautiful for our imaginations and thoughts to describe or decipher, and I killed the dream, the vision, the truth, through deliberate sin. I had no plans or visions for a mansion in Heaven, I just wanted to be there with Jesus. I was so happy to live in a little hut by a stream and be forever mesmerised at the beauty of the flowers and the greenest grass.

Satan was smirking as I walked through the park in Pollok with the father of my daughter after my grand fall. Satan had won, he thought. He had managed to pull me from the Kingdom of Heaven for a time and he didn't have to lay one hairy demonic finger on me to do it. He used deceit, not gold, silver, finances or apples, just plain old deceit. I was deceived, his favourite trick in his book. He plays mind games. He is a whisperer, he suggests and, when we're not armoured with The Word of God, he springs up and into the tiniest gap that is exposed. Any chink in the armour will do. In my case it was loneliness. I was waiting, impatiently, for my husband, and stepped out of line. I hadn't perfected patience and timing. I could hear God's still, small voice but chose not to wait on Him. I fell from God's grace and it was my own fault. I blame no one but myself. It was my fault and I knew it, I blew it.

Rab (Sarah's dad) and I walked through the woods one dark autumn evening, me with Toto, and Rab's German Shepherd, both on leads, where I saw Satan. After cutting through the path to some spare ground, my eyes came across something that was unusual and creepy. My heart was heavy, as I thought about Jesus constantly. The weight of sin crushed every part of my being, physically and emotionally, because I loved Jesus, yet I had become the one who crucified Him. I was daily consumed by grief and regret. As we strolled further on, I saw someone sitting on the ground and holding a high pole of some sort. As we walked towards the 'person', I was silent in my own thoughts. Although it was dark, I could see someone sitting on the ground with his legs crossed and wearing a loose black outfit that covered his knees, and his right arm was stretched up as though he was holding a staff, not curled at the top, it was poker-straight. On his head he was wearing a tall pointed hat, which was crumpled and twisted down to the rim. His face was very dark but I could see he was ugly and grinning. His face moved away from us as he turned to look towards his staff, I'll call it, then back again towards us, facing us. A staff, or crook, has a bent curled top, which is used for grabbing the neck of a lamb or sheep in order to gather it close and out of danger. Satan's pole was different, like a spear for poking, stabbing and maiming.

He was very old, wrinkled, dark, and as ugly as sin, I was now seeing him in his true form, not as a handsome being. The closer we got to him, the more menacing he was becoming. He was shuddering as though sniggering, that I saw clearly when he turned to the right. My legs started to shake and felt like jelly. I heard no sound but he acted as though he was sniggering and was pointing towards us. Just as we were almost before him, I slowed down in my pace. Rab said nothing and I realised he couldn't see Satan, even although he was sitting right in front of us. I thought I was going to pass out and took hold of Rab's arm to steady myself before I collapsed with fear.

'Look!' I said to Rab. I pulled on his arm and searched his face for help as we got right before Satan. When I faced the front again, Satan had completely vanished. He quickly disappeared into the cold night air. I couldn't speak, and said nothing about Satan. I saw Satan and he saw me. I had been aware of his presence from childhood and saw him on the hill many times, I knew him and there is no doubt in my mind, he is real and does exist.

Someone asked me recently if I believed in Satan. I told her, 'I don't believe "in him" (I don't put my trust in him), I believe he is here and lives on Earth, though.' I've seen him and his menacing works, in swirls up on the ceiling. I've met many intelligent people throughout the years and the ones who concern me most regarding their salvation are the ones who visit mediums, fortune tellers and other evil spiritual events. I've had people tell me, under protest, 'But they told me something no one else in the whole wide world knows, only me.' Well, that is just not true. God knows! Satan and his demons know! God warns us via the bible to stay well away from mediums and soothsayers and Satan even quotes the bible, he knows what it says in there more than we do. He is in it, why wouldn't he know what's going on in the Spirit and on the Earth, where he lives?

'How do you know it is not God providing the information?' they ask. God does not deceive, lie, sit with a round glass ball, dress weird, mumble nonsense and charge you a lot of money to tell you half-baked truths or unbaked lies. God does not have a stammer, it was Moses who had a stammer. God does not narrow his eyes and say, 'I see someone in your family, beginning with the letter J. Is it Julie? John? Jeremy? Jack? It begins with a J. Jemima!' The devil is a liar and his greatest trait is deceit. He can also be very handsome, and masquerades into a being of light to deceive us, a trait he still uses, his beauty, and I saw him. There is nothing beautiful left in him. There is no love. Don't forget, most people have posted their whole life on social media. Not just their own family's, nearest and dearest, friends', births, deaths and marriages. It is much easier to find information today than it ever was.

Back to that secret no one else knew. There are people who worship or serve Satan and they open themselves up to the spirit world. No one has to look far to seek and find Satan, he is already here hovering around, as he has access by millions of unseen doors and avenues.

Hundreds of years ago poor people had a glass ball hanging from their windows, with the belief that any evil passing, be it a witch or demon, would see itself in the glass ball and fly by, 'knowing' evil already lived in there, so they wouldn't bother visiting. They thought the glass ball would protect them. I have glass balls at home, they are called paperweights. I don't use them as paperweights, I only collect them because they have a nice glass design on the inside and they're pretty, that's all. My husband would go a little further and call them dust collectors and that's true too. Be warned, you will find what you are looking for because Satan is waiting to fill the ears and eyes of any person searching the future, because he is in the Spirit world. He will tell you and give you what you want because he wants your Spirit in Hell. He does not and cannot love you. He hates his demons and they hate him. I thought I was talking to my sister on the telephone. I thought it was her I was hearing as 'she' spoke back. It was evil who thought it was funny to play stupid games. Be double warned, Satan is alive and kicking and it's you he will more than kick if you play with him. Do not dance with the devil. The people who are playing with Satan and charging you money are no wiser than yourself. You could, if you so desired, pass yourself off as a medium or fortune teller and so could I. It's wrong and forbidden, don't get involved. You will find yourself trapped in a web of evil and out of favour with The Almighty God, who became flesh and dwelt among us (Jesus). Satan and his weedy followers will take the flesh from your face when they call for you to go with them when you leave the earth. Be warned, don't go there.

I was speaking to a man not much younger than myself, who told me he has never gone to bed with the light out because he is afraid of the dark. I didn't share my childhood experiences with him because he was already living in fear, but who told him he was frightened? What happened in his life that has made him so insecure when alone at night? I didn't get the opportunity to have a deep conversation with him as he was with his girlfriend, it wasn't the right time and place, and I didn't want to embarrass him. The horror I saw as a child was not for everyone to witness, God let me see it.

Third warning: Stay well away from all kinds of evil, especially subtle little nosy pokes, such as reading your 'stars'. Pannie, my younger sister, recently told me her bed moved too, she was so shocked when I told her that little part of my testimony for this book. She thought she was alone with this Satanic encounter and told not a soul until I mentioned it first. We shared the same room and it was when we were sleeping in single divans that we were 'visited'. She volunteered the information without coaxing when I told her some of the contents of the book. I believe her because I know through my own personal experience that it happened. As far as the devil is concerned, we don't need to dabble with him for him to find us. Stay away from him and all of his nasty and tasteless devices. There is no nourishment, either physically or spiritually, in dabbling with the occult.

The road to God is via The Lord Jesus Christ all the way and there is no other way. Life without God is not life, it's death, eternal death. There is no living if God is not in us and the death we walk in continues after the death of our bodies, to the area where Satan exists. Furthermore, Satan is entitled to us when we don't choose the life God has prepared for us. If you have given your life to Satan, served him, worshipped him, sought after him or not chosen the narrow road to salvation, then Satan already has claims on you. There is nothing left to say, we choose where we are going, we choose life or death. In order to stay with God, we must be 'born again' in the Spirit because we are naturally excluded through sin. We are separated from God and we must confess 'Jesus is Lord' to get back to our Heavenly Father. We are lost for all of eternity if we don't. Jesus is the Sacrificial Lamb whose blood was poured out for all of mankind, there is no other sacrifice available. Jesus is one with God. God is one with The Holy Spirit. God has seven Spirits! That's too deep even for me. I have spoken to hundreds of people who have said they would never have shouted, 'Crucify Him' if they had stood beneath His cross on the hill of Golgotha. We still shout, 'Crucify Him' when we sin. We are partakers of that same crowd every time we tell a lie, cheat, steal, swear or murder. Sin is sin. We are separated and need to get back to Our 'Abba' Father. Neither Jews nor Romans killed Jesus, they were merely assistants to a greater master plan, Our Master's plan. It is important to remember that Jesus was not *killed* for our salvation in the way the world thinks, He *chose* to lay down his life. It was the great master plan, which happened right under Satan's nose, and he didn't understand what was happening. What a beautiful love story. God became flesh and dwelt among us, He experienced our difficulties, trials and traumas and He still knows how hard it is.

When I was in my teens I cried out to God in anger one day and told him, 'It's all right for you, you don't know what it's like for us on Earth, you haven't lived here!' God opened up and showed me He came as a newborn baby and experienced our lives on Earth. He did know what it was like, He walked the same earth and suffered the same difficulties. He showed me He kept his eyes on The Heavenly Father at all times and prayed nonstop. He was tempted too but He never succumbed to the temptation. His actions spoke much louder than words. When I realised it was true, that He even came to Earth and had a taste of how difficult it was for us, I was completely remorseful and humbled. There has never, nor will there ever be, a greater love story. He wants us back. He came to this earth to collect us and He's not giving up. No matter what we have done, He wants us back. I finally accepted that God was right when I saw and realised I had been deceived and went back to another church and repented, telling myself I was doing it for my children, at the very least. It was painful but I did it. It was too painful for me to continue without God, He didn't deserve my sin. It was the sorriest time in my life, much worse than being abused mentally as a child. I deserved death and Hell. It pained me to open up and confess that I had walked away. I appreciate God, Jesus and The Holy Spirit much more now, more deeply than when I first received him into my life. At first I was so in love but now I have a gratitude that will never fade and I will never deny him, even if it means death. I've tasted and seen, see, that The Lord is good. He has made mention in His word that backsliders have to come back to him. It's really hard to do when we are so ashamed that we cannot face Him but He is waiting and He will receive us. There is no sin so great or small that can keep us away. He is waiting with open arms. We have to get back, it really is a matter of 'Do or Die', forever. Right now is the day of your salvation, put the book down, He wants you to come right now . . .

The Angels in Heaven rejoice when we are saved and enter

into the fold of Heaven. It's a tough walk but not a tough choice. A little note to the victims of the appalling sin ripples that hurt us: people do dreadful things on Earth that cause us to recoil in horror and say, 'I can never forgive that person who did . . .', whatever it is they did to hurt and destroy your soul. They too have to live with their actions and they will see, feel and know even again, what they did on Earth, on Judgement Day. They will feel the other person's hurt, and even the hurt they caused to surrounding families and friends. We will be so aggrieved at their actions and words as they watch their lives unfold on Earth, we will see how stupid and reckless they (and I) were. It's easier said than done, let go and 'let God'. It's not easy to forgive and forget when grief and despair has broken us and when sin has destroyed us to the point of not wanting to live any more. There are people among us who were never destined for Heaven. Sin is laughing at us every day in the form of Satan but God alone is the author and finisher of our faith, He is The Judge too, let go. Then one final day we will be reunited with our loved ones and it will all be forgotten. It's all right to say I will forgive but I'll never forget, because one day we will forget and God will make it better. He is the Great I AM, who will put that spiritual sticking plaster on us and heal us. He will make us better, that's what Daddies do. God is not just any old Daddy, He is The bona-fide Daddy. We will run and laugh in Heaven with the family members we lost in tragic circumstances. Do not let Satan destroy your thoughts, emotions and dreams and keep you from the true blessings God The Father has in store for you. God's agape love poured upon you will destroy all fear.

I went along to a small hall in Cardonald, on the south side of Glasgow, which was packed to capacity with believers. Arthur O'Malley was the pastor and his wife Linda welcomed me with open arms. A girl at the church asked me if I knew Jesus and I replied, 'Yes, but I had backslid' and wanted to come back to church. She replied, 'Ooohh' in a derogatory way but I still went along nevertheless. She had her thoughts and I had mine. She was right, it was my own fault. Arthur and Linda didn't judge me, though, and I had a great time at his church until they moved many miles away, too far away to attend.

I never forgot Linda's laugh and zest for life. She came along to one of my plays (later on) with her friends and it was her I could hear howling with laughter right up at the back of the theatre. She laughed so much I had to have pregnant pauses before I could speak my next line and a lot of improvising was needed to fill in the time. She kept laughing at my facial expressions even as I waited on the laughter dying down and it made it even harder for me to act. Her laughter was like God laughing too and I finally forgave myself and moved on.

My personal faults happen most when I am in a supermarket and I have to warn myself to be good. I enter fine, breathe deeply and choose what I need so I can leave unscathed but I find myself in aisles I don't need to be in, looking for items I don't want. In order to get everything I have to traipse up and down every aisle to find it. I have a fair idea where to find things but, as seasons change, goods gets moved to different aisles, and that's why I have to travel up and down every single one. I come across the customers who stand still in the middle of the aisle so they can read what they are looking at and I can't get my trolley past their backsides. I breathe deeper. On the next aisle I bump into 'The Waltons', the group of people who haven't seen each other for months and assemble across the whole lane to chat, stopping everyone who wants to get past. Then there is the person who knows what she wants but she turns her trolley lengthways across the aisle so nobody passes her. There are the kids on their wheelie shoes, who travel at great speed and smash into you or your trolley, and the toddler who is having a tantrum in horizontal fashion on the shop floor. Speaking of speed, do I even dare mention the disabled person in the motorised scooter, who takes the skin off your ankles and drives faster than the five miles per hour stated on the supermarket car-park sign? Still, I keep taking deep breaths until I get to the last lane, then find I have to go back to some other aisles because stock has been moved, bumping my trolley over the boxes the staff have thrown behind them, deliberately. No wonder my retired supermarket manager husband doesn't do the shopping. The self-checkout point-blank refuses to assist me and demands I take the last item back out of my bag, then flashes a red beacon above my head. A long, long time later, an assistant comes but the invisible self-checkout entity does it again and again just to annoy me when she turns her back . . . and I've got Jesus, God help those who don't.

## Chapter Thirteen

# *AGAPE LOVE*

God took me back because He is Love. When I was pregnant with Sarah, I explained to the doctor on an ante-natal visit that I felt I couldn't carry her any longer and felt as though she was about to fall out. I hadn't seen her daddy for a few weeks, after I had repeatedly told him it was over and I wanted to go back to church. On turning into the hospital on the day I was to be booked for the 'inducement', I looked up at my rear-view mirror to see him driving in behind me. I was annoyed to find he was obviously following my movements and told him I was going in early to be induced because I felt the baby was popping out. We were civil to each other for a change and left it at that. Sarah was born at five twenty pm later that day. Five minutes after the injection to start my labour, she shot out into the world.

Later on, I got talking to a woman on the four-bed ward, who told me she came from Campbeltown. Chatting away, I was just about to tell her I had dated a guy from Campbeltown when I was younger and still at school. Just before the words came out of my mouth, the nurse came in and called her by her surname. She was only the wife of the fisherman I had dated in Ardrishaig! I was glad the nurse had turned up and called out her name and asked if her husband was coming. She said, 'No' (living so far away). I gulped and crawled under the bed sheet. I had a lucky escape there. I didn't want to see him. Not only that, her baby was ten pounds four ounces and was a natural birth. Ouch.

Sarah's daddy didn't live with us and, when he did, he would stay overnight on the spare bed settee. Sarah loved the very bones of him, and he her, and I loved her more than life. God had given me this beautiful little girl when I deserved nothing. I would look at her and cry, not only at her beauty, but at the fact God was so good and kind and graceful.

My brother Adam and his girlfriend Evelyn babysat a lot and Evelyn loved the bones of Sarah too. She looked after her to let me go out to work and would take her out a lot, even when I wasn't working. We called Evelyn Eve for short, so we could refer to them as Adam and Eve. After a few years I went along to Elim Pentecostal Church in Butterbiggens Road when Pastor Arthur moved away and it was there that Evelyn accepted The Lord Jesus as her saviour. Despite being with my brother for years, she fell for a bloke who also attended Elim and left my brother. I didn't see her again when she uprooted and left with her new man friend and I heard through the grapevine that she had passed away with cancer.

Elim Pentecostal's pastor was amazing, a great and humble man of God who let us cry on his shoulder. He told me it was all right when I apologised for wetting his jacket with tears one day and said his wife didn't mind, she always had to scrub the lipstick from his shirt collars, as females bowed their heads into his neck for a hug when unloading their heartaches. He was a hugger, a listener, a smiler, a prayer warrior, everything a pastor should be he was more than. The greatest thing about Elim (meaning 'an oasis in the desert') was that The Holy Spirit was always there. That's how good the leadership is and the music and prayer meetings are God-filled. It was in Elim that God Himself ministered to me most. People will think God (The Holy Spirit) is in every church, I know from personal experience He is not. Where two or three are gathered in His name, there He is, in the midst, but not every church has The Holy Spirit. Two or three can be gathered anywhere in His name and He will be there in the midst, as He says. It could be in a hospital ward, the roadside, a toilet, it could be anywhere where people are looking and praying for Him. He will come. I know this because there was one church I visited in the city centre which went through the rituals of religion.

As I sat in that church, I felt a horrible sensation of my skin crawling so badly I had the urge to get out and flee. I could feel 'Spikey Worms' trying to cut through my skin. The pews were packed and I was stuck in the middle of one, trying to behave and ignore the sensation, but I couldn't sit still and vowed never to set foot in that church again. When I explained how I felt to another Christian, she told me she felt exactly the same way in another church, which just went through the motions. It's horrible, you know when God isn't there and it's a terrible shame for the visitors and regulars who are gathered in His name, yet they are numbed.

The pastor in Elim Pentecostal never stepped out of line except for his handshake. It was all-powerful and crushing, which I laughingly gave him a row for. His sermons were always bang-on and God breathed. I had had many visions, words of knowledge and experiences with God in the past but at Elim it was as though Jesus was there himself, The Holy Spirit is most definitely there. It was there I saw miracles and saw the full manifestation of a woman with an evil spirit. She screamed and writhed with foam coming from her mouth as she lay on the floor of the church after falling out of her seat. The evil spirit was rebuked and fled.

I share with you now some other events with God that happened while I was at Elim. When I have a clear vision from 'The bank of Heaven', I now have the full confidence to tell any person involved and I know without a shadow of a doubt it will come to pass in the future. I write this because there have been times when I was too shy or afraid to come forward with the vision, only to find out later I was right. I heard God's voice before and said nothing. God says, 'My Sheep hear my voice, and they know me and they follow me.'

My brother Addie had visited us and was leaving to go down-stairs to his own house and was standing in my living room, holding onto the door. As he said, 'Bye', God showed me a crystal-clear vision of Addie carrying a wee boy on his right hip with his right arm wrapped around him. Evelyn was deperate to have her own children but was infertile and that's one of the reasons she doted on Sarah so much. I told Addie what I had just seen right there and then before he left. I said to him, 'God has just shown me He is going to give you a baby boy.' I added nothing else to the statement, just exactly as God had shown me. My brother was amazed as he and Eve couldn't have chil-dren, they had been together for a long time and let nature take its course. Also, as I said, Evelyn broke away from my brother and he now had no partner at this point. Addie eventually met someone else and his baby is now a fine strapping young man.

The exact same thing happened to my son. He was at the very same door, ready to exit, when I saw him wearing a white coat and a stethoscope around his neck. He was still in high school at the time. I told him what God had just shown me and that he would be wearing a white coat, dressed as a doctor, with a stetho-scope around his neck. I did not tell him he was going to be a doctor, I simply did what God told me to do and told him what I saw. This has not come to pass as yet but it will, my son is an actor and model. He is not a doctor but he will wear a white coat and have that stethoscope around his neck for one of his castings.

At the time of this vision I was at a Hogmanay party. I wasn't drinking, as it was difficult to get a taxi at this time of the year, and I had my wee daughter out late, so I drove. My son wouldn't come to the party, he just wanted to go to bed, which made me quite sad as Hogmany is a time for all family to be together. I was tired and I wanted to go home to bed too and was being a real party pooper. I sat and spoke to a woman I had never met before, which was nice, and we had a great time chatting away. At some point during the small hours of New Year, I saw a 'man hanging' vision in a flash but the after-effect lingered and would not go away. I couldn't hold back any longer because I was sick in my heart and thought it might be my son I saw. The strength and urgency in the vision upset me and I had to get home straight away without causing panic. I upped and got ready to leave but had to drive some others home who were annoyed at my departure and pressured me into giving them a lift, which had me feeling distraught, to say the least.

Back at the flat, Sarah's dad took his time coming up the stairs, as I fired up them two at a time because I had to get there first. There was no one hanging from the stairwell. I unlocked the front door and ran into my son's bedroom, practically jumping on top of him. He was fine, though shocked, as I fell on top of him. 'Thank God,' I repeated over and over. I didn't know who the man was but I couldn't shift the vision and fretted about it. After praying, I went off to bed to sleep. The man who killed himself was a cousin of Sarah's dad. He had just hanged himself on the first of January in front of his wee daughter, I was told later that same day. It was too awful but I thanked God over and over again for taking care of my loved ones and was heartbroken for the family of the man they had lost on the first of January.

Sarah, who attended nursery, was going with me to the doctor's for her pre-school assessment, which involved checking everything was well, from head to toe. About a quarter of a mile before we got to the surgery, I heard the inside voice, 'Heart murmur', very clearly. I was furious! I rebuked the devil and gave him a severe tongue-lashing. I warned him to stay away from my family and went on a righteous rant, banging my steering wheel. After I calmed down and was driving into the doctor's I heard it again, only much softer this time. 'Heart murmur.' That was it, I was raging this time, like a mother lion with her young cub. 'I warned you before, I will not tell you again, take your sicknesses and diseases and go to Hell, Satan.' I was so angry with him. 'Who does that thing think he is? I'll give him a heart murmur,' I assured him.

When we arrived at the doctor's and I had suitably calmed down, the doctor checked the little one's ears, tonsils, standing on one leg, then the other, hopping. 'Clap your hands above your head,' she said, before bending limbs and sounding her heart. The doctor listened for a while, then told me Sarah had a heart murmur. I was stunned. The doctor explained she had one herself and suspected it was innocent and told me hers had never given her any problems. We were referred to the hospital for a further check-up to find out what was going on in there. Not long after the doctor's appointment, we did go to the children's hospital for the check-up and everything was fine indeed. I was happy with the results, of course, but I was really dismayed that I had mistaken God's voice for the devil's. When the voice was softer the second time, I should have realised my Heavenly Father was speaking to me. I was so protective of my youngster that nothing on this Earth was going to harm her. I later laughed at the thought of giving the devil a verbal tanking for nothing because I thought it was him trying to suggest my daughter was sick. I am one of God's sheep and I hear His voice as He says, 'My sheep hear my voice.' That's what Satan gets, he shouldn't go about deceiving and imitating people's voices.

**'YOU HAVE A LUMP IN YOUR BREAST, NOT YOUR RIGHT BREAST, YOUR LEFT BREAST.'**

That's exactly what The Holy Spirit said after I had already gone to bed and done a quick self-examination, but I hadn't done it properly, to locate the pea-sized lump. Instead of being worried about the lump in my breast, I was happy because God had spoken to me before I nodded off to sleep. He could have told me anything and I would have been overjoyed because He had spoken. Not only had He prompted me to explore and examine the area again, I knew by the knowledge He imparted that He would make sure everything was all good and well with my body and soul. I did the usual under the circumstances and made an appointment with a female doctor at the surgery, who agreed the lump should be investigated further and dutifully sent off a letter of referral to the hospital.

'How do you know you have a lump in your breast?' the consultant asked, sitting forward and smirking. I looked at him in total disbelief. Duh! Are you for real? I thought, Is my own doctor stupid? Would she have asked for a second opinion or examination and sent me here if there was no lump? I gave him one of my long sighs, which says, I'm going to persevere here. The consultant shifted awkwardly in his chair as I looked him straight in the eyes and let him see I was thinking carefully about my answer. Why do you want to know how I found the lump, I wondered, are you waiting for me to say I was feeling my breasts? Hmm! I thought further, I'm not going to explain it to you the way you want me to, dirty boy.

I did do a self-examination, that was true, but I didn't find the lump. He wasn't going to like my answer but I couldn't help myself. I leaned forward to tell him, 'God told me. He said, and I quote, you have a lump in your breast, not your right breast, your left breast.' Up until then the doctor was still smirking. When I told him what God had told me, he shot back in his chair and suddenly became the professional person he should have been at the beginning. I knew he was going to look at me as though I was at the wrong hospital but I didn't care, nor did I care for his silly questioning.

For what it was worth, I thought he was in the wrong hospital and in the wrong department. The lump turned out to be a little fatty tissue, which was removed and left a minute scar.

The best thing was hearing God's voice, but that's not all. I got talking to a woman in the waiting room who was afraid she had cancer. Most of the women had their husbands or partners with them and I went along with God. As I spoke to the woman beside me, I told her not to worry and that the devil was a compulsive liar. I was so deep in conversation with the woman I hadn't noticed the smiles of the other woman in the room until I turned around to look. The mood really lifted from fear to faith in the waiting room that day. I hadn't really thought about why God had told me about the lump, or about the strange consultant who asked silly questions. The thing that struck me most was that God made me so happy by actually speaking to me and made the other women happy because I then spoke to them about God. He was in charge and was in the waiting room that day, ministering to someone. I don't know what happened when I left but God, being who He is, would have waited with them and would have been with them on every step of their journey. He is amazing for his insight, which He imparts to us and we have no shame, only comfort, when allowing him into the private parts of our bodies, which He created. We are fearfully and wonderfully made and He is the one true Father we can talk to about anything. My conversations with God never end, at the shops, in the loo, in the car, in the kitchen, when I'm nodding off. I ask Him what's for dinner, what do you think, Lord? Is that okay? I tell him everything and ask His opinion, as though He is right beside me, knowing full well He is there.

I was in the Southern General Hospital for three weeks with pneumonia, desperately ill with lung pain and a fever, my bed tilted backwards to help ease the pain and assist my lungs.

After a week the nurse suggested I should get up and she would assist me in taking a shower. There was only room in the shower for myself, and one chair, to get dried. While I was showering, the nurse sat on the chair. It was too hot in there and I struggled to breathe with the heat and steam, and felt very wobbly. The assisting nurse, who was sitting on the chair in the tiny area, lit up and smoked a cigarette, I am not kidding! I didn't want to get her into trouble and said nothing. I wished I had, because it played on my mind for years, but you know what? She did a stupid thing. I would need to borrow all of the fingers of my church members to count the stupid things I have done. Regretfully, in a moment of madness or not thinking straight, I have made some whopping blunders, like giving a complete stranger my BMW, which I never saw again.

A work friend told me her little girl was very badly burned from a boiling kettle, which had taken the skin from the sides of her chest. Her wee girl was screaming as she was sitting on a hospital bed and was adamant she needed to go to the toilet. Distressed with the burns on her chest, she sobbed uncontrollably. The nurse told her to be quiet while she was being assessed and told her she didn't need to go to the toilet. When her mother intervened and said she was taking her to the toilet, the nurse wasn't happy at being interrupted, and lifted the little girl from the bed by slapping her two hands on each side of her chest. 'She still has the nurse's moulded finger marks on her chest to this day,' my co-worker told me. There are thousands of terrific nurses and most of us know someone who is a great, caring nurse and good at their job, it's another case of 'If the cap fits'.

On another visit to the Southern, I was there to pick someone up who was in the Accident and Emergency. Without looking to see who was standing beside her for attention, she asked, 'Aye, whit dae ye want?' I didn't reply to the ignorance of a person who couldn't be bothered to look at me. After a while the silence disturbed her. When she looked up, I slowly made a point of looking at her magazine and crossed legs. That made her move to a standing position with a big stretch. Now I had her attention. How rude! Being playful and getting up to mischief in hospital was a must, anything to take your mind off sickness, disease and pain is most welcome. We had great nurses, some whom we knew and could have banter with.

When I had my son in the month of April in 1981, the weather was absolutely roasting. Being on the ground floor, we sat outside the back door of the ward in the scorching heat. A nurse came towards us and called out, 'Helen, your baby's crying.' Helen was my next-door neighbour to the left, in the crescent. The bold Helen tilted her head back and asked, 'Aw, nurse, gonny you get her, Ah'm too sore.'

'Aye, that'll be right,' the nurse replied. 'She'll no get a thimbleful of milk from me, move your Erskine Bridge,' helping Helen out of her seat. Helen replied tongue in cheek, 'See you, hen, you're just a wee cow', which had us roaring with laughter. The nurse then sat in Helen's chair for a wee while in the sun. We had a great laugh with the nurses and they too, with us.

In the maternity, there was an old woman, well into her eighties, who had fibroids that blew her stomach up to a horrendous proportion. Workmen hung around fixing the windows on the outside and the inside of the television room and we could see them staring but couldn't hear what they were saying. We often wandered around from the ward to the television room and visited each other's bays to swap magazines and suchlike. The hospital doctors kept us in for a lot longer years ago and we had to amuse ourselves one way or another. The hospital visiting hours were still only an hour mid afternoon and later on at quarter past seven, providing there were no delays or mishaps. It was a very long day and we needed to entertain ourselves and, boy, we did just that. The old lady would come and go just like us, shuffling along with her hand on her back for support, making her abdomen appear fully extended and noticeably visible. One of the workmen who was on the inside of the building whispered to a couple of us regarding the old woman, 'Surely that's not pregnant?', referring to the old woman. They couldn't keep their eyes off her. Workmen, referring to the old woman as 'That' instead of 'she' was cheeky, they were getting it.

'Of course she's pregnant,' we told them. 'Are you blind?' What would she be doing in the maternity ward if she wasn't pregnant?' The men were both stunned and horrified, their faces said it all. We could only imagine what was running through their minds and we let them go on believing she was pregnant without owning up. I would love to have been a fly on that wall as they told their cronies about the old dear who was just about to give birth.

The naughtiest thing we did had me roaring with laughter

in the years ahead. Actually, I didn't even do it, I was too sore. I was just one of the women who had tight lips again and kept the secret going. In another bay there was a woman who was having her haemorrhoids (piles) removed and we played a trick on the patients who were not in on the secret. Someone brought in dark cherries and we got a sick bowl from one of the nurses in order to carry out the plan. The cherries were stripped of their outer skins and squashed into an oblong shape, with the juice squeezed from the remainder to look like blood and placed down beside the toilet pan, covered with a piece of disposable blue towelling. 'How ur ye feelin', hen?' the patient who was in on the joke was asked when she came back round from her operation. 'Ah'm awfy sore, it was murder. Go and look and see the size of them for yersell, they're in the toilet.' The other patients did go and look and were up in arms at the sight of the piles in the sick bowl. 'That's terrible,' they shouted. 'Ah canny believe they've just gone and left them in the toilet, that's a disgrace,' they went on and on. They even called the nurses to complain about the haemorrhoids being left in the toilet. Everybody, everywhere, from all the bays came and had a look at the piles that were to stay in the toilet for the doctor to have a look at when he was doing his rounds.

'Where do you want us to keep them?' the nurses asked innocently. 'In the kitchen?' The women fell for it hook, line and sinker, and the bloody juicy piles were flushed down the toilet before the doctor came round in the morning. This time we did own up but we were in so much pain from laughing. It's true what they say in Govan about the Southern, 'You go in for a laugh and come out in stitches.'

I was standing close to my little daughter one day at the beach as she sang and danced to Jesus. Her arms were high in the air as she practised her sword dance, praising her little heart out, which made my heart swell with pride, because she loved Jesus all on her own account. I saw the incident before it happened, which gave me time, even just a millisecond, to turn my heart to God for help. She slammed her bare foot heavily on top of a sharp broken medicine bottle. The bottle was lying flat with the whole top side broken off, staged at exactly the way her whole foot landed on it. The sides of the medicine bottle were razor-sharp, like protruding shark teeth. I couldn't grab her in time to whisk her away, as her whole foot landed heavily on top of the bottle, but grabbed her immediately and swung her up and away to look at the damage. The sole of her foot should have been torn to ribbons and the bottle stuck fast. There wasn't a mark on her foot, nothing. No blood on the glass, and her foot was absolutely perfect. That's what happens when you praise God.

Some of the things I've written and told you about have made me cry, but not as much as this incident. It starts off many years before when there was a beautiful little girl who was abducted from a fairground in or near Edinburgh on the eighth of July, nineteen eighty-three, and the picture of her angelic face, posted in the media, never left my memory. As a mother, I have always been desperately saddened and sickened to hear a child has gone missing or has been abducted. The pain and heartache can never be forgotten. When both my children were taken, I was ill with worry and fear, but I got them back almost immediately, thank God. I can only imagine the ongoing pain and despair a parent feels when something horrendous happens. With this little girl, I couldn't shift the hurt I felt, it was as though I knew the little one personally and my emotions were in dark agony when I thought about her. I always wondered, 'Why?' I never found the answer until about nineteen ninety three.

The love I felt for this little girl was different from all of the rest who were missing or later found dead. With her hair pulled back (in media photograph) into a tight ponytail, and her tiny baby teeth, she was every mother's dream, every parent's very own little heavenly being.

On the first day of the 'Agape' love experience, I thought I was just being over-emotional, something that always happened as that certain time of the month came round. I was always interested (understatement) in God's love for us. I thought about Him all day and wondered how He could love us when we were wrong and so downright selfish. Then there were people who did dreadful things, how could He love them? God isn't just any old god though, He is the real, true One and Only, He is (and was, and who is to come) LOVE.

I was wandering about in my daily business as though I had taken some sort of feelgood drug because I was feeling euphoric happiness. Having never taken or known drugs to give that sort of effect or feeling, I was just happy not to have a migraine. Migraine medication never left me with the feeling that everything was wonderful and life was beautiful.

The love I felt made me extraordinarily happy and 'loved up' with everyone around me. I was very quiet as I stood still and watched people go about their business, and prayed for everyone. I felt tremendously close to God and felt as though I could float if I so desired. This was a new experience for me. This love I was experiencing was supercharged, much greater and purer than any other love I had ever known or felt, better than and different from being in love. I knew of the differences between the various loves, as I had previously been to bible school and did the Glasgow Bible Training Institute by way of correspondence. I had a little knowledge regarding the different names for love but hadn't experienced all.

I slept well on that first night but woke early on the second day with the feeling I was heavy, very different from the day before, when I felt I could float. The love I experienced was now much deeper and brought different emotions. The happiness was still there but the tremendous deepening love had taken over my body and soul. People I didn't know appeared as though I'd known them all of my life, and I felt drawn to them. I wanted to know them, care for them and do everything I possibly could for them. I spoke to people God put in my path. One woman I met and got chatting to was pushing her severely disabled teenage son in his wheelchair. She was upset and angry as she told me she got no help whatsoever from any agency, because she wasn't under the spotlight of the Social Work Department, and felt nobody cared or helped. She told me she never once got a penny from any of the charities who collected for children and who promised the money would stay in Scotland. 'Not a single penny or anything!' she said, as she stormed off, pushing her big boy up the hill with all her might, strength and skinny little arms. She was angry with life and the greed of the social system and charities. I could see she was tired and disillusioned, and had given her son her whole life, receiving no care or respite for herself. With tremendous compassion, I watched her bent back trudge away and wondered when she last had a holiday break.

Another woman approached me and told me she had woken up in the middle of the night to find a man standing over her bed. She lowered her head as she told me what happened next. She had never met him in her life and completely broke down in uncontrollable sobs as she told me the judge let him off with the crime of actual bodily harm, including rape. The panel on the jury laughed at her when she replied she 'made soup' during the day, when quizzed about her movements. She was laughed at by the judge and jury and her rapist was set free.

Broken people were everywhere and kept their traumas to themselves, hearts bleeding hurts no other person knew of. I didn't now the women who shared their heartfelt sorrows, and I saw they they needed a shoulder to cry on and for someone to listen to their pleas. They needed assurance, justice and Jesus. They weren't seeking astronomical special favours or gifts, they needed the love of God, and for Him to assist in their burdens and broken hearts. God was showing me how much He loved and cared about both of these women because, without the prompting of The Holy Spirit, I wouldn't have spoken to them of my own accord. I desperately wanted to help and make everything well for them. I was deeply grieved and had a heavy heart because they were upset and unloved.

Moving away from the car park, I found it impossible to concentrate on normal living with the experience of this pure kind of love. It was getting heavier by the hour and I could not get my head around the amount of ministering it would take to put someone's life right and onto the straight and narrow, to not only listen, but to mend. It was possible but the compassion in the 'agape' love was strenuous and required Heaven's energy and I found it really difficult, not only to comprehend, but to hold onto. The 'agape' love was lasting, forgiving, mending and healing. Dense, yet uplifting, concentrated! That's it, a deep rich concentrated love that was actually beginning to hurt my body because it was so heavy and dense.

By the third day I felt I didn't belong on this planet. I couldn't be in my earthly body of skin, flesh and bones and have this 'agape' love too, my body could not cope with it and my mind agreed. It was far too heavy, weighty, deeper than an ocean, higher than the never-ending sky. My body was buckling as 'agape' love was changing me. I felt I needed to lie down on the ground and pray. There was an explosion of love that was about to blow my body apart and I didn't know what I was supposed to do with it.

Sarah and I walked down to my mother's, her grandmother's, house, to find she wasn't at home. I sat on the front doorsteps and watched as Sarah went off to play and sing in the garden, pottering about, picking up stones and flowers and chatting away in conversations only understood by her and God. I watched her happy little face with her baby teeth and her hair pulled back into the ponytail I had brushed in the morning. The density of 'agape' love crushing me by this time, as it continued to deepen. Looking at Sarah, I remembered and saw the little girl who had been abducted from the fairground (5 years earlier). Sarah was, by now, around the same age. She was beautiful, smiling and laughing within the presence of God. She lifted her head up, but not to acknowledge me. There was a cloud surrounding her face which was brighter than that of the sun.

As I looked at Sarah, she was the image of this other little girl, as though they had melted and morphed together. Right at that very moment, I realised why God had given me compassion for a child I had never met before. She was real, alive, deeply loved, and very precious in His care. A picture of perfection, a child belonging to God, who was with God.

As I thought of her first school photograph, I saw she was almost identical to the little girl from the outskirts of Edinburgh. Sarah was born five years, one month and six days after the little girl and now, here before me, was my own precious little soul, laughing and singing away. I saw my little girl in the one who was abducted before she was born and clearly saw the one who was abducted was with The Heavenly Father, two little girls treasured and deeply loved by God. That was why I had so much compassion for a child I had never met.

Breaking down, I cried, 'Enough, Lord, take it away.' I couldn't hold God's love because it was far too powerful. It made complete sense to me when God says, 'No man shall see God and live.' He is far too powerful, His love, even just a sample of His love, would have consumed me. God immediately took His strong agape love away and left me normal, whatever normal is. He showed me a tiny part of how He loves and how He cares. I realised my own love was so shallow in comparison to His, yet I was sure it was deep at times. In showing me the little girl, He kept her in my heart to show me how I could and should love all people. God shared with me how He loves, yet after only three days I had to ask Him to take it away. His love had me breaking my heart with compassion for other people. It broke me like a shattered vase of precious oil, leaving only Himself and His love inside of me. My body of flesh couldn't hold His love. I also began to see that, if I did not have any love or compassion at all, then I would have been all consumed. My love has a very long way to go, a very long way to deepen, to mature and develop, and I doubt very much that it will ever come anywhere close to the agape love experience again on Earth. Love is all . . .

Taking you back to a familiar pattern here, I want you to 'Get it'. I want you to understand that God can do anything, any time, anyway, anyhow and anywhere He decides and desires. When a matter is absolute, He may show you it three times, sometimes in the exact same way, such as the way He showed me my interview, which still has not taken place yet, or three ways in complete contrast. If it is a definite future event, He will most likely show it to you three times anyway, regardless of how He does it. He doesn't have to show it three times, you might get it the first time. If you say, 'No way, God!', and He wants you to do what He is asking, then He will come back until you say 'Yes'.

This one is a real cracker. If you thought seeing Angels twice and having an Out of Body Experience was cool, this event wins hands up. I already have two children up to this point, as you now know, and I love the very bones of them to Heaven and back, it goes without saying. I do say, though, I had no plans to have any more. I say to God over and over again, 'Thank you very much for my beautiful children, I didn't deserve them, I don't deserve anything.' They both choked on a sweet and you saved them, God. Chris choked on a piece of fudge in the old Pollok Centre and Sarah choked on a hard-boiled sweet at home. Both were turned upside down and given the thumping of their lives to clear their airways. They were both stolen, wheeled away in their prams and, Lord, you gave them back immediately, when I was terrified.

Christopher was wheeled away from a shop in the Pollok Centre by a mother and one of her Irish daughters, and Sarah was wheeled away from the Housing Department, which was next to the police station on Brockburn Road, by a child and an older man. I gave chase away up the road and gave him hell, he knew fine well the child he was with should not have been taking someone else's baby away in a pram. Thank you, God, forever.

There were always fantastic expectations that God would do

something spectacular at Elim Pentecostal Church at Butterbiggens Road, not just natural births and new births (Born again), but spiritual births. Even men being pregnant (in the Spirit) is not a problem to God.

Again, like so many times before, I was sound asleep in my bed. I have to tell you I was in my thirties at this point, certainly not a youngster. From my deep sound sleep I suddenly found myself wide awake in a dark room, actually, I should say 'A dark womb'. I looked to the left and noticed there was plenty of room in the womb. As usual, God was behind me. It was so completely natural to be standing with God that I was intently looking at what He was showing me. I am standing before an unborn baby, inside another person's womb, honest! I look upon this baby and notice it's a very big baby. Although I can't see his penis tucked underneath, I know for sure and without being told that it's a boy. God told me the child is mine to look after, for Him. He told me the baby is special and precious and He has plans and a purpose for the baby. The baby is face down and curled up with his legs and arms tucked underneath and I could see the baby boy very clearly. I lifted both my hands without being told and laid them on the back of the baby's head and slowly drew them down his head, down the curve of his spine and round his bottom, that's how big the baby was. Even although I was in the Spirit, I deliberately cupped my hands together and felt him. I was able to run my hands down his anatomy. The Lord God watches me do this and says, 'It's going to be difficult, I can take it (the task) away if you want me to.' I replied, 'Yes, I'll do it, I want to do it, even if it is hard.' God gave me a baby to look after for Him and I knew I wanted to do what my Heavenly Father asked of me. Remember, The Holy Spirit went to a young girl before, named Mary, and told her she was going to have a baby, the baby Jesus (His Son). He did it before and He will do it again and again in the very way He so desires.

As soon as I agreed and said, 'Yes, I'll do it', I was back in my bed but I woke immediately and sat bolt upright and shouted, 'Oh, my God, that was real. I'm going to have a baby', but it wasn't actually my baby, it was God's baby, and I was inside somebody else's womb, not my own, with Him and the new baby. The mother didn't know I was on the inside of her with God, stroking her son before he was born. I touched him before she did. God was with me and watched and waited while I observed the baby, His baby. It was the most natural thing in the Universe to do, no questions such as 'How did I get here?', 'Whoa, who are you?' (to God). I knew that God was and is our Father, simples. I didn't fully understand, though. I knew it was going to happen, but how? Where? Why? When? It's funny how you stand with the very Majestic, amazing, almighty God of the Universe as one with Him, your Father, and utterly trust Him without comprehension, yet when you realise you're back in your body, you want an explanation. 'Wait! Hold on!' It was five am, I looked at the clock and it was Sunday morning, far too early for church. I was wondering when and how I was going to receive the baby boy. We had no room for another, that's for sure, although we could have made room. Where there's a will there's a way and all that and God would provide all my needs. I was chosen to look after the baby by God and was blessed and honoured, and happy.

I closed my eyes and nodded off to wake up at a respectable hour for a Sunday morning. We got up and ate breakfast before heading to Elim Pentecostal for the first service of the day. The church was always packed but this morning it was a little quieter, as Pastor Peat was away. You can imagine what it's like, people have their favourites and, when that favourite person is not coming, then they won't bother either.

We sang the amazing praise and worship songs and prayed before The Word was preached. Bibles open, the assistant pastor read out the title of his sermon, 'GOD IS BIRTHING IN YOU'. I gasped and nearly jumped up from my seat and shouted, 'I'M PREGNANT!' I couldn't believe what I was hearing. The

whole of the service was about what God was birthing in us.
He preached it right and not just for me, he went on to state
that men could be pregnant with God's expectation, whatever
that expectation was. I felt as though I was on a very fast roller-
coaster with God, my head was spinning. I had just gone with
God to someone's womb and the sermon was all about God
'birthing' in us. That's not all, the new monthly church magazine
was out and featured a testimony about a man being pregnant
with the deed that God was doing in his life. That was the three
ways God was confirming to me about 'being pregnant' in the
spirit. I had to tell a few people about my experience because
it was so fantastic, real and raw. I even asked for an audio copy
of the service so I could hear it again but I never did get it.
When I read the church magazine article later on, I was astounded
to read of the man who was 'birthed' on by God. His testimony
went on to say that he was pregnant with the will and Word
of God. Not a physical baby, of course, that would be ridiculous
to an unsaved person, wouldn't it? God took me inside a woman's
womb and told me I was to look after his baby.

Those were the three totally different ways in which God
showed me I was to look after this baby. He just never told me
when, though, and I had to wait and wait and wait . . . and
many years went by. Up to this point I only knew it was still
spiritual but I would ask God intermittently, instead of every
ten minutes, 'Where is the baby, God?'

It has just occurred to me, because I never ever gave it a
thought before, that God always spoke to me, or was with me
until about five in the morning, because that was always the
time when I came back and looked at the clock.

Satan didn't have to bother with me so much when I was
not saved, even though I knew he did everything in his power
to make me feel afraid and cause me to stumble. I didn't know
anything about a devil until my mother told me he existed one
night and it scared the living daylights out of me, but I'm so
glad she was honest and told me the truth. As soon as she told

me, the visitations made complete sense, even though I never told her I had them. I was always acutely aware of his various disguises and quickly recognised his evil cunning traits. I was also very aware that God was with me and provided protection. Whenever I was in doubt about whether something was not of God, He would give me that familiar 'punch' warning to keep me righteous and out of harm's way. It was also concrete proof that God was The Boss, The loving Heavenly Father, and I was/ am His child.

I had been attending a business session start-up with one of the women, Mags, from Elim Pentecostal Church as we pondered setting up a business together. Our business mentor instructed us in preparing a business plan and gave us loads of tasks to do by way of research. When Mags and I met often for a coffee to discuss our finances and itinerary, more often than not we would go to her home for a cuppa when I dropped her off. One morning, bedraggled, Mags told me she had the pastor and a deacon up at her house in the middle of the night because she was terrified. She went on to tell me she had woken up and sensed there was something horrible in her bedroom. She switched her bedside lamp on to find out she was right, Satan was sitting on her chair in the corner of her room. She described him perfectly as I had seen him, sneering and moving his head from side to side. 'Was he wearing a large hat with a wide brim that was pointed and had creases and crinkles in it?' I asked her. Her eyes were huge. 'How do you know that?' she asked. I told her I'd seen him too but I couldn't talk to anyone about it. I told her about the time I tried to talk about it to another Christian and was shot down, so I didn't ever mention it to anyone again.

'He's not much to look at, is he?' I asked her. 'And he's not worth talking about either,' I smiled. 'Forget it', I told her she must be doing something right for God's Kingdom, otherwise she wasn't worth bothering about either. She thought she was alone with this distressing encounter and was deeply troubled by her late-night experience but when she knew I had already seen him too, she went away laughing again with more confidence. I put it down to the Christian's occupational hazard, regarding Satan:

*YOU DO NOTHING*
*HE'LL DO NOTHING*
*YOU DO SOMETHING*
*HE'LL DO SOMETHING*
*FAITH OR FEAR*
*HE IS NEAR . . .*
*WHOM YOU'LL SERVE, MAKE IT CLEAR.*

There was an event, though, that mystified me for many years and shook me up because I had been deceived. It was not the deception alone that bothered me, it was the fact that Satan could be free to do this, that he knew what was going on in the world and in our lives and families. It didn't take me long to find out I had had a conversation with him.

My mother was dying, she had a duodenal ulcer that became cancerous, and she had a terrible time with it because she couldn't eat. Eating always resulted in unbearable pain, which had her bent double in agony, and that was in the earlier days before the stomach ulcer became cancerous. She was tall and thin already but was becoming a bag of bones before us.

One day my youngest sister asked me to keep an eye out for her because she had to go to work and she told me she would be back home at eight thirty pm. She would run straight home, she said. I told her to go to work and to tell my younger brothers to phone me immediately if I was required to go round to the house which was just around the corner from me. Looking out of my back window, I could see my mother's house and we would often wave to each other. There was no phone call from my brothers and I assumed everything was fine. At eight thirty pm my younger sister phoned me, absolutely frantic. She told me that our other sister, Kat and her boyfriend, Phil, had come and taken our mum out for a walk and she didn't know where they had gone. Our mum was far too ill to go out for a walk either by foot or in her wheelchair. Besides that, she had a morphine pen drive on, which pumped her medication every hour to keep the pain at bay and she could hardly sit up at times, let alone go out. 'Why would Kat take her out?' I asked. 'Especially with Phil. She doesn't even know Phil that well.' I was now anxious because it wasn't like Kat to visit and take my mum anywhere without asking first. Kat had only just started dating Phil, they weren't even a couple as such, so naturally I wasn't happy with this news either. Not only that but the rest of the family didn't even know she was dating a guy called Phil. My youngest sister was really worried and irate, it was only really her and myself who looked after our mother. My younger sister wanted my mother back into the house immediately. We talked a lot about where she could possibly be. 'Did she take the wheelchair?' I asked her. 'Go and look in the hall and see if the wheelchair is there so we know if she went out in it or in a car,' I told her and waited for her to return. There was a pause as she went to look. She came back and told me the wheelchair was there. I was a bit perplexed and mystified at the same time, listening intently to every word she said and keeping her calm, reassuring her everything would be fine. During our conversation God 'punched' me hard in the gut, that place he always gets me in and, as soon as he punched me, I thought to myself, 'That's not my sister!' As soon as I had the thought 'That's not my sister', the voice on the phone changed to a drawl and the caller said, 'Goodbye,' and put the phone down. When the voice changed I knew for certain it wasn't my younger sister who had called me, it went from a female voice to a 'melted record' trailing off sort of a sound.

'What on earth was that, Lord?' I said out loud. 'That's the strangest conversation I have ever had.' I was upset because God warned me that I wasn't talking to my sister and I was completely baffled because of the circumstances of my mother not being at home.

I threw my jacket on and marched round to my mother's to find out what was going on. Five or so minutes later, I was at my mother's house and saw my mother lying propped up on the settee in the lounge, and my sister standing at the fireplace drinking the tea she had just made them both when she got home from work at eight thirty, as she usually did on that evening.

'Where were you?' I enquired of our mum.

'When?' she asked. I looked at my sister and said, 'When you phoned me.'

'I didn't phone you,' she laughed. 'What are you talking about?'

I was annoyed and not in the mood for playing games because I was worried about my mum being missing and about the mystery of the phone call. I said to my younger sister, 'You just phoned me there and told me Mum was missing and that Kat and Phil came and took her out and you wanted her back!' Just at that, my mum stated she wasn't out anywhere and my younger sister was adamant she did not phone me. I was stunned. This phone call had just been taken no more than ten minutes before, but I knew by the way they were both looking at me, that they were speaking the truth. Also, if my mother had been out, she would not have been back and settled drinking tea in peace in the short time it took me to walk round to hers.

How could the caller imitate my sister's voice so exactly that I believed it was her? We are very close, I know her voice, her mannerisms, her ad-libs and strange half-baked Highland accent. The caller was a liar and a deceiver and God warned me and told me I was not speaking to my sister. How could Satan or his sidekicks speak through the phone? I know I saw him before but how dare he phone me, how was he able to communicate? No one else had the private information regarding Kat and her new 'date'.

I was absolutely furious with Satan and his lying demons

because I had been deceived. He can roam the earth as himself, live in a body, and can phone? Imitate and sound exactly like someone else! All the same, I was glad God was opening my eyes to his deceitful wiles and ways. I was glad He also let me see just how much of a foothold he has on Earth. By the way, I recalled the last caller number on the phone when I got back and it wouldn't connect.

One day the twins had their music turned up far too loud (as usual) and I had repeatedly told them off and not to do it, particularly as mum was resting. One of them was a DJ for the community occasionally and it was a hobby he loved but he could have used earphones. No one should be subjected to loud music, especially if it's music they might not even like or understand. I often told them to turn the volume down but they were fifteen years old and teenagers think they know best. Wisdom had still to catch up with them. All the next-door neighbour had to do was chap their door and tell them to turn it down but instead he punched my weak thin mother, who was dying (and wearing glasses), full on in the face because he was displeased with the noise, as she answered the door. Robbie phoned me and explained what had just happened and told me to come round straight away. I told him to put the music off, bolt the door and look after our mother because I had something really urgent to attend to, and he did what I said. I went to my knees at the foot of my bed and wept buckets before The Lord God, telling him I couldn't go round there. My mother desperately needed me and I couldn't go and comfort her, that hurt tremendously.

'What could I do against a huge bully of a drug dealer?' I cried. I sobbed my heart out to God. I was devastated, my mother was dying. I wept, 'How could he hit her?' I poured my insides out to God in grief. When I felt God had heard me and comforted me with peace, I thanked Him. That was the urgent task I had to do, to get before God. I didn't go round to my mother's until the next day, as The Lord had said, and she basically repeated what Robbie had told me. Her face was terribly swollen and discoloured, and he smashed her glasses too, which could have taken her eyes out. I told her straight to forget it. 'VENGEANCE IS MINE, SAYS THE LORD,' I told her. 'Watch God do what God does best, He is dealing with it.' Every time she mentioned it, I told her the same thing and put up my finger and warned, 'Shh, watch this space.' Love is not just a noun, it's a verb (an action).

I had no control over the situation and I wasn't involved in the gangster's downfall, but I was involved in the life of The Highest Power. 'He who sits in the Heavens shall laugh!' I reminded her. The drug dealer who lived by the sword died by the sword seven days later. He was murdered and it was nothing whatsoever to do with us. The common-law wife, who had his children, then gave her heart to The Lord, case closed. See what happens when you live with God, The real Father. Again I repeat, 'VENGEANCE IS MINE, SAYS THE LORD.' That was the wrong kind of punch and I wouldn't recommend using it on any one of God's anointed or their loved ones, end of.

My mother didn't come to church because of her circum-stances and trauma but she loved Jesus. Her mother, my granny, was a captain in the Salvation Army, I heard. My mother never spoke of her at all, she was a very quiet and private soul. She was kind and I know she hated her life, I hated it for her. She had no interest in fine things, she had no interest, period.

It was my youngest sister and I who stayed with her at the hospice overnight. We lay with our heads on her controlled mattress, which blew in air to stop her from getting bedsores and to relieve her of pain. She'd tell us to 'Get off' it as we were upsetting the flow of air. We quietly listened to the fireworks going off all around Glasgow when the New Year rang out at twelve, listening to the bangs and cheers of the celebrations around us. People rejoicing and having the time of their lives as they welcomed the brand-new year in. We needed this time with our precious mother and The Holy Spirit and we wouldn't have swapped it for anything in the world. The hospice was the most beautiful place to be in, in terms of hospitality. The staff were fantastic in their care, even in their Glasgow patter, with one of the male nurses often warning our mother, 'Right, that's it, Emily Baxter. If I have to come over to you one more time, you're getting it!' He made us laugh at the way he spoke to her and she loved it too. It was a sad yet beautiful time. The valley of the shadow of death is a beautiful walk when God is there. It sounds bleak, but it wasn't. It was peaceful, and full of Agape Love.

'What songs are you going to sing at my funeral?' our mother asked quietly out of the blue, with her eyes still closed. We couldn't answer because we were bawling our eyes out as my youngest sister and I looked at each other, shaking our heads and holding in sounds which would have given us away. We didn't want to cry in front of our mum and tried to be brave.

'I hope you two urny greetin',' she piped up after a period of silence, making us laugh and cry at the same time. Most times she would be asleep but we were told to talk to her all the time because she could probably hear us, she just didn't have the energy to reply any more. Every now and then she would blurt out a word or sentence, which had us in fits of laughter, at other times it was snot and tears. It was a beautiful time and thank God the hospice staff allow you in to stay for as long as you need to. One night, as we were nodding in the wee small hours, our mother let out a horrible wail, as though she had seen something nasty and was frightened. We held her soft skeletal hands and told her she was fine and that God had a bubble of protection and Angels all around her that the devil wasn't allowed to enter. We prayed and told the devil and his demons to flee. She settled back down and I could tell by her face she knew that, she was satisfied that whatever had troubled her had fled and she had another peaceful night's sleep. As I prayed, I looked around and wished I had the job of staying and praying with people who were at their end of life. The hospice had such a profound effect on me that I felt I had a calling from God there. I wanted to hold the hands of the dying as they left the Earth. To reassure them, Jesus has His arms wide open to receive them.

On the morning of the twenty-eighth of February, sis decided she needed to go and stretch her legs and I told her to go downstairs for some fresh air, which she did. We were sore and stiff with sitting and sleeping on hard chairs day and night. While she was on the steps, I went to the other side of our mum's locker and started to clear up some of her things by putting them into her toilet bag, just a general tidy-up of her bedside locker, and to throw away all the sweetie wrappers we had accumulated. Sis came back and let me go down to the front door for some air and a stretch. As I stood at the top of the hospice stairs, I had a growing experience where I became very tall. It was a bit like the Out of Body Experience I had previously had, except I didn't see anything change beforehand. I just became very tall and I felt and saw I was a giant. While I stood, amazed at the experience, sis burst through the door and told me to hurry up. We raced upstairs and ran to mum's bed, where she was smiling the biggest brightest smile I had ever seen on her face. She couldn't physically smile for over a week, she couldn't do anything as she was so heavily sedated, but she woke up one last time. Her face was absolutely radiant and filled with peace, joy and happiness . . . and then she went home to be with The Lord. She was unable to talk or smile for the last week of her life, yet she waited for me to come back, God could now take my beautiful God-given mother home.

The date of her passing was the twins' sixteenth birthday. They bounced into the ward and had just missed her leaving. God had finally taken her back home and I was ready. I agreed He could and should take her back. It was a beautiful time, even in death, as God was there. I have never known so much love in my life. My mother never cuddled me as a child but the love surrounding us in the hospice was tangible. Wrapped up in the package between God The Father, God The Son and The Holy Spirit in the ward around our mother, it was price- less. He did not forsake us or leave us. On the contrary, He lifted us up, because my sis told me she had the exact same 'Tall' experience I had when I told her what had happened to me on the stairs.

Some time later, when I was alone at home praying, I briefly had the thought that we were now orphans, an untimely lie from the devil. All of my siblings were younger and I knew I now had the job of keeping them on the straight and narrow. I didn't know if I had the strength or even the wisdom to do that and I felt so alone, even with God. My world, my mother, my head of the family was gone and now it was me who was the head, I severely doubted the daunting task. God intervened immediately and spoke to me in an audible voice and told me I was '**Not an orphan**', that was the first word. Guess what happened next! At Elim Pentecostal Church a guy stood up on the first Sunday after our mother's death and told us that God had given him a word, but it was only one word and the word was '**Orphan**'. He then prophesied and spoke out: '**GOD SAYS TO MAKE IT CLEAR THAT YOU ARE NOT AN ORPHAN, I AM YOUR FATHER SAITH THE LORD AND I ALWAYS WAS AND ALWAYS WILL BE YOUR FATHER.**' Seconded. The third confirmation was The Word that Pastor Peat preached, it was exactly the same, about how God was our Father and how he would never leave us alone or forsake us. I felt better and thought I could do this with God's help. When my mother's funeral at Elim Pentecostal was done and dusted, I left the church just as I had done when my Daddy died but this time I didn't backslide.

It wasn't too long after the funeral when Mother's Day was upon us. I went to the graveside and collected the large 'Mother' wreath of fresh flowers we had bought, took it home and pains- takingly replaced the withered flowers with plastic ones so it would last a bit longer. On another visit to the grave shortly after, I saw our 'Mother' wreath had been stolen. I knelt down and asked God to forgive the person or persons who took the wreath away. 'Maybe they didn't have any money, Lord, and their mother is every bit as precious to them as ours is to us, let them keep it.' I was happy knowing another mother, somewhere, had the beautiful flowers I made up. Mothers are precious, so be it. A mother's love is the most precious and greatest love I have ever known and experienced. I believe it is a life-saving love, a giving love, a healing love and a rebuking love too. I am honoured to know that precious and powerful love. It will never come close to the Agape Love, which I had to ask God to take away because it was all-powerful and all-consuming. You would have to ask God to take it away, or would you? Do pastors have that kind of love for their flock? If so, I will look up to a pastor with very different eyes because this Love is very powerful and bides with God, and is God. This is the Love Jesus had for us when He precariously walked to the cross and laid down His life. This Love has no end of depth, or width, or height, no end, full stop. This is the Love God loves us with. He loves us unto death on Earth only to swoop us up immediately, all to Himself. The love for, and of, my mother often tore my heart to ribbons. All of my young life I ached for her to be happy. At the same time, being a child who would occasionally get into mischief and do her head in. I grew up very quickly and learned this one thing, 'Love hurts.' Agape love hurts the most. It is the most selfless love anyone could ever experience. Thank you, God, Thank you, Jesus and Thank you Holy Spirit for Agape Love.

## Chapter Fourteen

# ALL WORK AND ALL PLAY

In the play *The Messiah*, I was cast in three contrasting roles. The first role was as a disciple, which I loved and milked as I gazed into the eyes of Jesus, throwing myself at His feet and kissing them while the other disciples just nodded to Him and smiled as we parted ways. I loved Jesus deeply and let that show in my performance, which came as naturally as I could portray because I know something of His character.

My second role was as The High Judge, where I was part of the pomp and piety of the false and twisted accusations against The Christ. I knew not, and cared not, whether He was innocent or guilty. I was part of that devilish ceremony where I strutted the stage menacingly in my cloak and fine jewels and gripped the audience in suspense before I announced my judgement. My decree was the final decision, holding the audience captive, in deathly silence, before I delivered the vile verdict: **KILL HIM!**, said with the deepest guttural sound I could find in my being and I meant it.

As a guard, I observed the nails being hammered into His hands and feet at close proximity, squirting the blood at that exact moment when they were pierced, leaving a cross trail of red liquid splattered across the stage, and I watched Him squirm in agony as He painfully hung from the cross. We cast lots for His garments and swore at His feet, laughing, snorting, spitting and throwing vinegar into His wounds. The filth beneath the cross only served to highlight the comparison between the guilty and The Innocent.

'How could you do that?' my best friend asked me later on. 'You're a Christian!' She had upped and left the performance at that point in the show, as did others because the play was too powerful and they were deeply offended at the brutality of the crucifixion. I wasn't going to pretend Jesus was in the Garden of Eden being fed grapes and fine wine. This love story is real and I had to act accordingly. I enjoyed what I did and put everything I perceived about The Judge into the words that ordered His execution. I am an actress, that's what I do, and I ask for the anointing to carry out my talent to get it right. It doesn't mean for a split second that I don't love Jesus. It means that after the experience of Agape Love, I have to 'keep it real' and I will, because His agape love is real. I cannot and will not lie, it was a very dark moment, dark day, when Christ laid down His life for the sins of mankind. What other way was there to portray that? Yes, it was awful, it was harrowing and heavy, a cross I couldn't have carried, yet there I was condemning Him to death. I would have no hesitation in doing it again to get the true unadulterated heartbreaking truth told time after time.

In my private time with God I didn't apologise, I simply asked God if I did it properly to get the message across and felt totally honoured to have been given the roles I had been given. Who else was better to take on the roles? I was qualified through the anointing of God and I didn't let Him down. I love Him deeply and in that deep love He has given me, I will tell the truth even when it hurts or offends.

Reports came back that it was the best performance ever presented. Even the hairs on the audience's arms and necks stood to attention. The ending, as we know, was/is a happy one. It did offend some, even Christians, but this is real, guys, I cannot make it a fairy tale. It was a dreadful harrowing true story of God's love for mankind. It was a grievous day all round and is still as meaningful today as we enter into The Last Days. It is written for all to read in the bible and sometimes we have to act it out to get the message across in any way we can. There are no apologies required for telling the truth as we all know it and it really did happen. It happened for you and for me, so we could be bought and brought back to God. Perhaps workshops are required, where the audience can take part in driving the stakes into the hands of the poor soul who has to play Jesus. Perhaps they could spit in His face (How filthy!) and sell His clothes for the highest price. Who would like to pierce His side or look up to His twisted crying face of agony? The death on the cross is for their sins. People who saw the show would realise that and read the bible with a very different understanding from then on.

**The third and final time God took me from my bed and onto the stage, where I watched myself being interviewed by the same man as before, I knew what was to come. As I watched myself being interviewed, I looked perfectly happy and at ease being there. God was behind me, just as he was at the last two briefings. I didn't once question how God could leave my body in my bed fast asleep, be with me on a stage and watch me being interviewed all at the same time. It was perfectly natural. I know that because I moved my head to the right to answer Him, and saw YOU! This time I said, 'All right, God, I'll do it, but you'll have to be tell me what to say.' I went from 'No way, God' to 'God, I can't do it, send somebody else' to finally agreeing I would do it.**

I haven't done it yet. I will one day and I'm going to make sure I go to the part of the stage where I was standing with God when he took me from my bed. Do you understand what this means? While I am sitting on that chair being interviewed by the man I saw three times, God (The Holy Spirit) will be on that very spot at exactly the same time! He was there with me and took me to that very stage when I was under eleven years old and I saw the audience on my right-hand side. Every person present was already there when I was a child. I saw them three times.

When my children were at school, I worked close by in the petrol station in Old Mearns during school hours and finished just in time to pick them up when the bell rang. We were just outside Glasgow but sometimes we would arrive to find sheep in the forecourt. In the Highlands, that's normal in certain areas, but not next to quite a busy road. Colin would kid the female customers on when they came in panicking with a flat tyre. 'Is it just flat at the bottom?' he would ask and they would innocently reply, 'Yes', then he would get thumped for taking the mickey. Then there would be the guys who told their wives they were taking the dog for a walk, I won't let on they were nipping in to Colin's office for a fly smoke. Oops! Well, I won't mention their names, but only because I can't remember. We had locals who would come into the back with Colin for a cuppa and a chat, like big Monty. He had a dog which was a real bruiser, a heavy muscled beast that looked like a real menace. Occasionally I would go to the car to say hello but I never dared stick my fingers in the window. I'd then shout over to Monty, 'Your girlfriend's looking rough today!' Monty would get me back by paralysing me with one hand on my collarbone when I got too close to him.

Monty informed us he lost his dog in Rouken Glen park one day. 'It's all right Monty' I said,

I don't think anyone will steal him' He informed me he got his dog back no problem. My knees would have collapsed if his dog approached me. It was a man's dog, a huge beast of muscle and teeth. Dogs I loved bit me, I sure wasn't taking any chances with one I wasn't keen on.

We were a close team and the job was great in the summer apart from the wasps, which were a pain in the neck. Colin, while he was doing the accounts, would call from the office, 'Get the kettle on.' I'd put it on and shout back, 'You're making it. I made it the last time.' He wasn't above making the coffee but most of the time I'd make it, despite the backchat. We had a great laugh, especially in front of customers, where we would act up. If Colin asked me to do something in front of a queue of customers I'd reply, 'What did your last servant die of?' The customers loved the banter too, especially if it was a first visit and they didn't know whether we were serious or joking and because of the 'tongue in cheek'. Many customers asked Collin if we were married and he always replied, 'No, but it feels like it. I have to hand her an unopened wage packet and I get nothing but attitude.'

I'll never forget that very bitter biting winter when it was minus eighteen to twenty-one degrees and hardly anyone could get to work. Most of the local shops were closed and all of the schools were closed anyway as it was between Christmas and New Year, and water pipes everywhere were frozen solid. I promised Colin I would be in as soon as my car sparked into life and it took me a couple of hours every morning doing the same thing. I'd get up extra early and fill every hot-water bottle I had in the house and put them on top of my water tank, radiator and frozen pipes, under the bonnet of my car. I would then squeeze, manipulate and soften the hose pipes until the ice melted so I could start the car. Once the engine was running, the heat from the engine would do the rest and away I would go, to the frozen petrol station to help everyone else. By the time the car was ready to go, I was frozen myself, despite wearing the warmest of winter clothing and a full ski suit on top.

Antifreeze would still freeze when poured neat over the windscreen but I refused to be beaten and I got the car started no matter how long it took. Being in Newton Mearns, many customers had heated garages, which helped start their cars, and some of the staff could walk to work, as they lived locally, which meant we could get the petrol station open for business.

In work I didn't change out of my ski suit because it was far too cold. The water and sponges I left in the aisles for windscreen cleaning froze within minutes and the freezing fog never lifted. Many people don't remember that year in nineteen ninety-five or so but I do. The carwash temperature gauges told us it was minus eighteen to minus twenty-one degrees over the freezing days, the coldest I ever remember it being. I would stand at the water tap for over an hour each time to get the water flowing but I didn't always manage to thaw it out.

As it was too cold to work outside, I was on the cash register this particular day, when an older man stuck his head round the door and asked why the carwash wasn't in operation. I told him it was frozen solid and none of the male staff could get it to work because of the ice. He went ballistic, absolutely furious, and stood red-faced, shouting. I was called every name under the sun we hadn't seen properly for weeks, and he made sure everyone else heard his rant. There was no talking to the guy, he wasn't having it. The other customers and I were stunned. He walked away cursing and the last customer to enter asked, 'What's up with his face?' I told him the carwash wasn't working and it was my fault. 'So it is,' he said, laughing. 'You make sure you get it working and don't do that again,' he ordered with a cheeky smile. I was so taken aback by the older man's behaviour that I told every person I was talking to when we were on about how cold it was.

The next day the same thing happened. I got up early and put hot-water bottles on my engine, manipulated the frozen rubber pipes by rubbing, squashing and melting the ice. I had to scrape my windscreen over and over again because the freezing fog made visibility impossible. Being just after Christmas, we wished every customer a warm-hearted 'Merry Christmas'. Hugs, smiles and festive greetings kept our hearts cosy, even if our fingers were frozen and numb. I was on the cash register again with about four people waiting to be served, who were quite happy to wait as we had the door heater on and the small shop floor had an extra heater blazing to take the chill out of the air. All was well until the same older man burst through the door and marched straight to the front of the queue, having no regard for any of the other customers. He bawled at me, 'Is the carwash fixed yet?'

'Oh, are you the same man who came in yesterday and went off his head because the carwash wasn't working?' I asked him. He stood in front of me and the queue and blew up again. This well-dressed respectable older man with his collar and tie and long dark grey winter overcoat lost control of his emotions and topped the day before's outburst.

I stood still and waited for him to finish his rant without interruption while he shocked the rest of the customers and finished his tantrum. God had put me into silence mode, as though He had turned the sound off and I could only see. I had heard it before and expected it was more of the same complaint, something to do with the carwash not working again. Sometimes when people are screaming, shouting and talking too fast, I hear it as a foreign language, because there are too many sounds bouncing, but this time I heard absolutely nothing, as though watching from a distance. It was only him I was watching, in detail, his face, emotions, actions and hatred. When he stormed off, the sound came back. Customers were astounded and asked if I was all right.

'Och, I'm fine, he did it yesterday too,' I told them. I was totally calm and smiled away as I served the customers again, each one remarking on which way they would have belted and booted him up and down the forecourt if he had spoken to them like that. It was a good job Monty and his 'girlfriend' weren't there because Monty always told me I was to tell him if I was ever in trouble, or if I needed his help, to let him know, but Jesus always had my back. Mentioning 'back', embrace this one.

Going back a little, in the few weeks running up to Christmas I was busy on the shop floor. I was securing the Christmas cards the staff and customers had given us onto the door between the shop floor and the office for all to see. When it came to my card, I looked at the large gold embossed Angel on the card, which I thought was beautiful. Smiling, I touched the outline and stuck it to the door in central position because it was so special. As I stood admiring my expensive foil card, someone put his hand on the small of my back and I thought it was because one of the staff wanted to go into the office. As I stepped aside to let him go in, nobody went past me. There wasn't a soul on the shop floor. I went home and told everyone an Angel touched my back, I felt it and moved out of the way.

There was a yearly competition which Texaco held in three stages. Our petrol station was very old, with antiquated pumps, not like the modern ones we have today, where you can pop your card in and pay as you go. So long as we informed the 'High head ones' of the difficulties we faced with having an old station and shop, we were allowed dispensation. A lot of petrol stations were brand-new builds and we had to work extra-hard to have any chance of winning. The officials came in groups of five with their clipboards and scrutinised every aspect of the station, which had to be immaculate. We shook hands with them before the inspection took place and we couldn't have met nicer people. Being a perfectionist, I made sure every tin, can, packet, bottle, or whatever the item was, was highly polished and facing the right way and the exact distance apart, positive there was not a speck of dust to be found. I'd polish and tweak and warn other staff not to touch anything. Colin's 'baby' was the confectionery and crisps. No one was allowed to touch his things. We all mucked in and Hamish was forever hosing the front of the forecourt to make sure there was not a drop of petrol or diesel to be seen on the ground. The chrome flashings on the pedestals were so highly polished they looked like mirrors. The cleaning was my job alone but, when judging was due, every member of staff mucked in and pulled their sleeves up.

As I went about my daily business, I spoke the same Word of God over and over again: 'God shall make me the head and not the tail.' I didn't stop saying it from the minute I arrived at work to even after I had gone. I spoke to the sheep in the field beside us, I said it to packets of cornflakes and tins of spaghetti: 'God shall make me the head and not the tail.' I said it to myself when I saw my reflection and to people I was waving off, and they didn't even know what I was saying. I spoke to every single living thing, to birds and cows, trees and leaves, bushes: 'God shall make me the head and not the tail.' I didn't tell a soul what I was saying or believing. I would look up to the sky and tell God His own Word. I said it when I woke and when I was going to sleep. The people on television copped it, the radio, the sun, rain, moon, everything, everywhere. All day and all night I quoted the same scripture under my breath, in song, speaking out loud: 'God shall make me the head and not the tail.' I had to have this competition in the bag, I was spearing for it and I was taking it by The Word of God.

Round one came and, a few weeks later, when judging had commenced all over Britain and all was deliberated, guess what? HALLELUJAH! We came first, of course, because I said it just the way God said, speak it out. I spoke that Word out. Round two came and I did everything as before, not forgetting to claim it by my mouth and by The Word of God. I spoke to the wind, the water, if it moved I spoke to it: 'God shall make me the head and not the tail.' When all was judged, Colin would be the proud owner of a brand-new car and we were to be rewarded financially. I had already had fifty pounds from round one. I was having this for Colin, for the staff, for myself, for God, and I kept my eyes and mouth on The Word. On round two we slipped back a little and came second. That was the kick on the backside I needed to spear for first place again and I knew for certain and with the faith I had in God that this was ours for the taking, for the glory of God.

'You have got to be joking,' I wailed to Colin when he told me the competition had to be withdrawn, owing to financial cutbacks. I was absolutely gutted. I already knew we had won this competition, where were our prizes? I couldn't do anything about the current financial state of affairs but I knew how to use The Word of God, and what's more, I saw first-hand that The Word does what it says in the book and that was more important to me. I had won because of The Word. Still, I became fed-up and began to moan a bit to God, telling Him I was tired and poor, as far as I was concerned, I was just bringing forth my 'Good causes'.

While working outside, I told God it wasn't fair because I tithed my ten percent faithfully and gave my gifts and offerings as well and it wasn't right that I should be living like this. 'I speak your Word, Lord!' 'I'm a child of the Most High God,' I told him. 'I'm your daughter!' I went on and on muttering under my breath in prayer, then walked into the office, still fed-up. Crash! I got the fright of my life when Jim banged something hard and heavy onto the stainless steel sink. 'Esther,' he greeted me. 'Look at this.' He unwrapped two large frozen fish he had brought me from his freezer at home. 'I kept them for you,' he said. 'Two beautiful trout.' He told me his friend had gone fishing and he had already eaten one, stating it was absolutely delicious. 'Oh, thanks,' I said, not overly excited. Just at that, Colin yelled from his office through the back, 'And you can take that bread up the road as well.' I said 'Thanks' and went to get a carrier bag to put it in. As I put the bread in the bag I counted the loaves, there were five. I said to God, 'Five loaves and two fish? You're very funny, God!' I didn't know whether to laugh or cry. I smile now when I think of God The Father as having a great sense of humour. That taught me to stop complaining and do something about my needs, in action.

We hadn't long had the lottery up and running and at the beginning it was very busy. People had all week to put their tickets on but a Saturday evening was chaotic with punters leaving it until the last minute to enter their tickets. Cars would screech into the forecourt like the Keystone Kops to try and get their ticket on before the machine cut off automatically at seven thirty. Some made it, others didn't.

I had been learning full Psalms off by heart when I didn't have a script to learn. I uttered a different scripture from the last one, which was: 'My leaf also shall not wither and whatsoever I do shall prosper.' I wasn't praying for anything in particular, I was quoting The Word to keep me strong in The Lord and because I knew God had the power to better my living circumstances. My car tyres were being slashed periodically in the area we lived in and I ended up having to park my car miles away, which was inconvenient, having to get up very early in the morning, as I needed the car for the school runs and I was working for nothing every time I had to pay for new tyres. Then there was the night-time drama of having to go away and park the car again, meaning I'd have to walk home in the dark, along lonely roads with no street lights for quite a bit, and I was too tired physically and mentally. I was sick to the back teeth of living next door to drug users who didn't work and who moved in when my good neighbour Kathleen moved out. Their music was horrendously loud, until four or five in the morning, when they pushed their windows wide open and let the whole street suffer the abuse. Our house always had to have a sitter or they would have broken in and emptied it. I had been there before and found out who broke in and emptied my flat when he left his flat. I found some of my personal belongings in the street, which could only have come from my flat. I truly believed God would help so I didn't stop saying the same thing over and over again: 'My leaf also shall not wither and whatsoever I do shall prosper.' When I refuse to listen to my thoughts and batter them out with The Word of God, I have the most rock-solid determination, which no one can talk me out of.

At the last minute, on my shift at the petrol station, a customer came in for a lottery ticket. He held up his pound coin then looked behind at the sweets as if deciding whether to buy some, but he changed his mind and asked for a lucky dip. He was just in time, as the machine cut off after his ticket was produced. It was my day off on the Sunday and when I went back into work on the Monday, there was a flurry of excitement about the lottery agent coming for the readings from the machine. I had work to do and got on with it, popping in and out of the office when I needed to. The conversations were hyped with 'I bet it was me that sold the ticket', the guys arguing among themselves with ridiculous stories. Colin informed me someone had won a half share of the nine million pounds draw and the winning ticket was now narrowed down to the Saturday. I finished my shift and had to get round to the primary school for the bell ringing. By Wednesday the arguments were still flying around as to who had sold the winning ticket, I had my work to do and got on with it as usual. I had sold far too many tickets to Joe Public to imagine who it might be. On one of my shifts I saw two bottles of champagne on the sink. 'What are these for?' I asked Colin. 'They're Jim's,' he told me. I thought nothing of it and moved them to the back of the sink because I needed to use it. The banter was the same as usual and we were all happy at our work. As in every establishment, there are those who hang over counters and talk without working. I usually worked without talking except to The Lord. 'My leaf also shall not wither and whatsoever I do shall prosper,' I sang as I cleaned outside. Come the Saturday, I was on the lottery again until the machine cut off at seven thirty. As I went to take over the machine, the boys were still gassing about who had served the winner, coming away with ridiculous stories like 'Aye, he came in with a pocket full of ones and twos and slapped them down on the counter.' 'Who are you talking about?' I laughed. Then they said his name. 'I served him, and it was a pound coin he gave me, by the way,' I told them. They knew it, the time was on the machine for the exact date and purchase of the ticket, which tallied with the person who was on the shift. They had been waiting for me to own up but we weren't to discuss the winner until it was common knowledge who had won. I never told a living soul and, when reporters asked, I walked away. I understood from the gossiping young men, there were handshakes of congratulations and a gift of six bottles of fine champagne for Colin, Hamish and Jim, who were just members of staff like me, but why did they get champagne? I wondered.

I gave my full attention to detail and worked under the ethos of The Word of God.

I was really deflated. For the first time ever, I couldn't even afford to buy my precious little daughter new shoes because the ones she had were hurting her toes and that made me feel bad. I went to God in prayer, dejected, and told Him how disappointed I was. I felt really left out in work and I asked Him why I didn't prosper in the way I believed I should have, especially since I trusted in His Word so much. I went on to say I was also really disappointed in the way I was left out of the lottery when I had been one hundred percent depending on Him to get me through and on top of His Word. I wasn't expecting to win the lottery, even although it would have been fantastic if I had, maybe, maybe not, as it could have taken me down a path of life and away from God and I didn't want that, not for all the money in the world. The lottery win wasn't mine and I had no qualms about not winning it. On the contrary, I didn't want a lot of money, I wanted to prosper by the work of my own hands and with God, Jesus and The Holy Spirit by me and with me. I felt as though I was getting nowhere, though, and I opened up to God and told him so. I also questioned why His Word didn't work this time. It worked the last time but The Devourer stopped the blessing.

The Lord told me to look at His Word again and 'Strip it apart and think carefully about it'. I went straight to the part 'And whatsoever I do shall prosper' and did what The Lord said, vowel by vowel, consonant by consonant, and even into the syllables. 'Whatsoever' served to highlight 'my leaf shall not wither'. I was happy with that statement, I would bear fruit in season and I understood it, I got it. I understood 'I do', that was simple enough. 'Shall prosper' – will prosper, I understood the will/shall but I wasn't satisfied with the word 'prosper'. It seemed to suggest prosperity on its own with a promise that we would prosper but it wasn't enough until I realised the word 'prosper' was a verb, a doing word. When I read it as 'whatsoever I do, WILL DO,' I finally understood that my action went on to do what The Word of God said it would do. (I've gone too deep for myself here, lol!) I understood that God's Word did what He said, again. I would prosper and that's exactly what happened. It just so happened that on that evening, I was in charge of a machine that had to obey The Word of God because I had full superiority and authority over it because of His Word. I had been repeating it continuously and He had to honour His own Word from my very mouth. The Lord then asked me, 'Did I lie to you, did I do anything wrong?' I told him, 'No. Lord, I understand the "Do" part. You were right, my action of the "doing" worked. I pressed the button on the machine for the lucky dip and it had to work under the law of your Word. My action was the "Do" part, and what I did, did indeed prosper, as You said.'

The peace I had when I finally realised that Our God was indeed a miraculous, all-knowing, all-seeing and all-'doing' God, was phenomenal. His Word worked and it would always work as we spoke it out and used it. It could never return void.

The Lord also gave me a 'Real dream' and 'A Word', which added weight to the part of the matter where I felt I was being snubbed, as far as the thank-you or gifting for the lottery scenario went. I dreamt I was in a living room, which was tastefully decorated and furnished with a three-piece suite, a coffee table, pictures and curtains, just like everyone else's living room, with a few ornaments and photographs. It was a very real dream and I knew it was of God, in order to explain something to me. I was in this living room with, believe it or not, a huge grey baby elephant! I was trying to look after this massive but young elephant and I couldn't control it. It was barging around and I couldn't even get my arms around its neck to pull it away because it was far too strong. It stomped into everything, jumped onto the couch and the coffee table and did a wobbly circuit because it was young and too big for the living room. It was so real that I woke up and asked The Lord what it meant. The next day I went to church for a bible training session and the pastor said something that floored me. He said, 'There's an elephant in the room.' I immediately asked him what that meant, which surprised him. 'Have you never heard of the saying, there's an elephant in the room?,' he asked me. I said I hadn't and shared the strange dream from the night before and I asked him what the dream and the saying meant. He told me that basically someone disagrees with a decision and they don't want to discuss it again in public. They have made their mind up and won't budge on the subject, and it's referred to as 'An elephant in the room', a bulky big weight no one can shift, move or change. I was floored by these events, The 'Word working', the elephant dream and the pastor using that very phrase the following day. I also saw that God took His time to make the events clear to me so I could understand His ways in the world. He unravelled and dissected the whole situation and I was content with His reasoning and thought no more of the lottery hype, I had other things to do for My Father, God.

One thing I always secretly desired was a big old church bible. I just wanted one and I would always look for one when we went to antique shops. On a visit to Inveraray one day, there was a church fair at the top of the street. On one of the stalls there were three huge old bibles, the cheapest one was seventy pounds, but it was battered and broken with loose pages. The desire to have one of my very own never went away, it was just my secret heart's desire.

I didn't like Christmas much, and often told God so, but He said something which floored me, 'It's the only time of year some people come to me', and I changed my mind. One Christmas, when I was doing my rounds at the petrol station, I spoke to The Lord God in my heart. I thought, 'Lord, I would love a gift from you, I'm not naming the gift, I want you to search into my deepest heart and give me a gift that no one else knows about, a gift only you know about, Lord, one that would take my breath away, one that I would truly appreciate.'

I thanked Him and thought nothing more about it. When I walked back into the petrol station, Jim told me he had something he thought I would like, a big old bible, right there and then after I had spoken with God. He said he had it at home and would bring it in for me. No person in the world knew about my secret heart's desire to have a huge old bible and, immediately after I had this silent conversation with God, He prompted Jim to tell me he had one for me. I was stunned. God had listened to my deepest thoughts and pulled out this secret desire, which I had totally forgotten about, to have one of those big old bibles. Sure enough, Jim brought in that big old church bible and handed it to me. It was in perfect condition and didn't cost me a single penny. That was the one prayer that floored me most. He heard me, He knew my heart, it was a total secret between The Most High God and myself and He acted on it. He even ministered to Jim to tell him to give me it and Jim doesn't know to this day what happened. God knows our deepest secrets and enjoys our thoughts and our friendships.

As I have written earlier on my childhood, I was always prone to colds and flus and had had them constantly since primary school, which didn't bother me so long as I didn't have a fever. The shadow on my lung had now become COPD and I had lost all of the elasticity in certain areas around my lungs, and still don't (or can't) shiver. Being flu-ish was what I knew growing up and have lived with the condition fine. I also went on to develop asthma and a lifelong cough, but that was just me, I always had it and never knew any different.

All hell broke loose on a doctor's visit in 2009, when I explained to the doctor I felt awful and had just come back from holiday. I felt feverish, cold one minute and hot the next, flu-ish as usual, but I also had a splitting headache that I couldn't shift with any amount of medication and I was exhausted, done in, so to speak. Swine flu was rife, so the doctor protected herself with gloves, mask and apron and went into decontamination mode, putting my husband out of the back door of the surgery, to his surprise, as he was closer to the front door. I was tested for Swine flu (H1N1) but the test came back negative and I was told to go home and stay indoors until the doctor called to see how I was, but during that time I got much worse and asked my husband to get my sister. She took one look at me and phoned the hospital detailing my symptoms and said she would bring me down instead of calling the doctor or waiting for an ambulance. I was put into isolation and tested again for Swine flu, and this time the result came back as positive. My antibiotics were given intravenously, which constantly upset my stomach, meaning I couldn't keep any food or drink in me. It took a few days for me to begin to get back to the real world.

I remember the exact time, it was four fifty am, because I lay wide awake watching the clock at the tower of Battlefield Rest, which I could clearly see from my hospital bedroom window on the ground floor of the Victoria Infirmary. I always knew when someone was coming into my room, as the wash-hand basin would be turned on. The mask, apron and gloves were put on and the bin lid would clatter as something was dropped into it. I could hear the spray being used and sometimes there would be chit-chat if there was more than one person entering.

At ten minutes to five in the morning my door opened and someone came in without scrubbing up and the door closed behind the 'person'. I heard footsteps coming towards my bed and my mattress went down as the 'person' sat on my bed behind me. I don't know why I didn't turn around. I was so peaceful I just stayed the way I was positioned, looking out at the big clock outside and across the road. I lay there contented and enjoyed the gentle rub on my back and was waiting for the 'person' to speak but no one did. He or she got back up and walked to the door and closed it on leaving. Who was that? I wondered. I thought it was really odd as I had a sign on my door saying, 'No admittance'. I asked every person I saw and knew of if they had come into my room in the early hours of the morning at ten minutes to five and they all said 'No.' There were only two staff on night duty and they were adamant no other person came into the ward and spoke to them. I told everyone an Angel had visited, or maybe Jesus, yeah.

I have always looked out for my 'baby' sister because of the circumstances with The Daddy, and felt protective of her. It was when I was still working at the petrol station, I knew I was leaving to move on. She was working for the Church of Scotland in Newton Mearns as a caretaker. However, I knew she had something better to do and God showed me that she had my job and she was to move on to her calling. I told her straight out, God said, 'That's my job, so go in there and tell them you're leaving and I'm taking your place.' She looked at me as though I'd suddenly sprouted a unicorn horn. I explained she was to do something else and that she would need to leave and move on. Each day I asked her the same question, 'Did you tell them?' 'No, not yet,' she said. She must have felt quite silly. It's not every day you walk in before your boss or board members and proclaim, 'I'm leaving and my sister's taking my place.' I told her not to worry about what they would say, as God was in charge. One evening while watching the television, I casually asked her if she'd told them yet. 'I'll tell them tomorrow,' she said, and she did. She came bouncing back with the reply that I was to go in and shadow her so I knew the surroundings and knew what to do. Easier done than said. She faltered a bit before doing it but God has a plan for everyone and He tells me things.

When we obey him nothing will be able to stop us getting to where we are supposed to go. It took her a little while but she did it eventually and has grown from strength to strength in the job she now has. At the time, she probably thought I had kicked her out. Well, I did in a way, but she has two great feet of her own and knows how to land on them. Time is shorter than we think, we all have that special something to be getting on with and if I see that little bird stalling, well, I'm just going to help it out. The testimony always makes me smile. It reminds me of the time Jesus told one of the disciples to go and get Him a donkey, just take it and tell the owner Jesus says it's all right. There is a saying in Glasgow, 'God helps those who help themselves, but God help you if you get caught!' Make sure God has told you first.

As I was praying one time, The Holy Spirit showed me, in a vision, an area from Inveraray to Glasgow where there was going to be a terrible road traffic collision and He told me to tell my younger sister, who was leaving from Ardrishaig not to leave that night. He told me to tell her the two words, '**DON'T GO**'. I was not to tell her anything different, just to say The Lord said, '**DON'T GO**'. She was working in a small hotel as a breakfast chef and had some time to take off. Normally it wouldn't have taken her long to come to Glasgow and that's why she intended leaving just after seven pm. She wanted the benefit of the full day off and had every intention of leaving that evening. I phoned her and told her what God had told me to tell her and also told her she wasn't to leave that evening, but to travel the next day. I made her promise not to leave and she said 'Fine!', even although she didn't want to wait. It meant she was at a loose end but I warned her severely not to travel that night.

It wasn't long after she returned home the next day that we found out there had been a terrible road traffic collision, where there were fatalities. We roughly calculated that, if she had left Ardrishaig when she intended to, she would have been at that very place when the accident happened. She doesn't always listen to me but thank God she listens to Him. When she fully realised she had been saved from the dreadful collision, she was grateful and so was I.

Three things I always pray for are wisdom, knowledge and understanding. Most of the time I am wise and make good judgements about my paths and journeys in my daily life, prompted by The Holy Spirit, of course. I'm totally reckless left to my own devices. God's knowledge is all I need, as He never withholds any good thing from me. He knows what is good for me and His grace is sufficient for me, as He says. To understand comes with totally accepting that God is good and He is *always* right. He works in magnificent ways and never ceases to amaze me. I accept with simple gratitude that God, Jesus and The Holy Spirit know me better than I know myself. These baffling events left me confused and awestruck at the same time.

I had was seeing people I knew well when they were supposed to be somewhere else. I knew for certain they were far away in another country, on holiday or in hospital, for instance. I actually told God, 'That's weird, that person driving that car is the spitting image of so-and-so!' I was positive I had just seen that person, who I knew for certain was somewhere else and I was fair puzzled. To make it even stranger, the car driver (I knew) would slow down and look me right in the eyes and that is why I was so adamant and positive it was actually them and I accepted it was them. How could it be, though, when I knew for certain they were miles away at the same time? Bewildered, I began to pay more attention to the cars, the passengers and their drivers. They were all male, either alone or with the car full of other men.

I stood on a corner of a pavement one day and looked at the car before me, occupied by four men. I knew the driver well but he was ready to pull out at the give-way sign and paid me no more attention after gazing at me. Maybe he didn't have time to talk to me, I thought. When I caught up with him later, he point-blank denied it was him! We both saw each other.

On my way back home with Sarah, my daughter, who had been at her Highland dancing lesson one evening, we got stuck in a traffic jam under the Nitshill railway bridge. Both lanes of traffic had come to a complete standstill. Right beside us in the other lane, was Michael, known as Mick to most folks, Sarah's uncle, sitting in his pale green Volvo estate. There was the long rusty gash along the middle front of his car bonnet and I could see he was wearing his grey woollen Icelandic zipper cardigan. I knew he wasn't going to be travelling too far as he was going to meet up with his brother (Sarah's dad) and us an hour or so later, as was the usual Wednesday evening routine. We were practically face to face, I was looking directly at him and his face was facing mine with his eyes looking down, as though peering into the compartment of his car door. I had my hand up to wave to him and was smiling like a Cheshire cat. His face was radiant and happy, probably as his car was now going, I thought, as his legs were painful after an awful road accident many years ago. I have written the following conversation in script form the best I can remember. I am in the driver's seat and my daughter, Sarah, is sitting in the back, behind me. I didn't know how long we'd be stuck in the traffic jam, so I just sat there waiting for his response, certain he would look up. As I sat there watching him, it seemed like an age had gone by. I really felt he knew we were there. He'll lift his eyes in a moment, I thought for certain, he certainly couldn't miss us. We were laughing and joking about the fact he wasn't looking up and waving to us. Mick's eyes were smiley, his whole face was glowing as though very content. He stayed so still, face towards mine with his eyes looking down. Again I thought, he's going to lift his eyes any second and see us! He did lift his eyes and looked straight out of the front windscreen and drove off with the moving traffic, then we went ahead in our lane. I couldn't believe he didn't see us. I knew that he knew we were sitting there. It was more like he was pretending we weren't there. What was going on? Where was he off to now that his car was repaired?

MUM: Look, Sarah, there's Uncle Mick!
SARAH: Where?
MUM: In the car, wave to him. I wonder where he's going?
SARAH: I don't know.
MUM: He's not looking.

SARAH: Is he coming up?

MUM: I don't think so. We'll probably go down with Dad after dinner, they'll be going out as usual. He can't see us. What's he looking for? Hello! [chapping on my window]

SARAH: [Shouts] Mick!

MUM: Chap the window! He's smiling, he knows we're here. I can't believe he's not seen us. He's looking at something. [laughing] What's he doing?

[Mick looks straight ahead and drives off]

SARAH: Oh!

MUM: Can you believe that? He didn't see us. He can't be going too far, maybe up for a gas canister or something.

[We get home and have general chit-chat about the dance lessons while preparing the dinner]

MUM: [To Rab, Sarah's dad] We saw Mick, by the way.

RAB: Mick? Where was he?

MUM: Under the bridge in Nitshill, heading towards Darnley.

RAB: Darnley?

MUM: Yes, towards Darnley, but I don't know where he was going.

RAB: Darnley?

MUM: Yes, could you move your butt. You're right in my road! [Trying to make dinner]

RAB: Darnley?

MUM: Oh, for goodness' sake I said Darnley, you know, where Mary Queen of Scots snogged the face off Lord Darnley? I don't know any other Darnley, do you?

RAB: Are you sure it was Mick?

MUM: Yes! He was driving his car.

RAB: He wasn't driving his car!

MUM: He was, you know. He was driving his car. I don't know where he was off to.

RAB: Are you sure it was Mick?

MUM: Yes, I just told you so! It was Mick in his car. He was wearing his knitted zipper. He never saw us, did he, Sarah?

SARAH: I didn't see him.

MUM: What? You couldn't miss him. Wait a cotton-pickin' minute. What do you mean?

RAB: I can assure you it wasn't Mick. His car's not working, you know that. His alternator's goosed and the bonnet's stuck because it got dented so he can't get it fixed.

MUM: I know that, but he's obviously got it repaired. Maybe he was taking it for a run to recharge the battery.

RAB: It wasn't Mick.

MUM: [I peer right into his eyes] It was Mick, I bet you a hundred quid it was Mick and I'll take your money right now, pal!

[After dinner I drove Rab and Sarah down to Mick's]

RAB: [To Mick] Where's your car?

MICK: Where it always is, at yours. [Parked up on private land]

RAB: [To Mum] See, I told you.

MUM [To Mick] We saw you earlier under the bridge at Nitshill, when we were coming back from the dancing.

MICK: Me? It wasn't me!

RAB: See, I told you so.

MUM: [To Mick] I saw you. I saw the car. The registration plate. The car driver behind you saw you, or why would he leave such a massive gap between you and the next car if you weren't there? You were there. I was watching you for ages, ready to wave. I saw the rusty part on the bonnet and you're wearing that same zipper. I saw you!

MICK: [Quietly spoken and genuinely serious] It wasn't me.

MUM: Oh, forget it.

RAB: Forget it? Forget it nothing, you owe me a hundred quid!

MUM: Is that right? Well I'm not stumping up! I SAW MICK! I was there, watching him for ages when the cars got stuck under the bridge.

I never got over this incident because I know I saw him with my own eyes, not that I could have seen him with anybody else's eyes. I saw him and I'm sticking to my testimony forever until that day when the truth will be revealed. Mick was telling the truth too, though. His car was fully taxed, M.O.T.'d and insured but was still off the road because his bonnet was stuck. The car needed a repair that couldn't be done until the bonnet was released. The rusty dent on the car bonnet was caused by something falling on it, which jammed the release catch. I am absolutely certain, then, that I saw an Angel driving a copy of his car. That explains the fact that the Angel knew I saw him. The Angel was radiant, glowing and smiley. I knew the Angel also knew I was watching him (the being, he looked like a he, looked exactly like Mick) and wouldn't interact as 'it' was obviously on a mission. I began to see that the other people I saw driving cars were Angels too. How could a person be in hospital or abroad and be driving their car in front of me at the same time?

It happened again for certain. God was showing me clearly that Angels are right beside us and using cars that are legitimately licensed for road use. After picking my daughter up from primary school in Newton Mearns, just shortly after the school bell rang at three fifteen pm, I drove into the petrol station where I worked, for a few items and sweets for Sarah. I spoke to Callum, my colleague, who was on duty by himself and he told me he was finishing shortly. After being served, I was then to go and pick my sister up at four pm from the Clockwork Orange, where she worked for friends of my late mother, about five miles away. In small chat, Calum told me he had his mother's car but I wasn't really paying attention as I didn't want to be late in picking my sister up. He had to wait for the other member of staff to turn up before he could leave was all I really took notice of. We chatted for a few minutes before I left, saying, 'I'll see you later.'

While we were sitting outside the Clockwork Orange waiting for my sister to appear, we saw Calum in the waiting traffic across the road, in the other lane at the traffic lights, which were on red. 'How did he get here so quick?' I said out loud. I was quite amazed that he was there because he was still working and waiting for the other member of staff to turn up and let him leave his post. I actually said to Sarah, 'There's Calum.' Sarah was too busy eating her sweets to take any notice. I sat there resting in my driver's seat and watched him until he pulled away when the lights changed to green. When I next saw Calum at work, I casually asked him how he got there so quickly. 'Where?' he asked. I told him I saw him at the traffic lights near the Clockwork Orange. He looked at me puzzled and said he hadn't been there. I told him I saw him in his car (which I knew well). He reminded me that he had his mother's car because his had broken down. He also reminded me that he had told me that when I was in the petrol station but I didn't take the information in because I was in a hurry. I just thought he had swapped cars again, because he was driving his own car. As I went on and on about 'seeing' him, I could see by the look on his face that he thought I was nuts. Having been there before, I just shrugged and said, 'Oh, never mind.' He said it wasn't him and his car was still sitting in the garage for a repair. That's two of the cars I have seen when the car is off the road awaiting repairs. Angels are not only using the likeness of the car driver but are using the actual car, which is clearly taxed, insured and M.O.T.'d. That way they will not get stopped by the police. Supernatural God and Angels are allowing me to see they are at work, on earth. I knew I had been seeing 'people' when they couldn't possibly have been there. Now I had concrete proof as I began looking out for them, even although no one believed me.

In my account and testimony of these two events I have a crystal-clear memory and have no doubt whatsoever in my mind as to whether I may have made a mistake. I saw them both. Angels are on missions and driving cars, or at least imitations of people's cars. I won't ever go back on my word or testimony. I knew I saw people when even they themselves argue and say it wasn't them. I believe them . . . but get this, Angels are working beside and along with us, not only in The Spirit, but appearing as though in the flesh. At times when your legitimate car is off road, it may also be somewhere else too . . . on Angel business.

I also suspect without a shadow of a doubt that Satan and his 'flying ones' are using them too. We must not be deceived, they are using cars too. The one I saw with the petrol can was a demon. A punch in my gut from His Majesty warned me not to stop and help him.

Every time God does something I'm either in awe, stunned, flabbergasted, humbled, amazed or even shocked. Sometimes I just stand there in silence and wonder, God what are you going to do next? Who is like unto you indeed? How come you love us so much? He just never ceases to surprise and amaze me.

Mick had brought along his speciality, 'Castle soup', which Kevin and Sarah named, homemade soup, so thick it would hardly come out of the flask, along with sandwiches, crisps, drinks and other picnic goodies. We were hundreds of miles away from home on this particular day. The soup was finally shaken out of the flask, tea and coffee for us adults, juice packs for the sprogs and, to top it off, it was a beautiful and warm sunny afternoon. Kevin and Sarah squealed with laughter constantly, at every little thing their imaginations threw at them, especially when Mick got talking to a pretty policewoman who sauntered through the gardens. Kevin and Sarah danced and circled him with a creative new song: 'Big Mick's got a chick!' What a pair they were. When we had all been fed and watered, I packed the picnic away so we could head into the castle while Kevin and Sarah were pretending to drive and pressing all sorts of buttons on the dashboard.

'Right, out, you two,' I called over to them, letting them know it was time to go. I closed the boot and the other car doors after shooing Kevin off and casually walked to the driver's side to take the keys from the ignition but before I could shout 'Noooo!' Sarah bolted out of the car like lightning and slammed the door behind her, running off and laughing with Kevin.

'I can't believe you just did that,' I shouted after her. I tried the car doors but they were well and truly locked. Putting my hands to my face, I mumbled, 'No way, please tell me that didn't happen.' Kevin and Sarah stood like statues, trying not to laugh. 'Oh, God!' I said. 'I haven't got the spare key.'

'Look in your bag,' Rab said.

There was no point, the spare car key was hanging up on the key holder box at home, I could visualise it. We were too far away from home, in the countryside well away from a bus route. To go back for key would take forever and would have put a real downer on our day out.

'Oh, God!' I repeated. 'What am I going to do?' Deflated, I slowly looked through my bag, knowing full well the other key was hanging up in the house. I fumbled through the inside of the bag for nothing and that's what I found, nothing. There was a tiny zipped compartment on the outside of the bag, which I never ever used as it couldn't hold anything significant, so I just tapped it with my hand, nothing to be felt there. The only reason I opened it was because I didn't know what else to do and inside this tiny useless compartment was a key from an old Volvo I had many years before. Taking it out, I held it up and looked at it and said, 'Never!' as I wondered if, just maybe, it would fit the car doors. Of course it didn't open the doors, why would it? I just said it out loud but I did try anyway. The last door to try was the boot and when I put the old key in the lock, it clicked!

'Oh, my God!' I squealed out loud, which started Kevin and Sarah off laughing, dancing and chasing each other all over again. Before they got too far away, I shouted and pointed to Sarah, 'You, get over here!' She came skipping like a young joey, all radiant and glowing. I lifted her into the boot of the car so she could climb over the back seat to get into the front and open the driver's door. No problem, she pulled the handle to open the door so I could get the car keys out. 'Get out of here,' I jokingly scowled as I watched her running away and squealing with laughter again.

That single Volvo key opened all of the doors of the old car, including the boot. My current car key opened all of the doors, including the boot. I couldn't understand why the old key only opened the boot of the new car. Why did I even have that old Volvo key when I had got rid of the car years ago? Who put it in my bag? Me? What prompted me to look in that useless tiny zipped area of the bag I never ever used?

*I do not know*
*I do not care*
*I called on God*
*And He was there!*

Staying with the theme of cars and God's help, We were all camping in a very remote area in England, many miles from nowhere except for a small guesthouse.

Rab had Mick, his brother, for company. Sarah and Kevin had each other for adventure and laughter and I had Jesus and the dog, Milly. We were staying in a large mobile home that was like a small cottage and we had everything we needed in the way of provisions.

On a jolly around the countryside my exhaust snapped in two, leaving the pipe scraping along the ground. I was grateful the exhaust broke the right way at least, trailing on the ground, it could have snapped and jammed as it dug into the road if it had broken the wrong way. As usual Sarah and Kevin thought the noise of the broken exhaust was hilarious and Rab and Mick didn't give two hoots. There was no garage for at least forty miles and I couldn't bear to drive the car for that long looking to find one. It was also a Saturday evening and the chances of finding somewhere open on a Sunday were very slim. With all of the hilarity and carry-on going on in the car I felt alone, even with God as my anchor. In the middle of this nowhere I asked God to help me. I loved camping and rolling around the countryside, but not alone. The family were as useful as a chocolate teapot and the calamity was mine to attend to because it was my car. I drove on to the tiny petrol station, hoping and praying it wasn't closed. It wasn't a garage but at least it would have a phone if nothing else, I thought. I couldn't even hear my thoughts through the noise from the exhaust and the 'squealers' in the back of the car but kept praying, 'Please help me, God.'

The petrol station was open. Sarah and Kevin leapt out of the car and ran to the sweets, Rab and Mick stood outside the petrol station to admire the view and take in the scenery and fresh air with Milly, and I went to the corner of the tiny petrol station shop to see what they had, still groaning for God's help. I bought two huge steel clips, an exhaust bandage, black sticky exhaust hardener and a tin of soup for the children, and had an idea God had given me.

Once Sarah and Kevin had chosen all they wanted, we drove back to the mobile home, where I told them they were getting the soup before they were eating their sweets. Mick heated the soup for them while I cut the other end from the soup can and carefully slit it lengthways too. I squeezed myself under the car (without ramps) and fitted the round clips on to each end of the broken part of the exhaust, then attached the soup can around the exhaust to hold it back together. After tightening the clips at both ends of the soup can, I wrapped the sticky exhaust bandage around the can and clips and covered the whole thing with the sticky goo which was to harden from the heat from the exhaust. There was nothing else to do but to trust in God to hold it together. It worked a treat, in fact it worked so well it was solid in no time and I didn't bother taking it to get properly mended.

Three years went by and, when I finally went to get a new exhaust, the mechanic asked me who had fixed it the last time. 'Me,' I told him. I should really have said it was God, because he helped me. 'Why?' I asked the mechanic out of curiosity, thinking he might have thought I had made a right mess but he stated he couldn't get the exhaust off at that part because it was absolutely rock-solid. No wonder I love God! Again, what would I have done if I didn't have The Father I could talk to?

There wasn't anything seriously wrong with my car this day. I can't remember why I even had the bonnet up, maybe checking the oil or water or something minor. From out of nowhere, an older man appeared beside me with his Border collie dog. The man was slow in walking and was hobbling around me, aided by his walking stick and his black and white dog shadowing faithfully by his side. I paid more attention to the dog because I'd had the Border collie many years before. Just mentioning her again reminds me of her faithfulness.

The old man was popping his head under the bonnet where I was looking but he wasn't giving me any sound engine advice. Oddly, he kept telling me he was an archaeologist. I didn't know what to say to that. The only other archaeologist I knew was the young man, John, who worked shifts at the petrol station with me and he always told me he hadn't been on many 'digs'. He did go on a field trip once when I was working at the petrol station but he also told me he never made any money out of it. On the contrary, it always cost him money, hence the reason why he worked at the petrol station.

The old man hovered about so much he was getting in my way so I closed the bonnet and got the children and friends back into the car. It was only me he was talking to and I didn't want to seem rude. I was on a mission to somewhere and said goodbye to the old man. He still kept getting in front of me and really wanted me to take this information in, 'Remember this,' he repeated over and over. 'I'm an archaeologist!' When we got into the car to drive off everyone was mimicking the old man and telling me to do this. 'Remember this, I'm an archaeologist!,' they kept laughing. 'Stop it, you lot,' I told them as we drove out of the forecourt. Kevin and Sarah were rolling about laughing and even made up a song, singing 'I'm an archaeologist, I'm an archaeologist.' They laughed at everything together and the old man started them off again.

The Ayr road is very long and I was watching the old man and his dog as they left slowly and turned the corner. They were only out of sight for a few seconds but, by the time we turned the corner, both the old man and his dog had totally vanished. 'Where is he?' 'Where did they get to?' 'They can't just disappear!' I said in total disbelief. None of us saw him, he wasn't anywhere to be seen up that huge stretch of road and he couldn't exactly sprint.

To this day I still don't know why I've to 'Remember this, I'm an archaeologist.' I can only assume the dear old man was an Angel – as well as an archaeologist.

Our little Cairn terrier dogs, Toto and Milly, always got their last walk at around ten thirty pm. On the way back to the house in the dark of the night with the dogs, I was alone. Not another soul was around and our crescent wasn't a true crescent, it was a one-way back road. Something knocked into the left side of my back really hard, along with a strong wind and a whooshing sound, causing my long hair to fly over my face. It happened with such a force it was strong enough to knock me slightly off balance and I turned round and said 'Sorry,' even though I was the one who was bumped. I was astounded there was no one there and was convinced it was an Angel on a mission so, when I got into the house, I immediately opened my bible while asking God about it. The words that were given to me had me sitting in awe. God confirmed it was an Angel. I read in Hebrews 1, v 7 'But about the Angels God said, God makes his Angels winds, and his servants flames of fire.' Wow!

God is with us at all times and will intervene when we are in trouble. He knows when trouble or evil surrounds us and sees what that evil has planned as we innocently go about our business. We can be totally unaware of the dangers ahead and The Holy Spirit has our backs when we are vulnerable. He is all-knowing and all-seeing and often intervenes on our behalf.

At the top of the Old Mearns Road one night I was doing the usual, taking Toto and Milly for their last walk of the evening when an estate car which was heading towards me at great speed suddenly screeched as the driver slammed on his brakes and pulled in to the bus stop on my side of the road. I got a terrible fright and immediately wondered why the driver had seemingly done that, for no reason. I stood my ground and continued very slowly, at a snail's pace, as Toto and Milly sniffed away at their leisure but I was close enough to see that the driver was rolling something in his fingers while peering over his half-cut specs. His face was very bony and muscular, and from what I could see he was well-built, strong and looked very menacing. I could also sense he was an opportunist and I knew he certainly wasn't stopping for a picnic.

It was late autumn, windy and dark. There was not a soul around but him and me. I turned away and pretended I wasn't fazed or alarmed but all I could think of was the huge hedgerow swaying beside me which had an eerie feel to it. I could visualise a body, battered and lifeless, in the thorns. It was too easy to grab me and if he had a weapon, well, nobody would have known as the houses were so few and far between.

He was scrutinising my every move and I was acutely aware of what he was doing but I didn't have a battle plan. He would have won the battle, with or without a weapon. I used the only weapon I knew I had. I deliberately lifted my head and looked to the darkened sky and prayed, making it obvious I was speaking to God. I then lowered my eyes and spoke very loudly in tongues (The Holy Spirit language). I have never done that, ever, before an unbeliever but I felt compelled to. This night was an evil, dangerous night. I felt I stood in a place where many thousands of younger women and men had stood and I could feel the fear they had felt. The driver looked down as though he didn't know what to do next and looked more scared than I was. The tide had turned. He mistook me for easy prey until I stood tall in the power of The Holy Spirit. He stayed put in his car as I walked casually back home with the dogs in tow. I have no doubt in my mind he was full of evil intent and I was his intended target. It was the same scenario, like the time I asked God to keep the three boys on the wall. This time was much worse, the evil destroyer was out to kill, not just maim. I didn't pray for God to keep the strongman in his car. I don't know what I prayed because this cry out to God needed more than the request 'Keep them on the wall, Lord!' Is anyone with me? This was not the first time the strongman had hurt youngsters. I could smell the fear, I could sense it, feel it, I could see a lifeless body lying, decaying, in a hedgerow of thorns and shrubs. I turned my back on the evil and walked back home, it didn't matter that he was behind me and I couldn't see what he was doing. The matter was dealt with. Evil was once again put in its place and there it would stay. I reported him to the police as I knew he was evil.

Toto was the dog Christopher and I had bought for my mother as a pup for Christmas and named him Toto, short for Totus Tuus which means 'Totally yours' in Latin. She cried when we handed over the tiny ball of fluff, which we'd kept hidden for days and tried to get everyone to keep it a secret. Milly was a real bitch in more ways than one, supernasty. My mother, in turn, bought me Milly when she was fully grown. Milly had fought viciously with her own mother, resulting in the owner having to sell her on. Most of the time Milly got on well with Toto. She knew she was in deep trouble when I backed her into a corner and gave her 'what's for' by way of a pointed finger. She knew I was the boss, put it that way, but she was still one to watch. I had seen her in action when she was in one of her ravenous kinks and it was horrendous when she was in a bad mood. She had a vicious temper without mercy. I have no doubt in my mind that she would have chewed the legs from the hard-faced man, had he got out of his car and come close to me and Toto would certainly have joined in. That man was blessed that night and he doesn't even know it. It was him who was saved from an attack. I'm not suggesting that's the reason the strongman stayed put, it is just a 'By the way'.

Flashing hazard lights at the side of a very quiet and lonely road caused me to slow down and pull in one night. Standing at his passenger side was the driver, who looked visibly upset. I stopped and asked if he was all right and asked if there was anything I could do to help. He explained he had run out of petrol and needed to get to a petrol station. His wife and children were in the car. That's why he was at the other side of the car, as he had been talking to his wife from that side. The man told me his wife wasn't well and had been attending hospital, although he didn't go into any detail about her illness, and he didn't want to leave her alone with their young children. I offered to run him to the petrol station but he didn't want to leave his family on the lonely, dimly lit back road. I told him there was a petrol station two miles down the road and I gave him my petrol can. I suggested he should stop a taxi, as he might not be allowed to purchase the petrol without a vehicle. I also told him I wouldn't leave his family until he got back, so I sat in my own car, behind his, and waited for his return. It wasn't too long before he came back in a taxi, as I had suggested. We said goodbye, I wished them well and I left them to get on with their journey.

I continued along the dark road until I got to the traffic lights at the junction at The Hurlet and turned right, taking me onto Nitshill Road. It only took me about three minutes or so to get to that point. At the edge of the pavement was a very tall, handsome smartly dressed man in dark trousers and a white shirt, who gave me a terrible fright as I thought he was going to walk in front of my car in order to get me to stop. In front of me, he smiled broadly while shaking a fuel can in the air. I don't know what car he had, all I can tell you is it was gleaming, long and black. God punched me and warned me not to stop. This was not a real man, he was 'the deceiver'. I drove on by him, shook my head and said, 'Get lost, Satan.'

An irritating friend had a dreadful habit of grabbing my left knee and squeezing it hard while I was driving the car and it made me mad, to say the least. If I had to tell him once to pack it in, I had to tell him a thousand times. There was also the emotion of surprise or shock which made me lift my foot from the pedal as I shrieked in pain. I was so angry with him one day I actually drove off and left him when he got out of the car to go an errand and quite far from home too. Sometimes he would drive the car. One day I was in the passenger seat, relaxing, minding my own business and looking out of the front window, as you do, and I gently laid my right hand on his left leg. I positioned my hand carefully above his knee and wrapped my fingers around his leg muscles. I massaged it and toyed with the idea of gently squeezing it but I didn't have the strength he had and I had no intention of doing to him what he often did to me. As I tightened my fingers, without any protest from him, I suddenly felt a tremendous surge of power go down my arm and into my hand. I gripped his leg like a hydraulic vice until I felt I would break his leg if I didn't pull my hand away. It took more power for me to let go than to squeeze as I loved this feeling of strength and wanted to carry on. I had to throw my left hand over to grab my right hand to help me stop, as I knew I was hurting him when he squealed like a piglet. The terrific surge of power I experienced was so fantastic I wanted to continue but I was breaking his leg with just my finger tips. During this 'power surge' I didn't once take my eyes off the road ahead, I undertook the whole experience by touch only and kept on looking out of the window. I was completely relaxed as the power intensified and the supernatural power flowed through me. Afterwards he said absolutely nothing at all, neither did he ever squeeze my leg again. The Holy Spirit gave me a supernatural 'Samson' experience which put an end to mortal man's efforts.

One of my aunts didn't have a paste brush for brushing the paste onto the wallpaper. I stood back and watched, amused, as she slapped a load of paste in her cupped hand and wiped it around the wallpaper in circles, carefully reaching the edges so as not to miss any. She was a 'dab hand' at it, I thought. I thought she was a bit too thin. She and my uncle had been trying for many years to have a baby. When I got home I prayed for her in a really matter-of-fact way. I got down on my knees and prayed that God would bless her body, bless their marriage and marriage bed. That was all. Nine months later my aunt gave birth to a beautiful little girl, and she really was beautiful. She won a beautiful baby competition in Elder Park, Govan, across the road. This was not a freak of nature or a coincidence. My aunt and uncle had been married for seventeen years before the baby came along. It just didn't happen for them but I knew who was The Jehova Jira (The Lord God Provider) of the world. Now they are grandparents to a beautiful wee boy and new granddaughter. Sometimes my simple little 'off-the-cuff' prayers happen quicker than long-drawn-out ones, Praise God.

On that same note, I got talking to a woman I knew quite well in our tennis club, who was also desperate to have a baby. She was in tears as she spoke to me in the ladies' toilet one evening and was gutted every month when she realised there was no baby for them to look forward to. Despite being on hormone replacement therapy, nothing happened. I related the story of my aunt and uncle and told her I would pray for her, as it is God who breathes the breath of life into the tiny little newborn, it's Him who gives the baby, and gives the baby its spirit. I urged her to pray too as she was the one needing to speak to The Heavenly Father.

I haven't seen her since that last discussion a few years ago now. She is probably far too busy looking after her husband and cats . . . and her little girl!

Whatever the prayer is, He hears every one, and everyone. I have just written something that I have found to be very true in prayer. If the prayer glorifies God, then He will most likely say yes to the request. Amongst other things, the answer is granted according to our motives. Here's a tip: Keep it pure and simple, be yourself and don't try and puff up the words in the request because you think He will want to hear them, speak to him sincerely.

Perception and knowledge are amazing and great tools, if I can call them that. There have been many occasions where God has saved me from road traffic collisions by warning me beforehand about what other road users intended to do. I have been saved from some crackers. People pulling out of 'give ways' seems to be the most common occurrence, it's almost as though folk just don't see the car. Also, I always know when something is going to go wrong with my car because God forewarns me and He is never wrong.

I remember God showed me a washing machine breaking down and I thought it was going to be my own. No fewer than three people I knew well had their washing machines break down at the same time. God often shows me a picture of what needs attention and I pass it on.

I needed a car and I didn't have the money to purchase one. I sincerely asked God for one and I knew it was His great pleasure to hear me and to give me one. I was to act alongside Him for the manifestation of my prayer request and I bought a new toy car and wrapped it up and put it in the offering basket as a thank you and an action, in humility to The Heavenly Father. I had discussed it privately with God and confided in my Christian friend, who then mocked me and told other church members what I had done. She belittled me no end but God gave me my car, then another one, brand-new with the tax, Insurance and M.O.T. all free. I'm not suggesting everybody fills the tithing bowl with toy cars, I was desperate and it worked.

The police have been mentioned a few times in my testimony book, God obviously wants them here, so thank God for our police and for all of our emergency services.

I was pottering about in my kitchen, sorting out the laundry and listening to Gospel music, when God gave me a clear vision of two policemen at my door. I thought nothing of it and carried on with my chores, and immediately after the vision the door was chapped. On opening the door, I saw two policemen and was so shocked that I stood there with my mouth wide open. One of the policemen put his hand up and said, 'No, it's okay, we're only here to ask about your neighbour.' They must have thought that I thought I was about to get some bad news but I was just so shocked because God showed me the vision of them at the door and it transpired immediately after I saw it.

Before my wonderful next-door neighbour Catherine moved away, I was in the kitchen again as usual when God told me to pray for her. I felt it was urgent as a heaviness swept over me but I didn't know what or why I was to pray so I thought I would just do it later. I hadn't seen Catherine all day and I didn't think anything was wrong or I would have heard about it. The truth is, I was busy and didn't do what I was told straight away, I won't mince my words. Later on, I was just about to pop into hers when she came to the door and I put the kettle on for our daily chat, which we always did. Her Samantha and my Sarah were the same age and were always out playing together in the garden or on the balcony.

Catherine was in dire agony with a swollen face, and staggered over to lean on my radiator as she always did, so she could see her children from the window. She was tormented with pain and holding her head and ear. She told me she was at the doctor's the day before because of severe earache, then came home and went to her bed after taking her strong painkillers. No amount of painkillers were dulling the pain. It was the worst pain she'd ever had, she groaned, but she had more to tell me. At the same time as The Lord laid her on my heart to pray for her, she said she was terrified in her bed and told me this:

'I was in agony, the worst pain I've ever felt. I went to the doctor and he packed my ear again after pulling out the dressing, which never seemed to end. I felt sick with the pain, the tablets and the sight of the dressing covered in gunge. I had to go home and lie down. At teatime I was delirious and went to bed but couldn't sleep for the pain. I felt something walk up my quilt and stand on my chest. I thought it was Jasper (the dog) but Jasper has never done that before. I lifted my head a bit and opened my eyes to see what was going on, Esther, I was terrified, there was a huge black demon on my chest and it was staring into my eyes. I screamed and screamed until Danny (her husband) came rushing in. When I told him what had happened, he said I was just dreaming. Esther, I know what I saw, I was awake with my eyes closed because I couldn't sleep. I know what I saw and it was horrible.'

I now saw why The Lord God had put Catherine on my heart. She needed me to fight her corner when she was ill. I didn't go and see her, nor did I even tell her that God had told me to pray for her right there and then. I was one of those young mothers who had a million things to do and had not fully accepted I was supposed to be ministering to others. There were far too many times when God had told me do something and I chose not to. I should have known better and was now in a position to stand up and fight with the army of God to do His will. I had met this demon face to face as Catherine had, but I was much more experienced than her and should have helped her in her time of need. I hadn't fully accepted I was a warrior and not a child, I saw then why I was allowed to see the demons as a child.

## Chapter Fifteen

# THE WORLD IS A STAGE

*

**'Look at her!' 'Here comes the actress!' 'It's Glamour girl!'**
I was deeply ashamed and embarrassed in secondary school by one of my male teachers, who ridiculed me at every opportunity. He, like my Daddy, made everyone look at me and made a point of giving other teachers and pupils my character. I wished the ground would open up and swallow me whole, yet I failed to see he was calling out my destiny.

I studied Acting and Performance for three years, where stupid me received excellence in an HND. It was terrific fun but very hard work. I had dancing feet in contemporary dance and learned how to fence. My circus skills weren't that great, I couldn't get the hang of the unicycle, but I could sew up some amazing costumes, make rostrums, hang the fresnels, and work the lighting cue and sound cue switchboards. The Alexander Technique and every other technique of the theatre was taught from acting to stage managment, writing and directing, and I loved the learning curve and all of the adventures throughout the journey.

My acting Curriculum Vitae more than quadrupled my working history and I had terrific fun and laughter 'starring' in pantos, plays, SCDC, festivals and competitions. Photoshoots and advertising campaigns for the police (mothers, wives and girlfriends against knife crime), Council, Education, political campaigns, television and radio advertisements are ongoing commitments as my agent sources my work.

I was also attending an AOG church where I was in the praise band and was a deacon. I should perhaps say 'deaconess', even go further and call an actor an actress (again) when she is female. The 'ess' seems to have been stripped from the female titles as though she doesn't mind. Well, actually, I do mind, I am an Ess, it's in my real name too!

I met this pastor when I joined my first church in Dennistoun and used to see him with his long dark leather coat and dreadlocks and his dog, which had the same dreadlocks. He was unsaved at the time and I had no idea he would eventually become my pastor. I would go to speak to him and wanted to tell him about Jesus but he was on his way to the pub and I only spoke to his dog. He would never have remembered me and I didn't own up and tell him this. When I did go to his church, I was there for years before I realised it was him, until he showed me a photograph of himself before he got saved. He looked completely different from the man who was down and out. I was interested to hear his testimony because he told me that, like me, he had had an Out of Body Experience, but he never did tell me about it. It then dawned on me that the pastor's testimony may not have been about Heaven, but about Hell. I'll probably never know now, not on Earth anyway.

Many of the congregation would come in on the Sunday morning, late, stinking of the wrong kind of spirit, the alcoholic kind, and others continually turned up terribly late, just for the spread of food. I met an older man who was an alcoholic until he accepted Jesus into his life, what a fantastic transformation and regeneration he had. He died shortly after he got saved and I was really blessed, privileged, to run him home after church a few times. His face shone and he loved Jesus so much I was blessed by just looking at him, what a brand new creature he was, a real treasure. The shine on his face was uncanny and I now wonder if the same shining glow was the shine the prophetess, Anna, from Dennistoun saw in me when she wouldn't open the door wider to let me in when I was fasting. I am looking forward to seeing him again because he was beautiful, so much so that I was quite sad to see him leave my car every

Sunday but it only made me happier to see him the following week.

I was always grieved to find people fell out with the pastor and weren't coming back to church without my knowledge, as they were walking out of my life with no explanation, they were just gone. They hadn't fallen out with me, nor I them, yet other church members had to suffer the loss too. I missed many church members because of fall-outs, what does that say about church and the Love Paul talked about? If we can't sincerely and genuinely love in church, then we're not obeying The Word and instead preaching another Gospel. What's the whole point then, of sharing The Good News? We must continue to love unconditionally without strife. If we saw someone burning and screaming in agony, we would (surely) do everything in our power to save them. I know I would, even if it meant I might die to save them from the fire. It's that real, we have to save, dress wounds and heal minds and hearts, not chase people away. I saw Satan, he is alive and kicking and Hell is real. I don't like to preach hellfire and brimstone but I will because I can't help anyone once they are in the furnace of flames. We must hold tight onto Love because our lives depended on it.

I went along to church dutifully because I went to give, bless and lead in the ministry of praise and worship, and loved worshipping God in His Holy presence. When we were reverent, The Holy Spirit was there in that old school in Christian Street where I saw many healings and heard fabulous testimonies of the faithfulness of God. There were many characters who were flippant about church but The Holy Spirit still came. He came as a help and a comforter, He came as a rewarder of those who diligently seek him, He came to those who were still in the world as far as booze and drugs went, He came and poured Himself out over the heartbroken. He always came to meet us as we gathered, expecting Him and He was never late. If He didn't show up, I would have gone elsewhere and sought Him.

Cupping the left side of my face in my hand one Sunday

morning, I was wishing and praying the pain and the pressure on the inside of my mouth would cease to be. The agony of the abscess in my gum left me dopey as I tried to silence it with gels, mouthwashes and painkillers to no avail. My face was very badly swollen and I felt quite seedy because of the amount of medication I was taking to ease the pain. I briefly told the pastor in mumbles that I couldn't sing as I was in too much pain, but I also told him I would stand in my place anyway and just play the guitar, so I wasn't totally shirking my responsibilities or giving up, or in.

'Come on out here and get prayed for right now,' the pastor said as he slipped his hand in his pocket for the little bottle of oil. I was at God's mercy. The beating pulse of the throbbing monster was bringing me out in beads of perspiration. The pastor assured me he wouldn't put his hands on my face because of the swelling. All he did was put his three fingers very gently on the back of my neck, spoke to the abscess and basically told it to 'leave, in the name of Jesus'. He didn't mess about and I didn't want to hang about. Sometimes something's got to hurt really badly before you go after it with a spear and The Word of God and that's what was happening here. My spear was my guitar, even in terrible pain I refused to bow out. If you can't help yourself, thank God there are others who are standing in the gap watching and waiting to help you. As my guitar and everything else was set up I wandered back to my chair to sit on it and, when I lowered my head through the bend to sit, I heard a big pop! There was a taste of blood and the pressure and pain fled, my gum healed right there and then. The swelling went down immediately and there I was singing and praising God again. Nothing to do with me, that was one of the best services we ever had at New Wine church, so powerful The Throne was before us, or vice versa. Other people got healed when they saw my face was back to normal and Satan was thrown out of the church by the power and the anointing of The Holy Spirit.

On most Sundays at church, someone would be asked if they would like to testify about something great God had done for them during the week. I was always up testifying about an event, about someone getting saved, or something about anything, but I often felt it was always me who spoke and I didn't want to put anyone else off, so I waited, and waited. Nobody got up, as usual, so I stood up and shared this silly, but true story.

I was in one of those moods where I was totally fed up and wanted a God cuddle and told Him so while I was sitting in my car in between jobs. I have already explained I talk with God at all times, especially in my car and when I am alone.

I parked up near the boating pond in Rouken Glen Park because I have didn't enough time to go home. Sometimes I would go shopping but that often meant spending money on things I didn't need. There I was, talking away to God as usual, saying, 'I'm fed up sitting here, God. I want a cuddle, why can't you just give me a cuddle, God?' I was waiting for Him but there was silence, of course. 'Do you even hear me, God?' 'I can't stand this waiting about,' I told Him, as I was getting cold. 'Well, can you at least hold my hand then?' I asked as I lifted it up to Him through the open car window, not caring what anyone would have thought on seeing me. No answer was the big loud reply. I got fed up asking and let my hand drop down outside the car door . . . SLAP! 'OH MY GOD, WHAT WAS THAT? GOD, IS THAT YOU? WHAT HAVE YOU DONE?' I was too scared to look. My heart was beating loud and fast as I lifted it up slowly to find the hugest, most perfect, green, shiny waxed leaf with points had wrapped perfectly inside my hand, the points of the leaf curved and closed around it. It looked like another hand holding mine firmly, closely grasping until fingers met. I couldn't stop laughing and knew He did hear me. I spoke to Him and said a few things but I did make it clear I wanted some comfort from Him. I wanted proof He was there and that He could hear me and I got it. Of course I knew God was there, I was just having a little moan.

The pastor loved my testimony and stated, 'That is so like God.' He has a great sense of humour with those who walk with Him. He is funny, a side of Him many Christians and others don't know. He is everything, fiercely jealous, with compassion, and a protector, but still funny too. Most of all He is 'The Daddy.'

Jim was a volunteer at our church charity shop in Pollokshaws, Glasgow, an older retired man, who was very enthusiastic, honest, respectful, consistent, compassionate, cheerful, and hands-on at work. He did his Portable Appliance Test, enabling us take in electrical goods. He was funny and kind, a real gentleman, but whenever anyone spoke about The Bible and witnessed to him about Jesus, Jim would say, 'Oh, I don't know about that,' or 'I don't believe that,' which made me giggle because I love the honesty in people. He never once argued about God's Word, he just gave you the 'look' that said, 'What are you talking about?' He didn't give me that look, though. Everyone in the charity shop already knew about my Out of Body Experience, as I go on about it to anyone who listens. I just can't keep it in, especially when other people start talking about God and the air gets infectious, it's like an upper room experience. During a discussion about the bible (The Word) with other members of the church, Jim was in his usual defence mode, arms folded, closed body language, pursed lips and piercing eyes, until I told him my testimony about my Out of Body Experience. His eyes lit up and he said excitedly, pointing, 'Now that I believe, that's the stories I like.' Jim became full of enthusiasm when I told him my testimonies, saying cheerfully, 'I love to hear people have had their own personal experiences in life with God.'

I kept it up, always telling him about what God did in my life daily and this ultimately pleased him. It meant he could tell me things about the events in his life. He said himself, 'That's the kind of thing that touches my heart, to me that's reality.' He believed in God and in His Word and encouraged me to keep telling my accounts of what God, Jesus and The Holy Spirit did in a day-to-day account. He was fascinated with the real live 'now' God. People need to know that or they won't meet Jesus today. We can always tell people what's happening 'today' because it's brand-new news and it's important that they get to see God is real right now.

Jim is no longer on this planet and I very much look forward to seeing him again and shouting, 'I told you so!' Bless God. We either sow, or reap, sometimes both. In telling someone about Jesus we may feel we never get anywhere but it's not our job to worry, it's only our job to testify about what Jesus has done and is still doing. If God, Jesus or The Holy Spirit has done nothing, then fair enough, He will one day, you just haven't let Him prove His love and devotion to you. I love meeting people and saying, 'Wait until I tell you this!' I always have news. Sometimes I mention God, sometimes Jesus, often The Holy Spirit.

My favourite times are when I am gathered in a room with a few folk, then they open up and tell me a story of a time when . . . and off we go. Even before we realise it, God is right there too. He is more than real and more than loves to be with us. People are afraid of God because they have sinned, just as we were afraid to approach our parents when we did something wrong but they didn't kill us when we owned up. Our loving God-Father won't kill us either.

There were some people I felt I couldn't get through to. I tried to help but this task was much bigger than I was and years of damage were so deep-rooted in a broken soul who needed expert help. When I first met 'Kitchen Girl', I fell in love with her immediately (not in a sexual way!). I felt a deep rapport with her, which was pure, the way God loves all of us, men too. I love everyone, some people are easy to love and some are hard work, but still, Love is Love and Love is all.

Kitchen Girl told me about her abysmal life as a nameless child. At the tiny and tender age of just six months, she was placed into Quarrier's orphanage, unable to yet walk or talk and was 'free' to leave when she was seventeen years old. It was not considered right for a daddy to have custody of girls back in her day and her daddy was working full time anyway and couldn't look after her in the way she should have been cared for. Her daddy paid for her keep – remember this as you read on – her daddy paid Quarrier's orphanage to keep her safe, warm and fed, to look after her wellbeing, physically and emotionally.

Over gallons of tea and hundreds of tears, she told me of her horrific ordeal as she was growing up, thinking she was an orphan because they told her that's what she was. When she left the orphanage she discovered she had a twin brother, who lived nearby in one of the other cottages. That was a terrible shock to her, not a soul owned up and told her he existed.

Here are some of the stories Kitchen Girl told me as we went for tea, shopping and days out, through a broken heart and red inflamed watery eyes. The heartache never left my older lady friend and I did the best I could to lighten her up. We did have some laughs at our misfortunes, as I told her about my cheeky ways growing up and the names we gave to teachers, such as 'Ten to Two feet' because of the way they walked along the corridors. The fact we both had teachers called 'Ten to Two feet' had us in stitches and we laughed as well as cried as we recalled our daft younger selves. I believe it's called 'self-preservation'. Kitchen Girl told me:

'I was always so cold, my fingers were numb with pain as we scrubbed the cold brick floors with our bare hands. I was terribly underweight and the food was filthy. There was a tin for old breadcrumbs, which were saved up from bread the children didn't eat, and the bread inside the tin was blue with mould. I had to make bread and butter pudding from the old bread stored in the tin. I showed the house mother the mouldy bread and she told me to get on with it. The meat we ate was nothing like meat, it was all fat. If we didn't eat it, we got slapped across the back of the head with such force it knocked you off your feet, and told we were ungrateful. We wouldn't get another thing to eat until we did eat it, then we would be sick and get battered for being sick. I couldn't eat, I had no appetite and I was always sick. I made myself sick to empty my gut and soul out. I was ill, physically, emotionally and mentally. We hid our food in our knickers and threw it away on the ground going over to the school or to church, where the birds would pick it up and save us from another hiding.

'One morning I didn't feel well, more unwell than usual. I always didn't feel well but this particular morning I was dizzy. I was slow in the kitchen this day because I thought I was going to faint and had to pace myself while the house mother kept ringing her bell and shouting "Hurry up!" The house mother was lying in her big warm bed upstairs. My fingers were hurting as I got her breakfast tray ready to serve her breakfast in bed. The bell kept ringing and ringing and I was crying. I got the boiling water into the solid silver teapot but the tray was too heavy and everywhere was turning black all the way up the stairs.

'I could still hear the bell ringing in my ears even when it wasn't ringing and had to stop at the top of the stairs and put the heavy silver teapot on the varnished tallboy because of the weight, then rush in with her breakfast tray.

'"Where's my tea?" the house mother screamed. I told her it was outside the door as it was too heavy and I ran to get it. I always had to run. I'd had no breakfast myself, we didn't get anything until all of the kitchen tasks were done. I was so dizzy I thought I was going to pass out but I tried with all my might not to,' she told me as she bowed her head, her voice broken and quiet. The memory of being alone and needing a competent adult to assist her was obvious in her voice and she too doesn't remember ever being cuddled. I fondly remember that one solitary cuddle my mother gave me.

'By the time I went to get it, the boiled tea had made the solid silver handle of the teapot roasting and unbearable to touch. I was horrified when I discovered the heat from the silver teapot had melted the varnish on the tallboy and the teapot was stuck fast to the unit. The tallboy was higher than my chest and I couldn't get it off. My thin dress couldn't reach up to cover the hot teapot handle. She beat me to within an inch of my life and made an example of me before my other house girls by grabbing me by the hair and screaming into my face. That melted varnish ring was still there when she left Quarrier's,' Kitchen Girl told me.

I was horrified, imagine asking a wee girl to lift a heavy roasting hot solid silver teapot with naked hands while the house mother lay in her bed demanding to be served. Words failed me often when conversing with Kitchen Girl. Her words broke my heart as she testified to the ugly truths she had witnessed and endured. She broke my heart because someone had broken hers and the ripple effect continues to bubble out, touching other hearts. She went on to tell me the house mother knew fine well the bread was mouldy and, as Kitchen Girl was in charge of the mouldy bread tin, it was her place to make sure it got topped up from scraps, not just leftover enders, but leftover half-eaten bread too because nothing got wasted. We both cried together as she recalled a lot of the stories and told me the one of the little girl who was told to stand all night long because she had wet her bed. The little girl was still standing in the same spot in morning, cold and stinking of urine, and was made to stand on that same spot for the rest of the day without food or a drink.

'Call on Jesus,' one of the part-time house assistants whispered as she passed the little girl. 'He will come.' A lot of the part-time house teachers and assistants were sacked or sent away if they interfered with the running of the institution. The wee girl who was ordered to stand all through the night and most of the day collapsed when she could no longer stand upright. She was taken to hospital, where she was given food and a warm bed, all because she called on the name of Jesus. That was all she dared to say, one word, 'JESUS'. She called His name and remembered no more as she hit the floor.

This was what I was trying to communicate to Kitchen Girl, who was heartbroken with God, all because she was marched into church, made to learn scriptures and sing 'Safe in the arms of Jesus' while being sexually, physically and mentally abused. She was even placed on television each Christmas to sing joyfully for the nation, with new clothes, which were immediately taken from her when the recordings were finished. All for an appeal for the poor orphans from Quarrier's Village and they were forced to sing for their supper.

I told her I vaguely remembered the orphans singing on television at Christmastime and I thought it was lovely they were so well looked after and was glad they were loved. I knew, thought I knew, they got everything going, cakes, biscuits, food, clothing and cash, because it was a well-known fact that people gave mightily and wished Quarrier's well, yet the children were beaten and starving. Kitchen Girl told me the nice things were never seen and the staff had the best of the food. When she was asked what she would like for Christmas by one of the television presenters, she told me she only asked for a pair of gloves, thinking she desperately needed to keep her hands warm because her fingers were painfully bent. She was belted on the back of the head when she got back to the house, she said, with a bible and told, 'This will suit you better!' She was called the spawn of the devil and a reprobate. Her father paid for her keep, remember, she was neither a charity case nor an orphan, yet she was led to believe she was both.

Kitchen Girl also had me rolling about with laughter on occasions but the laughter had a hidden common denominator of abuse and hurt and I knew the tears lasted longer. It was a much welcomed breakthrough on my part, and I hoped to reach her with the love of Jesus. She spoke to me of the love she had for her husband and how dreadfully she missed him, so much so she couldn't live without him. He was her first and last love, the only love she had ever known and now that she was alone, life was too painful without him.

Love was alien to her but she found a glimpse of it through meeting and marrying him. She shared with me the story of how they met and she truly believed that they all had to get permission from the police to go out with anyone, she was dreadfully naive. If the police saw you alone they would arrest you, she really believed that and was afraid for her future. She learned it too as she watched the police bring back 'runaways' all too often and no one told her any basic facts of life, not about welfare or marriage, only that no one would have her. As for sex, menstruation and having babies, well, she was totally clueless and didn't know the first thing about relationships and conceiving a child. She didn't know the basic facts of life and believed it was sinful to have any such thoughts. Neither did she even menstruate until she was older than seventeen because she was so underweight. I could relate to that story all too well.

I lay down in script the story she told me on meeting her first and only love, who became her husband. Here is the first time Kitchen Girl meets a boy who likes her. I am both blessed and flabbergasted at her innocence. When she is finally free of Quarrier's, and working, she meets a boy who tries to ask her to go out with him on a date, a handsome young man by the name of Jack.

Jack: How are you doing?
KG: How am I doing what?
Jack: My name's Jack, would you like to go out?
KG: I'm out!
Jack: Would you like to go out with me?
KG: Out where?
Jack: To the pictures.
KG: What pictures?
Jack: Any pictures, we could go and see something new.
[really suspicious of his motives as she didn't realise pictures meant cinema]
KG: New pictures? Can you not go and see them yourself?

Jack: I'll let you pick what you want to see, I don't mind.

KG: Oh, will you indeed? I don't need you or anybody else to show me pictures. If I want to see pictures I'll go and pick pictures for myself to look at.

Jack: Eh?

KG: The pictures! What's on these pictures anyway?

Jack: I don't know what's on but I'll find out.

KG: You don't even know what's on the pictures?

Jack: What pictures are you talking about?

KG: What pictures are you talking about? You're the one that's going on about wanting to see some pictures and you don't even know what's on them!

Jack: I like you and I was wondering if you would like to go to the pictures with me to see a film?

KG: Oh, why did you not say that in the first place? I thought you were off your head! Yes, I'd like to go to the pictures.

. . . And so they did, dated, got married and lived happily ever after, until Jack was taken home to be with The Lord.

Kitchen Girl didn't know love, she hadn't ever experienced it. As a baby, she was brought up by the other little girls who were in the orphanage, as part of their duties. They were just youngsters themselves, who had to feed, change, bathe and rock to sleep the little scraps of humanity placed in their care, when they needed the same care themselves. All of the girls had been allocated tasks, some were looking after the younger babies, others would have toilet duties, and so on. As part of her task as the kitchen girl, she was always up very early and couldn't leave the kitchen until every duty was performed until late in the evening.

Kitchen Girl despised Jesus because she thought He was part of the heinous plan when she got hit on the head with the bible when asked what she would like for Christmas. If it wasn't for Christmas, the birthday of the baby Jesus, then she wouldn't have got belted as she stood beside a real fir tree with baubles, glittering and sparkling, singing Holy songs. She didn't want much, a pair of gloves to keep her tiny cold, cracked fingers warm, that was all. She knew not to have any grand ambitions or dreams. SMACK! 'You'll get a bible and you'll read it, Scum, that will do you a lot more good than a pair of gloves.'

She told me another thing, which was astounding. The staff who didn't live in the area of the cottages were normal mothers, who never witnessed the abuse at night, as they would have gone home to their own warm houses. They were outsiders and were watched like hawks when at work. It was them who often reported the abuse but they got sacked, meaning they had to keep quiet so the abuse was ignored. Many needed their jobs and it was better to say nothing. That way they could still have access to the children.

One of the visiting staff hand-knitted a cardigan for Kitchen Girl, which she couldn't ever wear. She didn't want it to get ruined, she had nowhere nice to go and it was too precious. She kept it in the tissue paper all of her life. She would open it up and cry as she gently ran her fingers over the wool and thought it was the most beautiful garment in the world.

'I couldn't understand why she had hand-knitted me a cardigan. It was too precious to wear, it was too good for me.' Why can't I read about the hand-knitted cardigan without bubbling? I thought my life was hard as I watched the orphaned children on television while I was living in the house of evil with the swirls on the ceiling and The Daddy being a monster, but I now see there were children worse off than me.

'It was soft, the colour was beautiful and the design took my breath away. It was too good for me. I just looked at it and cried because it was so precious. Why did she knit it for me?'

People didn't show her love, she had never met love before. At the age of just six months, she remembered nothing but grief, screaming and yelling. Love was not a visitor to Quarrier's, especially not at Christmas. She spoke very highly of the kind woman who hand-knitted the cardigan especially for her. It blew her away and messed with her emotions at the same time. Like me, she was told she was useless and believed every negative word spoken.

I won't pretend to read Kitchen Girl's mind and thoughts as she continually opened the tissue paper to stroke the cardigan made with love, with her skinny little cold bent fingers, the cardigan she never wore because it was too precious and she had nowhere to go. We never knew, when we watched the Quarrier's orphans on the television as children ourselves, that there was a horror story behind the eyes of the children. We had no idea, when we saw the orphans on the television singing Christmas carols, that they were really poor, hurt, miserable and despondent. They looked happy and well-fed. I thought everybody (except us because we were poor) was giving them money and food. I didn't know the staff were keeping it to themselves. As I already wrote, we often cried and I told her Jesus wept too.

I was desperately trying to reach her but I couldn't find her. There was too much baggage and she was so badly damaged that I could only relate her testimony to that of Jesus's. I told her He was abused too, wounded for our transgressions when He was sinless. Thankfully, she understood but she still didn't want to stay on this Earth.

I spent a few long nights at the Accident and Emergency in Victoria Hospital, where she promised me she hadn't taken an overdose of medication and I ran to her home for essentials. One night she did fill herself with medication in the way of strong pills and I never saw her again, as she was placed in her highly polished coffin. It was a very dark lonely night and I wasn't there for her. She didn't phone me as she usually did and she had promised me she would. She had promised me she wouldn't swallow all of her medication again. I was heartbroken for her plight when everyone else turned away because they were fed up listening to her story about her childhood and abuse, with her crying eyes. Jesus didn't turn away. At the very least I was able to tell her that Jesus loved her. I hope to see her again in Heaven some time in the near future. Perhaps she is the one who is the friend on the wall as Jesus passes by to walk down into the city of lights, below. No one had time for her but I couldn't leave her or let her down. Jesus wouldn't let me. I miss her so much it still hurts.

There are many 'Kitchen Girls' in this world who need our help and I pray I meet as many as I possibly can, even if I do cry and bubble like a baby. I may not be able to help wipe away the horrible memories but I know The Lord who can. He is the same God of yesterday, who is active today, and fashions our tomorrows. That's another reason why I love him so much, not just because He hears and helps me, but because He is deeply and affectionately The Father of mankind and He wants us all to come back to Him.

Over thirteen years had passed from the time God had taken me from my bed (while attending Elim), and had taken me inside the womb of the mother having the 'big baby'. Throughout the years I continually asked God where my baby was, the big baby I ran my hands over and said, 'Yes, I'll do it.' I always wondered, where, how, when and why? I knew without a shadow of a doubt it was going to happen but I had sort of resigned myself to leave it to when God was ready, or when I was ready too, I should say, God would do it. I had learned to be reasonably patient and God's timing was perfect. All I had to do was to be silent and not bleat on about it. I never forgot it though and wondered when it would happen.

In the meantime I had entered into the business of Health and Social Care to help a friend out, a very private business where not a word is uttered about any part of a person's personal life. Once this is drummed home, any information regarding a person's private life stays private. Kitchen Girl was not one of my clients under this regime, therefore I could freely speak of our conversations.

I received many children to care for who were demanding

and required, in my opinion, two carers. I had a very difficult time with one such child, a real bruiser of a young lad, who was built like a wrestler, so big and strong he had joined a rugby club. My heart would pump out of my chest when I was with him as I found minding him a very difficult and laborious task. His voice was powerful, turning every head at both ends of the shopping centre with a boom.

He would punch me 'playfully' but it was really sore as he pointed his knuckles out and would nearly knock me into 'next week', bouncing me off store plate-glass windows, which caved slightly in bending, but didn't break. I was covered in bruises from the beatings, as he didn't realise his own strength. He popped a good strong cap gun full on, in my ear, causing damage, so that I heard a ringing sound for a few days, accompanied by a dull pain. He often ran away and left me, causing panic as I searched for him. He had dreadful temper outbursts and would yell and shout just because he felt like it, causing everyone to 'tut-tut' as they watched his unreasonable performances. He would scream, 'Paedophile!' and 'Child molester!' at the top of his voice when I laid my hand gently on his back for guidance, as instructed by staff. People would turn around to find me close to tears with embarrassment as I bowed my head in his presence.

'Please send someone else, a man perhaps, to mind him' fell on deaf ears. I spent much of my time sweet-talking him round and spent my wages on him to keep the peace because he hardly ever had money on our outings. I had to buy him socks one day when he went ballistic because he couldn't find any without holes in them. He broke many items in my car, like good pens, and would open the car door while I was driving, nearly giving me heart failure. He grabbed the steering wheel while the car was in motion and slapped the windscreen mirror from its holding. Eventually, I had to stop my car before picking him up and hide everything his eye might spy. By the time he was dropped off home, my car was in a terrible state, the passenger side of the car was a riot of broken biscuits, crisps, sweetie powder of some sort, sticky toffees and drink cans or bottles, which he shook vigorously so the gas would splatter on the car roof and windscreen before it was pointed at my face for a sticky wash. He laughed his head off at his own antics. I prayed to God to help me cope because I was shattered.

My young client stabbed me with a school compass because it made him laugh and he always had a lighter for setting things on fire, mainly my clothes. Trying to take things from him would have been perceived as abuse if I laid a finger on him. He was banned from several shops and warned by the security guards that he would be banned from the whole of the Avenue if he didn't behave, but I always stuck up for him and took his side, explaining I was his Personal Care Assistant and promising we would be fine.

I went home and burst out crying one evening as I emptied tiny sticky sweets from my clothes and picked at the ones that he had deliberately spat, out of my congealed hair. My hair came out in strands as the sweets were dry and stuck fast. He covered me with spray foam and silly string from the counters of shops that had left them out for a free trial, and thought nothing of slapping something, anything, full on in my face, mindless of the fact I wore glasses. Just when I thought we would be having a good calm day, he would jump on my back, knocking me to the ground, or put me in a headlock for fun. All of the public witnessed the humiliation of a middle-aged woman in the shopping centre as he paraded me around in that way until he decided he would let me go. The security cameras must have seen some sights when we were in, as I was being abused. My clothes were torn, not only by him admittedly. I had other younger children who were very strong to look after. The three-year-olds could certainly kick out but this guy was ten years older and his beatings led to the aches and pains I felt the following day.

My office wouldn't help and I was forever beaten down in condemnation by his family and my bosses, for not doing this and that, or I would get into trouble for actually doing something I wasn't supposed to be doing. If I was doing such a bad job, why didn't they send someone else to do it, as I pleaded? No one else could or would do the job. 'Not for all the tea in China,' one reported and another said, 'I don't get paid enough for that crap!' Some tried so I could have a holiday break but changed their mind after only one 'shadowing' visit. I would start work at five am to let his mother get to her work early in the morning, so getting up at four am and working until eleven pm sometimes.

The big bruiser told me he wanted to go up in the lift to the top floor of the Silverburn shopping centre for a look. I explained there was nothing up there but a car park, which was used for teaching young people to drive, and was not open to the general public. A full blown rant was coming on and so, to keep the peace, I agreed and up we went in the lift to the top floor of the four-storey building. When we got there, he saw I was correct, there was nothing to see. It was a freezing cold, dark December evening and the bitter biting wind stung my cheeks in the open air of the roof of the building. I asked him to come back down in the lift as it was far too cold but he refused. It was an eerie dark place to be with very little lighting and I needed him to come down because I didn't think it was safe or wise to be there. I would have got it in the neck yet again if anything had happened to him. I stood back against the plate-glass door with my arms folded to keep warm as I watched him throw himself over a waist-high barrier to do somersaults. As I stood and watched him I spoke inwardly to God and said, 'God, I'm fed up with this carry-on, I want out, I can't do it any more.' God said to me right there and then, '**THAT'S THE BABY I GAVE YOU!**' The baby turned fourteen years old about six months after I was allocated him. He was the big baby God had taken me to visit inside his mother's womb before he was born. I saw him before he entered the earth. I stood inside his mother's womb with God behind me and I touched that big baby before he was born. I deliberately turned and looked over to the left and it was dark, while I was with God. There was plenty of room in the womb, everything was larger and I was standing up. I was completely relaxed and when I looked away from the left, I focused on the big baby boy and paid attention to what God had asked me to do. He said, as I looked closely at the big baby, '**IT WILL BE DIFFICULT, I CAN TAKE IT AWAY IF YOU WANT.**'

I was with God's big baby for all that time and it never dawned on me for a split second who he was, I was looking for a big baby, not a fourteen-year-old, fourteen years later.

I knew then I was supposed to look after the big boy who was the baby I was taken to visit inside his mother's womb and got on with the business of doing so without any further complaint about doing the job, because God was with me every step of the way. I took the beatings, physically from him and verbally from all sides, my bosses, his family and outsiders who had nothing to do with his care.

I never told his mother I was inside her womb with God, that would have gone down like a lead balloon under the circumstances. Neither did I tell my big (baby) boy. I did tell him Jesus loved him, though, something that I was not allowed to do, being forbidden to share my faith. He asked me a ton of questions about God and I gave him the answers I knew. When I didn't know the answers I told him so and found out. We had many long conversations about God and he loved to go there. I didn't just do the job I was supposed to do at work, I did the work of God I was asked to do, especially when I realised who the baby was. The task ended after a couple of years, two birthdays and Christmases went by. When the time was right he was taken away from the system and I was given a final written warning, just short of the sack, for giving his small female best friend a lift in the car, with her grandmother's permission too.

God was right, it was really hard but I did it. Before I realised who I was looking after I kept demanding that the office send somebody else and they wouldn't do it. Now I knew why any of the other staff weren't appointed, God had given me the task thirteen years before. There were tears as my big baby boy was taken from me. I was actually heartbroken by the abuse from all around him and my own office but he wasn't lost with God, he was on another part of his young life cycle that would take him in the correct direction. God has plans for His big baby and maybe one day I'll get to hear how he is getting on, hopefully. It was a hard task but I offered to do it. I could have said 'No', but who wants to say 'No' to our God when He always gives us everything we ask and need? Even our secret heart's desires no one else knows about. It wasn't so hard it disabled me permanently or killed me, the task had me in floods of tears many times, but God stood up for me and healed my broken heart. What a mighty productive God we serve.

On stage we were taught there was no room for two at the centre. Centre stage houses one person only and the Follow Spot is on them. For two people the stage becomes split, unless of course the two people are joined as one, or are as close as that. We had been taught that if we were being masked then it was our own fault. 'Move out of the way because the person standing in front of you doesn't realise you are being masked and cannot do anything about it,' we were enlightened. 'Move yourself out of the way if you want to be seen.' Each person has a part to play on Earth and you do not have to be at the centre of the stage to be seen. The person at centre stage wouldn't be there if it were not for the hard-working folks in the background making it happen.

There are fresnels to shine and light you up. There is someone qualified who is working the 'Follow Spot'. That person knows exactly what he or she is doing and has already received the director's lighting instructions. It doesn't mean our job, work or words aren't important, they are. We have to be in the right place in order to do that job, but not necessarily always centre stage. Patience and silence (with God) will help us understand His perfect timing.

I knew it was pointless for me to seek my own will and try and be centre stage at any time of my life because I always knew I was supposed to stay with and care for my parents. My whole world evolved around God and if I could imagine where I was in relation to Him being centre stage, I wouldn't even be in the chorus line. Also, the person at centre stage would not be there if it were not for the props, costume, lighting, sound, scriptwriter, director, choreographer, backstage hands, chorus and fellow actors. Where am I then as I wonder where my part is? I'm writing another one of many thousands of scripts, stories, testimonies and writings, that have been written before me. Not so long ago God told me to write my book or someone else would do it. That made me mad! No one could write my personal testimony, but they could have written their own and used my title. I wasn't having that. I got my head right down and got on with it. I have to say reservedly that I didn't write it on my own. The Holy Spirit sat with me and helped me to remember and recall.

I've had some terrific laughs on and off stage and had a fantastic time performing in pantomimes, and also wrote and directed my own pantos in keeping up with the times, which included an audition in *The X Factor*. There was a Simon Howl on the panel, what a laugh. The script is named *Cinderella and The Time Warp*, where characters from other pantos and shows occasionally got lost and turned up in the castle. I even managed to hire a Dalek with some help but we couldn't get it up and onto the stage, because was a real Dalek, you know.

Children from all over asked me if it was a real Dalek. What could I say? 'Yes, of course it's real,' I told them. Word got about fast and we could have sold the tickets ten times over. The Dalek had to enter and exit down between the audiences because Daleks don't do stairs very well, slopes yes, stairs no. Dr 'You Know Who' had an awful time trying to peel children from the

Dalek as it passed by the audience. The poor guy inside could hardly control it, the fact that he couldn't see out didn't help, and I had to invent a part for the Doctor. The Doctor is not the Daleks' best friend. For the panto, though, I had to pair them up and needed the Doctor to guide the big Dalek in and out. The children were practically exterminating the Dalek as it tried to pass feet, shoes and handbags. It drove the theatre staff daft but what a brilliant time that was. Word got around there was a real Dalek and many disappointed children missed out. On that note, the more children who attend make the production less profitable, as the ticket prices are cheaper for children, hence the reason the pantos can be adult-based with 'slapstick'.

I have to tell you this while it's on my mind. I thought I was going to collapse laughing this day, I needed oxygen and couldn't get at it. I have never ever 'corpsed' on stage, only in rehearsals, I'm very disciplined on stage. This Christmas panto was the one where a young Peter Pan was flying around the stage. It was the third years' final exam in college. We as second years had to assist in every aspect of the production and I was put into the costume department. I came up with two beautiful mermaid costumes with sewn-on individual fins on the tails, along with the Alligator, who had a green dyed costume with scales. He had a cracking head with red flashing lights for eyes and the rest of the cast had spectacular costumes too. Our costume depart-ment had a great crew and the other departments such as props would come and squeeze into our department because we had a laugh.

We cordoned our area off with the black curtains and made a huge den, furnishing it off with tables, comfortable chairs and a kettle for our tea breaks, as well as the required sewing machines and costume rails for the third-year real Actors.

Aye, that'll be right! This is where the so-called actor got his or her real character assassination. The second years decided who was great, a prima donna, or a useless twat! The actor/

actress received the nomination according to their behaviour, not for their acting ability. For anyone interested in Acting and Performance, Musical theatre, Stagecraft, Director, Choreographer, sound or lighting, it really is not a nine-to-five job, not even in college, be well warned. Also be warned that about twenty-four potential actors are chosen from hundreds of applicants in first year for NC. One has to audition again for your second year, where numbers drop to around eighteen at HNC and if you make it to the HND (by audition again), then there is no guarantee of work at the end of your three-year slog. You will still be an actor, an out-of-work one, or as we say in this amazing creative industry, RESTING! And don't bother going to the Jobcentre and explaining you are an actor or performer because you won't like the positive feedback. You will sweep the streets like everyone else, and if that doesn't keep your feet firmly on the ground, nothing will.

Our snug was like a cosy living room but before we knew it, every Tom, Dick and Harry would come in for the banter. We also had to be part of the third year's chorus, which meant lots of rehearsals and time being pulled from our costume making, which also meant I had to take the costumes home. I would often be up until four in the morning sewing the costumes, as they had to be finished and approved for the Christmas production. If they weren't done properly, they had to be done again. The actors were so impatient and wanted their costumes as soon as possible, soooo ungrateful by the way! Now you can see why their characters were assassinated.

Our costume preparation was interrupted once again for a chorus call and off we went and climbed up on the back of the huge ship, singing, 'What shall we do with the drunken sailor?' for what seemed like the millionth time of going up and down the huge perfectly built ship. We started and stopped dozens of times and had to get up the makeshift ladder of the ship the carpentry department had made and walk along a ledge at the back of the ship, which couldn't have been more than six inches wide. As I was always last up there was no more room on the ledge of the ship for me and I got to stay on the top of the ladder. To make matters difficult, we needed both hands for the ladder and had to appear with our swords in our mouths and look menacing, making singing, in our harmonies, difficult but not impossible.

Up and down we went as the stage hands tried to fly Peter across the ship to land on a very specific spot. They had to get it bang-on right but the problem was the stage hands couldn't see to the other side of the stage as the ship was so huge. Over and over, day in and day out, from early morning until last thing at night this difficult manoeuvre was practised. There we were again then, up in our places, singing away at the tops of our voices, brandishing our swords with one hand and holding on tight to the unsanded wood of splinters with the other.

We heard a thud as Peter was smashed into the breeze-blocked wall at the far end of the stage by the stage hands. The silence was tangible. The Principal, Stage Director, Head of Stage Carpentry, Choreographer, Musical Director and other tutors were absolutely furious as they watched the scene from the front row. Poor Peter could have been seriously injured, they echoed in surround sound and disgust. The stage crew couldn't possibly see the spot at the end of the ship, where Peter was to land. The air was blue, Peter's face was red from the smacking and the chorus were tickled pink because they thought he was a twat anyway. As the rage of the shouting and bawling was dying down, one of my chorus muttered the most unforgivable state-ment ever to be breathed on a stage . . . 'Peter Pancake!' Oh no, help! I managed to bend down the ladder, thus hiding my face, but the others couldn't move because I couldn't move any further down with just one hand on the ladder. I could hear the painful groans and whelps of the others as they tried to keep the laughter in, as their faces were at high mast for all to see. I was in hysterics as I bent down and hid behind the ship, thank God, because laughter is highly infectious and unfortunately I catch that infection a lot, I now name this infection on this ship H0W11.

'Peter' was fine, of course, but the others were in agony trying not to laugh. It is agony holding laughter back and pretending something's not funny when your insides are screaming with delight and happiness, making acting harder than you could think or imagine. Crying on stage is much easier than holding back laughter because laughter becomes uncontrollable.

The unfortunate crewmate who muttered 'Peter Pancake' got a real ticking-off from the rest of the chorus for making them laugh. Nevertheless, they still laughed about it for the rest of the production and I was glad to be last up and first down the ship.

I have had a few unfortunate mishaps on stage, which I hope have gone unnoticed. Only experience helps one to bow out gracefully without further misadventure. Every care is taken to make the production run smoothly but it's common knowledge that we must always look out for naughty and malicious misadventure, such as the sewing-up of trouser bottoms that an actor might have to wear on stage. It goes without saying that it should never happen but it does. A raw egg in a boot is a favourite, so it breaks and squelches when the actor puts his foot in it. Magazines and books have to be continually checked on the prop table because someone will, eventually, put a naughty picture in the middle of the pages, particularly on the last performance, which could make you laugh or completely throw you off your line.

I had my own mishaps without anyone's help, thank you. In a play where I was a loose landlady, I was to wear false eyelashes, which were a hideous silver colour and way too long. I only wore false eyelashes once in my life and I couldn't stand them, so I didn't bother doing it again. Needs must, though, for the benefit of the character, naughty Mrs Husk.

Everything was going great throughout the performances until my left eye got stuck with the eyelash glue one night and I couldn't open it. Trying not to panic, I wiped my eye and tried to unstick it during the play, only to realise I had nearly pulled off the long eyelash, which was now flapping. My left eye closed completely with the glue and the huge silver eyelash was hanging over my cheek, like a caterpillar hitching a ride. As if that wasn't bad enough, it became excruciatingly itchy and I needed to scratch my face. We have all been there, I'm sure. Trying not to scratch an itchy area drives you mad, getting itchier by the second.

My character was a drunkard, who was to swig from a bottle of booze. That's another thing we had to watch out for, vinegar in a drink which was to be consumed on stage. The drink was bad enough as it was, usually strong dark cold tea and whatever else was used to colour it. Sometimes a mishap actually helps to get you right into character. I had to hit the bottle quicker than I should have by swigging it and pretending the drink was going straight to my head. That bought me time as I got drunk quicker and allowed the hanging eyelash to become part of the character, a hussy of a drunken landlady with low morals. Everyone thought the acting was brilliant but I was really improvising because I couldn't see properly and my character got funnier and drunker as the show went on. One of the best acting skills you can have is being able to improvise and think quickly on your feet without disrupting the cast. Stealing the limelight or changing the lines of a script is a definite no-no unless you own it.

In this same play I was also wearing very long nails and at one point I was to grab a new lodger by his belt, undo it, pull his fly down and get his trousers down to his knees, but on the first night I couldn't get his belt undone with the fake nails on. He was to protest and stop me doing so by holding on to his belt but, because I couldn't get his belt undone and his zip down, he had to help me to get his own trousers off without anyone noticing. When I saw him on the television in *Taggart*, I laughed and told my husband, 'I've taken his trousers down.'

In a serious play I stuffed my bra with watery 'chicken fillets' as I was wearing a long black matronly dress and I wanted to add emphasis to the small waist of the dress by enhancing the chest area. Somewhere along my lines I was to lose my head and stomp around the stage in a furious outburst of anger. As I did my jumping and stomping around in anger I suddenly felt one of the chicken fillets come bouncing out of the bra, which was too big, and it would have hit me on the chin were it not for the tight collar of the dress. Then it would have fallen straight to the floor from under the long dress. As I had no belt on this dress, I quickly threw my arm across my waist to hold it there but I had suddenly become disabled. I didn't dare take my arm away from the front of my waist and let the fillet fall to the floor, I would have been mortified. The stage was set in floor space which meant the audience, who were in a circle, could see absolutely everything, even the hair on my face because of the lighting. People noticed the carefree character blowing her top had changed, I could sense the shift in dynamics, and also that of the audience, and I had to 'act' quickly and not panic. Instead of going mad with anger, I had to change quickly into a sinister fiend by moving slowly so as to hold on to the chicken fillet, yet continue acting. I narrowed my eyes and growled through gritted teeth. I don't know who was more scared, the other characters, or the audience. It worked a treat and added a surprise element to the character but I wasn't always so lucky.

The shoes I was given for another serious play had heels much higher than I would ever have worn and I felt way out of my depth (or height), quite literally, as I tottered around in them. Actors have a little say in their costumes if they don't fit but that's all, you have to wear them. They can be taken in or let out, but not changed once the ASM has passed them.

At one point in this serious play I was to crouch down and peer into a grave to say my goodbyes, but on the way back up one of the spiky high heels cut through the black lace of the dress behind me. As I tried to walk away with the rest of the bereaved I had the most massive humph and a limp and nearly fell over. With the shoes being so high I couldn't get to balance on the one foot to try and free the dress from the other shoe's heel. I was in so much trouble this time and it was obvious to everyone I was struggling to free myself. I couldn't get out of the dilemma without sitting on the floor (ground of the grave-yard) and quietly breathe (panic!), feeling a change of colour on my face as I took a few moments to gather my thoughts. No matter how much I pulled at the lace of the dress, the shoe wouldn't come free and everyone noticed the disaster. I had to pull my foot from the shoe and release it from the dress, which the audience clearly saw. Everyone else had left the stage where I was supposed to follow, being last as usual. I got back up and smiled, wriggled my foot back into the shoe, and walked off. The audience noticed every bit of the unfolding drama and gave us the best applause because of the incident. It was a big 'Uh Oh' moment I couldn't improvise with because of the serious-ness of the play. We were never allowed a prompt and had to learn our lines (and everyone else's) because it was our respon-sibility to do so. We were quick to assist and help each other vocally but not where footwear was concerned unfortunately.

In the play, *The Steamie*, which I have appeared in many times now, I was to get dressed quickly and get 'my man's boots' on as soon as possible. No matter how hard I tried I couldn't get them back on and tied up before my next lines were to be delivered and had to do it while speaking, wobbling all over the place as I tried to squeeze my feet back into them. We even-tually put elastic laces in the boots but it was still a difficult task. I'd be walking about with one foot or the other breaking the back of the boot until I had time to get it on properly, stamping on the ground, trying to get it on without a drama or a notice-able crisis.

This footwear story might have you gagging, so here is a WARNING before you read on. Running late one day I missed the beginning of a rehearsal and was told to 'Hurry' with shouts of 'You're on!' I leapt onto the stage without getting changed and grabbed the chair set for the ugly sister. Shut it, you! It wasn't my fault there weren't enough men to play the parts of the ugly sisters, lol. I started immediately with my line, 'Oh no, it just doesn't fit,' as I was to pretend to squeeze the glass slipper on. I threw my left leg up and grabbed my trainer and started shouting 'OH NO! NO! NO!'

'Aw, she's really good,' people in the wings were saying, not so, I can confirm. I had stood on dog's dirt on my way to the theatre and had only gone and slapped my hand right tight as you like around the mucky stuff as I grabbed my trainer. A huge clump fell off and landed on the stage and when everyone realised what was on my hand and trainer, they ran quicker than lightning, gagging. I was hopping on one foot and holding my right hand out, completely matted and covered in dog poo. Nobody would help me and they wouldn't want to come back to the stage until it was seriously washed and disinfected. They should have put 'Esther-NO FRIENDS' on the programme, because they kept their distance all day.

My worst ever mishap was on the day I auditioned for Acting and Performance at Langside College. I took my two contrasting monologues to a friend, who said they were great but far too long and he cut them back. I then did the monologues before him for his approval, to make sure they suited me because I chose to perform them, all good.

He said they were great but told me to make an impact, to do something the panel would remember me by. I took his great advice but took it too far. At the end of my second monologue, when I was changing into different characters, I was to go before the auditioning panel and bang on the desk right in front of the three judges, peering into their eyes. Yes, I thought, I'll do that, I can make an impact. Again, the monologue was great and was indeed a total contrast from the first one. I came thundering out from behind my chair and, after firing my imaginary rifle, I ran to the desk and battered it with my fists, giving my last line as a warning to the panel, according to the script. It was fantastic up to that point and I knew I had done really well, but . . . on banging my fists on the desk, their cups of coffee went flying through the air and landed upside down onto the paperwork from the previous auditionees.

'That's all right,' I told them and quickly ran for paper towels to clear the mess up. I thought I had blown my chance of getting in. They certainly didn't forget me, I'd made sure of that. We weren't told how we'd got on until the letter landed behind our front door, six months later. Over three hundred applicants apply for just twenty-four or so places. Not only did I get in, I was to meet in the 'Emmanuel' studio. I told everyone what had happened and how I was to meet in the 'GOD WITH US' studio.

I have said at the beginning of the book that the World is the stage, God is the producer, Jesus the director, and The Holy Spirit is the prompt, and we have the book of Acts. We are told how to act through God's Word. We are all actors, some for ourselves and some for others, some by ourselves and some beside others. One day we will be given a prize greater than any Oscar. I was acting before I did my HND and have come across many actors who don't have training. The truth is, you don't need it if you are already an actor. It helps with confidence but it's not imperative. It was spoken and prophesised to me from primary school and I didn't see it for myself. I was good at it but I wasn't leaving my mother to seek my own will. I was so backward at coming forward that I could never have imagined myself acting or performing, yet people saw it in me and told me what I was going to do. When it was prophesised I was to write a book I replied, 'no way'. On looking back I can clearly see what other people saw in me, some people believed in me and I wasn't that stupid useless person I was also led to believe.

I have also shown there is a great comparison between The Earthly Daddy and The Heavenly Daddy-The Father, after all. This staged life is only for a little while and we will all bow out soon. In one of the plays we wrote ourselves in college, I made a suggestion that we should all stand in a line at the end of our strange showcase and applaud the audience. It was the most bizarre experience as we looked at the audience in close proximity and applauded them for watching us. They found it strange too but highly amusing. I've had my fair share of applause and credits in the media but once again, I applaud The Father, The Son and The Holy Spirit. There is no script greater than that of The Love Story where The Very God of The Universe became flesh and dwelt among us, then laid down his life for every one of us. That script is Holy and is called 'The Bible'.

## Chapter Sixteen

# HALF-HOUR CALL

Serenity. Serene. Serena. I often pondered about which name to choose before I could share this story with you because I am not at liberty to use the young lady's real name. Also, five of the women in my testimony have the same name, posing the obvious problem, you might forget which one I am on about. I can have you thinking, 'What are you talking about?' I don't need to throw a spanner in the works by having you also think, 'Who are you talking about now?' So, sitting quietly and pondering with The Lord, I thought something along the lines of serenity, as my client was quiet, peaceful and asleep most of the time. Well, in the morning anyway.

Serena was sight-impaired (totally), unable to speak, paralysed and bedridden. Her only way of communicating was to groan or by the noticeable distress signals on her face, which would become bright red. Her closest family knew what the groans meant, whether or not she was happy or angry, and could tell by her slight facial expressions and her moods if she was comfortable. There inevitably had to be communication somehow and, in the silent moments of personal care, her closest family even knew the rhythm in every one of her heartbeats. Serena could not squeeze our hands or even wiggle her toes. She gave each of us quite a scare many times when she stopped breathing. One time in particular, she seemed to be gone for too long. I held her hand and wrist often and even put my ear on her heart waiting for the next dull thud to confirm she was still with us, when unsure. Most of the time she was sound asleep in the morning and we were always worried in case she was 'off'.

The peg-feed in her abdomen would sometimes block, resulting in back-up or overflow, which was the cause of much distress for her, obvious by the flush of her face.

Infection control was an hourly, as well as a daily battle. Bedsores, when she had them, were bloody and pus-filled when infection won. Her body was scrutinised at every wash, looking for any telltale signs of a sore and every red pimple was noted, creamed and recorded. There were bowel blockages to contend with, as her body was unable to apply any pressure to push and assist with the natural bodily function of waste. The severe cramp of menstruation, headaches, diverse pain or that overwhelming irritating itch would be around to bully Serena, who was unable to communicate vocally.

The inflated balloon at the end of her feeding tube would sometimes pop out and refuse to re-enter her swollen abdomen. We would tell Serena she was playing hard to get when we struggled to insert the small balloon and tube back into her abdomen. I'm sure I detected a faint smile on her face many times as we became frustrated at our attempts to make sure we weren't hurting her.

Her head was often slightly elevated on arrival so she wouldn't choke on her saliva or any acid reflux. Quite often the aspirator would be used to remove the foamy phlegm from her mouth and throat to keep the fluid away from her airways, leading to her lungs.

On entering her home, we had to wait twenty minutes for our hands to heat up as Serena slept naked except for her simple linen sheet, pads and any pressure dressings. The shock of anything that was not at body temperature was unacceptable on her largest organ, the skin, therefore, we would be allowed to put the kettle on and make ourselves and the house owner a tea or coffee. Sometimes we went for the milk or brought biscuits in for the tea or coffee. Her sister had enough to do, not getting to bed until well after two am and back up at four am to care for her Serena.

I was a relative newcomer, having only been with the family for two years. The casting process for this job was simple, one chance only to prove your worth, although new staff were very rarely required for Serena. Even then, every move, action, attitude and word was scrutinised. We weren't there to impress with false eyelashes, two-inch stuck-on painted nails, hair extensions, pure white veneered teeth, tattoos, fish lips and silicone implants. Some of the carers in particular will know all of those mentioned are their characteristics. Not only were those attributes not required for the tasks ahead, they were not welcome in this household and many others. Only real, down-to-earth, honest and reliable people were invited. The love of one's own self before that of Serena was deeply frowned upon. Serena couldn't speak to answer back but her sister certainly could and commanded, quite rightly, that we still converse with her and not treat her like a piece of meat, ignoring her. She had as much right to dignity and respect as the next person and carers were told that.

The carer had to be a dog lover too, as there were two completely opposite canines to contend with, the minute one ruling the roost. There was a parrot in the house somewhere, as it was always told to shut up because it barked like a dog. I thought there were three dogs in the house for months before I was informed the parrot thought it was a dog. That was just a little general information on the household in case you had built up a quick picture in your mind of clinical waste, antibacterial wipes, hand sanitiser and boxes of pads, lotions and other medical necessities. Sure, those things and images were evident but this was not just a house where a disabled lady lived in the back bedroom, this house was a home with real love and laughter. The front door was always unlocked for family, friends, guests, carers, nurses and other health professionals alike.

Like so many other dwelling places in Glasgow, it was a real down-to-earth fixed abode, where love and humility lived. Honesty, truth and respect were paramount. What went on within the four walls of any person's house was private and confidential.

Aye, right. If 'It' was happening, going on somewhere, then we had it dissected, probed and analysed verbally so we could take the juicy gossip into Serena and tell her all about it. It was vitally important to keep her clued up on what was happening in the outside world. She was a long, long time in her bed and it was imperative we bring the outside world and local happenings in to her.

We would be in the kitchen, talking away one minute and in the next minute Serena's exhausted sister would be fast asleep, leaning on her arms at the table. Serena's care package required that we always arrived in twos for the personal care, though not always at the same time. Whoever was in first got the kettle on and the cups prepared for the morning cuppas.

We were frisk-searched by the family's humungous golden Bull Mastiff, after he finally let us go from the wall in the hall near the front door, that is, on entry to the house. His greeting didn't stop the interrogation until we were seated at the kitchen table with our brew. We had to turn our pockets inside out to prove we had nothing in them for eating and if we had, well, it was confiscated by him in a flash.

He was taller than us and had paws that stapled us to the wall for our morning face bath and routine slobbery welcome. Our cries of protest and help did not completely fall on deaf ears, though. There was another canine hot on the heels of the big yin. The 'Rug Rat' or 'Yap' (as the owner called her) bounced and barked at the top of her lungs at the sight of us being loved and slobbered to death by the big yin.

We were very much loved and welcomed by the huge beast, which made sure we would scrub up well before the shift commenced, lest we had forgotten. Grown men who delivered medical supplies were understandably unsure and afraid of the beautiful beast and the window cleaner was terrified in case the dogs were let out into the garden. I never knew if he was afraid of the bark or the bite from the big yin or the wee yin. It was customary for the window cleaner to chap the door first to let the owner know he was about to clean the windows, not only to keep the dogs inside, but to make sure Serena was half decent and not in the middle of her bed bath.

The tiny Yorkshire terrier often fought with the massive Mastiff and got into trouble for doing so. She didn't care, she was the boss and she knew it. She would literally trample all over him, paws in his eyes and ears whenever she was on the move. Instead of walking round the huge beast, the tiny Yorkie walked on top of him to get to where she wanted to go, up and over his huge mountain of muscles. He never flinched or looked up. On the contrary, he looked as though he was enjoying the airy massage by her tiny nailed paws. The owner stated he was just a great big 'pie' for letting her walk all over him. His body took up all of the remaining kitchen floor space, making our journey from the kettle to the fridge on the opposite side of the kitchen, treacherous. I often wondered if I would make it back to the fridge in one piece with the milk carton as I stretched over his body. What if he stood up? What if the door went or the other carer walked in? In a split second I would have been carried away over his back as he shot out to meet and greet his next victim. To commune with him only resulted in another full-face slobbery wash. Although he was huge, he was still a youngster, soon entering into his early daft boisterous teenage ways. When he wanted up for a cuddle, he thought he would just go right ahead and get up onto the kitchen chair with you, impossible. As he grew, there was only room for his great big head on your lap. A friendly paw was agony because his claws were thick and sharp and his pads like the roughest grade of sandpaper. I bore many a raw fresh slash when he ran his paw down my arm for attention, he didn't mean to hurt us and just wanted a cuddle. When I looked into his massive loving eyes and stroked his face, I knew I loved him dearly. That said, my love was still not an invitation for the bruiser to sit upon my knee. I actually felt so sorry for him because the tiny Yorkshire terrier was always on her mummy's knee, gloating, and the big yin still wanted an embrace, a cuddle, a time of comfort. Mummy would eventually give in and allow her big baby to get up on her knee for a couple of minutes, making 'Yappy' mad with jealousy. The dog fighting was always one-sided. He would annoy her by sticking his great big bulbous head under the owner's kitchen chair, where the little one's bed was and she would go ballistic. In the stramash that inevitably followed, the Yap would nip the nose off the offending culprit in a raging fury. He, not to be intimidated or outdone, would grab at her fluffy bed and drag it to the centre of the kitchen. All of this taking place under the owner's feet, her chair slowly but surely screeched and slid along with the dog bed jammed underneath and with mummy still on it, kicking and screaming that she was going to kill both of them for their nonsense. Although 'The Big Yin' started it, it was always 'The Wee Yin' that got into trouble for keeping it going.

'Did you hear that carry-on this morning, Serena?' I would ask her, and explain what happened to fill her in on the canine combustion front. I loved making the story very descriptive and coloured in the facts to create an exciting picture.

Serena heard what went on but I made sure she knew every action, movement, reason and outcome so she could see in another way. The kitchen looked like the setting for a Carry-On film at times, it was hilarious.

Serena's care package required two confident people, one to wash and the other to hold her body still and secure when she was on her side. While she was on her side I would massage handfuls of the skincare cream onto her back from her neck to her waist, gently rubbing the areas of her back she could only imagine reaching. Having been trained in the structure of the bones and muscles in the human body came in very handy when Serena was having her massage. I leaned towards her face so I could listen and hear her faint moans of appreciation and reminded her in whispers that she owed me the massages back when we were in Heaven. Sometimes she stayed fast asleep throughout the whole bed-bath routine, which I thought was amazing, this is how gentle we were with her. I would catch her with a peaceful smile as though in a great dream. Once cleansed and padded, her thin bed sheet was tucked under her arms and pillows bolstered all around for comfort and protection, her long dark brown hair brushed, cascading down around her.

The massive Mastiff would sometimes come into Serena's bedroom for a visit and to do his nosy. After a good sniff around, he would lie under the mechanical bed, having stolen one of the used towels to chew on. He wasn't allowed into Serena's room while we were there working but it was impossible trying to physically push him to get him out. Just one word from Serena's sister, though, with the Yap circling around her feet with little authority, got him told. When he got into trouble, she would second the opinion. Despite the owner giving her a row for making a noise so early in the morning, the Yap just would not 'SHUT IT!'

'Right, missy, that's you gorgeous again. I'll see you in the morning. Don't be getting up to any mischief or sneaking in any undesirables through that window now, do you hear?' She did hear. She had the look of serenity on her face, a glow, peace. I would then switch her small television on for the next detective story, her favourites. I leaned closer to have a private word and say a little prayer before leaving her with 'God bless you and Jesus loves you'. I then moved her tall thin stainless-steel cannula holder, which also held her chimes and little glass angels hanging from coloured ribbons people had given to her as gifts. She couldn't see or hold them but she could hear them as they chimed when we moved them closer to her bed. Before leaving, I always told her I would be back soon for her next massage, giving her a very gentle hug and a kiss on the forehead. 'See you soon, babes,' I always said on leaving the room.

With no travel-time allowance to get to the next client, the job was very demanding and I often felt like a pressure cooker ready to explode. We would get phone calls asking where we were because we were 'late', allegedly. So why are you phoning me for twenty minutes, droning and complaining and making me even later? I would think, sitting at the side of the road or inconveniently bumped up onto a pedestrian walkway, so as not to use the mobile phone while driving. Hands-free phones couldn't be used as the private conversations could often be heard outside the car by passers-by. I always gave the same diplomatic answer, 'If you can find anybody else to drive within the required miles per hour as stated in the Highway Code and get them to be at the next client six miles away at exactly the same time as I have left the last client, then go right ahead and give them my job!' 'You are telling me to break the law,' I kept complaining. 'If I get a criminal record, then I can't work for you.' I would often have to sit with the phone well away from my ear because they were being so unreasonable. I would jokingly ask for a time machine because that's what is needed in the care industry.

Carers got hell from all sides. I couldn't believe my ears one afternoon as I sat in a hospital waiting room waiting for a client to come back from his consultation. There had been dreadful abuse of some dear old lady at another care home. In another country, I might add, not even in Scotland. A man in the waiting room was with his elderly father when he spotted my uniform and asked him if he had seen the abuse on the news. The family of the old lady had installed a hidden camera in her bedroom, which clearly showed the pensioner being slapped and punched by a carer. Even worse, the second carer, who stood at the other side of the bed, watched and laughed at the cruelty inflicted on the defenceless old lady. It's bad enough one behaving in a despicable and criminal manner, but for the other to stand and watch without intervening is appalling.

My own sister, a paramedic, was booted between the shoulder

blades by a Council carer who was blind drunk and wasting emergency services time. After having looked after, without prejudice, the drunkard and got her to hospital, she lashed out when my sister turned her back, resulting in time off work and years of physio. The off-duty carer was charged by the police officer in attendance, who arrested her in the Accident and Emergency Department. That carer was stinking drunk, not a great role model as a carer and a letdown to the Council who employed her. Apart from her, I know of no other carer who is abusive and I know that Scottish women will not tolerate abuse of any kind, that's why I love my 'Ain folk'. Our emergency services do the most amazing work to keep us safe. Thank you, all of you guys.

The man in the hospital waiting room made sure everyone heard his conversation, aimed at me because of a uniform. I was a carer, therefore it was my fault, and we carers were all branded by the same iron. One day he will know what that felt like, alone and with no defence, to be blamed for the sins of others. It was a very heavy and hurtful burden, nasty, humiliating and degrading. Head bowing, hands outstretched in the mind's eye to receive every word and thought of condemnation without the chance of a defence. To receive the accusations because of the wickedness of others really hurt. To be falsely accused, marred and tarred because of the love and compassion for the infirm and elderly was distressing to say the least.

How heavy it was for Jesus then to have taken on the burden of sin for the whole world, He who was without sin, He knew no sin. He became very ugly and was not nice to look at because of the disgusting filth of the sin of mankind.

Family members blurt, 'She's only in for five minutes when she's supposed to be there for half an hour.' I explain to them the carer is run ragged and the families agree it's not their fault. Carers often found a client in a great deal of distress, messed, or on occasion, deceased. The client cries, the carer cries, does anyone have a heart? How can the carer be in for half an hour when he or she has had to drive seven miles to get to the next job in rush-hour traffic (some jobs as far away as eleven miles and even outside of Glasgow). I am no mathematician but our local speed limit is generally thirty miles per hour with many of the school roads depicting a strict 'Twenty's Plenty' zone so as to be mindful of our youngsters. Also taking into consideration the time it took leaving from the last client and sitting at a junction where no one is in a hurry to 'give way' because everyone is selfish.

Roadworks, complete road blocks and diversions due to the laying of huge sewage pipes, potholes like craters, floods, snow, trees, ah yes, I remember the tree that fell on my car in slow motion. I made it in time to witness the tree slide down the back of my car in a storm (Thanks for that, Lord). Then bearing in mind we occasionally had five minutes to get from A to B, very often we would have no minutes or be in the black with minus minutes to make up if the last client required more care. The delegated starting time of the next client would often be the same as the finishing time of the previous client. I am not joking.

The families then argue (re the food), 'It only takes a couple of minutes in the microwave.' Really? The frozen-solid package states ten minutes with two minutes standing as the food is still cooking, twelve minutes gone in my calculation, without adding on the time to plate up and serve on the tray when the client is made comfortable after having been hoisted for PC and washed. Aptly named a convenience food for obvious reasons, it is a pathetic excuse for a dinner – limp, soggy, tough as leather around the edges and tasteless with any nutritional value destroyed in the micro blasting. The families are as proud as Punch to be seen paying a fortune to delivery companies for this excuse – labelled food. My dog eats better with real cooked chicken and fish. Even his foil tubs look much more appetising and succulent than the dinners put down to the infirm and elderly. The carers also have to deal with the medication too, which must not be hurried, and carefully fill in both the comment and medication sheets. All other business, queries, complaints and general health, making sure the client isn't unwell and having a chat while assisting the client into nightwear if there is no tuck visit, has to be undertaken. There is no joy in cajoling an older person, trying to hurry eating a roasting-hot micro meal so he or she can get ready for bed at teatime. Teatime, by the way, can be from three thirty to six thirty. It is not the carer's fault she/he has no time, she/he will be stressed to the hilt. By the time the carer has done all of this, she/he is exhausted, gutted, disillusioned, cold, tired, hungry or perhaps needing to spend a penny? There are service users who will not allow outsiders to use their toilet, and that's the truth. It's a thankless job in an industry that is desperately seeking carers and always will, failing to explain you will not be paid if you are more than seven minutes late if there is a phone-in.

There are beautiful clients (Wee Fiona C x) who are the salt of the earth, as are some of their families (Anna, Rose and family), who will cook and prepare proper meals for the week ahead, even if they are to be frozen. Anything homemade is always much tastier than the dull bland non-nutritious manufactured takeaway and processed conveyer-belt ready meal.

While the family of the loved one is having a ball in their own home at Christmas, I have stood in the kitchen of the client preparing his or her slither of turkey, mushy sprouts and hard roast potatoes, which got binned. Merry Christmas. Why do carers bother, given that there is no overtime on Christmas Day? LOVE! What else could it be? It's certainly not for the money, that's for sure. While the families are living abroad, as some are, the carer is there to love, hug, wrap up, keep warm, lend an ear, shower, assist in personal care, nurture, reassure and often go well beyond the call of duty. They are the most unappreciated and underpaid workers I know of. Then, as usually happens, the client passes away and the carer is left deeply saddened, as he or she remembers the quiet last moments of their service user's end of life and all is gone. Never a thanks forthcoming because that's their job, that's what they were supposed to do. Their very own half-hour call. No one knows the last conversations between the client and the carer. More often than not, it was a beautiful moment in time between two people. Time was short but it was powerful in action and word. Holding a hand or letting an aged or disabled person hold onto your arm for stability is priceless. Sometimes a twinkle would be seen in their glazed eyes. Yes, priceless is the right word. No amount of money can capture that moment, but caught and recorded it is. Carers keep people out of hospital and are terribly undervalued.

It was the day after I came back from one of my holidays abroad that I heard the chimes in my car, behind the driver's seat. I waved my hand behind and under the seat when I stopped at the traffic lights to catch the chiming culprit but I couldn't find anything, periodically trying to see behind the seat to find out where the chiming music was coming from.

'What on earth is doing that?' I asked myself. I stopped the car and looked in the boot to see if there was a toy or something that was making the noise but there wasn't anything in the boot that could give off a sound like chimes. It wouldn't have been unusual to find something in my car that made a noise, as people were always giving me goods for the church's charity shops and I would thank them and tell them to just put whatever it was into my boot. After searching the whole car, I didn't find a thing in my car that could possibly chime. I sat bewildered, wondering what was going on. I knew I wasn't imagining it because the chimes were so loud. 'Right, God,' I said. 'Who do I know that has chimes, because I am obviously hearing them and there's none in the car?' The only person I knew who had them was Serena.

'Is she all right, Lord?' I prayed for her to make sure, just in case. 'I don't know what's wrong, Lord, if anything. Please keep her pain-free and comfort her, look after her and bless her in the name of Jesus Christ, Amen.' I missed her and was looking forward to getting back to work for our happy chats and to catch up on the family gossip.

I ran up Serena's path, expecting to get into her house, but the door was locked. The family member who answered the door was astonished I hadn't been informed that Serena was in hospital, as I was in attendance daily. I was told she was fine and had been admitted to the hospital for a minor procedure, which required observation and monitoring.

The nursing staff had no idea about the intensive-care package Serena was accustomed to and a team of us had to take turns on the ward, usually just visiting because her sister, as usual, had her in tiptop condition. Serena was given the best pampering sessions in front of all the patients and visitors, as it was a long ward with many beds. Serena loved every minute of her stay, as there was chattering and always something going on. She still had to be specially fed via her abdominal tube and had separate tubes for all of her medication, which her sister administered every day, and night. Even younger family members in their teenage years knew how to care for Serena perfectly. They knew how to insert her abdominal tubes, clean the equipment and give the medication, which was varied and in liquid form. One of the teenagers has now gone on to study Health and Social Care.

Serena could hear the different noises in the ward of staff and visitors alike and had a great time, unable to move her head, but she could hear what was going on. She got special and personal treatment from her nearest and dearest and we were allowed in at any time, day or night, to attend to her. Serena hadn't been out of the bedroom she slept in for over twenty-five years, so this was like a holiday for her and she loved it. She heard new voices from the nurses and doctors and we teased her endlessly about getting fresh with them and told her to behave herself. We all loved winding her up, although she couldn't respond. Her face said it all as I stated earlier. A simple change in environment was a Godsend. The Lord God was telling me through the chimes that it was 'Serena' I was to pray for and they stopped chiming when I found out.

On another one of my holidays, The Lord God took my Missy Serena home to Heaven. When the office phoned to tell me I told them, 'I know.' God told me before I got the call. Given that we will have a new body there, I don't think I'll get my massages back but I still can't help wondering again, who is that girl I am talking to on the wall as Jesus passes by on the way to The City of Lights below? If it's not Kitchen Girl, could it be Serena? I'll find out one day in the near future. My heart has been deeply touched as I have sat and held the hands of the dying and I know Heaven is beautiful, we are in for a real treat, for all of eternity.

One of the many ways God communicates with his children is by actually speaking to them, as in you would hear an audible voice. Another way is to hear on the inside, that voice is generally known as the still small voice, the private voice only for you. That was the way I heard Him say 'Heart murmur'. Yet another way, I'll call 'mental facts', which came out as knowledge as though reading a fax without seeing it, that's the way He did it when He told me, 'You have a lump in your breast, not your right breast, your left breast.' I have had this method used often. No matter the method He uses, His information is always crystal-clear. Many times, though, it's outside the ears, like the way I heard the chimes behind me in the car or music in the wind.

Not hearing a voice is not unusual. There is communication by way of thought, even when it's one-way thought. Have you ever asked a question in your thoughts like, 'I wonder what time she will eventually turn up?' Who are you addressing that question to? Yourself? It's not that weird, is it? You still know what you said and thought in your own head. So why should it be weird when God communicates with you that way? Every time you have thoughts and speak inside of your own self you are communicating via your soul and not your body (lips). We must guard our thought life every bit as much as we guard the words that casually roll off our tongues. Malice, lust and hatred can easily be identified when we get to Heaven, remember, it's only our body we are leaving behind. We will, without fail, testify against ourselves and we don't even need to open our mouths to do it.

If you are a new believer, unsaved, a nonbeliever even, or someone who has been a Christian for a long time and has never heard God's voice, you may find this incomprehensible. His greatest voice comes from His Word, The Bible, which is alive. Speak 'with Him and not just to Him'. God desires to communicate with us at all times, through prayer. Having already heard God's voice, I would be gutted if He never spoke to me again. What daddy doesn't speak to his child, even in anger? It's still communication and I live to hear God's voice. I have written of hearing chimes, music, choirs, the Morse code and every other thing The Holy Spirit brought to my heart (and memory) under his anointing and I've asked Him to disallow anything He doesn't want in my testimony because it's all about Him.

Since my Out of Body Experience, my hearing has been exceptionally acute. I've stunned many people by saying, 'I heard that', when they've lowered their voice so I'm not supposed to hear. I only say it when they have been joking about me, of course, never when I have heard anything unsavoury. I pretend I don't hear so as not to stir up confrontation.

God generally takes me from my bed to the place when He wants to show me something as well as tell me, now that is amazing. At the time, though, it is as natural as cleaning your teeth.

The God of all of The Universe, who created The Heavens and the Earth, the moon, the stars and sand without number, every hair on every person's head counted, every living creature, kings, queens, judges, foreigners, so on and so forth, speaks to me, an awful sinner saved by Grace. If God was not speaking to me I would be very unhappy, especially if He was speaking to everyone but me. He is my Father and as His child I command his attention.

I'm writing to you as a friend and I don't know if you're saved or unsaved but I know we will meet some time, somewhere, maybe on Earth but definitely in Heaven at some point. Life is hard for many and some of you have had remarkable life-changing experiences, some good and others dreadfully bad. The Christian ones will know that God has their back. That doesn't mean you get off lighter with the trials and tribulations of life on Earth. It simply means that The Light of the world comforts us, taste and see that The Lord is good and He will prove it. Get your talents out there, not just for yourself, but for The Glory of God and of course you will also enjoy and reap the benefits too. That secret little talent has to start somewhere. When you make up your mind to start what God has given you the ability to do, He will help you succeed. Writing this testimony book is one of the easiest things I have ever done and I have thoroughly enjoyed every moment. I've sat with The Lord and laughed and cried as I remembered the sad moments in my life. I've held the picture of that sad wee girl (me) at three or four years old and told her I feel so very proud of what she has come through. There are thousands of children (like me) secretly crying into their pillows. There are people looking for redemption and salvation, 'Trying to find themselves'. There is no place too dark for God to find you, Jesus is The Light of The World and knows all. Remember He was with you before you came onto the Earth and He will never leave you or forsake you.

Jesus says, Behold, I stand at the door and knock, if anyone hears my voice and comes to me, I will come in and sup with him, and he with Me (Revelation 3, v20).

I can't bear the pain of Satan (The liar) having power over you. He had his chance in Heaven and he blew it. Come as you are, You won't be entering into religion, you will be entering into a relationship. That empty space inside you was predestined and created just for God to come in and live in you. It's free, by God's grace. It was not free for God, it cost Him the life of His precious Son. He gave us the very best sacrifice of everything He created. Sure, everything belongs to God, as we know, but to have the full reality of what that action meant, would we give our own son up to be sacrificed? Every single person I have asked has looked sorrowful and said, 'I couldn't.' That is how much we are loved. I cry in shame when I know I still hurt Him to this very day because I should know better. Me, who ran and played with Jesus. Me, who is a partaker at the bottom of the cross shouting 'Crucify Him!' because of my sinful life. Me, who is exactly the same as every other. Me, who is saved by Grace. I could say me, me, me, all day long but it's not about me. It's about Jesus and His pure blood (Lamb) sacrifice. Thank you, Good God in Govan, for being just that, always and only Good, in *Sunny Govan* and the rest of the world.

I cry because I want to go back home. I cry because of my 'stupid' and selfish words and actions. I cry because people I loved and do still love dearly, don't love me any more. Jesus said they wouldn't love me and it hurts. They have accused me and whisper behind my back. Their hater so-called friends are only too glad to repeat their words voiced in private conversations. I cry buckets because I cared for you and spoke highly of you but it gives me a little glimpse of what Jesus means when He says we will be despised for following Him. People laugh at me and still think I'm stupid but I know who I am in Him. One day we won't even remember the first Earth's tribulations and sorrows. I appreciate life is horrendously difficult but Jesus will make it better. It's not easy to follow and obey but always remember, day or night, no matter where or what, He will show up when you call His name. When He shows up, don't be afraid, because meeting Him is the most natural thing you will ever experience. How could going out to play with Jesus be natural? How could it be natural to be taken to the top of a hill to watch flying demons or be taken inside another woman's womb to touch her baby before it is born? It is, it just is. That's the beauty and wonder of our Supernatural (Father) God. Should I have said the events were supernatural then? No! It was completely natural to be with God. If I was not in the natural way with The Supernatural God, I'd be unnatural. I didn't once question why I was in His presence or look around the womb and shout, 'Wow, hold on, where am I?' I was where I was supposed to be, with The Heavenly Father. He is the one who is Supernatural, Earth was meant to be natural but life here became unnatural through sin. We just totally accept who God is when we meet Him because He is our natural Father, yet Supernatural God. Sin makes us hide, just like Adam and Eve in the garden beautiful. The blood of Jesus (The Lamb) covers our sin. He paid the highest price for us to be redeemed (brought back). Come, '**Act now.**'

I leave off for the time being with a puzzle God allowed me to see not so long ago. The road I was travelling along, on the south side of Glasgow, became like some sort of 'pixels' with extraordinary shapes which fitted into each other and couldn't be moved, except by His hand. I was going straight ahead at the crossroads and stopped the car to look at the puzzle in detail. No other traffic came and I sat and watched the pixel puzzle from left to right, for a while. The whole area before me was in a dimension I had never ever seen before, similar to a giant transparent jigsaw puzzle but with intricate joints. I have nothing to compare it with and find it difficult to explain what God let me see. The Lord God showed me the puzzle by taking one piece out and replacing it with another piece when I went the wrong way, making my life right, heading in the direction I was supposed to go in. If I disobeyed He would fix it. If I got lost He would sort it. If I broke the rules, sinned, had a bad mood, made bad choices, He mended it. He showed me He was right in front of me, in the world, to sort out my life, road and journey before Him. He is always here. I no longer have to worry or fear about what I'm doing or how I'm going to get where I am supposed to be, He has my life already written and mapped. That's God for you. That's you for God? Love you forever, Good God in Govan.

SHH . . . SHH . . . Be quiet . . . let Him hold you as you cry out to Him . . . SHH . . . AL . . . VAH . . . SHH . . . I am waiting to hear from you when you want to give God the glory and I have a whole page for your personal testimony for my, or should I say *OUR* next book, the book that is dedicated to your testimony.

---

**GOD BLESS YOU IN JESUS' NAME**

THIS IS THE DATE YOU RECEIVED

JESUS AS YOUR SAVIOUR

I _____ Believe that JESUS CHRIST died on the cross for my sins. He is the SACRIFICIAL LAMB, who shed His blood on the cross at Calvary so I can be saved, healed and BORN AGAIN. I declare before mankind and confess that JESUS CHRIST IS LORD. My Earth date of birth is _____ and my BORN-AGAIN date of birth is _____ PRAISE GOD, THANK YOU JESUS!

---

# Glossary

Achnamara . . . Village in Argyll

Aff . . . Off

Ain . . . Own

Annie Rexia . . . Anorexia

Askits . . . powders, painkillers

Aye . . . Yes

Bampot . . . Stupid person

Banshee . . . Wailing woman

Ba's . . . Balls (playing ba's on the wa's)

Battered . . . Punished or hit severely, beaten up

Bissom . . . Young girl, Scots word for a broom

Boaty McBoatface . . . Fibreglass boat in lounge built by The
Daddy in 1968

Bogey man . . . Contents from nose picking (bogey)

Brek . . . Break

Burds . . . Birds

Candlewick . . . Bedspread of thick, sculptured, patterned wool

Caramacs . . . Cheap sandshoes with sole same colour (light
brown) as Caramac chocolate

Catweazle . . . 1970s TV character played by Jon Pertwee

Chinkies . . . Game with elastic bands secured together in 1960s

Clype . . . Tell on

Coonsil . . . Council

'Cos . . . Because

Crabbit . . . In a bad mood (nippy, like a crab)

Dae . . . Do

Diz . . . Does

Doin' . . . Hammering, as in getting a doin'

Doon . . . Down

Dreepin . . . clambering down

Dug . . . Dog

Dunbeg . . . Village in Argyll

Dunny . . . Dungeon

Eg (Language) . . . Secret 1960s language of children, adding one 'Eg' per syllable

Fa' . . . Fall

Fag . . . Cigarette

Faither . . . Father

Fornethy . . . Residential school in Tayside

Gaun . . . Going

Geeze . . . Give

Gingies . . . Glass bottle, also known as 'Jeggie'.

Glesga . . . Glasgow

Goat . . . Got

Gonny . . . Going

Gorbals . . . Area on the south side of Glasgow

Govanites . . . Residents of Govan

Greetin' . . . Crying

Hawkeye . . . Eyes like a Hawk

Heid-The-Ba' . . . Person who thinks he/she is of high importance

Hen . . . Female Scottish pet name

Irn-Bru . . . Scotland's national soft drink

Linthouse . . . Area on the south side of Glasgow, opposite Elder Park

Manky . . . Filthy

Meccano . . . Miniature steel construction toys

Merriment . . . Happiness

Messages . . . Shopping

Mind . . . Remember

Nits . . . Head-lice, eggs

Oan . . . On

Och aye the noo . . . It's all right just now

Oor . . . Our

Palin's . . . Railings

Pea'd . . . Used the pea'd to insinuate Pee'd (urinated)

Peely-wally . . . Pale in the face (possibly sick, off colour)

Piece . . . Sandwich

Queerie . . . Strange person

Rottenrow . . . Maternity Hospital

Sandshoes . . . Cheap canvas slip-ons with half-moon elastic at front

Scullery . . . Kitchen

Segs . . . Metal shoe protectors, usually for heels

Skelped . . . Slapped

Skint . . . Having no money

Sleekit . . . Sneaky

Staun . . . Stand

Stookie . . . Hardened arm plaster cast made by bandage and plaster of Paris

Stour . . . Dust

Suffering General . . . Southern General, now Queen Elizabeth University Hospital

Swill . . . Pig's food

Tap . . . Borrow

Tellin' . . . Telling

Tick . . . Bloodsucking arachnid.

Tick . . . debt from borrowing, 'Ticked off' when paid

Toon . . . Town

Tottie . . . Potato

Trenchcoat . . . Waxed raincoat

Wa' . . . Wall

Washin' . . . Washing

Watter . . . Water

Waxcloth . . . Linoleum

Wisnae . . . Wasn't

Wull . . . Will

Wummin . . . Woman

# School Playground Songs

**Telltale tit**
Yer mammie cannae knit
Yer daddy cannae go tae bed
Withoot a dummy tit.

**The game's a bogey, the game's a bogey**
The man in the lobby
Come oot, come oot
Wherever you are . . .

**Ma faither's a lavatory cleaner**
He works in the lavvies at night
And when he comes hame in the morning
His boots are all covered in shi . . .
Shine up yer buckles wi' Brasso
It's only a penny a tin
Ye get it fae Woolworths for nothin'
Providing there's nobody in . . .

**Diz yer maw drink wine,
diz she drink it a' the time?**
Diz she get a funny feeling,
diz her head hit the ceiling?
Diz yer maw drink wine, diz she drink it a' the time?
Diz yer maw drink wine in the mornin'?